PLAN

B

Jonathan Tropper

St. Martin's Griffin
New York

PLAN B

This is a work of fiction. All the characters and events portrayed in this novel
are either fictitious or are used fictitiously.

PLAN B. Copyright © 2000 by Jonathan Tropper. All rights reserved. Printed in
the United States of America. For information, address St. Martin's Press, 175
Fifth Avenue, New York, N.Y. 10010.

www.stmartins.com

Book design by Michelle McMillian

Library of Congress Cataloging-in-Publication Data

Tropper, Jonathan.
    Plan B : Jonathan Tropper.
        p.   cm.
    ISBN 0-312-25253-6 (hc)
    ISBN 0-312-27276-6 (pbk)
    1. Male friendship—New York (State)—New York—Fiction.   2. Young
men—New York (State)—New York—Fiction.   3. New York (N.Y.)—
Fiction.   I. Title.
PS3570.R5885 P57   2000
813'.54—dc21   99-056148
                                                               CIP

10 9 8 7 6

For Lizzie and Spencer,
who make it perfectly fine to be thirty.

ACKNOWLEDGMENTS

This book might never have been finished were it not for the support and encouragement I received from a number of people:

My parents, who never stopped quietly urging me to keep writing. My wife, Lizzie, who was always gracious when I woke her up to talk me through the intermittent attacks of doubt that invariably struck in the wee hours. Simon Lipskar, for snatching my manuscript out of the oblivion pile and believing in it so forcefully that I had no choice but to believe in him. Kelley Ragland at St. Martin's Press, for championing this book from the beginning, while helping me to make it a better one. And finally, all of the friends who continued to express interest in my work, utterly convinced that it was destined for publication.

In the course of writing this book, I was aided in my

research by Edmond Cleeman, M.D., and Abraham Schreiber, M.D., and while most of their contributions landed on the literary equivalent of the cutting room floor, I am nonetheless grateful for their enthusiastic assistance.

PLAN
B

1

Jack was a movie star, which meant he was granted some latitude in the outrageous behavior department. Nevertheless, when he showed up sweaty and stoned to Lindsey's thirtieth birthday party, punched the overly solicitous maitre d' in the nose, and vomited into the potted gladioluses lining Torre's knee-high windowsills before passing out into a chair at our table, no one was amused. Not Lindsey, who said, "Screw this," and walked over to the bar for another shot of vodka. Not Chuck, who tossed the ice from his drink and mine into his napkin and, cursing Jack under his breath, ran into the kitchen to tend to the maitre d'. Not Alison, who jumped out of her seat and anxiously began trying to revive Jack by gently slapping his face and applying a wet cloth to his forehead, urgently saying over and over again, "Oh my god, Jack, wake up." And not I, who, lacking any other positive course of action, got up from the table and walked through the disapproving hush of well-dressed diners to join Lindsey at the bar.

Well, to tell the truth, I was somewhat amused. How often, after all, did you see that sort of thing in real life.

"You okay, Lindsey?" I asked, as she threw her head back and killed the vodka shot. Somewhere in the background, what sounded like Yanni or some other music on sedatives was being faintly piped into invisible speakers.

"Comparatively speaking, I would say I'm doing great," she said, casting her eyes in the direction of Jack and Alison. "What a shithead."

"Two more," I called to the bartender, who managed to stop ogling Lindsey from under his eyebrows long enough to comply.

"You think anyone recognizes him?" I said, looking out across the restaurant.

"Who cares?"

"Here's to you, birthday girl." We clinked glasses and downed the shots.

"I think they'd be making a bigger deal if they knew who he was," Lindsey observed. "It's not every day you get to watch a bona fide movie star destroy his life."

"He's lucky he hasn't been arrested."

"The night's young."

"I hope the maitre d' is okay," I said, grimacing as I recalled the lurching punch, the snapping sound Jack's fist and the maitre d's face had produced in their collision. Jack's punches usually had the benefit of accompanying THX sound effects. In real life the sound was startling in its lack of resonance, but somehow more imbued with violence because of it.

"Do you think it would be possible," Lindsey said to the bartender, "for you to stop staring at my breasts for a little while?"

The bartender, a fortyish guy with a goiter and a handlebar mustache, gasped and quickly moved further down the bar. He pulled out a dish rag and began meticulously scrubbing an invisible dirt spot. "You sure you're okay?" I asked.

"He wasn't even being subtle about it," she said, annoyed.

"So it wasn't the staring, but the sloppy execution that bugged you."

"Shut up, Ben."

At that point, Chuck returned from the kitchen, his forehead dappled in sweat beneath his receding hairline. "Sweet Jesus, it's hot in there." He ordered a club soda on ice, which is what he always drank when he was operating the following morning. The bartender served him without making eye contact, and then quickly retreated to the other end of the bar.

"How's the maitre d'?" I asked.

"He'll live. He's got a contusion on the bridge of his nose and it'll hurt him to sneeze for a few days. I told him I'll phone in a prescription for him. How's Hollywood doing?"

We all looked over to the table, where Alison had finally revived Jack, and was force-feeding him a glass of water, most of which was ending up in dark, damp spots on his brown shirt. The restaurant's dim lighting lent a jaundiced pallor to his already ashen complexion, making him appear gaunt and sickly. "He's looked better," I said truthfully.

"Dude, I've seen homeless junkies that looked better," Chuck snorted.

"Spare us the lurid details of your social life."

"Eat me," Chuck said with a smirk. Chuck had somehow missed the stage where we all outgrew salutations like 'dude' and 'eat me,' and he clung to those anachronisms tenaciously, as if they might somehow slow down the balding process.

"There's a shot for the tabloids." Lindsey interrupted us, turning back to the bar, the track lighting picking out her blond highlights in a glimmering halo as her head moved.

3

"I think we'd better get him out of here," I said. "If someone recognizes him, we'll be watching this on *Entertainment Tonight.*"

"It would serve him right," Lindsey said as we got up from the bar.

"What's the point of being a famous movie star if no one recognizes you?" Chuck grumbled.

"Look at him," I said. "I barely recognize him myself."

It was true. Jack's usually bright blond hair was in a matted, greasy mess above his Gucci shades, and he wore four or five days' growth of a beard. It was hard to believe that this was the same man whose face (and body, always the body) had been on every major magazine cover at one time or another over the last few years, the same guy who reduced tabloid journalists to trite adjectives like "heartthrob" and "hunk." But his grungy appearance that night would have done nothing to change that perception. Jack often went out looking like he hadn't showered in a week. It was a Hollywood thing. All the stars were doing it lately, if the candid shots in *Entertainment Weekly* and *Movieline* were any indication. It was their way of saying, "Even when I look like shit I'm beautiful." Which, in Jack's case, was undeniably true. His essence shone through the layers of grime—the perfect green eyes, the exquisitely carved cheekbones, the casual, unconscious grace with which he threw his lean body around. On your best day, you'd be lucky to look like Jack with smallpox.

As we approached the table, Alison looked away, but not before I saw that there were tears in her eyes. I nudged Lindsey. "Take her outside."

After the women left, Chuck and I took seats on either side of Jack, who was now sitting up, looking bleary-eyed but only slightly befuddled. "Do you think we can get out of here without any further incident?" I asked him.

"Sorry, guys," Jack said with a sheepish, million-dollar smile. Then, concerned, "Did I hit someone?"

"You whacked the maitre d'," I said.

"What was he doing?"

"Bleeding, mostly."

"Shit." He examined his knuckles with contempt, as if they had acted independently of him. "I knew I was too wrecked to come, but I really wanted to make it to Lindsey's party."

"Mission accomplished, dude," Chuck said.

"Fuck, my head hurts," Jack said, leaning back and rubbing his temples.

Chuck suddenly leaned forward and squeezed Jack's nose between his thumb and forefinger. Jack bolted upright in pain and swatted away Chuck's hand. "Asshole!"

"I thought that might hurt," Chuck said, with a modicum of satisfaction.

"Cocaine?" I asked.

"Definitely, man," Chuck said. "Leaves the nasal passages very raw."

"Not heroin?"

"Could be," Chuck answered. "But his behavior is much more consistent with a cocaine habit."

"Shit, Jack," I said, instantly depressed. "Coke?"

He was spared the necessity of a reply because at that moment the manager arrived, accompanied by two burly kitchen workers, to kick us out of the restaurant.

That was when we first thought Jack might be in serious trouble.

Of course, it wasn't the first time it had crossed our minds that Jack might be something other than drug free, but how do you distinguish a genuine addiction from standard celebrity behavior?

What major Hollywood star didn't trash the occasional Plaza suite, or get snapped by the paparazzi outside the Viper Room looking dazed and unkempt? If the warning flag went up every time a movie star cut a little too loose they'd have to install revolving doors at the Betty Ford Clinic. Still, in retrospect, Jack had seemed somewhat withdrawn over the last few months, hurried and antsy on the phone, speaking the way you do when you've got a long distance call on the other line or you'd just stepped out of the shower when the phone rang. He was distracted and tense, not at all like the Jack we knew. But an asking price of twelve million per film is bound to come with some pressure. The tabloid vultures had been circling for months now, searching (read: yearning) for any sign of a meltdown, but as Jack's friends we felt duty-bound to ignore the reports. No one wants to believe they need the mass media to stay in touch with a friend.

The irony was that Jack had never been interested in acting. For him, stardom came with the same serendipitous ease that everything else did. In college he would wander aimlessly into a party on his way home from a late evening jog, unshaven, his hair plastered to his scalp with sweat, visible pit stains on his ratty NYU sweatshirt, and he'd leave an hour later with any one of the multitude of girls who practically climbed over each other to make themselves available to him. He didn't plan it; he never planned anything. Things just happened for Jack. If he ever thought about it, he would have assumed that it was the same for everyone. But he never thought about it. You wanted to resent him, or even hate him a little, but how could you begrudge someone his innate gifts when he wasn't even aware of them? He lived in complete oblivion to his own charms, which, of course, made him all the more charming.

In our senior year Jack took a part-time job waiting tables in the Violet Cafe. His financial aid agreement stipulated that he work twenty hours a week. One day he served a frappacchino to some guy who was on the fast track at one of the major studios. The guy knew someone who knew someone, and within a few weeks he'd arranged a screen test. It was almost inevitable. Right after Thanksgiving Jack got a S.A.G. card and a walk-on part in a Harrison Ford thriller. Some on-site rewrites gave him three additional lines and a twelve-second gunfight sequence in which he blew away a Chinese body-builder before getting shot himself. It took three weeks in LA for Jack to shoot his scenes, and he came back disappointed that he didn't get to meet Harrison Ford. "He wasn't even there," Jack said bitterly. "He's already working on another movie."

A casting agent working on a modestly budgeted action movie for Miramax called *Blue Angel* saw the Ford movie when it came out a few months later and liked the way Jack held a fake gun. Jack was cast in the lead role for *Blue Angel* for which he was paid scale, and he flew out to Hollywood to begin preproduction. *Blue Angel* was the sleeper hit of the year and the trades anointed Jack Hollywood's next great action star. None of us was greatly surprised when he didn't come home to graduate.

I once asked Jack what he'd been planning to do before he was discovered. "What do you mean?" he asked.

"You were majoring in sociology, which is pretty much the equivalent of majoring in unemployment," I said. "What did you plan on doing after college?"

He frowned at me, clearly perplexed by the question. "I don't know," he said, running his fingers through his perfect hair. "I would have thought of something."

"Don't you ever worry about the future?" I asked.

Jack shrugged. "This is the future," he said.

When we left the restaurant Jack, one of *People* magazine's Fifty Most Beautiful People of 1999, puked all over himself, so Alison got him into his limo to take him back to his hotel, insisting, as he climbed in on all fours, that we didn't have to come along. Lindsey, Chuck, and I went to Moe's, a bar Chuck knew on the Upper East Side, one of those places that carefully spreads sawdust across the floor every night so as to seem like a genuine dive. For a surgeon, Chuck certainly got out a lot. He seemed to know the majority of the women in the place, and got a kiss hello from the bartender, who looked like a supermodel fallen on harder times. Jack may have been the movie star, but Chuck's life was a movie. Or at least a beer commercial.

While Chuck hit on some barely legal girls at the bar, Lindsey and I took a table in the back and ordered some kamikazes and a pitcher of Sam Adams to chase. "How's Alison?" I asked. I had to shout above the jukebox, which was playing one of those annoyingly catchy novelty songs that have slowly been replacing real music on the radio. The fact that I occasionally discovered myself humming along only intensified my dislike for the music.

"Still loves him, for all the good that does either one of them," she said, pouring beer into the plastic cups. "She thinks he's reaching the breaking point."

"What do you think?"

"I don't know. That was a pretty ugly display, even by movie star standards."

I nodded in agreement. "He's seriously messed up."

We drank in silence for a minute. "How's Sarah?" she asked.

"Are you inquiring into her health?"

"Forget it. I'm sorry."

I looked over to the bar, where Chuck was laughing it up with a brunette in a sleeveless blouse so tight I could make out the outline of her navel from where I was sitting. The light was causing a gleam on Chuck's head just above the point where his hairline continued to defy the daily assaults of Rogaine. He was in a desperate race with his hair, determined to bed as many women as possible before it disappeared altogether.

A few weeks earlier Chuck and I had gone down to Atlantic City for the weekend and I'd come into our room at the Trump Casino Hotel to find him standing in front of the bathroom mirror in a towel, using an eyedropper to apply Rogaine across his scalp. It was like inadvertently stumbling upon a deeply private ritual, like that scene in *The Empire Strikes Back* when the officer walks in on Darth Vader with his mask off. Chuck's hair, still wet from the shower, was standing up in jagged spikes, his pink scalp visible through the pithy strands like exposed tissue. He turned to me with an embarrassed grin, the eyedropper still poised over his head like a conductor's baton and said, "What have I got to lose?"

"It must be nice," Lindsey said, indicating Chuck. "He's able to find someone to hit on everywhere he goes."

"To a man with a hammer, everything looks like a nail," I said. Her eyes smiled at me from over the rim of her beer glass.

"What do you think he's after?" she asked me, putting down the glass. I shot her a look. "Other than the obvious," she said, correcting herself. "I mean, why do you think he's so determined to sleep around so much? In college, okay. It's an acceptable rite of passage, but at thirty it's a tad . . ."

"Juvenile?"

"More like pathetic," she said.

"I don't know," I said wearily. I took a sip of beer and held it in my mouth, letting the microscopic air bubbles tickle my tongue as they popped. "Maybe Chuck just hasn't found the right person."

"How would he know? He's gone before the sheets dry. He's got more of a Peter Pan complex than you do. His actually includes flying out the window before daybreak."

I laughed. "First of all, shut up," I said. "Second of all, I think it's more of a James Bond complex. He's not doing it to keep feeling young. I think he does it to feel like a real man."

Unlike Lindsey and Alison, who only met him in college, I knew that it hadn't always been this way for Chuck, which was probably why I cut him more slack than they did. We'd grown up together, gone through elementary school and high school together, where things had been anything but easy for him. From early childhood through our junior year of high school, Chuck was easily the most overweight kid in the class. Not grotesquely fat, but comically plump in a way that always made him look somewhat unkempt. He wasn't singled out for persecution the way it happens in those John Hughes movies, but he still suffered, especially when it came to girls. His wit made him popular with them to a point, but when it came to pushing for a girlfriend, he got the "just friends" speech every time. In high school he finally experienced some growth spurts, which, combined with some brutally disciplined dieting, brought his weight down into the normal range. But by then it was too late. He'd been a blimp for the first two years of high school, and that's how he was universally perceived for the last two. At sixteen, perception is nine-tenths of the law.

College, though, was a clean slate and Chuck was like a horse right out of the gate. Maybe it was compensation, or revenge on all women for past rejections, or maybe it was just the store of repressed sexual urges that he could finally have gratified with someone else after years of flying solo, what he shamelessly referred to as "roping one off." However you wanted to explain it, Chuck couldn't believe how easy it suddenly was to get laid, and he went about it with reckless abandon, as if he'd been granted a free shopping spree.

At some point toward the end of college, Chuck began losing his hair, and in his mind it was as if a giant clock had started ticking. It must have seemed terribly unfair to him that he'd worked so hard to shed one physical obstacle only to inherit what he perceived as another, completely beyond his control.

Lindsey and I watched as Chuck drew the girl closer to him and whispered something to her. She laughed with her entire body and gave him a quick kiss on the cheek. "Well, he's got some skills," Lindsey said. "I guess you have to give him that."

"If only we could get him to use his powers for good," I said distractedly and drank another swallow of my Sam Adams.

"You look sad," she said.

"I'm just pensive."

"What are you thinking about?"

"Whether or not to be sad."

"Same old Ben."

We drank in silence for a while.

"We're getting divorced," I finally said.

"Oh!" She seemed genuinely surprised. "I knew you were sep-arated, but I thought it was just a temporary glitch. That you'd worked it out."

"I don't know," I said, even though I did. "I think maybe the working it out was the temporary glitch."

"I'm sorry," she said, truly meaning it.

"Subject change, please," I said.

"How's your writing going?" she asked. Wrong subject.

"At *Esquire*?" I said. "Fine."

"You writing any features yet?"

"Nope. I'm still the list-maker." *Esquire* was big on lists. *7 Crucial Stomach Exercises. 10 Little Grooming Tips For a Big Night. 30 Things You Should Know About Your Money.* Before they let you graduate to real articles, you had to put in your time on the lists.

"And your novel?"

"Haven't touched it in months."

"What's the problem?"

"I have a tendency to procrastinate, but let's talk about that some other time."

"Ha."

"I don't know," I said, grinding an ice cube between my teeth. "I think it's the protagonist. He's too autobiographical."

"Meaning?"

"No motivation."

"Poor Ben," she offered.

"Poor Alison," I returned.

"Poor me," Lindsey said. "Thirty years old. Can you believe it?"

"I know," I said. "I turned thirty last month."

Her jaw dropped slightly in surprise, and then she turned to me with a sad smile, taking my head between her hands. "Oh shit, Benny. I totally forgot." She leaned forward and kissed me softly on the lips. "Happy birthday, Benny."

The kiss and the nickname brought me back six years, to when Lindsey and I were still together. It's an axiom of group dynamics that no circle of friends can remain a truly cohesive unit unless a handful of them are in love with each other in some twisted fashion or other. Twisted because if it were simple they'd pair off and that would be the end of the group. There was Alison's unflagging and unrequited love for Jack, conveniently disguised as maternal concern so as to keep things from getting uncomfortable. Chuck was happily in love with himself. And then there was my love for Lindsey, which started as simple lust when we first got friendly in college, but blossomed into a full-blown, hurts-so-good love that remained unspoken until after we had graduated. We both knew it was there, and we both knew that we both knew. It was evident in the way, when she kissed me hello or good-bye, that she always managed to get just the corner of my mouth. Or in the fact that whenever the five of us went out, Lindsey and I always seemed to wind up sitting together. And I was the one who walked her home at night, even though Chuck's dorm was closer. But still, despite all of the hints, neither one of us was willing to let it grow during college. I think we were afraid of not having each other anymore if it didn't work out. Or at least, that was probably her rationale. I would have been willing to risk it, if I weren't so sure of a gentle but firm rejection. I didn't get laid in college as much as Chuck, and certainly not as much as Jack, who might as well have been listed as a course requirement for entering female students, no pun intended. But I did okay for a somewhat bookish, Clark-Kent-without-the-alter-ego type, and the reason for that, I think, was that all of the feelings I had for Lindsey that were being stirred to a slow boil inside me needed somewhere else to go in the meantime.

At a party the day after our graduation, Lindsey and I were dancing, as usual just a wee bit closer than the legal limit for just friends, when she asked me, "So, Benny, what are you going to do now?"

"I told you the plan," I said. "I'm taking off a few months to write, and then I'll start interviewing at some publishing firms."

"No," she said, her lithe body coming to a complete stop as she pulled back to look me in the eye. "I mean, what are you going to do about me?"

We were together for two perfect years, the kind that would get a sixty-second montage of film clips set to a Harry Connick Jr. song like in *When Harry Met Sally*. Walking through the park, kissing in the rain, clowning around at a street fair, et cetera. Two years, which was long enough for me to believe it would never end. Of course it did, though, when Lindsey panicked and decided that at twenty-four she was much too young to be settling down and it was time to get out there and see the world. She quit her job as an elementary school teacher and launched her world tour, facilitated by a brief stint as a flight attendant, and I eventually rebounded into Sarah, who had a career, goals, and a more highly developed nesting instinct.

Lindsey moved back to Manhattan around the time I got married. Over the next few years she was in a constant state of career flux, from advertising, to diamond trading on Forty-seventh Street, to teaching aerobics classes at Equinox. Mostly she temped as a receptionist while she was between jobs. Whatever it was she'd been looking for when she took off for parts unknown, she hadn't found it, which should have made me feel vindicated but only made me sad. I saw her periodically, when all of us went out, but we never got together one-on-one. Lindsey never would have suggested it since I was married, and I was scared of being alone with her because it would make it harder to deny that I'd married the wrong person. So we met in the safety of our little group, stayed in touch intermittently, and tried not to see the tragedy in the casual acquaintances we'd become.

"Ben?" Lindsey asked, bringing me back to the present.

"Yeah?"

"You're crying."

"I'm just drunk," I said.

She put her head on my shoulder and wrapped her hands around my arm. "Poor Ben."

2

The next day I got a call at work from Alison.

"Hi, Ben, is this an okay time?"

Alison was an attorney, and probably a damn good one, although she wisely chose not to be a litigator. She has too peaceful a nature. Still, she was about five years away from a partnership at Davis Polk, so it was nice of her to ask me, an articles editor and chief list maker for *Esquire*, if it was an okay time.

Whenever I wanted to indulge in some quality self-pity, I would recall painfully how excited I was to get hired at *Esquire*. How on my first day I sat down in my pathetic little cubicle with its unfettered view of the wall, put my legs up on the Formica board suspended between the two front walls that served as my desk, and smiled to myself at how I'd made it to the big time. I was so sure that it would only be a matter of months before I blew them away with my writing and was elevated from my proofreading and issue compilation duties to loftier writing assignments. Maybe I'd even get them to publish one of my short stories. By the time I finished my novel, I would have no trouble snagging an agent and the interest of major publishers based on my solid credentials as a writer for *Esquire*. Even after I learned that most of the serious articles weren't actually written by employees but by contributing writers, I was confident that my abilities would eventually be recognized.

It took me a few years to realize that nothing was happening for me. Nothing doesn't happen all at once. It starts slow, so slow that you don't even notice it. And then, when you do, you banish it to the back of your mind in a hail of rationalizations and resolutions. You get busy, you bury yourself in your meaningless work, and for a while you keep the consciousness of Nothing at bay. But then something happens and you're forced to face the fact that Nothing is happening to you right now, and has been for some time.

For me it was a short story I was asked to proofread about a man driving through Florida with his younger brother to attend the funeral of their estranged father. Their car breaks down at an alligator farm and while they sit there watching the locals wrestle and herd the alligators, they review the dissolution of their family and the demons that drove their father to abandon them. *Esquire*'s fiction editor Bob Stanwyck, known throughout the office simply as "The Wyck," favored literary narratives with travelogue sensibilities and little if any ultimate resolution, and this selection was perfectly typical of him. It was also emblematic of why he consistently returned my own short stories to me through interoffice mail with courteous rejections scribbled on yellow sticky note papers.

After finishing the story I happened to glance at the author's bio and discovered with a start that he was twenty-six years old and this was the third story he'd published. I was twenty-eight at the time, and all I had to show for my efforts was . . . Nothing. Suddenly the gray, threadbare, carpeted walls of my cubicle seemed ridiculously small, and the foam dropped ceiling with its tiny brown craters seemed lower than before. That was the day I realized I hated my job. It would still be a few months before I came to understand that realizing it and doing something about it were two very different things.

When Alison called I was sitting in my cubicle, considering the metaphorical implications of *Star Wars* action figures for an article that would never be published. I was reworking the assortment of figures that adorned my overhead file cabinets to include a new Luke Skywalker with Yoda attached to his back (thank god for office accessorizing, the last playground of the reluctant adult). I was nine years old when *Star Wars* came out, and like so many of my peers, I never outgrew it. And now, twenty-two years later, with the release of *The Phantom Menace*, they had come out with a line of reengineered action figures from the original trilogy that I felt a strong, posthypnotic urge to buy.

It seems to me that action figures have come a long way in twenty years. Their colors are brighter, they're made with greater detail, and in some instances they actually resemble their actor counterparts. They have better accessories, they're slightly larger, and they're more anatomically correct. Real people, on the other hand, seem to lose color and detail as they get older, and after they hit middle age will sometimes even begin to shrink. Luke, Han, Leia, and even Obi-Wan seemed to be aging much more gracefully than the rest of us. *Thirty . . . shit.*

I told Alison that it was a fine time to call.

"It's about Jack," she said. She sounded nervous. "I think he's really in trouble."

"I've been thinking about that, too," I said.

"He's addicted, Ben. He needs help."

"Did you discuss it with him?"

"You saw the shape he was in," Alison said. "As soon as we got back to the hotel he fell down on his bed and went to sleep. I checked his shaving kit and found two bags of coke and flushed them down the toilet. He was so furious when he woke up, Ben. It was like he was another person. He tore the room apart looking for drugs and cursed at me. He said I . . ."

Her voice broke there and she couldn't go on. Sweet Alison, who never had a bad word to say to anyone, who had loved Jack selflessly for almost a decade, had to listen to him curse her out as he came down.

"You know he didn't mean anything he said," I told her. "It's the drugs doing the talking."

"Then Seward came in," she continued, struggling to get control of her voice. Paul Seward was Jack's agent and an absolute control freak. To hear him tell it, he'd conceived and delivered Jack and single-handedly nurtured him to stardom. "He practically pushed me out the door, told me to wait in the lobby and he'd get Jack straightened out."

"So what happened?"

"I waited down there for an hour and then I called up to the room. No one was there. Paul must have taken him out through another exit."

"Bastard."

"Yeah. He is."

"Did they go back to LA?"

"I guess so."

She seemed to be waiting for me to suggest something, but my mind was a blank. I picked up R2-D2 and began absently twisting his domed head around, a long-standing habit of mine. The clicking the ratchets made as the droid's head spun soothed me. "I'm not sure what you think we ought to do," I said.

"I don't know either," said Alison, and I could hear the weariness in her voice. "But I know that agent won't do a damn thing for him. Jack's his meal ticket."

"Maybe if we spoke to Paul and tried to make him see the larger picture," I said. "Jack might make a lot of money for him now, but at this rate he could crash and burn at any time. If he takes him out of circulation to get him cleaned up, he's investing in a longer future." Even as I said it, I realized the fallacy in my approach. Hollywood was not a place where you bought futures in anybody. Jack was a star here and now, and if you were his agent, you struck while the iron was hot. Next year, if Jack's career went to shit, Seward would have a substantial nest egg to live off of while he searched for the next Mr. Thing.

"We're his friends, Ben."

"I know."

"All of his friends out there have a piece of him, you know? We're his only real friends."

"So what do we do?" I asked.

"I think maybe we should have an intervention," said Alison.

An intervention. The surprise party of the millennium. Pick a place and time, invite the guest of honor, and have all of his friends waiting with light refreshments and some tough love. Surprise! You fucked up and we all know it.

"Do you think Jack will really respond to something like that?" I asked, returning R2 to his spot next to C-3PO, his golden sidekick.

"I don't know," she admitted. "But we have to try something. I could never forgive myself if we just stood by and something terrible happened."

"An intervention, huh? Aren't we supposed to have a professional drug counselor do it with us?"

"Probably," Alison said. "But whatever slim chance we have of Jack being receptive to us will disappear if he sees we brought in an outsider."

"You're probably right."

"What? What are you thinking?"

"It just sounds so . . . dramatic. Like a made-for-TV movie starring some has-been sitcom actor, or one of the *90210* girls."

"If you can't get dramatic for a movie star," Alison said, "then who?"

I had to concede that she had a point.

"So this guy is dating three women, okay?" Chuck was saying. "And he knows he needs to commit to one of them, but he isn't sure which one to run with."

"Why do all of your jokes sound autobiographical?" I asked.

"Because his life is a punchline," Lindsey said.

We were on a conference call, arranged by Alison, to discuss the viability of a friendly intervention for Jack. Chuck, Alison, and I were at work, and Lindsey was in her apartment. Alison had to put us on hold for a minute to handle another call, which gave Chuck the opportunity to treat us to this latest installment.

"You're both just jealous," Chuck said. "Anyway, he decides to give them each ten thousand dollars, and based on how they use the money, he'll make his choice."

"Perfect," Lindsey said.

"So the first woman comes back and she's used the money to buy him a new motorcycle. The second woman says, I can't take so much money from you, I'll just take five grand, because that's all I need to pay for the cruise we'll be going on. You with me so far?"

"Unbelievably," I answered.

"The third woman takes the ten grand and invests it in an I.P.O. for some dynamite Internet stock. A few weeks later she's got eighty grand, which she splits with him, forty a piece. So," Chuck paused for a moment. "Who does he marry?"

"I give up," Lindsey said instantly.

"Me, too," I said.

"The one with the biggest tits," Chuck announced triumphantly.

"Oh, lord," Lindsey moaned.

"I knew it reeked of autobiography," I said.

There was a click and then we all heard Alison's voice. "I'm back."

"And better than before, hey la hey la," Chuck sang.

"Okay," Alison said. "I've pretty much had the same talk with all of you concerning an intervention for Jack. We all agree that it seems to be the best course of action right now."

"Best course?" Chuck said. "It's our only course."

"Which makes it the best," Alison snapped.

"Okay," I interrupted. Chuck and Alison tended to rub each other the wrong way. It had always been like that, even back in college. Chuck's brash and often crude manner didn't mesh with Alison's quiet, refined nature. He viewed her tacit disapproval of his often inappropriate behavior as a challenge, prompting him to even further extremes, which in turn made her feel every outrageous thing he said or did was a personal attack on her. Once they started in on each other, there was no stopping them, so the rest of us had learned over time to interrupt them as soon as they began to disagree. "So how do we go about doing this?" I asked.

Alison explained that Jack had called her to apologize a few days after the Torre's incident, told her that he'd be coming to New York a week from Tuesday for a premiere, and offered to take her out to dinner. "I'll have him come pick me up at my apartment," she said.

"And we'll all be waiting there," Lindsey said.

"Yeah," Alison said.

"He'll be pissed," Lindsey said.

"Let him be pissed," I said.

"He'll be ashamed," Lindsey said. "It sounds kind of cruel. It's like we're all conspiring against him."

"He has to know we're doing it out of concern for him. Out of love," Alison said.

"Lindsey has a point," Chuck said. "Maybe it shouldn't be all of us. That might be too much for him to handle."

"If you don't want to come—" Alison began.

"That's not what I said," Chuck said hotly. "But you have no idea what you're dealing with, so why don't you let me give you a clue. Cocaine screws up your endocrine system. It triggers a hypersecretion of norepinephrine in the brain, which will often cause the addict to suffer hallucinations and psychoses, the most common of which is extreme paranoia. It's a textbook symptom. Lindsey's right, there's a good chance he'll misinterpret our intentions."

"I'm sorry, Chuck," Alison said. "I didn't mean it like that."

"Whatever."

"Listen," Lindsey said. "We have a few days to decide if there's a better way to do it. For now, I think we should agree that we'll all be there for him." There were murmurs of acquiescence. "But I think we should all accept the severity of this intervention," Lindsey said.

"What do you mean?" I asked.

"We may lose him," she said softly. "if he gets angry enough, or is so far gone that he can't face up to it, he'll storm out of there and that might be the last we see of him." She was saying "us," but we all knew that she was really talking to Alison. "What I'm trying to say is that I don't think this is one of those things that may work or may not work, but either way we're all back to being his buddies a month later. There will be consequences."

"I agree with Lindsey," said Chuck.

Alison let out a deep breath. "Look. As far as I'm concerned, he's on the path to self-destruction. We can't sit idly by out of fear that we'll lose his friendship. What's the point of staying friends if he's dead in six months?"

"Could it really be that serious, Chuck?" I asked.

"It's an idiosyncratic drug," Chuck said. "It affects everyone differently, and I don't even know how long he's been on it. He could go another year or he could already have an edema in the brain, which is bleeding. He could die of a hemorrhage tomorrow."

That silenced us all for a minute, and all that could be heard was the static hiss of Bell Atlantic. Someone began nervously tapping their desk with a pencil. We'd all smoked our share of weed back at NYU, obtained in twenty- and fifty-dollar bags from the Rasta guys that trolled Washington Square Park, but we were completely inexperienced when it came to anything harder. Nancy Reagan had taught us to "Just Say No," and we'd been trained instinctively to loathe drugs, but that didn't mean we fully understood the dangers. Hearing Chuck put the drug into concrete medical terms that involved the possibility of death made it suddenly a much more real and imminent danger. I remembered that commercial from a few years ago, the one with the egg and the frying pan. *This is your brain, this is your brain on drugs. Any questions?*

"We're his friends," Alison finally said. "We have to do what we think is best, regardless of how unpleasant it may be." She sounded like she was trying to convince herself along with us.

"So we're going to do this," I said. "We all agree?"

We did.

On my way home from work that day I actually spent sixty-five bucks on a full-sized Darth Vader mask, the kind that goes completely over your head. There was no rational reason for buying it. I saw it in the window of the Star Magic Shop and just walked in and bought it. It had that delicious smell of new plastic, the smell of childhood. When Luke Skywalker unmasked Darth Vader in *Return of the Jedi*, I felt as if something had been stolen from me irretrievably. Allowing Vader to relinquish the Dark Side of the Force would forever compromise his evil presence in the first two films. *Star Wars* and *The Empire Strikes Back* would never be the same for me, which meant one more link had been severed between me and the boy that I was.

Over the years, though, Vader had weathered the storm, and managed to establish himself as the most prominent icon from the trilogy, and while I did take some comfort in that, it didn't make me feel any less self-conscious about my purchase as I handed the teenage salesgirl my American Express card. I walked home with the mask in a bag, feeling embarrassed, nostalgic, and strangely insubordinate. When I got to my apartment, I pulled it out of the bag and put it on my kitchen table, and we just stared at each other for a little while, as if neither of us could quite figure out what the other one was doing there.

3

Thirty . . . shit.

That was my silent mantra during the weeks leading up to my birthday and following it. As far as I knew they hadn't removed any hours from the day or days from the year, yet the milestone had sneaked up on me, like a giant, silent wave swelling behind you while you're facing the shore. It had come way too fast. Some days it felt like I was still thinking like a nineteen-year-old, and here I was, more than a decade older.

Star Wars was over twenty years ago. I can still remember seeing it in the theater when it first came out. I went four times. In 1977 VCRs were still a few years away from the mainstream, and you never knew when you would get a chance to see a movie again. You had to internalize the film so you could take it with you.

Thirty . . . shit. It was like one of those inane lists I compiled for *Esquire*. Mick Jagger, Roger Daltry, and the Beatles are all over fifty. Billy Joel and Elton John are pretty much there, too, as are Harrison Ford and Sylvester Stallone. Gary Coleman and all of the Bradys are grown men. Magic and Bird are retired, Jordan's already retired twice, and Shaquille O'Neal is six years younger than me. I graduated college eight years ago. My parents are in their sixties, which is the age I always associated with grandparents, not parents. Any day now I'm going to walk into a doctor's office and discover that he's younger than me.

If I were an athlete I'd be past my prime. If I were a dog I'd be dead.

Thirty . . . shit.

It's a nice round number to arrive at if you have it all together. Success, love, a family, the overall sense that you actually belong on the planet. If you have all that, you can wear thirty well. But if you don't, it feels like you've missed the deadline, and suddenly your chances of ever getting it right, of ever achieving true happiness and fulfillment, are fading fast. You realize that all your hopes and dreams up until this point were actually expectations that, still unrealized, have become desperate prayers to a god you were certain you didn't believe in anymore. Please, let me have an easy mind and a pretty girl to hold my hand, or however the song goes. Is that so much to ask?

Thirty . . . shit.

Old enough to suddenly see forty, the Prozac birthday, shimmering on the horizon in your rearview mirror, a metallic, glinting speck, gaining steadily. Old enough to start seeing the small, subtle signs of aging in your friends and in your mirror. Old enough, needless to say, to have a friend with a cocaine habit, and to realize that everything might not be all right in the end.

Thirty . . . . shit.

Alison lived on Central Park West, five blocks downtown and three blocks east of my apartment, but it might as well have been another world. I lived in a walk-up on Ninety-second between West End and Riverside, a nice enough area during the day, but at night it became a sinister trading post for drug dealers and pock-marked, anorexic junkies who transacted intimately on the stoops and sidewalks. Whenever I uneasily walked that gauntlet at night to or from my apartment, I felt like a conspicuous interloper, and prayed not for happiness and fulfillment, but simply to be left alone.

Over on Central Park West, you didn't have any of that. The co-op boards wouldn't stand for it. Each building lobby had at least two doormen to keep the neighborhood peaceful and the sidewalks clear of the urban dredges that found my neighborhood so appealing. Alison's neighbors were Mia Farrow, Diane Keaton, Tony Randall, Carly Simon, Madonna, and a host of other celebrities who could often be spotted between their canopied lobbies and their taxis, hailed for them by uniformed doormen with silver whistles. There was even a button in Alison's elevator with a little car etched onto it that signaled to the doorman that you wanted a cab, so that by the time you stepped out of the elevator, depending on how high up you lived, he was already out there hailing you one. If you lived in the penthouse, there might already be a taxi waiting for you by the time you got down, which was only fair. To get a cab from my apartment you had to walk over to West End and flag one down yourself, but more often than not you just walked up to Broadway and used the subway.

Alison's apartment was an expansive two-bedroom deal, with a separate dining room and eat-in kitchen, two large bathrooms and a view of Central Park. It had been a gift from her parents, so she didn't even have rent to worry about. Not that she *would* have worried about it with her six-figure salary and trust fund portfolio. The rich really do get richer. Her furnishings were spare but tasteful, although I'm sure the jade green, L-shaped leather couch in her living room had probably cost more than every stick of furniture in my apartment, stereo and VCR included.

When I got to the apartment, Lindsey and Alison had been sitting on said couch, under a framed Magritte, drinking apricot sours. Lindsey was casual in black Banana Republic jeans and a sleeveless denim vest, still sporting a fading summer tan, while Alison wore a short plaid skirt and a white T-shirt, with her hair back in a loose pony tail. Both women were beautiful, I thought, but like night and day. Lindsey was sexy but intimidating, while Alison was inviting but vulnerable.

"We were just saying," Lindsey said, "that our generation is the first for whom pop culture is our sole frame of reference. The way we assimilate every experience is through the lens of pop culture. We've been raised on it to the point that it's all we have to draw upon."

"Give an example," I said, joining her on the couch and resisting the impulse to kiss her. I settled for inhaling her perfume while I ordered a rum and soda from Alison. I had seen Lindsey only a handful of times in the past two years, so I still experienced a bittersweet flutter in my chest each time I saw her. The bitter-to-sweet ratio varied depending on my mood, but not surprisingly, bitter had been coming on a bit stronger lately.

"I know what she means," Alison said, getting up to mix me a drink at her bar. "It's like when we describe people in terms of movie stars. Our parents would never have described someone in terms of a movie star unless there was an uncanny resemblance. Movie stars weren't as universal, and there weren't nearly as many."

"And back then, not everyone would necessarily know what every star looked like," Lindsey added. "But now, thanks to the media-fed hunger for celebrity news, we're confident that when using those types of descriptions, anyone we speak to will understand. We might say someone is extremely large and muscular, but we can just as easily say he looks like a Schwarzenegger. People's names are becoming common, descriptive nouns that are universally recognized. Our language is evolving along with our frame of reference. It's becoming less descriptive and more visual. We don't describe with words. We describe by referencing a comparable image."

"It's an interesting notion," I said. "But it isn't exclusively limited to images. We can also describe people based on the kind of music or movies they like, or the books and magazines they read."

"Right," Alison said, handing me my drink and curling up on the other side of the L. "If you're telling me about a guy and you say he reads *Soldier of Fortune* magazine and listens to Van Halen or Anthrax, I begin to form a picture and an opinion in my mind, and I already know enough about him to know I wouldn't like him."

"Chuck loves Van Halen," Lindsey pointed out.

"I know," Alison said in just the right way to make us crack up.

Chuck arrived a few minutes later, still wearing his scrubs, although I was sure he'd had enough time to change. It was pure vanity, but after going through seven years of medical school, I figured he was entitled. He looked at our empty glasses on the coffee table and said, "Is it good form to get plastered for an intervention?"

"Definitely," Alison said.

"Especially if it's an intervention for you," Lindsey said.

"Can I get you a drink, Chuck?" I said.

"Well," Chuck said, "I guess if Jack's going to show up high as a kite, we have to do something to level the playing field."

After I'd made Chuck a screwdriver Alison announced that it was time to discuss strategy. She wanted us all to be at the door when she let Jack in, but I thought that doing it that way, we might never actually get Jack into the apartment. Lindsey suggested that Alison let Jack in and tell him we were all in the living room and wanted to talk to him, but Chuck thought that gave him too much of an edge. "I know it sounds odd," he said, "but we do need to catch him off guard." In the end it was decided that Alison would open the door alone, and then walk Jack into the living room, where we would be waiting.

Alison went to mix herself a second drink. Chuck lit up a cigarette, and when Alison didn't snap at him to put it out, I knew that she was extremely agitated.

"We're all nervous," I said quietly, coming up behind her at the bar. "It'll be okay."

"I passed nervous about an hour ago," she said. "I'm somewhere between sheer terror and calling the whole thing off."

Just then the buzzer rang twice, Oscar the doorman's signal. We all looked at each other, suddenly feeling a little ridiculous and greatly out of our depth. Even Lindsey, usually unflappable, looked uncomfortable. A minute later the doorbell rang.

"Showtime," Chuck whispered, and plopped down on the couch.

We heard Alison open the door and Jack's voice came floating into the living room. The three of us on the couch looked at each other, the guilt and unease we were feeling readable on our faces, a tangible manifestation that thickened the air of Alison's living room. Jack was our friend, and we had conspired against him and now were hiding from him. As Alison's and Jack's footsteps approached the living room, I actually felt a shiver in my stomach lining, as if I'd rubbed velvet.

And then, suddenly, he was there. Wearing blue jeans and a navy blazer over a white oxford, Jack looked every inch the movie star at ease. He was clean shaven and freshly showered, a far cry from the greasy, puking mess he'd been when we last saw him. I suddenly wondered if we'd made a huge mistake. Jack looked at us, his face a blank mask. He was clearly surprised, but managed to keep his cool and look only slightly puzzled. His eyes were only slightly hidden behind the green, minimally tinted lenses of his black-rimmed Gucci shades, the hot new accessory of the post-modern celebrity, their message: "I don't have to hide behind dark glasses to remain inaccessible."

It occurred to me that we hadn't discussed who should do the talking.

"Hi guys," Jack said, his tone friendly, but guarded.

We all stammered out hellos. It was a testament to Jack's presence that, walking into a situation in which he was the one surprised, he could nevertheless render us all equally nonplussed.

"Well," Jack said, removing the sunglasses, "I know it's not my birthday." I noted his eyes were significantly bloodshot, a complex network of pink scribbling in the whites beneath the iris.

"Jack," Alison said, her voice not quite steady, "everyone's here because we need to talk to you about something."

He walked into the center of the room with no hesitation and took a seat on the rug, Indian style. "Well, by all means," he said. "Don't keep me in suspense."

Alison cleared her throat and looked over at us, her eyes pleading for someone else to take it from there. When we all remained silent, Jack's eyes shifted to me. "Ben?" he said.

I looked at him, then at Alison, and then back at him. "This isn't easy, Jack," I said. "But the first thing I think that should be said is that we all care about you and consider you one of our closest friends." Even as I said it I knew it was coming out wrong. To speak in terms 'we' was to put Jack on one side and the rest of us on the other. We needed to say things in a way that formed more of a circle, with all of us on the circumference and Jack in the center. Of course, knowing what to do didn't mean I actually knew how to do it.

"Are you breaking up with me, Ben?" Jack said, with a sarcastic smile.

"We're worried about you, Jack," Lindsey said. "We think you might need some help."

His eyebrows went up as the meaning behind our gathering finally dawned on him. "What," he said. "I get a little fucked up one night and you think I can't handle myself anymore?"

"You know it's a lot more than just that last night," Alison said.

"No," Jack said. "I don't. I'll tell you what the problem is here." He got to his feet, his face suddenly flushed with anger. "The problem is that my friends read all the Hollywood glamour trades, the bullshit magazines that don't know shit from a shoe box, and they read about how all these movie stars are getting fucked up on heroin, like River Phoenix and Robert Downey Jr. and Christian Slater. So naturally, if Jack shows up hammered one night, he must be in the same fucking boat! Poor Jack can't handle the pressures of stardom, got himself a little heroin problem, but then, he never was the bright one. Jesus Christ!"

"Cocaine," Chuck said to him.

"What?"

"It's cocaine. Your aggression and increased energy are consistent with an acute intoxication from a sympathomimetic-like drug such as cocaine. Heroin is an opiate. Much tougher to function with. You're keeping way too busy to be nursing a heroin habit. Not to mention the ulcerated tissue in your nose."

"Thank you," Jack said to Chuck as he began to back out of the living room, his eyes blazing. "That was genuinely informative, and I think we've all learned something. But I've got a show to get to and this is getting very boring."

"Jack, don't go," said Alison. "Please, stay and talk to us. We're your friends."

"Fuck you, Alison," he spat at her, and she winced visibly as if slapped. "Fuck you and your little feel-good therapy session. If you were my friend you'd be able to talk to me as a friend instead of ambushing me."

"You know that's not what this is," Alison said softly, her lower lip quavering.

"Hey!" Lindsey said, jumping to Alison's defense. "How the hell can she talk to you when you're either stoned, puking, or being carried out the back door by your agent?"

"You know what I think?" Jack said, turning to leave the room. "I think your lives are all so boring and empty that you'll do anything to create a little drama for yourselves, to feel a little better about your pathetic, little lives. Even if it means trashing mine."

"You know that's bullshit," I said, getting angry in spite of myself. "Just because we don't have glamorous cocaine habits like you doesn't make our lives pathetic."

"Really, Ben? Why don't you talk to me when you publish something a little more substantial than 'Five Essential Evening Accessories.' "

"Shut up, Jack," Lindsey said.

"I'll do you one better," Jack said. "I'm out of here."

He spun around and a few seconds later we heard the door slam. Alison, standing in the center of the room, stared after him, her jaw hanging open in disbelief. The rest of us sat on the couch, feeling like shit.

"I think we handled that pretty well," Chuck said.

4

Later that night I sat in front of the blank screen of my computer, as was my habit, waiting in vain for inspiration to strike. It didn't, as was its habit, and as my mind drifted I found myself remembering my earlier conversation with Alison and Lindsey concerning our generation's utter reliance on pop culture as our common frame of reference. It was like this game we often played back at NYU, describing people in terms of the movie star they resembled. If art imitated life, we wanted to make sure that we were all represented. We were big cinema-heads back then, which is probably what drew the five of us together in the first place. Movies tend to go out of style in college, especially for NYU students who feel a moral obligation to seek out the more avant-garde forms of entertainment available in the cultural smorgasbord of New York's Greenwich Village. Those of us who eschewed the drag-queen coffee shops, tattoo parlors and art-house flicks for good old-fashioned cinema were bound to find each other.

If Lindsey were a movie star, she would be a young Michelle Pfeiffer, with soft, mocha skin, emerald eyes, and an exquisitely full upper lip curling into a lazy smile that's somehow both seductive and sincere. When I met Lindsey in our freshman year, she was so wildly desirable that I instantly decided I had no right to be friends with her. Beneath her beauty and in-your-face sexuality was a sharp intelligence and spirituality, which did nothing to make her less desirable. If resisting sexual impulses toward a close friend was an Olympic event, I would have a few gold medals hanging on the wall next to my diploma.

Alison would be Mia Farrow in her early Woody Allen days. There's something about her that makes you want to kiss her on the forehead and tell her that everything will be all right. At twenty-nine she still seems impossibly innocent despite her Connecticut, white-bread sophistication, wide eyes, perfect teeth and a bearing that bespeaks a childhood of violin lessons and country clubs.

Chuck is Jack Nicholson, down to the widow's peak. He also has Nicholson's mischievous-bordering-on-mad smile, his infinite reserve of confidence and penchant for incessant flirtation. Chuck admits with no shame that he's in surgery for the money. He views the current trend toward what he calls the socialization of medicine with open distaste and quiet alarm. He is a staunch, unapologetic Republican to the point of caricature. He's actually read Rush Limbaugh's book. I don't know Jack Nicholson's politics, but somewhere in the eighties I read an interview in *Rolling Stone* where Jack said that he would vote for Gary Hart "because Gary Hart fucks and I think we should have a president who fucks." That's Chuck.

If I were a movie star, I'd want to be a young Mel Gibson, but who wouldn't? The cold hard truth is that I'm probably closer to

Dustin Hoffman in *The Marathon Man,* although without the schnozola, thank you very much. Athletic, optimistic, sarcastic, although my heart's not always in it, and only mildly introverted. On the plus side, like Hoffman, I, too, have had marginal success with women who, from a Darwinian standpoint, shouldn't have given me the time of day.

Jack is the easiest. If Jack were a movie star he'd be himself.

I looked up at the monitor in order to make sure that I hadn't gone into a trance and written some award-winning fiction while lost in thought, and after confirming that my screen remained stubbornly blank, I hit return for good measure and began to type a list.

After doing the lists at *Esquire* for a while, you get into the habit of thinking about everything in terms of lists, especially stuff like this.

Ten CDs you'd be likely to find in Chuck's car:

1. Van Halen: *Best of Van Halen*
2. Led Zeppelin: *4*
3. Foreigner: *Records* (A greatest hits album)
4. Guns N' Roses: *Use Your Illusion 1* and *2*
5. Kiss: *Greatest Kiss*
6. Aerosmith: *Aerosmith's Greatest Hits*
7. Def Leppard: *Pyromania*
8. AC/DC: *AC/DC Live*
9. Whitesnake: *Saints & Sinners*
10. Poison: *Look What the Cat Dragged In*

Lindsey *was* right. There might really be something to this whole pop culture thing.

Ten CDs you'd probably find in Lindsey's car:

1. Juliana Hatfield: *Become What You Are*
2. The Ramones: *Too Tough to Die*
3. No Doubt: *Tragic Kingdom*
4. Joe Jackson: *Joe Jackson's Greatest Hits* (My influence)
5. REM: *Life's Rich Pageant*
6. Barenaked Ladies: *Stunt*
7. Peter Gabriel: *Shaking the Tree*
8. Crash Test Dummies: *God Shuffled His Feet*
9. Liz Phair: *whitechocolatespaceegg*
10. Sheryl Crow: *Tuesday Night Music Club*

Here's what you'd find in my car, in the unlikely event that I had a car, and in the further unlikely event that it had a CD player:

1. Billy Joel: *The Nylon Curtain*
2. Joe Jackson: *Look Sharp*
3. Ben Folds Five: *Whatever & Ever Amen*
4. John Hiatt: *Hanging Around the Observatory*
5. Elton John: *Goodbye Yellow Brick Road*
6. The Beatles: *Sgt. Pepper's Lonely Hearts Club Band*
7. Elvis Costello: *This Year's Model*
8. Bruce Springsteen: *Born to Run*
9. Sting: *The Soul Cages*
10. Peter Himmelman: *Flown This Acid World*

Alison, predictably, is into what Chuck calls "vagina music":

1. The Indigo Girls: *Rites of Passage*
2. 10,000 Maniacs: *Our Time in Eden*
3. Jewel: *Pieces of You*
4. Sarah McLachlan: *Fumbling Towards Ecstasy*
5. The Cranberries: *No Need to Argue*

6. Lisa Loeb: *Tails*
7. Alanis Morissette: *Jagged Little Pill*
8. Shawn Colvin: *Fat City*
9. Stevie Nicks: *Bella Donna*
10. Lisa Stansfield: *Real Love*

The truth is, most of the music we listen to now is the same stuff we were listening to in college. Around age twenty-six, in an effort to stave off thirty, I began embracing the new alternative angst bands, like Pearl Jam, Nine Inch Nails, Bush, Stone Temple Pilots, et cetera, but at thirty, little of that remains. At thirty, you're back to the comforting sounds you grew up with. You have enough genuine angst of your own, you don't need it in your music.

5

Once, while we were visiting Jack in LA, he took Chuck and me to a party thrown by a producer friend of his in Beverly Hills. Jack had dressed us for the occasion in dark single-breasted Hugo Boss suits, Dolce & Gabbana loafers, pale shirts and no ties, and I felt like I had "impostor" stenciled on my forehead in bold ink. We shared a joint that Jack produced in the limo which gave me a sore throat but helped me to arrive at the party feeling loose and hip. The house was a single-story ranch surrounded by dense foliage, with stucco walls that had long since been colonized by aggressive ivy. You couldn't tell where the house stopped and the foliage began. We stepped through the front door and down three steps into a giant sunken living room that felt more like an auditorium, and everywhere you looked there seemed to be groups of tall blonde women in little black dresses. "Whoa," Chuck said appreciatively. "Hey mister, is this heaven?"

"Next best thing," Jack said with a smirk. "AMW's. Hollywood's greatest natural resource."

"AMWs?" I asked.

"Actress/Model/Whatever," Jack replied with a shrug.

"Amen," Chuck intoned reverently.

Jazz was being played much too loudly on the stereo. I noticed that there were clusters of men throughout the room, and most of them were dressed similarly to me. Weaving expertly in and out of the crowd was another class of men, all well built in tight vests over short-sleeved shirts, with sculpted hair and dazzling teeth. These men carried trays with colorful hors d'oeuvres, but they seemed to be socializing as much as everyone else. I turned to ask Jack if he had an acronym for them as well, but he'd already disappeared into the crowd, so rather than assigning them the same letters as the blondes; Actor/Model/Waiter, I designated them Pretty Boys.

I looked to my left and saw Jack approaching a group of four men in suits, the fattest of whom was beckoning to him frantically, waving his cigar around as if he was trying to spell something. "There he is," the guy yelled theatrically, and it sounded like he had pebbles bouncing around in his esophagus. He threw his arm around Jack's shoulders. "There he is! This guy! Let me tell you about this guy!" Jack was absorbed into a cloud of smoke and suits, leaving Chuck and me to navigate on our own. We made our way over to the bar, manned by one of the Pretty Boys, and Chuck got himself two drinks and carried them over to a bored looking AMW standing against the wall. He rapped to her for a bit and although her expression never changed, she accepted the drink even while her eyes continued to patrol the room over his shoulder.

Left alone at the bar, I had two quick shots of Absolut Citron to bolster my incipient buzz and then took a glass of something fruity to occupy my hands as I strolled around the house. It had been about four months since Lindsey left. I was still an open wound, and there was something intoxicating in the notion of hooking up with one of these exotic strangers for a night of dispassionate sex. Self-degradation as validation, or maybe some mis-directed form of revenge. Sex as Novocain. Either way, thinking about it reminded me that I was horny. I walked slowly past one of the dark leather couches, where an emaciated woman with skin the color of barbecue-flavored Pringles was complaining about her latest cosmetic surgery to a guy in a black blazer with Elvis hair and a unibrow. "It was so upsetting," she said. "I mean, he's sup-posed to be the best, isn't he? That's what everyone says. And then I wake up with this," here she indicated the left portion of her supernatural bosom.

"I don't believe it," the Elvis guy said sympathetically. "Is it really that pronounced?"

"Look," the woman said and pulled up her brown, clinging blouse, revealing a startlingly round bare breast that seemed to almost glow against the dark backdrop of the couch. Despite her vertical posture the breast didn't hang, but seemed to protrude independently from her chest. There was something erotic in that, and in the blasé way she unveiled it for inspection. I couldn't discern any defects, but Elvis continued to nod sympathetically, and I became aware that I was staring at the precise instant that they did. She flashed me a disdainful look and slowly lowered her blouse. There were rules here, I realized. You could look, but you couldn't show too much interest. Indifference was the currency, and without it you stood out as an alien, instantly exposed and summarily dismissed. Chagrined, I moved on.

There were French doors behind the couch, and the party had spilled out onto a wide patio that surrounded a kidney-shaped swimming pool. The only lights in the yard were those shining up from the pool, and in their dim glow the milling guests looked like shadows. I spotted a woman sitting alone by the side of the pool, one leg dangling lazily over the edge of her lounge chair. Cute, but not nearly as striking as most of the women at the party, which made me feel like I had a chance. With Lindsey's departure I had become a committed believer in the notion that a man's reach shouldn't exceed his grasp. I walked over and sat down on the adjacent chair. "How are you," I said, affecting a slightly midwestern accent for no reason I could think of.

"Great," she said guardedly. "You a friend of Ike's?"

"Ike?" I said, realizing too late that she meant the host of the party.

"Wow," she said sardonically. "What were the odds?"

"What do you mean?" I asked her.

"Nothing." She took a sip of her drink. "I'm just being a bitch."

I sipped my own drink. "It's Ike's house?" I asked her.

"Yeah." She leaned back in her chair and stretched. I could see a small strip of smooth, white skin below her naval as her shirt rode up. "I'm his sister," she said. "What's your excuse?"

"I'm just here with Jack," I said.

"Jack Shaw?" she said, instantly perking up.

"The same."

"Cool."

I hadn't deliberately dropped Jack's name, at least I didn't think I had, but I still wondered if it had gotten me anywhere. I sat back quietly, waiting to see what would happen next. It didn't take very long. "Could you introduce me to him?" she finally asked.

"Sure," I said. We got up and were headed inside when a technicality occurred to me. "I don't know your name," I said.

"Oh, right. It's Valerie."

"Nice to meet you," I said. She didn't ask for my name.

We walked into the living room where I found Chuck drunk on the couch, building a large pyramid out of about twenty used shot glasses. "Don't worry," he assured me. "They weren't all mine."

"What's going on?" I said.

"This party sucks," he complained, carefully adding another glass. "These girls are all seven feet tall and they won't talk to you unless you're like, Steven Spielberg or something."

"This is Valerie," I said.

He looked up. "You found the only short one," he said with a sigh. I looked to see if Valerie was insulted, but she was too busy scanning the room for Jack. "Have you seen Jack?" I asked.

"Downstairs," he said.

Leaving Valerie with Chuck, I found my way into the kitchen, where the Pretty Boys were fussing over some burners for the fondue, and I located a door that led to the basement. I followed the stairs down into a dimly lit, finished basement, which had a couch and some easy chairs all facing the biggest television I'd ever seen. The sound was off, and on the screen Bruce Lee was silently kicking Kareem Abdul-Jabbar's face in. The noise from upstairs was now muted, and I savored the quiet as my eyes adjusted to the dark. There didn't appear to be anyone down there, so I turned to head back upstairs when I noticed a door to the left of the television. Feeling suddenly like an intruder, I approached the door and pushed it open tentatively. At first I saw only darkness, but then, as what little light there was poured in from the doorway, I was able to make out bookshelves and a desk at the far end of the room. Jack was leaning against the far wall, his head tilted back as if he'd fallen asleep standing up. I was about to call out to him when I noticed that he seemed to be swaying slightly, forward and back; and as my eyes strained in the semidarkness, I was able to make out the form of someone else, a woman, kneeling between his legs, her bent form undulating as her head bobbed in and out of his groin. I let the door swing shut quietly and just stood there for a moment, slightly dizzy, my fingers resting lightly on the wooden door. Then I turned and went back upstairs, woozy from the pot and alcohol, which weren't sitting well together, and conflicted over what I'd just seen.

Chuck and Valerie were still on the couch, and the pyramid of shot glasses had now spread across the entire coffee table, six and seven cups high. I noticed one of the Pretty Boys giving Chuck a dirty look from over by the bar. "Did you find him?" Valerie asked.

"He's a little busy right now," I said. "We'll catch him later." I looked around the room, which suddenly felt too hot and crowded. "I'm going back outside."

"I'll join you," Valerie said, getting up from the couch.

"Go on, go ahead," Chuck said drunkenly, waving grandly at us. "You two kids enjoy yourselves." He always became a benevolent grandfather when he was wasted. He indicated the wall of shot glasses. "I'll be right here if you need me. Building my fortress of solitude."

We walked around to the side of the house, where Valerie showed me a small enclosure of high bushes that housed a Jacuzzi and two wooden benches. We sat down on one of the benches and for the first time since we'd arrived at the party I felt myself relaxing. I leaned back and breathed in deeply, inhaling the clean scent of chlorine and Valerie's light perfume. Eventually, we began making out, necking and petting like a couple of high school kids. It was actually kind of nice, but then she began groping at my belt, and something in the utilitarian way she worked on my buckle made me suddenly depressed. I grabbed her wrist just as she was lowering my zipper, feeling myself grow cold against her heat. "Stop," I said. I couldn't shake the picture of Jack in that dark room, his eyes closed as the anonymous woman serviced him.

"What's wrong?" she asked, both of our hands still poised over my crotch.

"Nothing," I said, releasing her hand and moving away from

her on the bench. I was disgusted with myself, with Jack, with Los Angeles. I felt a yearning for Lindsey so overpowering that it stopped my breath in my throat.

"Well," Valerie said sarcastically after an awkward silence. "This is something new."

"I'm sorry," I said, fixing my pants.

"Don't worry about it," she said. "I think I'll go back inside now."

"Okay."

She walked off, tucking in her blouse and looking slightly irked. I was irked at myself, too. Jack, of all people, getting head in the basement shouldn't have disturbed me, but it did. Somehow the image of him leaning against the wall like that had brought crashing home to me with stunning clarity that his immersion into this foreign society was complete, and had been for some time. That he'd taken a large and irrevocable step away from the rest of us. We were no longer best friends, we were simply old friends. Lindsey was gone, Jack was gone. It felt like I was slowly disappearing, bit by bit, and that soon there would be none of me left.

I needed to be around people. I felt a moment's regret over cutting short my encounter with Valerie, and headed back inside to join Chuck. As I stepped through the front doors, I saw Jack come through the kitchen doors across the room. He caught my eye, smiled and began moving through the crowd toward to me. He was almost there when I heard a shriek, followed by the shrill cacophony of breaking glass, as Chuck's shot glasses came crashing down on the coffee table. All conversation stopped, as everyone in the room turned to look at the couch. Chuck waved his hand weakly, as if acknowledging polite applause then looked at Jack and me, flashing a besotted smile. "I'm ready to go home now," he announced, then fell back on the couch and passed out.

6

Thirty . . . shit. Older than my parents were when they had me. I used to play basketball because I enjoyed it. Now it's just one more thing I do to stay in shape. Soon they'll have to start sending an annual search party up my rectum to check on my colon. When Mozart was my age he'd already written the bulk of his work. When Kurt Cobain was my age he'd been dead for two years.

What was Bill Gates doing when he was thirty? What was John Lennon doing when he was thirty? What was I doing two weeks ago? I can't even remember. *Thirty . . . shit!*

Two nights after our botched intervention I was home watching an old Stallone movie on HBO when Lindsey called.

"Hi."

"Lindsey?"

"Didn't recognize me?"

"It's been a while since we talked on the phone," I said.

"I never really felt comfortable calling when I knew Sarah was there. I don't think she really approved of me," Lindsey said.

"It was a case of retroactive jealousy," I said.

"I know," she said. "I had it too."

"Really?"

"Sure. Most women would like to see their ex-boyfriends dead and buried before they see them with someone else."

"Most women should have thought of that before dumping said boyfriends on their asses."

"Uh-huh," Lindsey said slowly, acknowledging the dig. "You're not going to get into all of that now, are you?"

"Sorry," I said, already regretting the remark. "I just felt like blaming someone for my current woes."

"Forgotten."

We observed a brief moment of silence in honor of our ill-fated past, our breathing resonating through the mild static of the phone lines. Staying friends after a breakup is fine in theory, but in practice it's a constant funeral, a sublimely tragic combination of wistful remembrance and perpetual regret. "I've missed talking to you," I said.

"I missed you, too," she said lightly. "That's why I called."

"Oh."

"So, when will you be officially divorced?" she asked.

"The lawyers have already drawn up the papers. We're getting together tomorrow for a signing party."

"I'm really sorry, Benny. She doesn't know what she's losing."

"She's got a pretty good idea, I think." Did you? I thought to myself, but thankfully managed not to say it out loud.

"Would it be bad timing to suggest dinner tomorrow night?" she asked. "Kind of celebrating your new status as a free man?"

"It would be excellent timing," I said. "But I don't think I should be out with a woman the night after my divorce. At least not one I care about. In that vulnerable state, I think my intentions might be misconstrued."

"By me?"

"By me," I said.

"I was just talking about a fucking dinner, Ben," she said, insulted.

Call waiting beeped. "Hang on a second," I said, grateful for the interruption.

"Turn on Fox News," Chuck said after the click. "Quickly."

I grabbed the clicker and flipped to channel five. And there was Paul Seward, Jack's agent, talking to a gaggle of microphones. I clicked back to Lindsey and told her to turn on the news.

". . . a minor incident that has been blown out of proportion," Seward was saying. "Jack Shaw does not have a drug problem. Everyone is entitled to an occasional bad day. I fully expect him to be out of the hospital and back to work within a few days."

The voice-over of a news correspondent came on. "Jack Shaw, whose last three movies have grossed a combined total of three hundred and forty million dollars domestically, became a major star after appearing in *Blue Angel,* an action film in which ironically, Shaw played a rehabilitated drug addict out to avenge the death of his family . . ." The voice droned on as they ran footage of Jack in *Angel,* firing a gun as he ran between moving cars on the California freeway.

The program then cut to the scene of what appeared to be a car accident on one of those winding roads in the Hollywood hills. According to the nauseatingly earnest news correspondent, Jack Shaw had driven his Range Rover into a tree at over sixty miles an hour, bounced back into the street and narrowly missed a school bus full of children before coming to a rest in a small gully by the side of the road. Predictably, the news was playing up the school bus angle.

"Shaw's car missed the school bus by inches, barely avoiding what could have been a major tragedy," the correspondent was saying. "Local police have released a statement saying that Jack Shaw was booked at the scene for driving under the influence and for possession of a controlled substance."

"Oh shit," Lindsey said.

The camera was now on the correspondent, who was standing outside of County Hospital in Los Angeles.

"Shaw is listed in stable condition at County Hospital, and his doctors expect to release him within forty-eight hours. But his legal battles are just beginning. For Fox News in Hollywood, I'm Rick Brian."

"I'd better call Alison," Lindsey said.

"Bye." I clicked back to Chuck. "Holy shit," I said.

"You missed the part where they interview the school bus driver. He gave this whole song and dance about how, if he hadn't jammed on the brakes, Jack would have taken them all out."

"Do you think he's okay?"

"They say he's stable. I've got a friend who's doing his OB-GYN residency over there. I'll call him and see if he can find anything out."

"Maybe this will shake Jack up a little," I said. "Convince him he's got a problem."

"Yeah," Chuck said. "Don't count on it."

By the time I'd gotten off the phone, I no longer had the patience to watch Stallone and his abs take on the Vietcong. I flipped on my computer and scrolled through the first few chapters of my latest literary attempt. I must have started half a dozen novels in my tenure at *Esquire,* all of which were really the same novel told from different points of view, none of which were working. I just couldn't seem to sustain a tone, the sense of emotional desolation I was trying to convey. I would read guys like Jay

McInerny and wonder at the ease with which he imbued his characters and the city itself with such a dark sense of casual futility. I wasn't trying to be McInerny. I knew I hadn't been to enough night clubs, dated enough models, or stayed up enough nights doing drugs with overeducated, preppy friends to even get near his subject matter. But I envied him his range of life experience and his ability to effortlessly draw upon it and make you feel you could relate, even when you couldn't. Not being part of any obvious subculture, I couldn't seem to find a setting in which to frame my characters. My failure to locate a context from my own life in Manhattan, even a dark dismal one, often left me feeling isolated and depressed. What the hell had I been doing for the last eight years and how was I going to write anything worthwhile without being able to access any significant pathos from my experiences?

Not surprisingly, I didn't feel like writing. I stripped down, briefly checking out my naked torso in the bathroom mirror, for what I don't know. I did a few perfunctory stretches and flexes, then caught my own eye and, suddenly bashful in front of myself, retreated to the shower. Showers for me are more than simply a place to clean off the accumulated grime of yet another day in New York City. They're more like those sensory deprivation tanks that Michael Jackson supposedly sleeps in. Put me in a bathtub, and I'm itching to get out after five minutes, but I can spend an hour in the shower. It's where I do my best brooding.

I thought about Jack and I thought about Lindsey. I wondered if there was anything I could do about either one. I thought about Sarah and wondered if I was sad because she was gone, or just sad because one more thing that was supposed to last hadn't. Was I grieving? Or was I just depressed that I wasn't? Friendship, love, youth, and fulfillment. All these impermanent things. When I finally stepped out of the shower, the tips of my fingers were shriveled like prunes, like the hands of an elderly man.

7

The first time I spoke to Lindsey was at a party at Aces and Eights in the winter of our freshman year. By then I'd been watching her for weeks, not so much frustrated by my inability to approach her as resigned to it. Every time I saw her around campus she was talking to one guy or another, always someone taller and edgier than me. I categorized them. Boris, the Film Student. Cyrus, the Anorexic Guitarist. Matt, the White Guy with Dreadlocks. Theron, the Stoned Poet. I fervently brainstormed for an oddball gimmick to make me something other than Ben, the Normal Guy, but inspiration never struck. They were hardcore rock and roll and I was a Bryan Adams guitar solo.

It was an utterly typical undergrad shindig. Strobe lights, pounding music, everyone blowing smoke into their drinks. Chuck and I were sitting in a corner doing vodka shots with these two girls I knew from one of my lit surveys but whose names I'd forgotten. Next to us was the requisite table of beer-soaked rowdies quoting Monty Python scenes verbatim, shouting to be heard above the music. "It's just a flesh wound!" "I'm Brian and so is my wife!" "Say no more, say no more. Nudge nudge, wink wink!" Chuck was arguing with one of the girls about what a dumb career move it was for Shelley Long to have left *Cheers*. The other one was telling me about some paper she'd written with the questionable thesis that Edith Wharton was the Danielle Steel of her day. I earned an impatient look for ironically suggesting that Henry James might likewise be compared to Sidney Sheldon. "Radio Free Europe" was blasting on the club speakers and I was getting progressively more nauseous. A "slammer girl" wandered into the vicinity wearing a bandolier that held dollar Jell-O shots in little test tubes. The Monty Python guys attacked her and in the ensuing chaos I managed to slip outside for some fresh air.

I walked to the corner and sat on the hood of a battered Honda, savoring the cold December air even as it made me shiver, breathing deep and slow to fight off the nausea. It was well past midnight and Broadway was fairly empty. The door to Aces and Eights flew open and Lindsey came out and began striding up the block in my direction. I was too buzzed to employ my usual discretion, so I just stared at her as she came toward me. She was wearing jeans and a black, fuzzy sweater, her face flushed and sweaty from dancing. It was the first time I'd seen her alone. I was drunk and she was alone and my chances wouldn't get much better than that, so I got off the car and said, "Hi, I'm Ben, I don't think we've met yet," or something equally witty, and she threw up on my shoes.

She threw up twice more on the way back to her dorm, and passed out before she could tell me which one she lived in, so I brought her back to my room. Carrying her down my hallway, I passed Jack and some girl heading outside. "Way to go, Ben," he said with a smile. "Maybe soon you'll work your way up to live girls."

"Shut up and help me with the door."

I laid her down on my bed and considered taking off her sweater, which had some dried vomit on it, but I didn't know what she had on under it and I didn't want my motives questioned, so I just rolled her up in my comforter and rinsed her face gently with a damp washcloth. She groaned once, then rolled over and fell asleep. I took a quick shower, popped a few Tylenols and sat down in my desk chair to watch Lindsey sleep. I spent some time considering some of the things I might say to her when she woke up, but when I opened my eyes in my chair the next morning, my neck knotted and my throat dry, she was already gone.

I didn't see her for three days after that. For a while I entertained the notion that she might call to thank me, but then I realized that I'd never even gotten the chance to tell her my name, which meant she couldn't get my number from the school directory. I didn't know her last name either, which saved me the bother of having to wimp out of calling her. I tried to hang out in all of the places I'd seen her before, but she never showed up.

It was a Sunday morning and I'd all but given up on parlaying our sleep over into anything when I looked out my window and saw her sitting in the snow. It was the first storm of the winter and by the time I'd woken up Washington Square Park was already buried under a few inches. The streets were covered, parked cars submerged, and the snow was still coming down, hard and thick. The park was deserted. Then I noticed her, on a bench beneath my window, just sitting and staring out across the park. Even from six stories up and without a full view of her face, I knew it was Lindsey. I threw on a jacket, some jeans, and Docksiders and ran downstairs, desperately afraid she'd be gone before I got there. When I got down to the lobby I looked out and she was still there, in black corduroys and a black and red ski jacket, her blond hair tied in a loose ponytail. I was horribly underdressed, both for the occasion and the weather. My resolve started to waver, more from habit than anything else, but I reminded myself that I'd watched her puke her guts out, and if puking wasn't enough of a social equalizer, nothing would be.

"Hi," I said, approaching the bench. "Remember me?"

She looked up and said, "Hi," which didn't exactly answer my question.

"We shared some puke?" I said. "You spent the night?"

"I remember," she said, with a grin. She had one dimple. "God, was I wrecked."

"Do you mind if I join you?" I asked with manufactured confidence.

"Not at all."

I sat down with her and we watched the snow fall together for a few minutes. We seemed to be the only two people around, except some guys all the way on the other side of the park having a snowball fight. Her hair was flecked with bulging snowflakes and I felt mine getting covered as well. The only sound was the barely audible, crystalline whisper of the snow as it hit the ground around us. I'd never thought of snow as having sound before.

"So," I said. "Are you waiting for someone?"

"No," she said. "I just love weather."

"Well you're in luck. There always seems to be some, you know?"

She smiled. "I mean, I like extreme weather. I like storms."

Whatever insecurities I had left were somehow buried along with everything else in the rapidly falling snow, and I was able to turn to her and look at her square on, without a wry comment to protect myself and say, "What else do you like?"

We sat there for about two hours, talking effortlessly. Homes, high schools, families, majors, movies. It was as if we were giving each other owner's manuals. The snow was like walls around us, enclosing us in a private room. She watched her breath in the cold air and swung her leg back and forth easily under the bench, and somewhere in it all I forgot to be thrilled that I was talking to her and just started liking her. My toes were frozen in my Docksiders.

"I guess it all boils down to the Peanut Story," she said at one point.

"What?" I asked. "Like Charlie Brown and Snoopy?"

"No, my Peanut Story." She turned to face me, folding her leg under to sit on her calf. There was really no getting around her beauty. It was like a warm liquid slowly spreading through my insides. "I have a Peanut Story."

"Lay it on me."

"Okay," she said, and took a deep breath. "Here it is. Now I don't actually remember this, since I was very young when it happened, but my grandmother has told it to me so many times that it feels like a real memory."

"Like *Total Recall*."

"Exactly. Anyway, it's more of an episode than a story. When I was thirteen months old, I found a peanut on the living room floor and tried to eat it. It got stuck in my throat and I began to choke. My mother heard me and stuck her fingers down my throat to try to get it out, but it was in too deep. By the time the paramedics came I had stopped breathing, and my face was as purple as a wine grape. They resuscitated me in the ambulance, got the peanut out, whatever. By the time we got to the hospital, I was fine. My mother was a wreck, though, and some asshole doctor gave her hell and told her she was an irresponsible mother and that I could have died and it would have been her fault."

The guys across the way now came tearing across the park, running past our bench throwing snowballs at each other. I realized that to them it appeared simply that Lindsey and I were together, and I had a vague, half-formed thought about how perception, however uniformed, could be the first building block of a larger reality. The notion didn't crystallize, but I enjoyed the proprietary sensation of being observed with Lindsey by strangers.

"Anyway," she continued. "I had a bit of a behavior problem toward the end of elementary school and in high school. You know, mouthing off to teachers, staying out all night, a lot of boyfriends. Just your general adolescent bullshit, I guess. But whenever I got into trouble my grandmother would always trace it back to the day I swallowed that peanut. She said my mother was never the same after that. She grew more and more distant from me, like she was afraid or had no right to show me any real love, because she'd almost killed me. I know my mother never yelled at me or punished me. My friends thought she was so cool, you know?" I nodded. "I think that night at the hospital she decided she didn't have the ability to be a parent. And my acting out was this pathetic attempt to try to shake her out of it, to force her to step in and punish me. To actually be my mom, you know?" She looked up at me then quickly down at her boot, embarrassed. "I sometimes think about what might have been if the peanut thing never happened." She flashed a sideways smile and raised her eyebrows. "Anyway, that's my Peanut Story."

I sat back and exhaled. "Wow," I said.

She gave a short laugh. "It just occurred to me that I've never told that story before."

This time my wow was significantly louder, but I only thought it. "Why now?"

"I don't know," she said, catching a snowflake on her mitten. "The snow. Whatever. I just thought you'd understand."

"Thank you."

"Don't thank me, tell me yours."

"What?"

"Tell me your Peanut Story. Everyone's got one, you know? Some seemingly innocuous event that in retrospect changed everything."

"I don't know," I said. "I don't think I have one. Maybe that's my problem."

"Come on," she said, giving my shoulder a friendly push. "Everyone's got one."

I looked at her through the falling snow and decided to chance it. "I guess maybe this, right here, could become my Peanut Story."

She didn't look away or make a face. She stared earnestly at me, searching for any signs of sarcasm, and then broke into a warm, brilliant smile. "You're going to be a handful," she said. "I can tell."

I blew into my hands. I didn't have a crush on her anymore. I was probably halfway to being in love with her, and I didn't trust myself to say anything more. By now a number of other people had entered the park, walking their dogs, playing with their children, or just strolling through the snow, leaving footprints. We sat back and took in the scene in companionable silence. Lindsey said, "This is nice."

I said, "Yeah."

Later, we built a snowman.

After our day in the snow, Lindsey and I became close friends, which wasn't exactly what I'd set out to accomplish, but it was fine. There was something intimate, and certainly romantic in the way we related to each other. We understood each other completely and reveled in the confidence with which we could navigate through each other's minds. It was exhilarating to know someone so well. I never pushed for more because I was so scared of ruining what we had. Which isn't to say that I wasn't in a constant state of wanting her.

You make certain assumptions about beautiful girls. The first thing I had assumed about Lindsey was that she'd never even talk to me. Once I got past that, I discovered that Lindsey defied my expectations at every possible turn. Where I anticipated a jaded smile I found one that was completely sincere. Where I expected a throaty, sexy voice I heard a soft, musical one. She had a dry, self-deprecating wit, but she never indulged in the vanity of false modesty. She had to have been aware of her innate gifts, but she somehow functioned independently of them. There was no denying her smoldering sensuality, which affected me even on a molecular level, but what ultimately seduced me was the indomitable zeal she put into simply living.

Lindsey did nothing halfway. She found something fascinating in every experience, and her enthusiasm was infectious. She drew me in with her ardor even when discussing the most mundane things, and when she listened it was with rapt attention and an unwavering gaze. She could make me laugh not only with a sarcastic remark but simply by laughing herself. When she cried at movies she cried hard, and I would inevitably feel my own eyes watering. When I was with Lindsey I came out of a shell I didn't even know I was in, and it was as if the world was suddenly in sharper focus, with brighter colors. She gave me leave to discard my insecurities, and buoyed by her wake, I felt as if I was finally getting my money's worth out of myself. I knew early on that if Lindsey loved me, she would bring that same passion to bear on me, and I spent countless hours in contemplation of that intoxicating possibility.

We were both aware of the strong attraction between us, and rather than avoid it, Lindsey embraced it. She was always hugging me, linking her arm through mine, holding my hand, kissing my cheek, cuddling. But we both understood that it wouldn't go any farther than that. We got involved with other people from time to time, but always with the unspoken knowledge that in some way we belonged to each other. Unspoken, because there was no way it could be articulated and sound rational. It was like we were saving ourselves for ourselves, which, as I said, doesn't make a whole lot of sense.

One night in our sophomore year Lindsey and I went out dancing. Both of us had just come out of short-term relationships, an event that always seemed to coincide for us. I had been dating an Israeli music major named Ronit, who liked to light candles and play the recorder in bed after we had sex. She was good-looking in an outdoorsy way, but I had no real reason for dating her other than because I could. I guess she caught on because one day she asked me to meet her for coffee and showed up with a Macy's bag full of every book and CD I'd ever lent her and whatever clothing I'd left in her dorm room. Lindsey had just ended things with Gordon, the Porsche Guy. Enough said.

We were at Rascals, slow-dancing to "Nothing Compares to You," and Lindsey said, "Ben, you know that you're like the only guy I know who hasn't tried to get me into bed?"

"I just work really slow," I said.

"You're the greatest friend I ever had, Benny."

I looked at her. "Is that what we are, friends?"

"You know we're more than that," she said.

"What are we then?" I asked, not angry but genuinely curious. "We're not lovers."

"We're more than that, too," she said.

"Well what does that leave? Platonic friends?"

She put her lips against my ear and said, "I don't think so."

We swayed back and forth while Sinead O'Connor moaned about her dying flowers. "Well," I finally said. "What are we then?"

"Why do we have to give it a definition? We're our own category. A new species."

"So we're a case of natural selection?"

"Something like that."

"Works for me," I said, pulling her close.

She laughed and hugged me tightly. "Well anyway, I just want you to know that I really love you. You take good care of me."

"I take good care of you and the other guys get to sleep with you. What's in it for me?"

She leaned forward and kissed me softly on the lips, something she'd never done before. "You get a kiss."

"Throw in some tongue and we'll call it even."

"Pervert."

"Tease."

"Are we going to talk or are we going to dance?"

We danced.

8

Sarah and our lawyers were waiting in her lawyer's office when I showed up to get divorced. She was wearing a light blue linen skirt with a matching jacket and a white T-shirt underneath. The fact that I knew she'd probably gone shopping for just the right outfit to break my heart when we signed the papers didn't make it any less easy to see her looking so good. I was instantly self-conscious in my jeans and polo shirt. No one had told me there was a dress code for divorce.

"Hey, Ben," she said, looking up when I was shown in by the receptionist. "You brought your copies, right?"

"I thought you had them," I said.

"What?" Her eyes flew open in alarm.

"Kidding," I said. "They're right here."

She smirked at me and crossed her tanned legs. Sarah's beauty was based on mathematics. There was a perfect symmetry to her face, the way the points of her eyes met just equidistant from the bridge of her nose which was, in its own right a paragon of geometrical supremacy. Her lips, too thin to be pouting, were pursed at the exact midpoint between the tip of her nose and the point of her chin. Every feature was a study in precision, the total effect one of order and logic. And when you looked deeply into her eyes, you could see equations.

We moved into a solemn-looking conference room and gathered at the end of a polished oak table that seemed much too grandiose for so intimate a proceeding. Sitting down, we began the ritual of flipping pages and signing on the lines our attorneys pointed to. It was a pretty simple divorce, seeing as how we didn't have very many assets to divide. I always knew not having a vacation home in Vermont would come in handy some day. Because Sarah, an architect, made more money than me, there wasn't any alimony to discuss. It was really more like a breakup than a divorce, except here there were legal fees.

For some reason I thought there would be some sort of closing ceremony when we were finished, a symbolic absolution from the vows we'd once exchanged; the burning of parchment, the drinking of sacramental wine. Something. But when we'd signed the last page the lawyers disappeared to have the papers photocopied, and afterward we simply took our copies and rode down in the elevator together. This wasn't how a divorce should feel. It was too civilized. It felt like any other thing we had done as a married couple. As a matter of fact, I never felt as married as I did when I was getting divorced. I felt a terrifying sense of emptiness, a panic slowly rising in my belly, and suddenly, I wanted to run back upstairs, tear up the papers and ask for a second chance.

"How's Jack?" Sarah asked.

"Jack?"

"I saw it on the news last night."

"Oh, yeah. Well, then you know as much as I do," I said.

She had never cared for Jack, or any of my friends for that

matter. She was just asking because it was the proper thing to do. Sarah was always concerned with what the proper thing to do was. She was the kind of person who was adamant about using chop sticks when eating Chinese food, claiming that it just didn't taste right with flatware. She insisted on using a French accent when pronouncing words like *croissant* or *Les Miserables* or *Gérard Depardieu,* and copiously studied the op-ed page every day, convinced that at any point there might be a surprise test on it. Remembering all of that calmed me down a little.

It was this borderline neurotic calculation that had drawn me to Sarah in the first place. She always seemed to have everything planned out to the last detail, was so completely sure of her direction. So when she determined that it was me she wanted to spend the rest of her life with, I knew that it was something she'd thought through, and that, unlike Lindsey, she'd never second-guess her decision.

Lindsey had treated life as an open-ended adventure where anything was possible. I loved her for the way she embraced the unknown, how she opened herself up to every experience. When I was with her she opened me up, too, stirred my passion and heightened my every sensation. Which was great, until she left me and all my heightened senses to deal with the heartache of losing her.

Sarah's outlook was that life was a course to be carefully plotted, with speed and direction calculated toward an ultimate, predetermined destination. It was like a book, where she could sneak a peek at the ending and plan accordingly. She knew where she was heading, and exactly what she'd have to do to get there. After what I'd gone through with Lindsey, Sarah's measured certainty was a welcome promise of stability and if that meant sacrificing some passion in the overall scheme of things, that was fine with me. Passion was dangerous anyway, and not conducive to stability. And so I cast my lot with Sarah, a well-intentioned, textbook case of rebounding. Of course, I didn't consciously recognize any of this at the time. I actually managed to convince myself that Sarah was very much like Lindsey, amorous and adventurous, but more prone to commitment. I reinvented Sarah in my mind, and it was like one of those posters with a hidden illusion that you can only see out of the corner of your eye. Once you looked directly at it, the illusion was gone.

It didn't take very long for me to start suffocating. I think it started going downhill shortly after our first anniversary. The same certainty that had first attracted me to Sarah was now threatening to stifle me. My life lay stretched out before me with utter clarity and it held no mystery, no hidden potential. Everything was completely scripted and there was no room for improvisation, no chance to say "what if?" Just an alarmingly increasing sense of what might have been.

And so I began to rebel. Quietly at first, almost imperceptibly, as if to test my own resolve, and then more aggressively. Maybe I wouldn't be ready to have kids by year four. Maybe I would quit my job at *Esquire* and write full-time, weekly income be damned. Maybe I did want to buy a house in the suburbs instead of buying and selling our way into an Upper East Side co-op. And don't you think we ought to get a dog? There was no shortage of issues to choose from. I met with resistance from Sarah almost immediately, as I knew I would, and reacted to it with surprised hurt, as if it was she, and not me who was suddenly changing the terms of our covenant. The marriage quickly deteriorated into a continuous barrage of petty arguments, memorable only for their escalating viciousness.

Afterwards, I would sometimes try to remember what was going on in my head during that awful time, to see if I made any attempts at reconciliation, but I can't seem to locate myself there at all. I was already gone, just another piece of furniture waiting for the movers. Our situation eventually became so adversarial that when

Sarah finally threw her battle-fatigued arms into the air and gave up, I actually felt elation, a sense of victory for which I was instantly ashamed. What made things worse was that from the minute we agreed to get divorced it was as if the bone of contention had been removed, and we instantly rediscovered our affection and respect for each other, which served to greatly magnify my already immense guilt and perfectly underscore the tragedy of the whole damn thing. Just in case I'd missed it.

"This feels weird, doesn't it?" she said, as the elevator doors opened and we stepped into the lobby.

"It just doesn't feel like anything," I said. "I always thought a divorce would feel more, I don't know, momentous."

She smiled sadly at me. "Your problem is that you always want everything to be so clear cut. You always want the situation to define itself in absolute terms. Otherwise you're scared you won't know how to feel."

It was true. That was one of my problems.

"Didn't I just sign something that says I don't have to listen to criticism like that anymore?"

"What?"

"We just got divorced," I said, trying to keep any trace of bitterness out of my voice. "Pay attention."

We stepped out onto Madison Avenue, into the world in which I was suddenly single again. Not only single, but a divorcé. I was suddenly less substantial than I'd been an hour ago. I had a scar to show for my travels, a mark on my permanent record. There was something oddly appealing about being damaged. I needed to get drunk in the worst way.

"Well," I said, thinking that there should be something more to say to her after having shared a bed, a bathroom, a bank account, and the occasional toothbrush for almost three years. A family of blond people in T-shirts and sneakers walked past us, holding hands and smiling like the Brady Bunch as they looked around. Tourists.

"Wouldn't it be nice," Sarah said, "if after a marriage didn't work out there was a place you could go, once in while, to just see the person, see how they're doing, and just kind of touch base with them?"

"That would be nice," I agreed.

"I mean, it's kind of hard to shake the notion that we are, in some way, still family."

We thought about that for a moment. There was still a sense of togetherness to us, in the way we were standing and talking, and both of us were having trouble breaking away. The aroma of sauerkraut came wafting over from a hot dog vending cart on the corner. I knew that now divorce would always smell like a hot dog. I would have to avoid barbecues for a while, which, given my social calendar, wasn't looking like it would be a huge problem.

"I'm sorry if I caused you any pain over all of this," I said.

She waved away the apology. "I guess it's just a good thing we did this now, while we're still young and there are no children. We'll be able to look back on the good times, you know?"

"I guess so."

She extended her hand and I shook it, and the absurdity of the gesture suddenly brought the whole scene crashing from the realm of the surreal back into reality. "Well," she said. "I wish you all the happiness in the world."

"Me too," I said. "And I hope you do okay, too."

"Ha ha."

"Take care, Sarah."

"You too, Ben. See you around."

"Yeah, see you," I said, but what I was thinking was, eight million people in the naked city, fat chance.

9

Chuck came over that night to get drunk with me. We sat on the floor with our backs against the couch doing shooters, two parts Sprite and five parts vodka, while watching the "News at Eleven." Sue Simmons had just told us about Louis Varrone, a twenty-three-year-old man in Brooklyn who had committed a sensational suicide. He had set up a lounge chair on the tracks of the elevated train, then listened to Beck on his Walkman and drank beer until the D train came in and pulverized him. His mother, who was not available for an interview, nevertheless sent word to the reporters that Louis had become increasingly despondent ever since the cancellation of *Star Trek: The Next Generation* a few years earlier.

"What a nut job," Chuck said. "Can you imagine what kind of loser that kid must have been?"

"I don't know," I said, letting out a burp that was two parts Sprite and five parts vodka. "I remember being pretty upset when they canceled *Battlestar Galactica*."

"Well, for Chrissakes," said Chuck, who was not quite as ine-briated as me, but getting there fast. "It's just a damn show. You don't go and kill yourself."

"I know. But I guess for some people, it's all they've got."

"Well then they might as well kill themselves anyway."

The news went on to show a fire that killed a family of five in Elmhurst.

"Have you ever noticed that the news is really just a glossy, overproduced body count?" I said. "I mean, why is it that death is all they think we really want to hear about?"

"It's human nature," Chuck said. "There but for the grace of god go I, and shit like that."

"They may as well just come on at the beginning and say, 'thirty-two people died today,' " I said. "Then do the weather and sports and be done in ten minutes."

"Yeah, and then they could show *Gilligan's Island* or some-thing," Chuck said.

"Or *Star Trek* reruns."

"Or more *Baywatch*," said Chuck.

"We could always use more *Baywatch,*" I agreed.

Chuck leaned back and closed his eyes. "There should be a Baywatch Network."

The secret vice of the nineties man. A mindless one-hour pic-torial with no depth to speak of, yet every man I knew occasionally watched it. You didn't plan to watch it. You didn't look at your watch and say, "Hey, it's six o'clock, time for *Baywatch.*" You just invariably found it while you were channel-surfing, and there you stayed, your finger poised over the clicker, as if you might change the channel at any moment. There was something undeniably com-forting about the show, especially at one in the morning when the emptiness of your life was keeping you awake. Endless sunny days, beautiful women, so accessible in their tight red bathing suits, clearly defined moral situations, weekly heroics and long romantic walks on the beach set to eighties-style love songs. Everything life wasn't. *Baywatch* was how your eyes massaged your brain.

At some point I dozed off, and dreamed that I was sitting somewhere outdoors with Lindsey. The air was the color of faded vermilion, and a soft breeze was blowing against our faces. I was holding her hand, but she didn't realize it. It seemed very important to me that she say something to me to show me that she knew we were holding hands, but all she did was talk about a temple in Luxor she'd once visited. As I grew more frustrated I tried squeezing her hand, but she remained oblivious. It was like I wasn't there at all, which didn't strike me as fair since it was, after all, my dream. Right before I awoke I thought to myself wistfully, maybe it's not my dream. Maybe it was her dream that I'd somehow ended up in, and that's why I wasn't having any effect.

I rolled over, seeing every fiber of the carpet with a drunken clarity, and looked up to find Xena, the Warrior Princess, scowling at me from the television and Chuck looking at me, cup in hand, a triumphant smile on his face. I could see a patch of stubble in the fold of his neck, where his razor had missed. "I know what we should do about Jack," he said.

Chuck's idea was simple in its premise, and damn near impossible to execute. What it amounted to was this: We would kidnap Jack, one of the most recognized movie stars in the world, take him to a secluded place where we could keep an eye on him, and stay with him until he kicked the habit.

"It would take forty-eight to seventy-two hours for his blood to be completely free of coke," Chuck said. "After that, we would just need to keep him there for a while to stop him from getting more. I don't think he's been on it long enough to have a full-blown addiction."

"What are we going to do, tie him up?" I said.

"If we have to."

We thought about it for a minute. "How do you kidnap Jack?" I asked. "He's always got an entourage with him."

"Don't fuck me up with details, dude," Chuck said. "I'm still talking big picture here."

"You're talking felony, my friend."

"I open people up every day," Chuck mumbled irrelevantly, closing his eyes and rubbing his temples. "I open them up and fix them." He suddenly looked up at me, as if he'd forgotten for a minute that he wasn't alone. "We can do this," he said. "It's not so crazy."

"You're talking about taking someone against his will—"

"Not someone. Jack. Our friend."

"Our friend who isn't speaking to us," I reminded him.

"Details," Chuck warned.

"The devil's in them," I mumbled. "Or is that god? I'm always getting those two mixed up."

"The devil's in the shit going into Jack's blood," Chuck said.

"I think we're both too drunk for melodrama."

"Fuck you. It's a good idea." Chuck heaved himself to his feet, groaning from the effort. "Jesus, I'm hammered."

"You leaving?"

"Yeah. If I begin my hangover now, maybe I'll be okay by tomorrow night when I'm on call."

I got up to walk him to the door. I was dismayed to discover that my brief nap had destroyed my buzz. "You going to be okay?" Chuck asked.

"Nothing's changed," I said. "It was just paperwork."

"Well, you two had some good times," he said weakly. "You shouldn't have any regrets. Do you?"

"None," I said. "Except I wish to hell I'd never gotten married."

He looked at me, not sure whether I was joking or not. I couldn't have said for sure myself. "Let me know when you're ready to get out there again," he finally said. "I'll hook you up."

"Thanks."

Chuck paused at the door. "My idea would work," he said. "Just think about it."

"Okay," I promised. "But I think it will sound a lot less reasonable without the benefit of alcohol."

"Bounce it off of Lindsey or Alison."

"I'll run it up the flagpole and see if they salute."

With Chuck gone, I set up shop on the couch and began the tedious work of reclaiming my buzz. Vodka in hand, I put the television on channel two and began a fresh wave of channel-surfing. Infomercials, Gary Coleman on the Psychic Friends Network, a movie from the early seventies about a prison break, the life cycle of the manatee on Discovery, fuzzy shots of body piercings on public access, a B-movie about radioactive high school kids with neon sweatshirts and bad haircuts on USA, stand-up comedy on the Comedy Network, an old *Happy Days* episode on Nickelodeon.

Finally, I found a *Baywatch* rerun on one of the local stations. Lieutenant Stephanie Holden was being held hostage in one of the lifeguard towers by an evil lunatic with a bomb. You could tell he was a bad guy because he didn't have a tan. Hasselhoff had to get under the tower undetected, so he was tunneling through the sand in his wet suit, digging out the sand in front of him and depositing it behind him with some gizmo he'd kept from his days as a Navy SEAL. He looked like a giant earthworm.

I was suddenly very lonely. For Sarah, for Lindsey, for a party to be named later—I didn't know. I had told Chuck that nothing had changed, but that wasn't true. Being an official divorcé brought late-night channel-surfing up to a staggering new level of depressing. I just wanted to belong to someone already. Thirty . . . shit.

The night before I got married, I ate dinner at my parents' house and afterwards spent some time in my old bedroom going through my drawers and bookcases, looking at all the stuff I'd accumulated growing up. Photos, birthday cards, ticket stubs, pocket knives, mix tapes, notes from old girlfriends. The bedroom was like a time capsule of the first eighteen years of my life, everything perfectly preserved as if I'd just left it the day before. As I went through my drawers, I was struck by how many items were still in the random positions they'd landed in when a younger me had discarded them to be dealt with at a later date. So many things I'd assumed I would revisit, oblivious to the hot breath of time on the back of my neck.

I sifted through all of my artifacts, feeling the need to touch every single one of them, to establish a tactile connection to my past. I found a green, elastic headband that belonged to Cindy Friedman, my ninth grade girlfriend and the first girl I'd ever seriously made out with. I held it to my nose and thought I could still detect the faint scent of her perfume. We'd climbed under my covers that night, quivering with anticipation, and she'd pulled it out of her hair and put it under my pillow. A little while later she had let me take off her shirt. I could still remember the sweet copper taste of her skin, the flawless texture of it against my lips. The next day I'd tossed the headband into my top dresser drawer, where it had remained undisturbed until that night before my wedding. Holding it again, I felt overwhelmed by a sense of desperate yearning, not for Cindy Friedman, but for the quivering.

At some point that night, while wishing that I could go to sleep in my childhood bedroom and wake up in high school again, I realized that I didn't want to marry Sarah. I'd actually realized it weeks before, but there, surrounded by the innocent souvenirs of my youth, I finally admitted it to myself. I loved Sarah, but I couldn't remember a single time I'd quivered for her. I must have sat on my old bed for over an hour that night, running through the different ways I could call the wedding off, all the while knowing I never would. High drama had never been part of my repertoire. I was terrified of facing Sarah, who would go ballistic, and my mother, who would have a coronary, but all of that was secondary to my primary fear, which was the knowledge that when the dust settled, I'd be waking up alone again. How long could you hold out for someone who made you quiver before the loneliness devoured you? My marriage might be tainted by pragmatism, but there was something almost reaffirming in precisely that. Almost.

And now I was divorced. I was waiting for the final feeling. The one that would come after the drinks wore off, after the depression and fear faded to faint background noise. The feeling that would stay. I wondered if I'd be elated or sad, liberated or just filled with regret. I had no idea, but I knew it was in the mail. I looked at a picture of Sarah and me dancing at the wedding of one of her friends. She was looking up at me with this wise and loving grin, as if I had just said something to her that only the two of us could ever understand. I wondered what I could have said to make her look at me like that. I was looking right back at her, but my expression was inscrutable, as if the camera had caught it in the middle of forming.

The booze wasn't doing anything for me, so I got up from the couch, scrambled some eggs, and thought about getting a dog.

A few hours later, as the first rays of sunlight came slinking into my bedroom, my mother called. I can always tell it's her before I pick up, as if there's a slight difference in the timbre of the telephone ringer when my mother's on the other end. This small psychic gift is matched only by her uncanny ability to call at the exact times when I really don't want to speak to her.

"Hi Ben, it's your mother." As if she's talking to an answering machine. Not "it's Mom" or even just a "hi" with the omission of identification that comes with familiarity. Always "it's your mother," as if we were strangers in need of introduction.

"Hi, Mom."

"Your father and I just wanted to see how you're doing." This was also part of her script, an apology of sorts for my father's poor communication skills. Not that he wasn't interested in my well being because he was, but in a passive, general way that didn't require details. As long as I was fine, that was all he needed to know, and he barely required confirmation. He was happy to assume it, unless he heard differently. A hard-working engineer his entire adult life, my father was a quiet, disciplined man, utterly unskilled when it came to showing affection or concern. I didn't take it personally, which isn't the same as saying I was thrilled to grow up with it.

"I'm fine," I said. "How's your leg?" My mother had recently begun suffering from arthritis in her left knee, an ailment that had taken on a much greater significance than it should have because to her it signaled the beginning of her old age.

"Yesterday was a killer. Today I took some Motrin and I'm getting by."

"Good."

"How's Sarah?" she asked. Although she knew we'd been separated for over eight months, she refused to recognize it for what it was, choosing instead to view it as an indulgence common to couples of our generation that we needed to get out of our system. Every time she called she determinedly asked after Sarah as if everything was completely fine, which somehow helped her maintain the illusion.

"She's good," I said, mentally gritting my teeth. "I actually saw her yesterday."

"Oh!" my mother exclaimed, surprised in spite of herself. "Is she back?"

"Uh, no. Mom, we got divorced."

"What do you mean you got divorced?" she demanded, as if I might be mistaken.

"That's it, it's over."

"You signed divorce papers?"

"Yes."

"With lawyers?"

"Hers and mine." The lawyers seemed to quiet her for a minute. I heard an electric whoosh as she put her palm over the phone and called out for my father. "Herb, get in here!"

"Mom?"

"When were you going to tell us?" she asked, which wasn't really the point, but she was reaching out for something to pin her disappointment on.

"We just signed the papers yesterday," I said.

"Yesterday," I heard her mouth to my father. I could picture her saying it, comically exaggerating every syllable so that he could read her lips, although he didn't need to since she was patently incapable of whispering, a failing that had embarrassed me in my youth on more than one occasion.

"Did you tell Ethan?"

"I haven't really felt like sharing yet, Mom."

"So what? He's your brother."

I willed myself to ignore the silent accusation in her mention of my older brother. She almost certainly didn't mean anything by it, but still I felt the familiar resentment rise unbidden, a bitter-tasting dryness in the back of my throat. Only four years older than me, Ethan was a partner in a small, highly successful venture capital firm. He was also married with two children and a third on the way, all of which added to his luster as the successful son. Basically, he was fulfilling all of her dreams and I was the screwup. She never said anything like that to me, never even hinted at it. She loved us both and would never consciously try to hurt either one of us. But still, it was apparent to me in the way her voice changed, ever so slightly, when she mentioned Ethan, in the subtle deference she paid him at family gatherings, usually in his immense house in Hewlett, Long Island. There was absolutely nothing wrong with the pride she felt in my brother's accomplishments, but I always found myself struggling against petty jealousy whenever I intuited that pride. Whatever I wanted for myself, I couldn't help feeling a filial obligation to be successful for my parents' sake, which may have been a silent factor in my decision to marry Sarah in the first place.

My mother had never been able to muster any real enthusiasm for my job at *Esquire*, and who could blame her? It was a steppingstone that had mushroomed into its own pathetic plateau. But Sarah had been my saving grace, because not only was I married, but I was married to an architect, and that was something my mother could sink her teeth into. My daughter-in-law the architect. My son the . . . husband. And now I wasn't even that anymore. I briefly wondered if speaking to my mother made me feel like a failure because that's how I appeared when I saw myself through her eyes, or because I projected my own feelings of failure onto her, and she was just an innocent bystander. Either way, I had to admit that my state of affairs had certainly plummeted to new depths if I was reduced to trying to figure out who thought I was the bigger fuck-up, me or my mother.

I sighed deeply into the telephone, telling myself that I was being too harsh. My mother was worried about me, that's all. Now that she understood the situation, some words of comfort would no doubt be forthcoming.

"Is she with someone else?"

Oh, Christ. "Mom, it was nothing like that," I said. "The marriage was just a mistake."

"Well you didn't think that three years ago."

"Obviously, or I wouldn't have gotten married then, would I?" I shot back, although I had my doubts about the veracity of that statement.

"Well," she said, after a bit. "I don't know what to say."

"Then don't say anything," I advised.

"We just want you to be happy," she complained, as if it were my sole intention to deny her that simple desire.

"Then really don't say anything."

"I'll put your father on." There was a minute's fumbling with the phone as they exchanged muted whispers, and then I heard my father's low slightly raspy voice. "Ben?"

"Hi, Dad."

"Hi . . ." I could picture him in his chinos and an undershirt, sitting at the kitchen table with his bran flakes and the *Times,* which he'd still be absently looking at through his bifocals as we spoke.

"Mom okay?" I asked, to give him something to say.

"She's a little bit upset right now."

"No doubt."

"Are you going to be okay?" he asked, clearing his throat as he did.

"I'm fine, Dad."

"Okay, well you know, if you need anything . . ."

"I know, I'm fine."

"Okay, very good," he said, not because it was true but because that was how he ended all conversations.

"I'll speak to you soon," I lied.

"Very good," he said again. I waited to hear the click of his phone before I hung up mine, which didn't click into place correctly, so I banged it in with my fist, hard enough to ring the bell. Two long cracks appeared in the plastic next to the number pad and I heard something small and metallic fall onto the floor and roll away. Very good, I thought.

10

Alison thought that kidnapping Jack was actually a practical idea. "We could use my parents' place in the Catskills," she said. "We all take off a couple weeks from work, and stay up there with him until he's better."

"I can manage a couple weeks," said Lindsey, who thought it was a ridiculous idea and therefore liked it immensely. "I happen to be between jobs right now."

"Shocker," Chuck said.

We were on a conference call discussing the possible abduction. Somewhere in the background I could faintly hear the P.A. system of Mount Sinai Hospital, where Chuck was completing his surgical residency.

"When do you want to do it?" Alison asked.

"The sooner the better," Chuck said. "I might be able to wrangle a little time off, but I'll probably have to drive in from the mountains every other day to be on call."

"How about you, Ben?" Alison asked.

"I'm not on call. I'm not even a doctor."

"Quit stalling."

"I suppose I could get the time off," I said hesitantly.

"What's the problem?" Lindsey asked. There was a slight coolness in her voice, which meant she hadn't yet forgiven me for our phone conversation two nights ago.

"Look," I said. "I like a good kidnapping as much as the next psychopath, but this isn't like kidnapping some nobody. Jack is famous. He has people who work for him, who represent him. He'll be missed."

"Who cares if he's missed, as long as he isn't found," Chuck said. "Next?"

"What do we do with him up there? Are we really going to tie him up?"

"That won't be necessary," Alison said. "My father's study can be locked from the outside. We can keep him in there. There's a sofa bed and a bathroom."

"So he's really going to be a prisoner," I said. "This doesn't seem a bit extreme?"

"Desperate times, Ben," Lindsey said. "Desperate measures."

"Alison," Chuck said, "not that I'm worried, but from a legal standpoint, where would we stand if Jack decided to press charges?"

"Well, criminal law is not my forte," Alison said. "But it's conceivable we'd be in some pretty serious trouble."

"I can't believe Jack would ever do that," Lindsey said.

"I can't believe we would ever do this," I said.

"So you're with us?" Chuck asked.

"It's not like I have a family to think about," I said.

"That's the spirit," Alison said.

I still thought it was a crazy idea, but the prospect of spending a week or two in the mountains with friends seemed like the perfect antidote to my current funk. Certainly, it beat staying up late on the couch by myself, studying my divorce from every angle like a new sweater I might want to return.

"So what's the plan?" I asked.

Everyone fell silent as the logistics of our plan instantly failed to take shape.

"Jack will be here next Wednesday for an AIDS benefit at Planet Hollywood," Alison told us.

"Do you think we can get invited?" Lindsey asked.

"What's the point?" Chuck said. "We can't grab him at a major media event. What are we supposed to do, whack him on the head and carry him out through the kitchen?"

"Sounds like a plan."

"Why don't we call that plan B," I said sarcastically. "Especially since Seward will be there, and he watches Jack like a hawk."

"I wouldn't mind whacking Seward on the head, while we're at it," Lindsey said.

"I don't think any of us really knows how to knock someone out," Chuck said thoughtfully. "You knock someone out with a blow to the head, its got to be a hard one, and nine out of ten times the victim will suffer a concussion. It isn't like those wimpy little karate chops to the back of the neck Captain Kirk is always using."

"What we need is a Vulcan pinch," I said.

"Are they referencing *Star Trek* again?" Alison asked.

"They are," said Lindsey.

"Why do they always have to do that?"

"Because they have penises."

"What about some sort of injection, Chuck?" Alison asked. "Like morphine or something."

"It's a possibility," Chuck mused.

"Or a stun gun," Lindsey offered. "I've been keeping one in my purse for over a year, and I've been dying to try it out."

"Too violent," Alison said.

"But more practical," Chuck said. "An injection is a hard thing to give to an unwilling patient in a public place. Besides, I don't like the idea of introducing something like morphine into a system that might be full of cocaine."

"Jesus, will you listen to us," Lindsey said, her voice smiling.

"I think Planet Hollywood is a horrible place to do this," I said. "They've got a whole security force there, and it will be wall-to-wall paparazzi."

"Where's he going after the party?" Chuck asked.

"I think straight back to the airport," Alison said.

"We could just invite him," Lindsey said.

"What?"

"Invite him. Say 'Hey Jack, we're all going up to the mountains for the weekend and we'd love for you to come.' "

"You're forgetting he's pissed at us," I said.

"So what? You don't stop being friends just cause you're pissed."

"He'll never come," Alison said. "He's way too busy. He's got to do looping on the movie he just finished shooting, and they're already in preproduction for the *Blue Angel* sequel."

"I still say we should use the stun gun," Lindsey said.

And so it went, for the next half hour. Finally, Chuck was paged and had to go, and we all agreed to think about it over the weekend and talk again on Monday.

As soon as I'd hung up the phone, it rang again, and I knew it was Lindsey before I picked up.

"Sorry I was such a bitch the other night."

"You weren't. Well, okay, you were, but I was being a little difficult too," I said.

"Well, you know, you're going through a lot right now, and I should have been more sensitive to that. I really am sorry."

"Don't worry about it."

"Okay," she said brightening. "How was the divorce?"

"Maybe the friendliest one in the history of the institution."

"Sounds good."

"Then I'm telling it wrong."

"Bad?"

"Yes. Divorce shouldn't be friendly. It just makes everything that much more confusing," I said.

"Explain."

"You know how Tolstoy says that every unhappy family is unhappy in a different way?"

"Okay."

"Well, I guess every bad marriage is different, too. Mine was the worst kind, a bad marriage disguised as a good one most of the time. We liked each other, had mutual interests, a good level of attraction. The unhappiness and dissatisfaction and whatever it was that made us fall apart just kind of caught me off guard because I didn't even suspect it was there. So you find yourself in a situation where you really like someone and can't point to a single thing wrong with the relationship, but at some point you've just stopped relating. And because nothing really seems to be wrong, you keep second-guessing your decision to get divorced. You keep asking yourself, why did I do this? Everything was fine. It's a good thing we didn't try counseling. They would have asked me what my problem was, and I wouldn't have known. Now I'm alone and I can't even think of a single thing that was wrong with the relationship."

"But obviously you can," Lindsey said. "Or why would you have gotten divorced to begin with?"

"I just kept thinking of this Chinese proverb. If you don't change direction soon, you're liable to end up where you're heading."

"Where'd you come up with that?"

"A fortune cookie."

She laughed. I listened to her do it. "So where were you heading?"

"I don't know. Somewhere really mediocre."

"So you did the right thing."

"I know. But I think that after a divorce it's probably healthier to feel a good measure of hate and anger, or at least contempt for your ex-wife. This lack of any definitive feelings is really messing up my head."

"Did you have such definitive feelings when we broke up?" Lindsey asked.

"I hated you for a year or two," I said.

"Oh," she said after a beat, clearly taken aback.

"I got over it," I said quickly. "I didn't so much hate you as blame you for my loneliness."

"I know what you mean, Ben, I really do," she said, sympathetic. "I know what it's like to be lonely."

"Hey don't knock loneliness," I said. "It keeps me busy when I'm alone."

"Very funny."

"Enough about me," I said. "What have you been up to lately? I feel like I don't know what's up in your life at all."

"That's because there's nothing to know."

"You're still temping?"

"You bet. I've elevated temping to an art form. It's the perfect metaphor for me. You know, never staying in one place for too long."

"What about teaching. You still have your license, don't you?"

"Sure. I've thought about going back."

"Why'd you quit in the first place? You loved teaching."

She sighed. "I know. I'm not sure. I don't think it had anything to do with teaching per se. I think I was just bothered by the finality of having found my career. It was like it defined me, and I was no longer a work in progress. I felt way too young to be a finished product. I mean, what did that leave for the rest of my life?"

Even though I knew she wasn't talking about why she'd left me, she certainly could have been. "So when you temp, you're still a work in progress," I said.

"I guess so."

"Well, you're right. That is the perfect metaphor for you."

"Thanks," she said. "I think."

"You're welcome."

She laughed lightly. "Let's get together soon."

"Definitely."

"Okay, bye."

"Bye."

Hindsight supposedly begot clarity, but whenever I revisited my relationship with Lindsey, trying to understand why we broke up, I found the opposite to be true. I would look at the relationship from so many different angles that on any given day I could come up with an alternate reason for her leaving. We had discussed it ad nauseum before she left, and yet when I tried to reconstruct those conversations in my mind, I drew a complete blank. Apparently, I hadn't been paying very close attention.

The easy answer was Lindsey's temping metaphor. She felt too young to settle down, and needed to get out and see the world. It was a recurring theme in our breakup and the one I chose to be the party line. A safe, acceptable notion, which didn't point to any serious flaws or deficiencies on anyone's part. But the assignment of blame was an inevitable component of my increasingly obsessive postmortems, and in my darker moments after she was gone I was haunted by the silent implication in that excuse, that she wouldn't have felt that way if there wasn't something lacking in me.

It wasn't that she didn't love me, I knew that she did, and that actually made it worse. If someone leaves you because they don't love you, it's a tough break, but as they say, life's a bitch, get a helmet. But if someone loves you and leaves you anyway, you enter a whole new realm of self-doubt and recrimination, what psychologists call the what-the-fuck-is-wrong-with-me syndrome. Spend enough time and you'll come up with an infinite list of answers. Emotional immaturity, sexual inadequacy, boring personality, body odor . . . you're only as limited as your imagination. There was actually one forty-eight-hour period when I seriously believed I'd been dumped because I had small, unmanly nipples.

My current and most promising theory was that from the minute we got together, I was never able to fully accept that Lindsey was truly mine. Having watched her romantic life from the sidelines for so long, developing an inferiority complex for every guy she dated, I had trouble believing that I was somehow going to succeed where so many others had failed. Lindsey was pretty wild in college and the guys she dated ran the gamut from athletes to rebels to foreigners to artists, but there was one thing they all had in common, none of them was me. And when it finally was me, the ghosts of all those men mingling in my mind with the ghosts of men still to come haunted me and left me in a constant state of anxiety, even while I thought I was blissfully in love. Lindsey was happy to have me, but I felt ridiculously lucky to have her. All of that had to be subliminally communicating itself to Lindsey, who may very well have read my insecurity as harboring a true personality deficit, making it something like a self-fulfilling prophecy.

It all sounds well and good, but at the end of the day, who really knows? It just as easily may have been the tiny nipples.

11

I was so deeply asleep when Jack called later that night that the first six or seven rings managed to get written into my dream somehow. Only by the eighth ring did I become conscious that my phone was ringing in real life. After a few seconds of groping around on the floor I found it.

"I didn't wake you, did I?" Jack said.

"Don't worry about it, I had to get up to answer the phone."

"Shit, I'm sorry," he said. "It's only around eleven out here."

There was a brief, awkward silence.

"So, what's up?" I asked.

"Can't I just call and say hello?"

"Sure. You used to do that all the time."

"It's not like you don't have my number, too," he said testily. He'd always been very sensitive about making sure he didn't become the cliché, the star who forgot the friends who knew him when. He grew defensive at the slightest implication that this was the case.

"You're right, Jack," I said. "I guess we've both just been a little busy."

"That night at Alison's house was the first time I've seen you in like a year," he said.

"Unless you count Lindsey's birthday party," I reminded him.

"Oh, yeah," he said vaguely, and I wondered if he had completely forgotten about that night.

"So, were you just calling to say hello?" I asked.

"Yeah, pretty much. And to make sure there's no hard feelings about the other night."

"No hard feelings," I agreed.

"I said some shitty stuff to you, and I'm sorry," he said. "I didn't mean any of it."

"It was probably the drugs talking," I said, steeling myself for a violent reaction. But Jack actually laughed.

"Maybe that's what it was," he said. "You guys are the best friends I have. I know you were trying to help."

For the first time in the last year, I felt like I was talking to the old Jack again. Jack my buddy, the laid-back jester of our little clique. He'd always been the most relaxed and amiable of our group, at peace with everyone around him at all times. He was the kind of guy who effortlessly formed a rapport with everyone he met, from store clerks to doormen to fellow students back at NYU.

We'd become friends basically because we lived next door to each other in the dorm. About two weeks into our freshman year he was walking by my open door and saw me struggling to move my dresser across the room. He knocked lightly on the door frame and said, "Hey man, need a hand?" I'd seen him around, always in a group, always the picture of easy confidence, and never figured that the trajectory of his orbit would ever intersect with mine.

The dresser, it turned out, was bolted against the wall, and it took about a half hour to get it loose. Afterwards, he sat on my bed, leaned back against the wall and said, "Whew, its Miller time." We went down to the Violet Cafe for a drink and ended up hanging out for a while. And just like that, we were friends. It happened as effortlessly as everything else in Jack's life. When we went to parties, Jack didn't wonder if he was going to meet someone, didn't scan the room until a girl caught his eye. He would just grab a drink and perch himself comfortably, and women would just gravitate towards him. It wasn't a conscious thing, it was just the way he and the world interacted.

One night, a while after we'd become friends, we were sitting in The Red Room, a piano bar that had become our favorite place to just mellow out, when Lindsey came in with some friends and stopped at our table to say hi to me. I felt a childish surge of pride that such a hot girl was coming over to say hello to me for once and not him, and a hint of fear at the prospect of Jack and Lindsey meeting. I was sure that those two would recognize each other instantly as soul mates, and when that happened I would cease to exist.

Nervously, I watched as Jack's eyes followed Lindsey back to her table. Still looking at her he said to me, "Is that the vomit girl?"

"Yeah," I said.

He nodded approvingly. "You got something going on there, Ben?"

"No . . . I don't know, maybe." He gave me a sharp questioning look and I said, "We're friends."

"Friends, huh?" He stared intently at me for a minute and then, as if he'd finally found something he'd been looking for, gave me a warm smile and hoisted his beer. "I guess we all need a friend like that," he said. He chugged his beer and banged it down on the table good-naturedly.

"Listen, Jack, there's nothing going on. If you want to ask her out, you can," I said, not meaning it.

"Hey," he said. "Don't get your panties all in a bunch. She's your friend, you're my friend. It's cool. There's plenty of other women out there." With that simple declaration he had offered up a promise that not only set my mind at ease about Jack and Lindsey, but somehow defined my friendship with him as the genuine article. Many things changed over the next few years, but Jack never wavered on the commitment he made to me that night. We never even discussed it again.

"How'd it go in court?" I asked Jack, wedging the phone between my cheek and pillow while removing a golf ball-sized bugger from my eye.

"I'll get off with a fine and probation" he said. "Probably have to do one of those public service commercials for MTV, telling all the kids not to do drugs."

"A typical celebrity first-offense deal," I said.

"They've probably already got a standardized script for it."

I decided to go for broke. "Jack, why don't we take a road trip, like we used to do every year after finals," I said. "We'll drive down to Wildwood or something, hit Atlantic City, just relax and have some fun."

"The summer's over," Jack said. "It's too cold to go to Wildwood."

"So we'll do it out there, go to Vegas or something. Just take some time off. Take a break."

"Ben, I don't need you to come out here on some errand of mercy."

"It's not mercy man. I need a break, too. In case you're behind on current events here, I just got divorced."

"No shit, really? When?"

"Two days ago."

"Oh, man. I didn't hear about it."

"We haven't alerted the media yet."

"Fuck you. Alison could have told me."

"I guess she's got other things on her mind," I said, although I felt a stab of resentment that Alison hadn't mentioned it. We all sat around worrying about Jack. Couldn't anyone spend a minute expressing concern over my sorry state of affairs? Even in matters of personal crises, Jack still got top billing. "Look, Jack, my marriage just ended and you've got a drug problem that's garnering national media attention. If ever a situation cried out for a road trip, this is it."

He exhaled deeply into the phone. "It's very tempting Ben, but I've got preproduction coming up on this film . . ."

"Fuck it, Jack. You need this break. You have a problem."

"It's not a problem," Jack said defensively. "I let it get a little out of control, I admit it. But the accident cleared things up for me. I'm off the stuff."

"Just like that?" I asked, skeptically.

"Just like that," he said. "It's not like I was addicted or anything. I was just working a little too hard."

"I hope that's the truth."

"It is, and you can tell everyone over there to cut out the theatrics," he said, a trace of anger now creeping into his voice. "I'm doing just fine over here."

"If you say so."

"I'm saying so."

"Okay, so there's no problem," I said. "I still think we ought to do the road trip."

"Now is just not a good time," he said, and now his tone was edged with concrete. He hadn't hung up yet, but the connection was already lost. He was back to being Jack Shaw, movie star and stranger. "Maybe in December."

If you're not dead, I thought, but I said, "Yeah. We'll go skiing."

"Say hello to Chuck and Lindsey," he said.

"You say hello to Sly and Arnold."

He snickered. "I'll do that."

"Hey, Jack?"

"Yeah."

"I'm here, man, you know? If you need me."

"Thanks, man. I don't. I'll speak to you soon."

"Okay."

I heard him sigh wearily. "Stop worrying so much," he said.

"I can't," I said. "I have to do your worrying too, otherwise it won't get done."

"Bye, Ben."

"Bye."

I rolled over, remembering how easy it had been for the five of us to hang out in the old days. Jack, Chuck, Lindsey, Alison, and me. No matter where we were, there was a level of comfort between us that let us all know it was the right place to be. Now we had to work to make ourselves fit into each other's lives, to maintain our relevance to each other. In college our collective friendship had been at the center of our lives, and now the centrifugal force of time had pushed it out to the perimeter, where it was in danger of spinning off the circle altogether. Thirty . . . shit.

The kryptonite green digits of the radio clock by my bed told me that it was just past two in the morning. Crap. I was up for the day. I padded into the living room and flipped on the TV. No *Baywatch*, so I settled for a National Geographic special on giraffes. In college, Jack and I always used to stay up late and watch the National Geographic specials and *Wild Kingdom*. We'd even discussed going on safari to Africa one of these years. As the giraffes lumbered across the Namibian plains, the inevitable British narrator explained that the average giraffe's heart weighed twenty-five pounds.

I knew how they felt.

12

Jerry Garcia might have been dead, but that wasn't stopping the band at Ruby's from killing him onstage again, with a thrashing, discordant set of Grateful Dead covers. I wasn't even a Dead Head and I was offended. The four of us sat at a table in the back, sipping at drinks and shoveling in free popcorn by the mouthful, discussing Jack's latest drug-induced public spectacle.

The night before, 911 had received a hysterical call from Jack, telling them that his house was on fire. LA fire fighters arrived to find Jack, clad only in his briefs, bravely fighting the flames with a garden hose. The only complication was that, despite their years of experience, none of the fire fighters could find any flames. They inspected Jack's Brentwood mansion from basement to attic and, with the exception of some water damage in the living room due to Jack's efforts with the hose, found nothing amiss.

Under normal circumstances, the firemen might have been pissed, but it isn't every day you get to meet a movie star of Jack Shaw's caliber. The fire chief, who one imagines had seen this sort of thing before, talked Jack down and walked him back inside. Later the crew all posed for pictures with Jack and then went home with an amusing new anecdote for their wives and kids. As it turned out, one of those wives just happened to work at the Los Angeles bureau of the Associated Press, and the story broke early the next morning. By noon they were playing the 911 tapes on every station across the country.

"He's in serious trouble," Lindsey said. "He's totally out of control."

Onstage, the band finished a barely recognizable version of "Sugar Magnolia" and began playing an even worse version of "Truckin'."

"He passed out-of-control months ago," Chuck said above the din. "The only question is if he's beyond our help yet or not."

"He called me," I said, and they all stared. "The night before he made the 911 call."

"What'd he say?" Chuck asked.

"Nothing," I said. "He sounded fine. Completely sober. He was angry that we thought he had a problem."

"What'd you say?"

"I said we should take a road trip."

"A road trip," Chuck repeated. "He's on the threshold of a personal and professional meltdown and you suggested a road trip?"

"It seemed like a good idea at the time," I said lamely.

"I don't think it was a bad idea," Lindsey said, smiling lightly. "A cinematic remedy for a cinematic figure."

"He must have looked real cinematic running around in his Calvins with a garden hose," Chuck said.

Alison put down her drink and looked at us. "I've come up with a new plan," she said.

"You still think we can do this?" I asked.

"I think we have to try," she said.

"So what's the plan?" Lindsey asked.

Alison told us. It was a hard and cruel way to go, and the fact that she had even thought it up was an indication of the pain this was causing her.

"Alison," Chuck said with a smile. "I never knew you could be so downright cutthroat. I like it."

"Until recently Jack used to call me every day," Alison said, staring down at the table. "No matter where he was, no matter what was going on, he would call to say hi and just, I don't know, check in. If he didn't get me, he'd leave me a message or call back again. Whenever I left him a message he would call back that day, even if it meant waking me up." She blinked back some tears and nervously crumbled some popcorn in her fingers. "I know you're all worried about Jack, but I'm more than worried. I miss him terribly. He's my best friend and . . . I want him back."

She covered her eyes with her hand and her body convulsed involuntarily as the sobs she was fighting to suppress imploded inside her. Lindsey reached across the table and grabbed Alison's other hand, squeezing it in her own, and I put my arm around her and pressed my forehead against her temple. Of all of us, she was the most uncomplicated, the most sincere, and I think it hurt us all to see that she was suffering so much. I felt a sudden, hot stab of anger at Jack for fucking up like this.

It had been through Jack that we'd all originally met Alison. He'd been having trouble in his statistics class which, for reasons known only to those at the highest levels of academia, fulfilled a core science requirement. Alison, who sat behind Jack, was good with numbers and offered to help him out. It's funny, or tragic, really, how an ordinary act like helping someone with their homework could be the inadvertent trigger for almost a decade of silent suffering. Alison's Peanut Story.

Alison at thirty should have been married with two or three kids, a nice house in Greenwich, and the whole Martha Stewart package. It was where she'd always been headed, her interest in law notwithstanding. She had three sisters, two older and one younger, all of whom had followed that path with nary a glance backward. In staying single Alison wasn't rebelling against her rich parents or some prosaic *Good Housekeeping* ethic that clashed with her own sense of independence. She'd unabashedly wanted that life, declared family to be her primary ambition, and was looking forward to it. She'd grown up in an idyllic home with loving, supportive parents, little if any friction between her sisters, and every possible opportunity and privilege. It was only natural that she'd want to recreate her own family in that image. But then she'd gone and fallen in love with Jack, a twist for which she was entirely unprepared, and that was all she wrote. Jack was the horse for want of which her kingdom was lost.

It was so obvious to all of us from the beginning how in love with Jack Alison was, he'd have to have been a complete idiot to miss it, and Jack was no idiot. Yet throughout college and the years after, he never made a single romantic overture, never seemed to even entertain the notion that there was gold to be mined in his friendship with Alison. I know how frustrating it was for Lindsey, Chuck, and me to watch, so I can only imagine what it did to Alison. Lindsey was the only one who was able to talk to Alison about it, to encourage her to move on and look elsewhere for love, but she never met with any lasting success. Her sessions with Alison could become so heated that the two of them would get into fights, sometimes not speaking for days afterward. "Any other guy here would die to have her!" Lindsey would say, her eyes bulging in disbelief. "They'd be fucking lining up at her door! And instead she has to fixate on the one guy who's too damn stupid to realize what he's got! What is she, a freaking masochist?!"

Alison did occasionally go out on perfunctory dates, but it didn't take very long for the new guys to figure out that they were competing against someone they could never beat. Lindsey, so independent and strong-willed, couldn't stand to see Alison in such a submissive state, and she rarely passed on an opportunity to plead her case. These periodic battles served to forge a strong bond between her and Alison, although it didn't do much for Lindsey's friendship with Jack. If Alison wasn't going to be pissed about the way he treated her, then someone had to be. Lindsey blamed Jack for not loving Alison, or for not letting her go, and while I don't recall her ever addressing the issue with him, I know she harbored a strong resentment toward him. "He goes out and does every girl on campus," she complained to me once while we were under the arch in Washington Square sharing a falafel between classes. It was winter, and her cheeks were burnished from the wind and I was wondering how much damage it would do if I leaned over and kissed one of those cheeks. "And then he comes home and goes out for coffee with his *friend*, Alison."

I remember thinking that there might be an obvious parallel to be drawn with Lindsey and myself, but in a rare display of discretion I chose not to point it out. "They really are friends," I said instead.

"Come on, Ben," she said. "He knows what he's doing. She's his, I don't know what, his safety net or something, and it's not right. It's emotional enslavement."

I know she wanted me to take issue with Jack, to talk to him about it and try to make him see what he was doing to Alison, but I didn't see things that way exactly. Jack rarely discussed his past, but I knew his mother had died when he was very young and he didn't get along with his father. Something he'd once said had left me with a vague notion of abuse, but I couldn't recall exactly what it was. Either way, there was clearly a powerful, ma-

ternal aspect in the way Alison cared for Jack, something undeniably nurturing. Jack took great comfort in that facet of the
relationship, and he wasn't willing to risk losing it by turning it
into something sexual. Even though it often looked to us like Jack
treated Alison poorly, I think he actually loved her more deeply
than any of us imagined, and her warmth and approval were his
sanctuary. To defile that with sex might have been unthinkable to
him, treating her like any other girl on campus. In a strange way,
I think Jack felt himself unworthy of Alison when it came to a
true, sexual relationship.

On some level, Jack must have realized that Alison had needs,
too, needs that weren't being fulfilled because of her unwavering
commitment to him. Maybe that meant there was an element of
selfishness to his relationship with her, but he rationalized it away
since she was too important to him to lose. I don't know if I
understood this then, or if I only had a faint notion and I'm im-
posing years of subsequent analysis on my memory, but I'm pretty
certain that both of them understood the true nature of their relationship. They were simply powerless to do anything about it.
Jack and Alison loved each other, but needed different things from
that love, which put them at tragic cross-purposes. Relationships
don't come with a warranty and being in love is no guarantee of
a happy ending. Just look at me and Lindsey. If anything, love is
just a starting point. Then life intrudes, along with the personal
baggage you've spent years packing, and things get royally and
irrevocably fucked up. You can get bitter or you can keep trying.
Most people do some of each.

I thought about all of that as I felt Alison's cries pulsating
against my forehead, and we all sat there in the bar trying to
absorb some of her sadness, to lighten her load just a little bit.
After another moment Alison wiped her eyes and offered us a grin.
"Sorry," she said. "I guess I've had that coming for a while."

"Well," said Chuck, lifting his glass in a mock toast. "To Jack's health."

Lindsey picked up her glass. "To saving Jack's ass from himself."

"To Alison," I said. "The lady with the plan."

Alison wiped her eyes and lifted her glass. "Plan B," she said. We downed our drinks.

"I'm reminded of a joke," Chuck said. "What's the difference between friends and good friends?"

"What?" I asked.

"A friend will help you move. A good friend will help you move bodies."

I once kissed Alison. Or she kissed me, I'm not sure. Some kissing took place though, in the Village East Cinema in our junior year. We'd gone together to see the director's cut of *Blade Runner,* which always seemed to be showing somewhere in the Village. It was something of an annual tradition for us since we had a long-standing argument over whether Harrison Ford's character was actually a Replicant or not. Alison said yes, I said no. We sat shoulder to shoulder, leaning on each other in a friendly manner as we watched Rutger Hauer beat the crap out of Harrison Ford in the not too distant future, and all of a sudden we were kissing, not long deep kisses but short, gentle, experimental ones. Upper lip, lower lip, open mouth, closed mouth, chin, nose. It felt good, but a little too unreal to get me going. It was like kissing through plastic. After a while the kisses tapered off and we were left forehead to forehead, looking at each other sheepishly. Alison finally whispered, "It was worth a try."

I smiled and kissed her cheekbone. "It would have been a nice way out, huh?"

She closed her eyes. "Yes." It was the first time either of us had expressed any frustration about our respective situations with Lindsey and Jack. Jack was dating some model/graphic artist from FIT and Lindsey was dating Boris, the Magician, and Alison and I were trading worthless kisses in an empty movie theater.

We turned back to the screen. Rutger Hauer was now breaking Harrison Ford's fingers. "Why do you think we take it?" she asked without looking away.

"You can't pick who you fall for," I said.

"That's lame," she said. "We're intelligent people. We should be able to see that something's not happening and move on. Why can't we do that?"

"Because we're artless romantics."

"Or blind optimists."

I thought about that for a few seconds and didn't come to any new conclusions.

"If I could just believe that he really didn't love me," Alison said haltingly. "If I could just make myself believe that, I think I could move on."

"But he does," I said.

"I know," she said. "And there's the rub. It's funny really. The great tragedy isn't that Jack doesn't love me. It's that he does." She was quiet for a moment. "What about you and Lindsey?"

"What about us?"

"I don't know. It's kind of the same thing, isn't it?"

"Not really," I lied. "I like the way we are."

"Oh," she said with attitude. "You do."

"Sure," I said.

"Oh please! You just kissed me more than you've ever kissed her. You're going to tell me that doesn't bother you?"

"Don't be so hard on yourself. You're not a bad kisser."

"Stop being evasive," Alison said, giving my wrist a squeeze.

"What do you mean? You brought up the kissing."

She looked at me for a minute and then smiled. "You're even evasive about being evasive," she said. "You've got it bad."

"I don't know," I relented. "I guess we're just being penalized for being such invaluable friends. There are worse things."

"If you really believe that, you're a better person than me." She sighed and leaned her head on my shoulder. I patted her leg and we watched the movie. A battered Harrison Ford was running and limping through a dim alley in the rain. I said, "It's always raining in the future."

13

MESSAGE

For: Mr. George Bernard.
From: Dr. Samuel Richter, Mt. Sinai Hospital
Date: October 4, 1998

Please call at once regarding instructions for emergency care of Alison Scholling.

Jack always used one of three aliases when he checked into hotels. We got it right on the second try and left the message. It was a jerky thing to do, but Alison insisted. He returned the call one hour later, to a number that actually rang at the desk of a receptionist at Mt. Sinai with whom Chuck was friendly despite his having dated her briefly. The call was routed to Dr. Samuel Richter, actually a candy striper who read from a script Chuck had meticulously prepared. Dr. Richter informed Jack that Ms. Scholling had been in a major car accident, sustaining head trauma as well as various internal injuries that he listed in jargon calculated to simultaneously confuse the layman and scare the shit out of him. Jack's name, he was told, was listed in her wallet along with her family, who had yet to be reached, since they were vacationing overseas. We were gambling that Jack would be too worried to wonder how the hospital knew to reach him at the Plaza.

As Alison had predicted, Chuck's beeper went off less than a minute later. It was sitting on a desk between the two of us when it began vibrating in an electronic jitterbug across the desk's scratched surface. Chuck caught it as it went over the edge, looked at the read-out and said, "It's him." He put it back on the desk and we waited sixty seconds until the beeper went off again. We were sitting in an unused office that Chuck said the interns used as a smoking room.

"Sounds like an emergency," I said, as Chuck pressed a button to stop the vibrating. We weren't going to answer the page right away. We wanted Jack to be as agitated as possible, and Chuck knew from experience that ignoring the beeper would do the trick. A minute later the beeper went off again. This time Chuck picked up the phone and dialed the number. When he got the Plaza's front desk he read off the room number on his beeper and Jack picked up on the first ring. I leaned in to better hear Jack's end of the conversation.

"Hello," Chuck said lazily. "Did somebody there page me?"

"It's Jack, Chuck," Jack screamed into the phone, prompting Chuck to jerk the receiver away from his ear. "Did you hear about Alison?"

"What about her?" Chuck asked.

"She's been in an accident," Jack said. "Shit, Chuck, she's in your hospital."

"What happened?" Chuck asked, finally putting a trace of concern in his voice.

"I don't know," Jack said. "A car crash or something. I'm coming over there now."

"Hold on a second, Jack," Chuck said. "Just calm down and tell me everything. How do you know she was admitted?"

"I got a call," Jack said impatiently. "Some Dr. Richter guy left me a message."

"Sam Richter?" Chuck asked. "From emergency?"

"Yes!" Jack said. "Samuel Richter."

"Shit. The guy's practically retired already. I'd better get down there."

"I'm coming now," Jack said.

"Hold on, Jack," Chuck said. "You can't just run into an emergency room here. They won't let you in. And besides, you're too easily recognized. You'll cause a commotion. Just stay there and let me check it out. I'll call you."

"No way," Jack said. "I'm coming over there now."

"Okay, okay," Chuck said, pretending to think about it. "But let's do it this way. Come in at the Ninety-eighth Street entrance, and take the elevator up to the eighth floor. My office is 812. Meet me there, and I'll take you to see her. By the time you get here, I should have more information."

"Okay," Jack said. "I'll be there in fifteen minutes."

"Fine. Two other things, Jack."

"Yes," Jack said impatiently.

"First, wear some sort of disguise, okay? We don't want to cause a scene down there."

"Got it. What else?"

Chuck took a deep breath. This was the part on which everything else depended. "Come alone. I don't think I have enough clout to get your entourage past the triage nurse."

"I'm on my way," Jack said, and hung up.

"He's on his way," Chuck said, flashing me a nervous grin. We were like two kids making a prank phone call.

"Terrific," I said without much enthusiasm.

Chuck reached into his desk and pulled out a small leather case that looked like a shaving kit. He pulled out a nasty looking syringe and a pear-shaped vial. Yanking the red plastic shield off the needle with his teeth, he jabbed it into the top of the vial and pulled back on the plunger, carefully watching as the liquid filled the syringe. When the syringe was three quarters of the way full, he pulled the needle out of the vial, pressed lightly on the plunger to squirt out a little liquid, and then replaced the red needle shield with his teeth in one smooth motion. Then, holding the syringe up in front of him, he flicked it twice with his finger, peering intently into the liquid.

"What are you doing?" I asked.

"Checking for air bubbles," he said, replacing the syringe in the leather bag.

"What is that?"

"Thorazine. Should take about five minutes."

"Couldn't you use anything faster?"

"Nothing except a blunt object to the head."

"What are we going to do with him for five minutes?" I asked.

"I don't know. You have any good jokes?" He reached into another drawer and pulled out a blue and green cloth bundle and threw it to me. "Scrubs," he said. "For our daring escape. You may as well change now."

As I climbed out of my clothing and put on the flimsy scrubs, I was overwhelmed by the surrealism of the whole situation. Here we were, two grown men, about to abduct another man and remove him from circulation. A major movie star was going to disappear without a trace, and we were going to be the ones behind it. This was big. I even had to wear a disguise. I looked over at

Chuck, who was wiping his hands on his white jacket. "All we need is the soundtrack to *Mission: Impossible,*" I said.

A few minutes later Chuck's beeper began jumping across the desk again. I grabbed it and looked at the readout. All ones. That was the signal from Lindsey, who was parked across the street in Alison's hunter green Beamer.

"Elvis is in the building," I said.

"Places everyone, places," Chuck said much too loudly, stepping behind the door.

My stomach felt like I'd swallowed a litter of rabbits as I took my position in the chair behind the desk. I was terrified of facing Jack, of seeing the look of betrayal in his eyes, when he realized what we were doing. My mouth was suddenly a desert, and my lips began to stick to my gums. I couldn't stop my right leg from shaking. I looked at Chuck and he stared grimly back. We were trapped in the moment, which seemed to last an eternity, but still it seemed as if the door was flung open way too soon.

Jack flew into the room with such force that I was scared the door would smash Chuck's face in, à la the Three Stooges. I had a momentary vision of Chuck slipping to the floor unconscious, the incriminating syringe still clutched in his fist, and Jack turning to me with the tough glare and half-smile he used in his action films and saying, "What's going on, Ben?"

But Jack just stepped up to the desk, gasping for air, and said "Ben, what's the story?" If he was surprised to see me there, he didn't show it, and he didn't seem to notice that I was wearing the scrubs. He was wearing Ray Bans and a purple Lakers hat to keep his face hidden. He looked flushed and was sweating heavily, as if he'd run the entire way, or at least up the eight flights of stairs. I felt a pang of guilt over making him worry like that, but I reminded myself that it had been Alison's idea. Desperate times and all that.

"Alison's okay, Jack," I said. "Why don't you sit down for a second."

"She's okay?" he asked, peeling off the shades and his hat, still laboring to bring his breathing under control. "You saw her?"

"I saw her, Jack," I said, standing up behind the desk. "Just sit down and I'll tell you what's going on."

Jack pulled the plastic, molded chair out and dropped down into it. The instant his butt hit the chair, Chuck stepped out silently from behind the door and, with no hesitation, jabbed the needle into the back of Jack's shoulder. Jack let out a yelp that was one part pain and two parts surprise and jumped to his feet, flinging an elbow back reflexively at his unseen attacker. The elbow connected squarely with the center of Chuck's face, and there was an audible crack as Chuck's nose erupted into a geyser of blood.

"Motherfucker!" Chuck yelled, falling on his knees, cupping his face as the blood flowed over his hands and onto the floor. Jack kicked the chair away and spun around, his hands up and his body squared in a very convincing martial arts posture. Jack had trained with various martial arts experts in preparation for a number of his films, and some of it had clearly taken.

"What the fuck's going on?" Jack asked, staring down Chuck. "What'd you just stick me with?"

Chuck stumbled to his feet, grabbed some paper towels from a shelf on the back wall and pressed them to his nose. "Jesus Christ, Jack!" he blubbered. "You broke my goddamn nose!"

"What the fuck is going on here?" Jack yelled again. "Ben!" He turned to look at me, his eyes seething. I noticed that the needle had broken off of the syringe and was sticking out of his shoulder. I made an instant decision. I decided this was a stupid fucking plan.

"Relax Jack," I said. "Everything's going to be okay."

Keeping one hand on his wounded nose, Chuck reached out to Jack with the other. "It's okay, Jack," he said, grabbing him by the arm, which turned out to be a grievous error in judgment. Jack, interpreting the grab as a continued attack, grabbed Chuck's wrist in an arm lock and spun him into the desk, which his thighs hit with a resounding thud. Chuck gave out a low moan and doubled over the desk.

"Jack, cool it!" I yelled helplessly. We were one minute into our plan, and it had already gone horribly wrong. I saw Jack glance at the door and realized he was going to make a break for it. "Don't move, Jack!" I screamed. "Don't fucking move!"

It worked. For about three seconds—and then he broke for the door, but before he could get there, it swung open and Alison walked in, closing it calmly behind her. When Jack saw her, his jaw dropped. "Alison!" he whispered, shock etched into his face.

"I'm sorry, Jack," she said, walking slowly towards him and opening her arms.

"You're not hurt," he said in a toneless, subdued voice, absently pulling the needle out of his shoulder.

"No," she said, putting her arms around his neck and holding him to her. "I'm sorry we had to do it this way, honey, I really am." He tried to move her back a little, so that he could see her face, but she held on tightly, whispering into his ear, while I looked on dumbly. Chuck was less concerned with Jack now and more concerned with stanching the flow of blood from his broken nose, so it was I who had to leap over the desk, scraping my left shin in the process, to help Alison catch Jack when he dropped into unconsciousness a minute later. He dropped into my arms so suddenly that I fell on my ass, with Jack sprawled all over my lap like a little kid who'd fallen asleep.

We all stayed like that for a moment. Chuck, leaning against the desk with the blood-soaked paper towels pressed to his face.

Alison standing by the door, her eyes opened so wide that her eyeballs appeared to be in danger of rolling out of her head, and me, sitting Indian style on the floor with Jack drooling onto my thigh.

"Phase one," I said. "Completed."

"Like clockwork," Alison said, her voice shaking slightly.

Chuck just let out a gurgling groan and leaned back on the desk. "My nose is broken. I can't believe it. He broke my fucking nose."

The next part was easier than we anticipated. Chuck produced a gurney and we put Jack under a blanket and wheeled him down the white hospital corridor and into the elevator. When we reached the ground floor, Chuck went into a closet and came out with a wheelchair and the three of us moved Jack from the gurney to the chair. We got a few strange looks from passing nurses and orderlies, but as Chuck had predicted, everyone was too busy to give us more than a passing glance.

We wheeled Jack down the outside ramp and across Fifth Avenue, where Lindsey was double-parked, the rush-hour traffic providing some welcome cover for us. Chuck and I hoisted Jack's unconscious bulk out of the wheelchair and into the back seat, while Alison ran across the street to return the wheelchair. The exertion caused Chuck's nose, which I noticed had swelled considerably in the last five minutes, to start bleeding again.

"Chuck, your nose," I said.

"Shit." He pulled off his white medical jacket and bunched it up to press against his face.

"What happened to him?" Lindsey asked, looking over her shoulder from the front seat.

"Minor glitch," I said. "Chuck, do you want to go back inside and get that fixed?"

"That depends," Chuck said nasally. "Do you want be double-parked on Fifth Avenue when Jack wakes up?"

"Okay," I agreed. "Get in."

"Just stop at a bodega and get me some ice."

We all got into the car, Chuck and I sitting like bookends on either side of Jack in the back seat while Alison took the driver's seat and Lindsey rode shotgun. Alison steered us down Ninety-sixth Street, stopping briefly at a deli for the ice, and then onto Harlem River Drive. As the adrenaline seeped out of me, I realized that I was soaked with sweat, so I opened the window and let the brisk fall air batter me dry. Every time a car passed us, I was sure that someone would look in and notice something irregular, but no one gave us a second glance. By the time the George Washington Bridge was looming in front of us, I'd accepted that we were going to get away with it.

"Well," Lindsey said merrily as we drove across the bridge into Jersey. "We just crossed a state line. I guess that makes it a federal offense now."

"You don't think Jack would really press charges against us, do you?" I asked.

"I would," Chuck said.

"You're just pissed because he broke your nose."

"No shit." He looked at Jack over his plastic ice bag, put his palm against Jack's head and gave it a disgusted shove. Jack fell forward until his head came to rest on the corner of Lindsey's seat.

"If it really came to that, I think he'd understand we're doing this for him," Alison said.

"Keep telling yourself that," Chuck said, his voice muffled by the ice pack.

"Music anyone?" Lindsey interjected, hitting the car stereo before anyone could object. 10,000 Maniacs came on, singing "These

Are Days" and all conversation came to a stop as we sat back to contemplate the enormity of what we had just done, or rather, whether what we had just done had any enormity to be contemplated. Depending on how you looked at it, we were either five friends heading up to the mountains for a vacation, or four criminals who had just kidnapped a major film star across state lines. Either way, the next few days would certainly be memorable. As I watched Lindsey's hair fly around her face in my open window's backdraft, I found myself overcome by a sensation of sweet anticipation that I hadn't felt in years. Natalie Merchant's syrupy, full voice filled the car as we drove into the pink-orange shadowlands of the Palisades Parkway at sunset. I decided that, come what may, I could certainly go for a few memorable days.

14

The Schollings's vacation home was a lakefront property on the outskirts of a small town called Carmelina, New York. The back of the house faced Crescent Lake, right in the bend of the crescent, which meant that just about every window in the place had a view of the lake. The house itself was a typical example of modern country architecture, a mixture of colonial and ski condo. Its exterior was stained wood, and there were slanted roofs, skylights, and windows everywhere you looked. The back of the house had a deck on stilts that looked out over the lake. The house and the surrounding forest made you feel as if you'd entered a J. Crew catalogue. It was exactly the kind of house I would have wanted to have if I had someone to have it with.

We drove up the long, narrow driveway to the left of the large front yard and parked close to the front door. Alison ran ahead to open the door and turn on some lights while Chuck and I carried Jack, still unconscious, out of the car. Jack had stirred once during the trip, and Chuck had given him another injection, this time Versed, straight into the vein. Chuck was confident that it would keep him out for the rest of the night.

The foyer was filled with our suitcases, which Alison had sent up the day before with Lucy, her parents' housekeeper, who'd been dispatched to prepare the bedrooms and dust off the house. She had also been charged with stocking the kitchen before she left, which was no mean feat when you considered that it was larger than my entire apartment.

We followed Alison up the stairs and around a short corridor to her father's study. The house had that slightly musty, pine smell that I always associated with summer camp. The study itself was rectangular with a mahogany desk and matching bookcases that lined three of the walls. A quick glance at the shelves revealed an *Oxford English Dictionary*, an *Encyclopedia Britannica,* hard-bound editions of everything from Shakespeare and Milton to more postmodern stuff like Pynchon and Barthelme, what looked like an entire shelf of old *New Yorker*s and *Commentary*s, and in between, stacks of papers and manila folders. The room had no windows. The fourth wall was devoted almost exclusively to family pictures. Alison and her sisters in various stages of childhood, always freshly shampooed and suntanned, as if the Schollings were only photographed in the summer. Beneath these photos was a convertible couch that had been opened up into a queen-sized bed. To the left of the sofa bed was a door leading to a small bathroom, also windowless. We laid Jack down on the bed, pulled off his shoes, and covered him with the blue comforter that had been left folded on the floor.

"He's going to be one unhappy camper when he wakes up," Chuck observed. His nose was now a misshapen clump, with a nasty purple bruise descending from his forehead to its bridge. He had to be in agony.

"We'll worry about that then," Alison said. She ushered us out of the room and from the top desk drawer produced one of those

old-fashioned iron keys, the kind that fit into keyholes. Closing the
door, she inserted the key and twisted it sharply to the left. I tested
the door by turning the knob and leaning into it with my shoulder.
It was a strong wood, maybe poplar or maple, and opened into
the room, so I was fairly certain Jack wouldn't be able to break it
down.

Alison placed the key on the top of the door frame and we
headed downstairs to the kitchen, where Lindsey was already for-
aging through the fridge. "Is anyone else starving?" she asked, her
voice echoing strangely from inside the refrigerator.

A half hour later, we had prepared a small feast of pasta in
marinara sauce, garlic bread, cheese omelets, frozen egg rolls, and
a large garden salad. There was something soothing about the four
of us preparing and sitting down to a large, home-cooked meal. It
somehow validated what we were doing there to begin with, added
a sense of normalcy to the whole affair.

"I feel like someone should say grace or something," I said.

"I know what you mean," Alison said, rolling her spaghetti the
proper way, with a fork and spoon. "It feels like Thanksgiving."

"Well, I'm thankful," Lindsey said. "I'm thankful we pulled off
what we did today without anyone getting arrested or getting
hurt."

"I beg your pardon?" Chuck objected, his mouth stuffed with
egg roll.

"Oh right," Lindsey said. "I'm thankful that only Chuck got
hurt."

"Fuck you very much," Chuck muttered, chugging on a Rolling
Rock and then pressing the bottle against his nose.

"Man," I said. "It feels like forever since we all just sat down
together."

"What are you talking about?" Chuck said. "We go out all the
time."

"This is different," I said. "We usually get together in a rush, and someone is always coming late or leaving early."

"Or punching out the waiters," Alison interjected wryly.

"That's why we need to eat out," I continued. "If we spent the time making the meal, half of us would be gone before it was ready. This feels, I don't know, slower. More personal. More relaxed."

"You mean it feels like college," Lindsey said, smiling at me. "All of us together, with no end in sight."

"Something like that." I said, spearing an eggroll with my fork.

"You always were the sentimental one, Ben," Chuck said.

"We're all sentimental," Alison said. "Ben just says it out loud." She flashed me an appreciative smile. Alison's spirits had been up ever since we left the city. It had been the helplessness, as much as anything else, that had been making her so despondent. After months of lonely agonizing over Jack's self-destruction, she was now finally doing something about it, and she was no longer alone.

"Well," Chuck said, finishing off the beer and spooning himself some more pasta, "I don't think our friend upstairs is going to view this as a happy little college reunion when he wakes up."

"You never know," I said. "Jack was always a pretty laid-back guy. Maybe he'll just say 'whatever' and take it all in stride."

"Yeah," Chuck said sarcastically. "If you're planning on seeing a carefree Jack tomorrow, I hope you packed a lot of cocaine, because that's the only thing that's going to keep him sane."

"He's right," Alison said. "I remember how crazy Jack got when I flushed his coke down the toilet."

"What about when he first wakes up?" I asked. "We didn't really think about this. How's he even going to know where he is?"

"We should leave him a note or something," Lindsey said. "Ben, you're the writer."

"You say that like it's a good thing," Chuck said with a grin. I nailed him in the face with my egg roll.

After dinner we all watched the late news, which was devoted to the aftermath of a catastrophic train crash in New Jersey. Thirteen dead. I remembered my comment to Chuck about the news being a glorified body count of the day's most sensational deaths. The really bad ones, I now noticed, even got their own logos. During the commercials I started to compose what I thought would be a brief note to Jack, but turned into a full-blown epistle. It never fails. When I have to write a thousand words on deadline I lock up after the first paragraph, but for an inconsequential note that will only ever be read by one person, the ink flows like a river.

Dear Jack:

Don't worry, you're not in danger. Alison, Lindsey, Chuck, and I have gotten together to form our own private rehab clinic, and you're our first and only patient. I'm fairly confident that when you wake up you're going to be very pissed about all of this. You'll be missing some important preproduction meetings and, no doubt, you'll be missing your coke, but we've been missing you for some time now, Jack.

You're always saying that I live too much in the past, that I'm always thinking that things were better back in college. "Live in the moment, Ben," you always used to say. "You'll never get it back." I remember how you once gave me a tape that just had one line from that Billy Joel song taped over and over again in a continuous loop. Ninety minutes of ". . . The good old days weren't always good and tomorrow ain't as bad as it seems." You told me to play it on my Walkman every night before I went to sleep, so that it would sink in. You always had an easier time with the present than I did, and I always envied you for it. Until now. Maybe I'm wrong when I think that the good old days were always good, but one thing I know I'm right about is this: The good old Jack was always good, and much better off than this one.

You were the most laid-back guy I knew. Cool as the other side of your pillow. Nothing could rattle you or shake your confidence. It was so easy for you to live in the moment because your moments were always so much better than everyone else's. You had your pick of the women, and everyone seemed to like you. You were the best kind of popular; you made no effort and couldn't have cared less. I felt lucky to be your friend.

And now, for the first time since I've known you, I feel better off than you. My life might not be where I want it to be, but it isn't literally dissolving right under my nose. You're constantly strung out, and your daily outings have become escapades, fodder for the tabloids. You're now the proud owner of your very own police record, and you're spending the majority of your time with people who don't give a shit what happens to you as long as they get their piece of the pie. Despite all of your success, the moment you're living in is killing you.

Somewhere in you is still the relaxed and happy Jack, the guy who lives life at his own pace, with his own rules. Don't you miss that guy? I know I do. We've brought you here to find that person again, for you and for us. We loved you when you were just a nobody, and we loved you when you became a famous nobody, which is why we can't sit idly by and watch you poison yourself.

Remember how we used to stay up late watching those nature documentaries in college? Well, I still watch them, and I recently saw one about a monkey called the bamboo lemur, so named because it safely feeds on poisonous bamboo stalks that no other animal can eat. The enzymes it secretes are specifically adapted to digest the poison. The problem is that the enzymes are so specialized that the bamboo lemur quickly loses its ability to eat anything else. It becomes completely dependent on the poisonous stalks. When the stalks are gone, the lemur dies. That's the price it pays Mother Nature for a steady diet of poison. What price will you have to pay?

I don't remember who first came up with the idea of this intervention, but we all agreed that we had to do something to get you off the poison. Chuck says it will take two to three days to get the coke out of your system, and another few days to get you to stop craving it. That means you're going to be our prisoner for at least a week, so get comfortable, and let us know if there's anything you need.

Every time I start to think we're crazy for doing this, I ask myself if you would do this for one of us, and I always come up with yes. In a minute.

Yours truly,
Ben

P.S. If it's of any comfort, you broke Chuck's nose in a spectacular fashion.

15

Somewhere around 5:30 in the morning, Jack began smashing things. I was jolted awake by the crash of a heavy object hitting the floor, followed by a cacophony of glass breaking against the walls. I staggered out into the hallway, where I found Alison and Lindsey already standing, ashen-faced in their shorts and tank tops, consciousness slowly bleeding into their eyes.

"What the hell is he doing?" I asked.

"Let me the fuck out of here!" Jack bellowed from behind the locked door. Alison began to approach the door, but jumped back when it shook with a resounding crash.

"That sounded like a television," Lindsey observed.

"I don't believe this shit," Chuck said hoarsely as he emerged from his bedroom in purple boxers and a ratty Springsteen T-shirt. The swelling around his nose had gone down slightly overnight, but the purple bruising had spread underneath his eyes. He looked like the Hamburglar from those old McDonald's commercials. From inside the study we now heard small flapping noises followed by lesser thuds, as Jack began throwing books across the room. It sounded like a squadron of kamikaze pigeons. Alison sat down on the floor, her back to the study door, and pulled her arms up over her ears.

"I guess we should have thought to clear the breakables out of there before we locked him up," Lindsey said, looking sympathetically at Alison.

"You think?" Alison muttered, rubbing her bloodshot eyes.

I tried to think of something to say or do, but my mind was still fuzzy with sleep. We'd been too wired about the abduction to get to sleep at a decent hour the night before, and even after we'd retired to our separate bedrooms—Alison and Lindsey sharing one while Chuck and I each had our own—I had lain awake for hours. I couldn't stop thinking that my bed and Lindsey's were separated only by a wall. It was unnerving to realize that for the first time in five years we were lying less than a foot apart from each other. I tried to feel her presence through the wall, and wondered if she was sensing my proximity on her side. It was past three when I finally nodded off.

"Get me the fuck out of here!" came Jack's voice, hoarse from screaming, punctuated by the sound of splintering wood. I remembered Mr. Scholling's mahogany desk and winced.

"He can't go on like that forever," Lindsey said.

"I should have thought to empty the room." Alison berated herself.

"You can't think of everything, Alison," I said. "We're all beginners here."

"Yeah," Chuck said. "And while we're on the subject, does anyone have any idea how we're going to bring him his food?"

"Oh shit," I said. We all looked at each other, last night's elation a distant memory. We were in uncharted territory here, and every minute seemed to yield one more glaring example of just how out of our depth we were.

In the study, Jack's tantrum seemed to have peaked. We heard something skitter across the floor, and then there was silence.

"Jack?" Alison asked tentatively. There was no response. "Jack?"

Suddenly, it was deathly quiet in the study. "Jack?" Alison called again, alarm in her voice. "You don't think he hurt himself, do you?"

"He's ignoring you, that's all," Chuck said.

"All that broken glass," Alison murmured. "He could cut himself, he could have fallen down . . . Jack!"

There was no response from behind the door. Alison suddenly reached up to the top of the doorjamb and pulled down the key. She was about to insert it when Chuck grabbed her wrist. "Don't," he said.

"He could be unconscious, or bleeding," Alison said, struggling to free her arm.

"He's playing possum," Chuck said. "You unlock that door and he'll tear out of there so fast you won't know what hit you."

She turned to look at Lindsey and me, her hand still on the doorknob, uncertainty etched into her face. "What should we do?"

"I agree with Chuck," Lindsey said. "He's just trying to scare you."

"It's working," she said, turning back to the door. "Jack, will you just answer me," she pleaded.

I bent down next to Alison and took a quick look through the old fashioned keyhole. There was darkness and then a sudden burst of light as Jack jerked his head away on the other side. "I saw you, Jack," I said, feeling a childish burst of triumph. "I saw him," I said, straightening up. "He's fine."

"Ben, you shit! Let me out of here!" Jack screamed.

"Not a chance," I said. "I'm going back to bed."

"Come on! Chuck! Alison! I'm hurt," Jack called. "I'm bleeding."

"We'll slide some Band-Aids under the door," Chuck said, rubbing his nose tenderly.

"Let me the fuck out of here!" Jack screamed, pounding on the door fiercely. "I'll get you all! You're all fucking dead!"

"Calm down, Jack," Alison said.

"Alison! Let me out of here now!"

"I'm sorry, Jack."

"Don't be sorry, be smart," Jack called. "You want me to go into a clinic? You let me out of here and you and I will go together. This isn't the way to handle this."

"I don't believe you," Alison said, pressing her palms against the sides of her head.

"I promise you, I'll do it," Jack said. "Come on. I'm hungry and I'm cut."

"I'm sorry, Jack," she said again.

"Alison, you stupid bitch!" Jack shouted. "Let me out of here right now you . . . cunt!"

Alison gasped, her eyes brimming with tears. Lindsey put her arm around her and gently steered her back towards their bedroom. "Ignore him," Lindsey said. "Remember that he's not well right now." Jack began pounding steadily on the door. "I suggest we all try to get a little more sleep," Lindsey whispered. "It's looking like today's going to be a long one."

We all headed back toward our bedrooms, but I turned around one last time. "Jack?"

"What?"

"Did you get my letter?"

"Fuck you, Ben!" he yelled, punching the door with what sounded like bare knuckles.

"Ouch," I said. "That had to hurt." I turned around and went back to bed.

I awoke again at 10:30 and gazed out my window. The trees surrounding the lake were a patchwork quilt of harvest colors, their yellows, oranges, and reds magnificently reflected in the pristine surface of the lake. For a few minutes I just sat up in my bed and watched a group of birds bathing on the near side of the lake, reflecting on how romantic and satisfying the view would be if there was a warm body tucked into the blanket with me. Now it just left me feeling like the sheets beside me, cold and empty.

There was a knock on my door and then Alison stepped in. "You up?"

"Yep."

"We're having breakfast."

"Sounds like a plan." I pulled the blanket off and rolled out of bed for the second time that morning. "He quieted down, huh?"

"I think he screamed himself hoarse," she said. "Is that a Darth Vader mask?"

"What? Oh, yes. It is." I had left it sitting on the night table. Alison looked at me questioningly. "I'm not sure why I packed it," I confessed. "I thought it might come in handy."

"You never know," she said.

Here's how we got the food to Jack. Alison made him scrambled eggs and ketchup on toast, which we put on a plate and into a ziplocked bag. We poured his orange juice into a Tupperware cup with a removable lid, and some coffee into a car mug with a lid that said Mystic Aquarium and had a picture of two dolphins in midleap on the side. All of this we placed onto a tray, which Chuck and I carried quietly up the stairs, tiptoeing until we were directly in front of the study door. I bent down and peeked through the keyhole, hoping that the mild groan in the floorboards would be muffled by the carpeting.

Jack was pacing the room like a caged animal, back and forth relentlessly. He was fairly close to the door, so all I could see was the area between his knees and his navel, but his body language was full of angry energy. I held up my left hand to signal Chuck, while silently inserting the key with my right. My heart sped up as I held my breath, concentrating on being completely silent. Chuck crouched before me, leaning in to where the door would open. When Jack turned around and headed toward the back of the room again, I dropped my left hand and in one quick motion turned the lock and pushed open the door, without letting go of the doorknob. Chuck instantly tossed the tray inside, its contents bouncing off of it as it hit the floor. I had time to see Jack spin around in surprise, his eyes raging under a tangled mane of dirty blond locks, and then, as he leapt forward, I slammed the door shut and turned the key. The knob shook in my hands as his body hit the door the instant it closed, and the key was knocked out of the hole and onto the carpet.

"Ben!" Jack yelled, banging on the door in frustration. "Let me out of here!"

"Shut up and eat your breakfast, Jack," Chuck called back pleasantly.

"You guys are going to go to jail for this!" Jack shouted. "I swear, I'll make you pay." He gave the door a final, resounding kick and then after a little while we heard him bend down to pick up the food.

"How'd it go?" Lindsey asked when we returned.

"No problem," Chuck said.

"He really sounds insane," I said, somewhat shaken by the intensity of Jack's rage.

"He's going through withdrawal," Chuck said. "He's used to

jump starting his day with coke. He's panicking now, wondering how he's going to get some."

"Panicking?" Alison asked.

"Imagine if you woke up one morning and found that your lungs could only get half the oxygen they were used to," Chuck said.

"It's really like that?"

"I don't know from experience, but I've met my share of addicts in the ER, and they'll do pretty much anything to get ahold of some drugs. They're surprisingly resourceful. You get junkies who have run out of drugs cutting off their ears or driving nails into their hands just to get some prescription painkillers."

"Jesus!" Lindsey said. "I think you can spare us the details."

"Okay," Chuck agreed, biting into an English muffin. "But I just wanted to prepare you."

"For what?"

"When he's done going crazy, that's when it will really begin."

"What are you talking about?"

"He hasn't had time to think yet. He's too panicked," Chuck said. "Once he calms down and assesses his situation, he'll start making his escape plans." He swallowed and looked around at us. "That's when things will really get hairy."

16

"I'm still at that age where people say 'she hasn't gotten married yet,' " Lindsey said to me later that day. We were driving Alison's Beamer into town to buy additional Tupperware for feeding Jack. We were on a two-lane blacktop that wound its way through the forest for about eight miles before it hooked up with Route 57, the main artery through Carmelina.

"You're only thirty," I said.

"I know. But I think it's time I started acting my age. Get back into teaching or something. Stop being so damn flighty. People might still be able to say 'she hasn't married yet,' but at some point in your thirties you cross some invisible line and then they start saying 'she never got married.' "

"I'm guessing you're not just concerned with the semantics."

"No." She was quiet for a minute. She breathed against the car window and began doodling with her fingernail in the fog her breath had created. "I want a family someday," she said quietly.

"What's bugging you?" I asked, the car's tires stirring up a patter of loose gravel as I swung onto Route 57.

"Nothing. I don't know," she said, running her middle and ring fingers through her hair in a gesture that was so familiar it brought a lump to my throat. "I don't have a career, I don't have a family, and I don't know what to do next. I've been so determined to escape anything permanent, and now I just feel like I'm nowhere. And what if that's the permanent thing by default?"

"That would suck."

"Thanks for your support," she said wryly.

On the side of the road an old man sat smoking a pipe next to a set of tables stacked with pumpkins. He wore a hooded sweatshirt under his plaid flannel shirt and the wooden sign behind him said, "5 days till Halloween." I saw that the "5" was on a removable slat, like those old scoreboards we had in Little League.

"We're all nowhere," I said, watching the pumpkin man recede in my rearview mirror.

"No," she disagreed. "You're working as a writer, Jack's a famous actor, Chuck's a surgeon, for god's sake. Alison's a successful lawyer . . ."

"Chuck's incapable of a serious relationship," I said. "Alison has not gotten anywhere with anyone she dates because she's still hung up on Jack. We all know how great Jack's doing. And I'm divorced, dissatisfied with my job, and haven't gotten one step closer to finishing a novel than I was when I got married. Thanks, now you've got me depressed."

"You already were," Lindsey said, smiling.

I said, "I guess one of the drawbacks to doing nothing with your life is that you're never quite sure when you've accomplished it."

Lindsey's smiled turned sad. "It's like we all set out so determined, so sure of our direction, and now we've gotten lost, and we're just wandering around in circles," she said, unclasping her seat belt as I pulled into the parking lot at Edward's. "We're all in this rut, you know?"

"The only difference between a rut and a grave is depth," I said.

"Jesus, that's grim."

"I just mean that we don't have forever to work everything out anymore," I said. "Sometimes I think to myself that I'm not lost, just behind schedule, you know? And then I feel this horrible pressure to catch up, but I don't even know the first step to take. Maybe that's why I rushed into a marriage." I turned to look at her. "I'm thirty years old. Shit. By now I was supposed to have at least one novel published. I was supposed to have a wife and a kid and house somewhere quiet, where you can hear the crickets at night. Somewhere out there is this whole other life that I'm supposed to be leading, and I just can't seem to find it."

"When you're in college you're just so sure that the future is going to unfold exactly how you want it to," Lindsey said.

"I know." I thought about if for a second. "The future just isn't what it used to be." She giggled.

"You laugh," I said. "But it's true. Nothing has gone according to plan."

"You know how to make god laugh?" Lindsey asked me as we got out of the car.

"How?"

"Make a plan," she said.

Carmelina's town center was basically two streets, Main and Maple that intersected at a cobblestone roundabout, the center of which had been turned into a small park with benches and a greenish copper sculpture of a Union soldier on horseback. Unlike Catskills towns further north like Roscoe or Monticello, Carmelina was not strictly a working-class town that relied on industry built around its "summer people" to see it through the grim winters. The town was close enough to the city to attract a significant population of middle-class families who lived there year-round. As a result, Carmelina's business district had a rustic, country feel without being at all decrepit. The streets were lined with a charming assortment of mom-and-pop stores with names like Curly's Comics, Parker's Five and Dime, the Carmelina Fudge Factory, Kids' Threads, the Itty Bitty Gift Shop, Rich's Hardware, Paperbacks Plus, and Mane Tamers Hair Salon. If you were looking for a Banana Republic or a T.C.B.Y. or a Sam Goody you'd have to drive back down Route 17 another thirty miles to the Middletown Mall.

It was the late afternoon shopping hour on Main Street, which meant that there were maybe thirty or so people on the streets, mostly mothers with small children and elderly couples. Everyone we passed either said hello or smiled a greeting, which reassured you that you actually had mass and took up space. It was a far cry from Manhattan, where a packed subway car could easily make you wonder whether you even existed.

"It's like a movie town," Lindsey observed, looping her arm through mine. "It feels like the opening scene of a Christmas movie." We strolled around for a little while, looking at the stores (Cora's Collectibles, Fat Man's Ice Cream Shop) and I enjoyed the sensation that, to all of the people we passed, we were just another couple. The small simplicity of the town generated a reality where the twisted nature of my current state of affairs couldn't exist. For this moment in time, we were a couple. I brought my elbow into my side, pulling Lindsey closer to me as we strolled down the sidewalk. She didn't pull away, and a quick, sideways glance showed the hint of an amused smile at the corner of her mouth.

Lindsey felt like walking, so we followed Main Street out of the business district, where it curved around a dried-up corn field and out of sight. The sidewalk disappeared and you could feel the real estate prices falling with each bend in the road. The houses we passed were single-story, prefab units, the kind that got delivered via the interstate by large flatbeds with flashing lights and "wide load" warning signs. Every driveway either had a pickup truck parked in it or oil stains to mark where one would be returning later in the day. The men driving those trucks would have hard expressions and callused, grease-stained hands. The kind of men who, by their rugged natures, made city slickers like me feel weak and unmanly.

"Did you notice any train tracks?" I asked Lindsey.

"No, why?"

"Because we somehow crossed over to the wrong side of them."

"It may be Carmelina, but it's still the Catskills," she said. I noticed that she was no longer holding on to my arm and wondered if that was unintentional or if she'd deliberately retracted it.

"I can't remember the last time we were alone like this," I said, which was my own uniquely nerveless way of broaching the whole general topic.

She frowned at me, confirming too late that the wiser course would have been to not say anything. "I'm sure that you can," she said, some sarcasm creeping into her tone.

The smart thing to do right then would have been to shut my mouth and keep walking, leaving the awkward moment behind, so I stopped and said, "What just happened?"

She turned to face me, her expression dark. "How about we just don't go there right now, okay?"

"Go where?" I asked.

She shot me a look. "You know damn well where. You always have to bring up the past. You can never leave well enough alone."

"What are you talking about?"

"Your lack of judgment, I suppose."

"No, I mean why do you think that?" I said, trying not to sound defensive. "I wasn't trying to bring anything up."

"Yes," she said angrily. "You were. You can't tolerate a single unexamined moment."

I must have looked pretty miserable, because her expression softened and she stepped closer to me, putting her hands on my shoulders. "Listen," she said. "I'm really glad we're spending time together now. I've missed talking to you terribly. But don't complicate things by dredging up old issues. You're not going to find any answers there."

We looked at each other for a minute. "Okay," I finally said, more by way of concession than agreement. I felt something inside my chest, warm and quivering, slowly deflate. It was absolutely ridiculous for me to be feeling heartbroken here, over this, but there it was. "I'm sorry."

"Forgiven," she said with a smile. She gave me a short hug, during which I thankfully resisted the urge to nuzzle her hair and kiss her. "Can't we just spend time together without complicating everything?"

"Sure," I said, knowing that it already was complicated. The damage was done. I'd forced the issue and been deftly shot down. I'd been kidding myself to think it might have been otherwise. Lindsey had hugged me and let it go, but the words were out there, a barrier that I'd unwittingly forced her to put up between us. The "just friends" speech at age thirty. A new and profound low.

"Come on," she said, turning around. "Let's head back." We turned and began walking into town. A growing rumbling behind us gradually turned into a roar, as a scary looking bearded guy shot by us on a Harley. The back of his T-shirt said, "If you can read this, then the bitch fell off," which normally would have been kind of funny, but I was all out of laughs for the moment.

We went into Parker's Five and Dime, kind of an everything store, and bought out the Tupperware section. The burly, middle-aged man behind the counter, whose name was almost certainly Parker, rang up our purchases on an antique cash register, the kind where a red sign that says "Sold" pops up when the final sum appears in the little window. "How are you today?" he said, bagging the plastic containers.

"Never better," I lied.

We drove home in silence, Lindsey looking out the window and humming softly while I dejectedly contemplated the order of things. The ink was still drying on my divorce, but all of my regret seemed to be directed at a breakup that had happened over five years ago. It occurred to me that there might be a peculiar balance to what I was feeling now. When Lindsey left me, I channeled all the feelings I had for her into Sarah, and now that Sarah was gone, those feelings were free to return to their point of origin. Then again, I might have been transferring my anguish over the divorce onto Lindsey simply because she was there. Less likely, but not impossible. I stole a quick glance at Lindsey, who thought I tended to complicate things. I remembered a literary anecdote about Kurt Vonnegut. When a visitor expressed surprise at his rather untidy office, he pointed to his head and said, "You think that's messy, you should see what it's like in here."

17

When we got back to the house Alison was sitting at the kitchen table, eating Ben and Jerry's Cookies and Cream out of the container and looking distraught. The Indigo Girls were playing on the stereo in the living room, but as far as I could tell that had nothing to do with it.

"He hasn't made a sound all afternoon," she said. "I've tried to talk to him, but he doesn't respond."

"He's either pissed or sleeping," I said.

"This isn't how I thought it would be," she said dejectedly. "I thought we'd be able to keep him company, to talk him through it. He's so alone in there."

"It's just the first day," Lindsey said. "We're in this for the long haul, don't forget. Things will change."

"I guess," Alison said, sounding unconvinced.

"Where's Chuck?" I asked.

"He rented a car and drove back to New York to get his nose taken care of and arrange for someone to cover his patients. He'll be back late tonight or early tomorrow morning." She stood up and returned the ice cream to the freezer. "I also checked my messages at home," she said slowly.

"Yeah?"

"There was one from Paul Seward. He wanted to know if I'd heard from Jack in the last day or two."

"It begins," Lindsey said dramatically.

"I figure we'll just ignore him," Alison said.

"Maybe, for now," I said. "Right now he'll probably just wait for Jack to resurface. Seward probably figures he went on a bender."

"It wouldn't be the first time," Lindsey said.

"I think they start preproduction on *Blue Angel II* next week," Alison said. "Seward will be frantic if he hasn't heard from Jack."

"Not as frantic as the producers and director will be when Jack doesn't show up," Lindsey said. "And given Jack's recent publicity, they'll instantly assume the worst."

"He'll get sued for breach of contract," Alison said. "And it will ruin his reputation. No one will want to insure him."

"We may have to talk to Seward," I said. "Maybe we can get him to work with us."

"Doubtful," Lindsey said.

Alison sat down and looked up at us. "We may be doing more harm than good here," she said.

"No," I said. "You have to believe we're doing the right thing. Whatever harm this may do to his career, it won't be as bad as what he would have eventually caused himself."

"He's right," Lindsey said. "We have to think long term here."

"I just wish he would talk to us."

"He will," I said. "Don't worry about it. He's in there somewhere."

"It's almost as if he doesn't want to get better," Alison said.

"That's why we aren't giving him a choice," I said, wishing I was as confident as I sounded.

That evening the three of us watched the news. None of us said it, but we were checking to see if Jack's disappearance was out yet. I was so relieved to see that it wasn't that I almost forgot to follow the body count, which was six. A power plant explosion in Monticello killed five, and an armed suspect was shot by a cop in a standoff over a domestic abuse call.

Afterwards, I went upstairs with Lindsey to bring Jack his dinner. Since our return from town, we were both doing our best to pretend that our earlier argument hadn't happened. We were lousy actors. I checked through the peephole and saw that Jack was sprawled out on the bed asleep. I continued to watch as Lindsey unlocked the door and, convinced that he was truly out, I slowly pushed the door in. Jack didn't budge. I took a minute to examine the room, which looked like a swarm of locusts had mistaken it for a wheat field. Torn and bent books were haphazardly strewn all over the place, and there were glass fragments everywhere. The mahogany desk was turned on its side, a feat of which I wouldn't have thought one man capable, and two of the curved legs had been broken off, giving it the appearance of some disfigured mythological beast. Behind the door in a pool of glass splinters was the television we'd heard Jack throw, a jagged crack running up the back of the black plastic casing. Little white electronic components were scattered around it on the carpet like dandruff on a dark suit.

Seeing this destruction was like looking into a truly tortured soul. I felt an icy breeze in my intestines when I looked back at Jack's prone form. I never would have believed that somewhere within him existed the pure and dark rage that had inflicted this damage. Looking at Lindsey, I could tell she was equally shaken. She was squeezing her lips with her right hand, her eyes wide with shock. "Jesus, Ben," she whispered, her voice trembling. "Why'd he have to do this?"

"I have no idea," I said dumbly. I placed the tray containing a turkey and cheese sandwich and a thermos of pea soup on the floor, scooping up what scattered remains of Jack's last meal were within arm's reach, and backed out of the room. Lindsey turned the key and replaced it on the doorjamb. I followed her somberly downstairs, wondering once again if we had taken on way more than we could handle. I wished that Chuck were there, to explain it all away as a symptom of withdrawal. At that moment, his unassailable confidence would have been a welcome antidote to my gnawing doubts.

By tacit agreement, Lindsey and I didn't mention the state of the room to Alison. She'd witnessed the same pandemonium we all had that morning and probably had a good notion of the extent of the damage, but a firsthand description might still be unsettling.

"How's he doing?" she asked when we joined her in the den. She was curled up in the corner of a large, burgundy couch, taking slow sips from a mug of hot cider. On the huge leather couch she looked like a little girl in her sweatshirt and leggings, and I wanted to curl her up into a ball and hug her. Instead I took a sip of her cider and sat down on the floor in front of her.

"He's sleeping," Lindsey told her. "With any luck, he'll sleep through the night."

"Good," Alison said softly, cradling the mug tightly between her hands as if she were fighting a chill. "Look what's on HBO."

I grabbed the clicker from the glass-topped coffee table and hit the power. And there was Jack, bleeding from a fake gash on the bridge of his nose, shooting an automatic pistol from the top of a baggage conveyor belt in a crowded airport. It was the opening scene of *Decoy,* one of the disappointingly average, highly profit-able action films Jack had made after the wild success of *Blue Angel.* Two bad guys went down, and two more fled up the stairs. Jack dove headfirst over a pile of suitcases in pursuit, knocking extras out of his way. He stopped briefly to help up a little girl who been knocked over, handed her the fallen doll she'd been searching for and flashed her a wide, white-toothed smile. "There you go," he said, and then turned to run up the stairs three at a time in pursuit.

"He hurt his knee filming this," Alison said in a monotone, staring at the screen. "He insisted on jumping off that baggage carousel himself, and he ended up twisting his knee so badly they had to shoot around his scenes for a week while he recovered."

"I remember," I said. "Jackie Chan was always one of Jack's heroes because he does all his own stunts."

"Didn't Harrison Ford hurt himself filming *The Fugitive?*" Lindsey asked.

"Yep. Same kind of injury," I said. "Jumping off a bus or some-thing."

"Hey," Lindsey said. "Harrison Ford to Jack Shaw in four mov-ies. Not counting the one they were in together."

"Easy," Alison said. "Harrison Ford was with Anne Archer in *Patriot Games.* Anne Archer was with Michael Douglas in *Fatal Attraction.* Michael Douglas was with Andy Garcia in *Black Rain,* and Andy Garcia was in *Blue Angel* with Jack."

"Good one," Lindsey said. "But I can do it in three."

"Do tell."

"Harrison Ford was with James Earl Jones in *Patriot Games.*"

"And *Star Wars,*" I chimed in.

"Good point," Lindsey said. "James Earl Jones was with Eric Roberts in *The Best of the Best* and Eric Roberts was in *Decoy.*"

"Julia Roberts to Jack in three," I challenged.

"Amateur," Lindsey said. "Julia Roberts was with John Malkovich in *Mary Reilly* . . ."

And so it went, well into the night. We played the game, we talked and reminisced and sipped our hot cider while basking in the soothing, blue-green glow of the television as if it were a fireplace. At some point I got off the floor and joined Lindsey and Alison on the overstuffed couch, the three of us splayed out in a tangle of throw pillows and the heavy, handknit afghan that had lain in a basket beside the couch. The smell of the leather couch mingled in my nostrils with the aroma of hot cider and feminine shampoo. I closed my eyes and leaned back, embracing all of the comforting sensations that surrounded me. For the first time in years, it felt like time was finally slowing down, at least for a little while. At some point we began drifting off to sleep, but rather than go upstairs we just pulled closer together under the blanket, like three newborn puppies, finding warmth and security in our proximity. I slept better than I had in months.

18

The next morning I awakened at what we used to refer to in college as the butt crack of dawn, disentangled myself from the sleeping forms of Lindsey and Alison, and, pulling on a jacket from the hall closet, took a walk down to the lake. Behind Alison's Beamer, there was a new looking Taurus in the driveway painted an electric blue that screamed rental. Chuck was already at the lake, sitting on a wooden bench beside the Schollings's dock and smoking a cigarette.

"Hey," I said.

"Hey."

"What are you doing?"

"I'm just lost in thought," Chuck said.

"I can see where that might be unfamiliar territory."

"Ha."

"When did you get back?"

"Around two or so."

"We didn't hear you come in."

"I know. I peeked in on you guys." He gave me a conspiratorial grin, blowing out a funnel of gray-white smoke. "Not bad, dude. Two of them at once, eh? You're a wild man."

"Your nose looks much better," I said.

"Yeah," he replied, rubbing it absently. "I had it set. Guy I know in ortho did it."

"It's a shame. I kind of liked the way it hid your face."

"Nice."

The sun was just coming up on the far side of the lake, a hazy, nebulous orb casting an orange hue on the surrounding blue. The mist rose lazily off the lake, seeming to muffle all sounds save the occasional belch of a bullfrog. I wondered where frogs went in the winter. Did they hibernate? Did they die?

Just then we heard a loud, whooshing sound from above and looked up to see a gaggle of geese coming in for a landing. There were about fifteen of them. In unison they circled the lake, flying across to the far side, and then came gliding down onto the lake, their webbed feet extended before them like landing gear. Within seconds, the once-still lake was bustling with activity. Chuck and I watched in wonder.

"That was pretty amazing," Chuck said, stubbing out his cigarette. "I feel like we should hear some British guy's voice-over telling us about the migration cycle of the speckled goose."

I smiled. "I guess for us, nature is just another thing you see on television."

We heard a door slam behind us, not from the Schollings's house but from the one next door, and turned around to see a young boy around eight-years old walking down toward the lake with a large golden retriever following at his heels. He looked skinny in his red and black flannel shirt and blue jeans, with dirty blond hair that had been recently cut. He hesitated when he saw us, but then snapped a leash on the dog and continued to come in our direction.

"Hi," he said, approaching our bench.

"Hello," I said, and Chuck waved.

"Are you staying at the Schollings's?"

"We're friend's of Alison's," I said. "I'm Ben and this is Chuck."

"Oh," he said, scratching the back of his dog's head.

"What's your name?" I asked.

"Jeremy," the boy answered. His dog came forward to sniff us, and I gave it a friendly scratching on its chest. "That's Taz," he informed me.

"Taz?"

"Yeah. Like the Tasmanian Devil. You know, the cartoon?"

"Sure," I said. Taz, it seemed, was a sucker for chest-scratching, and sat himself right down in front of me to get as much as he could, his eyes closed in pleasure. "Did you name him?"

"No, my father did." At the mention of his father, his eyes shot to the ground for a moment, and then came back up uneasily. "I came down to see the geese," he said. "They come every year at this time."

"Is that right?" Chuck said.

"Yeah. They're Canadian Geese, on their way to Florida. They stop here for about a week or so, and then they go. They also stop here on their way back in the spring."

"That's pretty cool," I said.

"What happened to your nose?" he asked Chuck.

"I got hit by a friend," Chuck said.

"You?" he asked me.

"Not this time," I said. "We all take turns hitting him."

"It looks like it's broken," Jeremy said. "You should go see a doctor."

"I see one every time I look in the mirror," Chuck said.

"Which is usually quite often," I added.

"You're a doctor?" Jeremy asked, skeptically.

"Sure am."

"Do you ever take care of people who have conas."

"What are conas?" Chuck asked.

"It's when you sleep and you can't wake up for a long time," the boy said earnestly. I noticed that his eyes were a startling blue, and that his left one sometimes winked shut and open again involuntarily.

"That's a coma," Chuck said. "C-O-M-A, coma. What do you know about comas?"

"My father has one," Jeremy said.

"Really," I said. "That's too bad."

"Yeah," he said, automatically. "He got hit by a truck while he was jogging. He's been asleep for almost three months now."

"I'm sorry to hear that," Chuck said.

"He never knew what hit him," Jeremy said, clearly repeating something he'd heard said before.

The back door of Jeremy's house swung open again, and a girl of about twelve came out onto the deck. "Jeremy, what are you doing?" she called to him.

"That's Melody," he informed us. "She thinks she's the boss now, because my dad's not around."

"Jeremy!" she called again.

"I'm just walking Taz," he called back to her.

"You have to come in for breakfast," Melody persisted.

"I'll be there soon."

"Mom says now."

He rolled his eyes with disgust, and gave Taz a slight pull with the leash. "I gotta go," he said.

"Sisters," I said with a sympathetic smile.

"You have any?"

"Uh, no," I admitted.

"You're lucky," Jeremy said, then turned to face Chuck. "Do you think you could help my dad?"

Chuck's eyes met mine for an instant. "I'm sure his doctor's doing everything he can," Chuck said. "Besides, I'm a pretty young doctor. I bet your dad's doctor is older than me, and much more experienced."

"I guess," the kid said, turning to go back up to his house.

"Hey, Jeremy," I called to him.

"Yeah."

"See you around."

"Yeah," he said, pulling Taz closer to him as they headed up the hill. "See you around."

"That poor kid," Alison said later, when I told her about our encounter with Jeremy over breakfast. "I had no idea. I didn't hear. We've known the Millers for years. I used to baby-sit Melody, when she was, like, two years old. My dad and Peter used to fish together." No one had felt like cooking, so we were eating Cheerios and milk, which I would undoubtedly suffer for later. Another symptom of my having turned thirty was a sudden increase in what had always been a very mild lactose intolerance.

"It doesn't sound good," Chuck said, gulping down some juice. "If he's been in a coma for three months, the statistics are not in his favor."

"I should go over and see Ruthie," Alison said. "She must be going through hell." She got up, threw on a sweater, and headed for the door. "Don't forget to give Jack breakfast," she called behind her.

When Chuck and I brought Jack his breakfast, we found him sitting up in his bed, still wrapped in his blanket. Because he didn't appear to be ready to make a leap for the door, I held it open a minute to talk to him.

"How's it going, Jack?"

"Okay," he said, without really looking me in the eye. "You guys going to let me out today?" He was bathed in a sheen of sweat, with little droplets forming on the bridge of his nose and at the corner of his eyes. His eyes were bloodshot, their lids rubbed raw.

I looked at Chuck. "I don't think so," I said.

"Jack, the first thing you'd do is go score some coke. It isn't even out of your bloodstream yet," Chuck said.

"I need something, man," Jack said. "Can't you give me anything? I don't feel good."

"You're going through withdrawal," Chuck said. "You'll feel much worse by tonight."

"Nice bedside manner, Chuck," I said sarcastically.

"You know," Jack said, shivering slightly under his blanket, which he pulled more tightly around him as he sat up. "You're doing some pretty serious damage to my livelihood right now."

"We're more concerned with your life right now," I said. "Try to get some sleep." I started to close the door.

"Ben," he said.

"Yeah?"

"You can't keep me here much longer."

"I know, Jack," I said. "But I wouldn't be me if I didn't try."

He was quiet for the rest of the day. I found it kind of eerie, picturing him just sitting in that bed, shivering, the blankets wrapped around him like an Arab, but Chuck said he was most likely sleeping. "His body is shutting itself down," he explained. "Coming off coke is an exhausting ordeal. Once the source of your strength is gone, the abuse you've been inflicting on yourself catches up with you. Some people sleep for weeks."

19

Later that afternoon I stepped out onto the Schollings's front lawn to get some fresh air. I saw Jeremy Miller shooting hoops in the Schollings's driveway and walked over to join him. I judged from the knapsack by the side of the court that he'd just returned from school. "How's it going?" I said, grabbing a rebound and dribbling out to take my own shot. Swish.

"Okay," said Jeremy, grabbing the ball and tossing it back to me for my courtesy shot. I noticed he was wearing a *Blue Angel* T-shirt that showed the movie poster, Jack on a motorcycle with a building exploding in the background. My next shot hit the back of the rim, but still managed to bounce in. "Friendly rim," Jeremy said by rote.

"You a big Jack Shaw fan?" I asked, taking a jumper that hit the front of the rim and landed in Jeremy's hands without a bounce. He dribbled it through his legs and back out to the foul line. He shot it the way little kids do, bringing the ball up from his belly and pushing it with both hands as he jumped. Swish.

"Yeah," he said, in answer to my question. *"Blue Angel*'s my favorite movie of all time."

"Did you see *Decoy?*"

"Yeah, that was good, but I liked *Blue Angel* better. You know, Alison's friends with him." He shot again, same motion, same result.

"Yeah, I know."

"Are you also his friend?"

"Yeah," I said, tossing him the ball.

"That must be so cool," Jeremy said wistfully.

I thought of Jack sitting up on Alison's sofa bed, sweating in his blankets between puking jags. "Real cool," I said.

He shot the ball, which hit the left side of the rim and bounced out of my reach. I was about to chase it when Jeremy said, "They're going to pull the plug on my dad tonight." I stopped in my tracks and dumbly watched the ball bounce off the driveway and onto the Schollings's lawn, where it rolled to a lazy stop. The reason kids can shock you so often is that they haven't learned to segue yet. They just blurt out whatever is on their minds.

"Really?" I said dumbly.

"Yeah. My mom says it's a good thing because if he woke up now he wouldn't be the same anyway. He had in his will that they shouldn't keep him alive with machines."

"I guess he knew what he was doing," I said, wondering what must have been going through this guy's head when he put that stipulation into his will. Probably anything but the fact that it would become applicable so soon.

"Yeah," said Jeremy. "I'm kind of glad." He stated it like a confession. "I pretty much knew he wasn't coming back, and I've been sad for a long time. Everyone in my family's been. It's getting harder to be sad now, you know? Do you think that's a bad thing?"

"No," I said, considering it. "I think that all people, if they're well balanced, healthy people, feel a need to mourn and then move on. You and your family have been stuck mourning for so long, and because the hospital was keeping your dad alive, you couldn't move on, you know?" He stared intently at me as I spoke, and somewhere in his eyes I saw that I was giving him affirmation that he desperately needed.

"My mother told me and Melody to write a letter to my dad, and she would read them to him before they pulled the plug," he said. "She didn't think we should be there. Just her."

"I think that's a really nice idea," I said.

"Yeah. I just hope Melody doesn't go all crazy. She can be a real drama queen."

"I'll bet."

We stood there in the fading light of the day, looking at our Nikes while we considered life and death. I looked at Jeremy and felt an overwhelming sense of warmth and admiration for this little boy carrying around so much grief and stress, stubbornly refusing to let it paralyze him, as I was sure it would me. "You're a trooper, Jeremy," I said. "You're going to be all right."

"I know," he said simply. "I just hope my mom is."

"You'll help her through it," I said. "You'll all help each other."

"Yeah," he said quietly. "You want to play one-on-one?"

That night, our third up at the lake house, Jack's disappearance made the evening news. A somber Tom Brokaw said the last time Jack was seen was by his agent after they'd checked into the Plaza Hotel in New York three days earlier. "Authorities will not speculate at this time as to whether Shaw has been the victim of foul play," Brokaw remarked, as the scene shifted to a press conference set up at the Fiftieth Precinct, where the Chief of Police was making a statement. "This afternoon at twelve-thirty, Jack Shaw was reported missing. At this time, we have no reason to think any foul play was involved. All I can say at this time is that his people are concerned and we are looking into the matter."

Brokaw then returned. "Although the police department says they are looking into the movie star's disappearance, a police officer who spoke on the condition of anonymity said that the police are more inclined to believe that Shaw's disappearance is drug-related. Over the last few months, Shaw's alleged drug addiction has made headlines across the country. Most recently, he was arrested and charged with driving under the influence and possession of a controlled substance, to which he pleaded no contest.

"As Hollywood wonders about the fate of its newest leading man, one famous director has been left holding the bag, as it were. Luther Cain spoke to us from the set of *Blue Angel II,* where Shaw's disappearance has halted the start of production."

Cut to a close up of Luther Cain on a soundstage. A tall, angular man whose complete baldness was accentuated by his comically bushy eyebrows. There was an artist-at-work intensity to his gaze, but his voice was soft and even. "We don't know where Jack is, and right now we're just worried about him. I hope he's all right, and that we hear some good news before tomorrow."

Back to Brokaw. "Cain, the Academy Award—winning director whose film *Blue Angel* launched Jack Shaw to stardom, would not comment on the financial implications of Shaw's disappearance, saying that it's only money and right now their only concern is to hear that Jack Shaw is safe. We'll have more on this for you as it develops."

We turned off the television and just looked at each other. Even though we'd known the story would eventually break, we'd all been secretly hoping that it somehow wouldn't. Now that Jack was officially missing, now that Tom Brokaw, for chrissakes, had seen fit to comment on it, we were somewhat overwhelmed by the enormity of what we had done. The trouble we might be in.

"Holy shit," Chuck whispered.

"That was pretty intense," Lindsey said.

"Maybe we should call Seward," I said. "Get him to call off the hunt."

"You can't be serious," Chuck said. "Seward needs someone to blame for this. If we tell him, we're his scapegoats to the media, to the police, to everyone. He'll want to do everything he can to show that this was anyone's fault other than Jack's."

"He's right," Alison said wearily. She'd spent most of the day with Ruthie Miller and seemed exhausted from sharing the woman's grief. "As it is, Jack was having trouble getting insured, but this is the first time he didn't show up for work. It will be virtually impossible to get insurance for Jack unless it was someone else's fault."

"So let me see if I understand this," I said. "We spend another week or so up here and Jack kicks the habit, right? Great. Now we have two choices. Jack can go back to Seward, and to the police, leave our names out of it, and he basically will never work again. Or, we step forward and admit our guilt, in which case maybe Jack gets to work, and we go to jail. Is that how this is going to play out? We choose between Jack's career and our lives?"

"Not exactly," Lindsey said.

"How's that?"

"I don't think the choice is ours. It's Jack's."

"Can I ask a simple question?" Chuck said.

"Why not."

"What the fuck were we thinking?"

We sat through the rest of the news in a somber silence that was periodically broken by Chuck, who muttered, "Tom-fucking-

Brokaw," to himself every few minutes, in a somewhat awestruck voice. I was so preoccupied that I forgot to keep track of the body count.

After the news we turned off the television and Alison opened up the mahogany bar in the corner of the living room and said, "Drinks anyone?"

"If you're pouring, I'm drinking." Chuck said. We went through the cocktails pretty quickly, and Alison got tired of getting up to freshen everyone's drinks, so she just mixed up a huge pitcher of vodka and cranberry juice and placed it on the coffee table. Lindsey fiddled with the stereo until she got the CD player working and put on an old Joe Jackson album.

"There's probably going to be a funeral tomorrow," Alison said. "They're pulling Peter Miller off life-support tonight. Ruthie told me the doctors don't expect him to live through the night."

"I'll go with you," I offered, thinking of Jeremy.

"Okay," Alison said appreciatively.

Chuck's beeper went off. He pulled it out and looked at the screen. "Who the hell is that?" he muttered to himself. I grabbed the cordless phone that was lying under the couch and tossed it to Chuck, who had dropped off the couch and was sitting cross-legged on the floor. He dialed the number and, after a few seconds said, "Yes, this is Dr. Nyman." We all smiled since it still sounded odd to hear him refer to himself as a doctor. Chuck's eyes suddenly flew open and he quickly covered the mouthpiece with his hand. "It's Seward!" he hissed.

The rest of us ran into the kitchen to put on the speaker phone, while Chuck remained on the cordless in the living room. ". . . on vacation," Seward was saying when Alison pressed the button. The phone was mounted on the wall beside the fridge, and the three of us stood there staring at it as if we could somehow see Seward through it.

"Yeah," Chuck said. "I'm just taking off a couple of days. How'd you get my beeper number?"

Seward ignored the question. "I've been trying to get ahold of Jack's other New York friends, and you all seem to be on vacation. I find that somewhat funny."

"You're easily amused," Chuck said.

"Come on, Chuck," Seward said. "Jack needs help. Help me get him that help."

"Oh, this is about the whole disappearance thing," Chuck said. "Wait a minute. Are you telling me you don't know where he is?"

"That's right," Seward said.

"Jesus. I just kind of figured you'd checked him into Betty Ford or Promises or something, and that you were trying to keep the media out of it," Chuck said, rather believably, I thought.

"Where are you right now, Chuck?" Seward asked.

"I just told you, I'm on vacation."

"I know, but I'm in New York now and I'd like to get together with you on this. You know, talk it over. See what we can do about helping Jack."

"Well, I'd love to do that," Chuck said. "But I'm actually down here in Florida, so I don't see that happening for another two weeks or so."

"You don't consider your friend's disappearance important enough to come back from Florida?" Seward asked in exaggerated disbelief.

"I'm as worried about Jack as you are," Chuck said, pretending to be insulted by Seward's remark. "But I don't see how meeting with you will help us find him. When Jack wants to be found, he'll turn up."

"Chuck, I'm going to cut to the chase here."

"I wish you would already."

"You're not in Florida."

"Excuse me?"

"You're not in Florida. You're calling me from the nine-one-four area code. I have Caller ID on my phone."

"Well aren't you just Sherlock-fucking-Holmes," Chuck said.

"Why don't you put Jack on the phone," Seward said.

"I would except that, in case you've forgotten, Jack's disappeared."

"Would you like my opinion?" Seward said. "I think you've got Jack up there, all of you. You tricked him with some bullshit message about Alison Scholling's health, and you have him somewhere where you think you're helping him out, while in reality you're actually causing irrevocable damage to his career and reputation." I grimaced, realizing that we had forgotten about the hotel message.

"Well, Paul," Chuck said. "You know what they say. Opinions are like assholes. Everyone's got one, and everyone thinks his own doesn't stink."

"Quit fucking around with me, Chuck," Seward was close to shouting now. "You're out of your league."

"Says you."

"Where's Jack?"

"I should be asking you that," Chuck said. "You're supposed to be his fucking agent."

"You have no idea what you're doing!" Seward screamed.

"That sounded like another opinion," Chuck said. "And you know what they say: Opinions are like assholes—"

"You fucking idiot," Seward screamed. "I'll have your balls on a spit when I—"

"—You can hang up on both of them," Chuck finished, clicking the cordless to terminate the call. I quickly leaned forward to disconnect the speaker phone. As I hit the button, I was dismayed to discover that my hands were shaking.

"Shit!" Chuck said, storming into the room. "He caught me off guard. I had no idea what to say!"

"It wasn't your fault, Chuck," I said. "You had to answer your page."

"He nailed me with that Caller ID thing," Chuck muttered.

"What do we do now?" Lindsey asked.

"We're screwed," Chuck said. "They know where we are now."

"No," Alison said. "Seward has a strong suspicion that we've done something, and now he knows what area code we're in. That's it."

"The police can track us with a phone number," I said.

"But I don't think Seward will go to the police," Alison said. "At least not right away."

"How's that?" Chuck asked.

"He wouldn't want it out of his control," Alison said. "He's still thinking he can salvage this situation and put his own spin on it. Once he turns this over to the police, he loses control and he loses the spin. In his line of work, that's the worst thing that can happen."

"So what will he do?" I asked.

"He'll try to find us himself," Alison said.

20

Thirty . . . shit.

Crows feet, jowls, love handles. I've started to see myself through the eyes of the teenagers I pass on the street, repeatedly shocked by the realization that they see me as older. So many of the things I've eaten with impunity for years suddenly give me indigestion. Nothing feels new anymore. Everything I see just reminds me of something else. I know now that there are certain things I'll never do in my life. A shirt I still think of as new turns out to actually be seven or eight years old. Seasons are quicker, holidays vaguely disturbing. Statistically speaking, I've used up more than one third of my life span, the healthiest third. And where are the tradeoffs? Where's the authority? The wisdom? The confidence that was supposed to have come with adulthood? I'm only experienced enough to know that I'm as clueless as I ever was.

We were all a little hyped up for the rest of the night, between Seward's call and making the evening news, and we didn't know what to do with ourselves. Sure it was scary, but there was also something undeniably exciting about being part of such a big story, about having the inside track. Forget Seward, we knew more than Tom Brokaw, for chrissakes! We *were* the news.

After a quick, late dinner of frozen pizza bagels and french fries, we retired to our separate bedrooms. Everyone seemed to need a little down time to reconsider what we were doing here. I took a fast shower and changed into boxers and a Ben Folds Five T-shirt and got into bed. Using the phone on my night table, I called my answering machine, more out of habit than because I was expecting any messages. There was a quick one from Ethan, sounding rushed and uncomfortable, telling me he'd heard about the divorce and was just checking in to see what was up. No return call necessary. After that was one from my mother, just letting me know that she'd told my brother about the divorce because she thought he should know, and really I should have told him but who knew when I'd get around to doing that, and besides he could tell something was wrong from her voice and he shouldn't accidentally hear it from someone else. The third beep raised my eyebrows, because I couldn't think of anyone else who would have called. A low, hoarse voice rambled on in Spanish for about sixty seconds before hanging up, and while my Spanish was usually limited to intuiting the meaning of the warning decals on subway doors, I was fairly confident in my conclusion that it was a wrong number, confirming my earlier suspicion that there was no one else who would have missed me.

The Spanish message was followed by three long beeps, which meant the machine had nothing left to say to me, so I hung up, remembering to hit the number seven first, which would erase those messages and leave a full tape for the next exciting batch. I could never understand the irrational hope that reflexively bloomed in me like a desert flower every time I checked my answering machine, as if I had all these friends I'd completely forgotten about who would eventually check in and refresh my memory.

I tried to read some Raymond Carver to clear my mind, but I still fell asleep thinking about Lindsey, and woke up with a start, my forehead stuck to the waxy laminate of the paperback cover, feeling the odd sense of bewilderment that comes from awakening in a lit room. I checked the clock on the night table, which read 2:12 A.M., and tried to recall what it was that had shaken me from my sleep. I rolled onto my back and lay still, listening, but the house was completely silent. Somewhere outside, someone was burning leaves, and the faintly acrid smell of smoke came wafting through my bedroom window. It actually took another minute or two of lying there, sniffing thoughtfully before it dawned on me that my window was closed. The smell wasn't coming in from the outside, it was already inside, and whatever was burning it wasn't leaves.

Jack . . . shit.

I rolled out of bed, nearly falling down on my face as my feet got tangled in the twisted blanket, and half hopped, half stumbled out into the hallway, which was already hazy with smoke. I flipped on the hall light and banged on the girls' door, yelling "Fire! Get up!" In the light, I could now see through the haze that the smoke was coming from under Jack's door. I had just located a fire extinguisher behind Chuck's door when he stormed out of it, practically colliding into me. "What the fuck?" he yelled, waving his hands in front of his face to clear some smoke away. Then the smoke alarm went off, a piercing whine that seemed to bypass my ears and go straight to the center of my brain, making my shoulders convulse.

"It's Jack's room!" I shouted above the din, as Alison and Lindsey emerged, looking dazed, their eyes swollen with sleep. Chuck grabbed the key from the door post, inserted it and pushed the door open. A wall of fresh smoke poured out of the room, momentarily stopping me in my tracks, and then I ran in, pulling the needle out of the extinguisher as I went. Jack had thrown a handful of open books into the center of the room and set fire to them. He must have found the matches in one of Mr. Scholling's desk drawers. I did a quick scan around the room, but couldn't find Jack anywhere. I turned the extinguisher full blast onto the pile of books, relieved to see that the actual fire was fairly small, surrendering immediately to the foam.

Chuck was two steps away from the bathroom door when Jack burst out in nothing but sweatpants and charged at him. Chuck hesitated and Jack tackled him, the two of them going down in a confusion of tangled limbs. "Jack!" Alison yelled. "Stop it!" I grabbed her and threw the extinguisher into her hands. "Empty it!" I said, and turned to help out Chuck. Jack had managed to extricate himself from Chuck's grasp and get to his feet. He stepped over him and then fell down as Chuck grabbed his foot and pulled. When Jack hit the floor I ran to get on top of him, but he flipped himself over onto his back and grabbed my outstretched hands, spinning me off balance so that I fell down next to him instead. Still lying on his back he kicked out wildly with his free leg, catching Chuck square in the chest on the third try. Chuck let out a sharp moan and released Jack, who scrambled to his feet with a crazed look in his eyes. I jumped onto his back as he was passing Alison, and the two of us spun furiously around the room, caroming off a bookcase and right into her. The extinguisher fell with a thud as Alison went down under our legs, and then we fell backwards over her. Jack landed on his back on top of me, and before I could catch my breath he was wrestling madly, his elbows inadvertently digging into my ribs as he fought to get up. Screaming, Chuck took a flying leap and landed on top of us, completely knocking the wind out of me, but Jack let out a yell of his own and pitched Chuck, head over heels into the sofa bed. "Fuck!" Chuck yelled as he collided with the metal frame. Jack rolled over so that he was now lying on me face to face, and I could see the crazed look in his eyes as he planted his arms firmly on my chest to push himself up. He had just gotten into a kneeling position when I heard a sharp crackling sound and to my surprise he toppled forward and fell on top of me. I steeled myself for another struggle but he was suddenly dead weight, his body lying limp across my chest. Only then did I see Lindsey standing above us, eyes wide, mouth open. In her hand, still clutched in a death grip, was her stun gun.

We stayed that way for a moment, four of us sprawled out on various parts of the floor, with Lindsey standing in the center, her stun gun still extended in front of her, as if she was presenting arms. Finally, I rolled out from under Jack and said, "Why is it that whenever we knock Jack out, he always has to land on me? I hate when that happens." I got up shakily. "Is everyone okay?"

"Not really!" Chuck yelled as he rolled away from the couch and slowly got to his feet. There was a trickle of blood coming from his left nostril, and he was rubbing his chest furiously. "Jesus!"

Alison got to her knees and crawled over to Jack, rolling him onto his back. "Jack!" she cried. "Jack, can you hear me?" If he could, he wasn't saying. "Come on, Jack, wake up! Chuck, I don't think he's breathing!"

Chuck walked over to where Jack was lying, leaned down and placed his fingers on the side of Jack's neck. "He's fine," Chuck said, leaning against the wall, still massaging his chest.

"Jack!" Alison screamed again. She turned and looked up at Lindsey. "What did you do?" she said angrily. "Look at him."

"Excuse me?" Lindsey asked incredulously.

"You didn't have to shock him," Alison said, propping up Jack's head.

Lindsey looked around the room as if searching for witnesses. "Are you out of your mind, Alison? Look at this room!"

"I don't care. You used a weapon on him!"

"He was burning your fucking house down!" Lindsey shouted, waving her stun gun in the air, and for one crazy second I thought she was going to zap Alison. Then she spun around, grabbing her hair in her fist. "Someone turn off that goddamn alarm!"

I ran out into the hall, pulling the leather desk chair out behind me. I got up on the chair and after a few tries managed to twist the plastic casing off of the circular unit on the ceiling. I didn't see any off switch, so I just yanked out the nine-volt battery and jumped to the floor. The instantaneous silence was so tangible, it felt like a whole other noise.

"I think we may have really hurt him," Alison was saying when I walked back into the room.

"Then we're even," Chuck said. The blood from his nostril had dried on his upper lip, and I realized that he might not even be aware that he'd been bleeding.

"He'll be fine," Lindsey said wearily. "He'll sleep it off." She bent down and pressed her hand to Jack's face.

"Leave him alone," Alison snapped, shoving Lindsey's hand away. Lindsey looked like she'd just been slapped. She stared at Alison in disbelief, her eyes filling with tears.

"I don't believe this," she said, her hands shaking. "He could have killed us all!"

"Ben and Chuck had him."

"Hey!" I said. "We didn't have him at all."

"It was more like he had us," Chuck said.

Alison ignored us, cradling Jack's head in her hands.

"You're on your own," Lindsey muttered, storming out of the room.

Chuck and I lifted Jack off the floor and lay him down on the bed. His body felt sticky with sweat, so we rubbed him down with a towel before wrapping him in a blanket. Chuck pried open each of Jack's eyelids with his thumb and looked at his pupils, then took his pulse again. I could see that Jack's breathing was shallow but regular. "He's okay," Chuck said softly.

Alison sat down on the floor next to the charred pile of books and began picking through them, crying quietly. Chuck and I looked at each other helplessly, not knowing if we should help her clean up or just leave her alone for a while. There was an abject misery to her silent weeping that made us feel unqualified to approach her. After a few moments Lindsey passed by the doorway, but stopped short when she saw Alison sitting on the floor. Hesitating only for an instant, she came into the room and got down on her knees behind Alison, throwing her arms around Alison's neck and leaning forward so that their cheeks were pressing. After a few seconds, Alison wordlessly reached up and wrapped her arms around Lindsey's and they just sat there, softly rocking back and forth as if to some slow, secret song that only they could hear.

21

I woke up at around 10:30, wondering if the previous night's entire episode had been just a vivid dream, but the faint smell of smoke still lingered in the air, and when I sniffed my shirt it stank of it. I rolled out of bed and headed down the hall for the shower. I could hear Lindsey and Alison speaking in hushed tones downstairs. I bumped into Chuck in the hallway as he was heading down to join them. "Good morning," he said.

"How do you feel?" I asked, remembering his collision with the sofa bed. So far, Chuck had taken the brunt of the physical abuse.

"I'll live," he said. "I'm just wondering what else he's got planned for us."

"You think he can top last night?"

Chuck shrugged. "Who knows? But I'll tell you this. The next time it's me standing between him and the open door, I'm just going to stand back and hold it open."

"I know," I said. "I don't blame you." He started down the stairs. "Chuck?"

"Yeah?" he said, stopping.

"Do you think he was trying to burn the house down? I mean, was that an escape attempt, or something more?"

"You mean suicide?"

"That," I said. "Or maybe some kind of revenge. I guess I'm just wondering if, you know, he would really try to harm us like that."

Chuck frowned, considering the question. "I don't think so," he said. "I think that he peaked last night in his withdrawal, and he wasn't thinking at all. He's scared, he's irrationally paranoid, and for all I know he's hallucinating. He's not in his right mind." I remembered Jack's eyes right before Lindsey zapped him and shivered. "Whatever that was last night," Chuck said. "He probably wasn't even aware that he might be endangering us."

I sighed and rubbed my eyes. "Okay then," I said. "So I won't take it personally."

"I did," Chuck said.

I climbed into the shower and leaned against the cool tiles as the scalding water pounded the back of my neck. After we'd doused the smoldering books with water, Lindsey and Alison had gone to bed, while Chuck and I stayed with Jack until he began to regain consciousness. We'd done a quick but thorough inspection of the study, looking for more matches and anything else that might conceivably inspire Jack to pull a MacGyver. Now, as I shampooed the smoke out of my hair, I wondered how Alison was going to explain all of the destruction to her parents. Between the damaged furniture, ruined books, and burnt carpet, the room was pretty much totaled. I didn't want to think about what might have happened if we hadn't caught that fire when we did.

I was walking past Jack's door, toweling off my hair when I

heard a faint, metallic clicking sound. I held my breath and tiptoed up to the door, listening intently. The noise came again, a squeaky scratching sound, barely audible, and I noticed the knob shaking a little. Quietly, I crept back downstairs and joined the others in the living room, where they were flipping around between various morning news programs that were doing stories on Jack.

"Does anyone know if Jack knows how to pick a lock?"

"What?" Alison said.

"I can hear him working on it from outside the door."

"That's an antique lock," Chuck said. "They don't work the same way as modern locks. There are no tumblers. I don't think, even if he knew how to pick a lock, that he could pick that one."

"Well, he's doing something."

They got up and we all stood silently at the foot of the stairs. At first we heard nothing, but then the metallic scratching resumed. Chuck went halfway up the stairs and stared intently at the door. "I don't think he's working on the lock," he informed us, coming back down. "I can still see through the keyhole."

"So then what's he doing?" Lindsey asked.

"I don't know," I said. "Maybe we should ask him."

"Jack," Alison called to him, walking up the stairs. "What's wrong? What do you need?"

The scratching noise stopped suddenly.

"Jack?"

Jack didn't respond, but a moment later the noises resumed. We joined Alison at the door, watching as the door knob rattled around in its casing. A moment later there was a loud, grinding sound, the sound of ratcheted metal being dragged across a wooden surface, and then, with a sudden snap that caused us all to jump, the knob popped off the door and landed on the floor, rolling lazily in an oval before coming to rest by Chuck's foot.

"What's he doing?" Alison asked, snatching up the knob as if it might disappear. From the inner center of the knob protruded the rectangular metal rod meant to go through the door and connect to the other knob, which is what Jack had managed to unscrew. "Jack!" Alison shouted, pounding on the door. "What are you doing?"

"I can't come out," Jack's voice came through the door. "Now you can't come in."

"That's just stupid," Alison said. "What do you want us to do, slide your food under the door?"

"Not my problem," Jack retorted.

"Jack!"

"Please try to keep it down," Jack said, sounding hoarse. "I'm going to try to get some sleep. I've got a big day today."

"Alison," Chuck said quietly, nudging her shoulder. "We can still open the door." He took the knob from her hands. "We just stick this in and twist."

But I had a feeling that Chuck wasn't giving Jack enough credit. "I don't think so," I said. "Why don't you try sticking it in now." Chuck took the knob and began inserting the metal rod into the door. He got about halfway before he hit the obstruction. "Shit!" he hissed, and began fiddling with the knob, but his attempts were clearly futile. "He jammed up the hole!" Chuck complained. "That stupid prick jammed up the hole."

"He's going on a forced hunger strike," I said. "He knows that if we can't feed him, we'll let him out."

"I say let him go hungry," Chuck said, tossing the door knob onto the floor in disgust. "You'd think we were doing this for our own health."

"Well," Lindsey said wearily as we headed back downstairs, "he has already gotten his breakfast, so I guess we'll figure something out later."

"American Cheese," I said. "Fruit Roll-Ups."

"What?"

"I'm just thinking of food we can slide under the door."

"Cold cuts," Lindsey volunteered.

"Wheat Thins," Alison said with a grin.

"I think we'll be able to find representatives of all the major food groups that come in flat packages," Chuck said, smiling wickedly. His competitive nature wouldn't allow him to be bested by Jack, even in this screwy situation.

"Of course, we can't make him eat," I observed.

"No," Alison said. "But we couldn't do that before anyway. It's like there are these unspoken rules. We've put Jack in that room. It's our job to feed him. If we can't, we have to let him out. But if we can, I'm pretty sure he'll eat it."

"Restraint was never his strong suit," Chuck observed.

22

Peter Miller's funeral took place at noon in the Carmelina Lower School's auditorium, just a few blocks out of the town center. The church had been deemed too small for the event. Peter had been a teacher at the local elementary school, so the place was packed with students and ex-students, parents, and faculty. Alison, Lindsey, and I sat in one of the back rows, feeling slightly out of place in what was clearly a community event. Lindsey had decided to join us at the last minute, leaving Chuck in the house to keep an eye on things.

The hushed din of a few hundred whispers was abruptly silenced as the pallbearers wheeled the brown, lacquered coffin to the front of the auditorium. As soon as the pallbearers had taken their seats, the minister, an angular man whose lips appeared to be fixed in a permanent grin, stood up at the podium. I was surprised by the sudden realization that I'd never attended a funeral before. Jeremy Miller, sitting up front sandwiched between his mother and sister, looking pale and scared, would carry this experience with him into adolescence, his teenage years, and his adulthood. I wondered if it would give him some greater depth, some wisdom or sensitivity that I as yet still lacked, if every thought he formed, every relationship would be in some way tempered by the grief he was now experiencing. I felt a pang of something that might have been a distant cousin to envy, but my subconscious banished it before I could feel ashamed.

"The Lord is my shepherd, I shall not want," the minister began. I couldn't help noticing that hanging directly above the podium was a large, dark blue banner with a basketball that said "Carmelina Jaguars, 1998 State Champions." The minister then paused and looked out across the auditorium, as if trying to establish eye contact with everyone in the room individually. "We hear this psalm of David read at every funeral," the minister continued. "It is a psalm of comfort, maybe because of its imagery, or maybe because of its familiarity. Hearing these familiar words over and over again at funerals, we recognize that death, too, is a familiar occurrence to us. Tragic though it may be, it is still a natural part of life and we recognize it as such."

He paused again, staring meaningfully at the front row of chairs, where the family members sat. "But when I read this psalm today, I will not read past the first line. Because I believe that right there, in the first sentence, there is a word that tells me all that I need to hear about Peter Miller. 'The Lord is my shepherd.' That is true. But it is an anthropomorphism, a personification of the Lord. It is the attribution of a human quality to God. We do this in an attempt to qualify God's divine actions, to somehow fit them into a category we can understand. And I now submit to you, Peter Miller was a shepherd here in our field, and in calling him a shepherd, I am referring to the exact human virtues and qualities that David was ascribing to the Lord when he wrote this psalm.

"Peter tended to our most valuable flock, our children. As any of his students and their parents can testify, he was so much more than an English teacher. He was a magnet to the students of the Carmelina Lower School, giving of his love, his energy, his enthusiasm, and his time well above and beyond the call of duty. As a substitute teacher here, I was privileged to work alongside Peter, and I cannot remember a time when I saw him walking down the hallways of this school alone. The children flocked to him, their shepherd, for support, for humor, for camaraderie. He made every single child feel special, and I know from experience that the children valued the distinctive nicknames he bestowed upon as many of them as he could." Here there was a light murmur from the crowd, and I looked around to see a number of people smiling at the reference. "When Peter gave a child a nickname, that child was reassured that he had a place in the school, that he fell safely within the shepherd's sphere of protection, and parents knew their flock was being tended by the very best."

I stared at the coffin and tried to develop a mental image of the man being described. Judging from the sniffling and tearing that seemed to be happening everywhere I looked, the minister's words were striking a true chord. I looked up at Alison, who was crying quietly, dabbing at her eyes with a tissue every few seconds, and at Lindsey, who was staring intently at Jeremy and Melody Miller.

"When I think of shepherds I think of Moses," the minister continued, "who led the Israelites out of slavery and into the promised land. As a young man, Moses grew up as an Egyptian prince, but he could not find peace living in the bustle of the big city. Instead, he fled Egypt altogether, and became a shepherd in Midyan. Only there, tending to his flock in the fields, was Moses finally able to find God, who appeared before him in the burning bush. Our Peter, who was born and raised in Manhattan, felt the same need to leave the city and find God and peace up here in the country. In Carmelina, Peter tended his flock, just as Moses did in Midyan, and I believe that he was blessed to have found his burning bush. To know him was to know a man of absolute contentment, a loving husband and father, a great friend, a God-fearing man whose ample intelligence did not serve to complicate him, as it does so many people. He had the wisdom to simplify his life, so as to better appreciate his world, and better serve his family, friends, and this entire community. And while his passing is tragic, we can take some measure of comfort in the fact that Peter Miller died a happy man. A man with more blessings than he could count, from his loving wife and beautiful children, to the friendship and admiration of every person in this room."

The minister paused, giving everyone a chance to digest all that he had said. Lindsey now had tears in her eyes as well, and when I looked around the auditorium I had trouble finding any dry eyes. "I would now like to call upon Mark Miller, Peter's older brother, to say a few words."

The funeral went on for another half hour or so, and then the coffin was wheeled out, followed by the bereaved. I saw Jeremy scanning the crowd as he followed the coffin, and suddenly felt unequipped to meet his gaze. Ashamed for reasons I couldn't understand, I looked at my shoes until he'd passed.

Driving home we sat in a subdued silence. I found myself thinking of shepherds. And trucks. Trucks could come out of nowhere and end your life, no matter who you were or what you were doing. I pictured Peter Miller, sitting in an expansive green pasture with his white robe and his shepherd's rod, when suddenly, out of the blue comes an eighteen-wheeler, scattering sheep right and left in its path as it veers toward him. And the look on his face, as the truck is bearing down on him, is one of pure exasperation. With the universe, with God, with life. Because if a shepherd in a field isn't safe from the cruel vagaries of fate, who the hell is? "Do you think he smoked?" I asked out loud from the back seat.

"What?" asked Alison, who was driving.

"Peter Miller. Do you think he was a smoker?"

Alison frowned at me in the rear view mirror. "I don't know," she said. "Why?"

"I'll bet he didn't smoke," I muttered.

Lindsey, riding shotgun, flashed me a perplexed look. "What are you babbling about?"

"We could all die tomorrow," I said glumly. "Any of us. We could all die at any time."

"That's what funerals are for," Lindsey said. "Contemplating our own mortality."

"Impending mortality," I said. "It's coming. Peter Miller is the statistical anomaly that proves it."

"What do you mean?"

"I mean, this was the last guy who should have died like this. He took himself out of the city and moved to a safe little community in the mountains. What do you think the rate of violent crime in Carmelina is? Probably lower than in any one city block in New York. He was a teacher and a father, leading a quiet, risk-free life in a quiet, risk-free community." I thought about it for a moment. "No way did he smoke," I said.

"And your point is . . . ?"

"He still died, a horrible violent death. Which means no one is immune. Every morning we wake up and assume it's just the next day in what will be a long series of days. But any one of those days can be it."

"Have you been to many funerals?" Alison asked.

"This was my first."

"Shocker."

No one spoke for a while. The weather was cooperating with our moods, with pregnant, gray storm clouds that obliterated the sky. "It's just that, you try so hard to get it right, you know?" I said. "To get your life to this point you've imagined in your head and you tell yourself that if I can just get to there, I'll be happy. You all accuse me of living in the past, but the truth is I'm thirty years old and I'm still counting on the future to bail me out. And that's a crock. You can spend years working toward something and get killed before you reach it, so what's the point?"

"Because you probably won't," Lindsey snapped at me. "Chances are you'll live until you're ninety, which is a lot of time to spend in an unhappy life. Peter Miller may be dead, but look at how many people he affected before he died. He lived in the present. You're worried that you might be wasting your time trying to achieve something when you might die tomorrow. You should be worried about getting your life together as quickly as possible so that if you did die young, at least you'd have lived. You're young, you're healthy . . ."

"Health," I said, "is just the slowest possible rate at which one can die."

Lindsey twisted around in her seat to glare at me. "Shut up, Ben," she said. I did, for a minute.

"I agree with you," I relented. "It's just that, you know, I was thinking about this guy. He was only around six or seven years older than me, and look at all he had to show for himself, all the people who cared, who will miss him. If I died tomorrow, I don't think I could fill three rows in the church."

"Well, you are Jewish," Alison said with a smile.

"You know what I mean."

Without turning around, Lindsey reached behind her and groped for my hand. "Well then," she said. "I guess you just can't die yet." I held onto her hand, wondering if the low vibrations I felt in our conjoined palms were originating from within us, or if it was the world that was shaking and we were perfectly still.

We stopped briefly in town, to replenish our food stocks and buy a paper. I was surprised to see that none of the newspaper vending machines had *The New York Times*. Lindsey said that all New Yorkers make the mistake of thinking that New York is America, which is ironic when you consider the map. We settled for a *USA Today*. The piece on Jack was mercifully small, something between an article and a blurb. Jack Shaw was missing, the police were concerned, but no one was speculating any foul play.

Shortly after we returned from the funeral, I was shooting hoops in the driveway when Jeremy came out of his house to walk Taz. Judging from the many cars still parked in the Miller's driveway and on the road in front of the house, there was still a large crowd at the wake. Jeremy was still in his suit and tie, which combined with his solemn expression and carefully combed hair to make him look like a sad little man. I always felt awkwardly unqualified to deal with the bereaved, or to even make eye contact with them, as if anything I said or did would be an intrusion into their privately painful experience. So I smiled at Jeremy, but turned quickly back to catch my own rebound. The sky still looked threatening, jammed with dark clouds, and the air was laden with the heavy promise of a thunderstorm, but the rain had yet to come.

"I saw you at the funeral today," Jeremy said.

"Yep."

"Why'd you come?" he asked. "You didn't know my dad."

"That's true," I said. "But you know, funerals aren't just about the person who has died. They're also about the people left behind."

"You mean my family?"

"Yep."

"But you don't know them either," he pointed out.

"I know you," I said.

"Was that girl with you your girlfriend?" he asked.

"What?"

"The girl who you were with, next to Alison. Is she your girlfriend?"

"That, my friend, is a very good question," I said.

"Well," he said, grabbing the ball from me and dribbling in for a lay-up. "What's the answer?"

"It's not that simple," I said.

"Oh." He put up another lay-up.

"Don't you belong inside?" I asked.

He looked toward the house, and for the first time I could truly see the grief in his eyes. Taz seemed to sense the boy's desolation, and bounded onto the driveway, reluctant to leave his side. "I don't feel like going in there right now," Jeremy said, rolling the ball between his fingers.

"I don't blame you," I said. "From what they said at the funeral, it sounds like your dad was a great guy."

"Yeah."

"I'm sorry I never met him," I said.

"That's a cool shirt," Jeremy said.

I was wearing a collector's edition *Star Wars* T-shirt with an artist's rendition of the characters all superimposed on a larger, translucent portrait of Darth Vader's face. "Do you like *Star Wars*?" I asked him.

"Yeah. We have all three movies on tape. The new versions."

"Me too," I said.

"Did you like *The Phantom Menace*?" he asked me.

I paused before answering. There was no question that I'd been terribly disappointed by the movie, which I thought felt like an overblown cartoon and contained none of the magic of the first three. But if the film had somehow done for Jeremy what *Star Wars* had done for me at that age, I didn't want to ruin it for him. "It's hard for me to get used to all of the new characters," I said weakly. "What did you think?"

"I liked it," he said with a shrug. "But I liked the first three better."

There was hope after all.

"I was around your age when *Star Wars* came out," I told him. "It became my favorite movie of all time."

"My dad, too."

"Hey," I said. "Hang out here a second, okay?"

"Yeah."

I ran into the house and came back out a minute later with the Darth Vader mask.

"Cool," Jeremy said, turning it over in his hands. I was pleased to note that he held the rubberized plastic up to his nose for a good sniff. He pulled it on over his head and made some harsh breathing noises. "Darth Vader," he said, trying to make his voice sound low and menacing. I felt a pang, maybe sympathy for the kid, or maybe because I missed being him. A fat raindrop fell on the crown of the mask and disappeared under the front ridge just above the black, styrene eyes. When he took off the mask, his hair crackled with static electricity, the thinnest strands floating up around his head like a blond halo.

"You can keep the mask," I said.

He looked at me. "Really?"

"You bet."

"Thanks a lot," he said, and he meant it. "This is great."

There was the sound of a door slamming from behind him, and his mother stepped out onto the deck. "Jeremy," she called. "Come on in now, sweetie, okay? It's going to pour."

Taz shook himself into a standing position and looked questioningly over at Jeremy. I looked across the front yard to Ruthie, feeling suddenly sheepish about standing outside with Jeremy, about the basketball, the mask, and my T-shirt. She was in mourning, and I was an overgrown child. I waved awkwardly and she waved back, the small, delicate gesture of someone not quite certain the world around them is made of the same things it was yesterday.

"I gotta go," Jeremy said.

"Go ahead," I told him. "I'll see you around."

"Yeah." He turned to go, and then turned back to me again. "You sure about the mask?" he said.

"Positive," I said. "It's not so smart for a man my age to have too many toys. It makes people uncomfortable."

He smiled at me, a sincere expression that seemed to contain more understanding than it should have. "Thanks, Ben," he said, and headed back up to his mother.

"Hey, Jeremy," I said, softly so that she wouldn't hear.

"Yeah?"

"May the force be with you."

23

There's something about the rain in the country that I find viscerally satisfying. The rain in the Catskills doesn't screw around. It comes down harder and more violently than in the city, with little concrete infrastructure to absorb its wrath. The trees hiss under the deluge, and it's as if you're hearing the collective sighs of all the leaves slaking their thirst, interrupted only by the thunder, which reverberates powerfully across the sky and rattles the windows. You're one with the trees and the grass, part of a living tapestry, unlike in the city where you're insulated and separated. Lindsey and I brought two chairs out onto the porch and sat there quietly, watching the rain and looking for lightning bolts over the lake. It was the first quiet time we'd shared since our ill-fated walk through town two days before.

"I'm sorry about our argument the other day," she said, putting her hand on my arm. "I overreacted."

"God, that seems like a long time ago," I said. "It was my fault. Don't worry about it."

"You've been distant to me ever since."

"I don't mean to be."

We sat there for a few moments and then she reached for my hand and I watched our fingers combine. I felt myself tremble slightly and realized that, despite the last few days' distractions, I'd still been seriously depressed about what she'd said and how it had left us. I opened my mouth to say something else, but then willed myself to stay silent, to hold onto her hand, listen to the rain, and be in the moment. And I was.

An hour or so later the clouds broke and the sky reasserted itself. I brought Lindsey down to the lake to see the geese. The sun was disappearing behind the trees, causing reflective glints on the dripping leaves and bleeding crimson streaks into the low clouds on the horizon. The still, dark water of the lake reflected the sunset perfectly. We sat on the bench, my right knee against her left, watching the geese go about the business of finishing off the day. Some continued to hunt for food, their posteriors pointed comically at the sky as they submerged their heads. Most of them, though, were selecting spots on the shore to turn in for the night. They would swim up to the shore and then, with a thrashing of their wings, leap up onto the land. The whooshing sound the geese's wings made was like a concentrated blast of wind, powerful and elemental.

"It's such a simple existence," Lindsey marveled. "They wake up with the sun, and they go to bed with the sun."

"And in between, all they do is swim, eat, and rest," I said.

"Not exactly a complicated lifestyle."

"You sound envious."

"I am."

"Are you worried?" I asked her. "About the whole thing with Jack, now that it has gone public?"

She thought about it for a minute. "Not really. I guess I just feel like it would be so absurd for us to end up in jail, you know? Who would waste their time putting us in jail?"

"I don't know," I said. "I mean, I can't believe Jack would ever voluntarily press charges . . ."

"Oh, quit worrying about it," she said, leaning into me. "It's just too beautiful here to be thinking about all of that."

"How do you think Alison's doing?" I asked.

"She seems all right. I think being up here is good for her. And, this is going to sound awful but, I think that the funeral wasn't such a bad thing for Alison, you know? It took her mind off Jack for a while."

"Poor kid. He doesn't deserve this."

"Jack?"

"Jeremy." I told her about my earlier talk with him.

"I always loved the way you liked kids so much," she said. "You know, I'm thinking of getting back into teaching."

"Really?" I looked at her. "That's great."

"Well actually, I'm done thinking about it. I've already decided."

"I'm glad," I said. "You love teaching."

"I guess I also want to be a shepherd," she said, smiling so that the lines of her cheeks formed perfect parentheses around her mouth.

We got up and began strolling at a leisurely pace along the side of the lake, taking care not to frighten any of the dozing geese. I kept sneaking glances at her profile, watching the way the cherry gloss of her lips rested so perfectly against her clean white teeth when she opened her mouth to breathe in the cool air.

"I cried the night of your wedding," she said suddenly, not breaking her stride.

"Excuse me?"

"You're going to make me say something like that twice?"

"Why didn't you tell me before?"

"It's bad form to tell a married man you're not over him," she said with a sardonic grin.

"Even when you know he'll never be over you?"

She stopped and turned to face me. "What would you have done, Ben? Really."

Her face had a rosy blush from the cold air, and as I looked at her, framed by the trees and water behind her, I knew that I would always be in love with her. It was a force coursing through my veins with the whooshing sound of geese's wings. "I would have done the same thing I did," I said. "I would have put all my energy into loving someone that wasn't you. I would have tried in vain, every day, to not think about you, and what could have been. What should have been. I would have tried to convince myself that there's no such thing as true love, except for the love you yourself make work, even though I knew better. I would have driven Sarah away by poorly pretending it was okay with me that she wasn't you, like I did, and we would have ended in a quick divorce, like we did."

"You got divorced because of me?"

"Well, you disguised as a whole bunch of other reasons. The bottom line is I never had any business marrying anyone who wasn't you."

She smiled sadly. "That's exactly what I thought when I heard you were getting married."

"Well, after you left . . ."

Lindsey looked down at her shoes as we continued to walk. "I have this problem," she said. "I instinctively mistrust any situation that seems to be working out too easily. I have no idea where I got it from, but I think it had a lot to do with why we broke up. Something in me just rebelled at the idea that it could really be that easy to find the right person. It's like I'm a film critic watching the movie of my life, and if the plot's too simple, the film's not believable." She laughed quietly, almost to herself. "And when you brought it up a few days ago, it was the same thing. I was so filled with regret, so sure we were over forever, and then suddenly, against all odds, here we are six years later with a second chance. It just seemed to have worked out too easily to be true."

"Come on," I said to her, turning to face her. "You have to think about the right kind of movies. Complex plots may be important for Oliver Stone or Quentin Tarantino, but the romantic comedies are never too complicated. If this were a Rob Reiner film with Meg Ryan and Tom Hanks, the critics would be saying that it's been way too complicated already."

"I know," she said, and I saw with surprise that she was close to tears. "I'm sorry. For everything."

"Look, you did what you had to do. I never held it against you."

"No," she pushed at the corner of her eyes with her index fingers. "You just let it wreck your marriage."

"Hey, it was all part of the plan."

"Oh yeah? Where'd it get you?"

"Right here," I said. "To this exact minute. My whole life, my divorce, my insomnia, Jack's drug problem, it's all been leading me right here, to this lake, to this minute with you."

We just stood there looking at each other, and the planet spun around a little bit more. It was as if we'd entered a daydream and forced it into focus. I felt the force of what I'd just said mingle with the power of the mountains around us, giving the air an electrical charge. "This is one of those moments in life," I told her. "When you know you're having one of those moments in life."

"I love you, Ben," she said, laughing as the tears came. "I really do." Although I hadn't been conscious of either one of us moving, we seemed to have suddenly gotten much closer to each other.

I was going to tell her I loved her too, but before I could she was in my arms and was kissing me so hard and deep that I almost fell over. She already knew it anyway. When Lindsey kissed you she really took you in, her tongue pulling, her soft, full lips pressing, consuming. This was not, I think, something you could learn. When we ended that first kiss, my knees were trembling, like I'd just run a race. I was quivering.

I caught my breath and said, "Does this mean you're my girlfriend?"

We came up the stairs to find Chuck sprawled out on the floor outside Jack's door in boxer shorts and a *Blue Angel* T-shirt, reading the paper out loud. The floor surrounding him was covered with discarded sections of the paper, a box of Entenmann's Pop 'Ems, and a bottle of Bushmills. "Hey guys," he said, bestowing an avuncular smile of inebriated benevolence on us as we ascended. "Welcome to the program."

"What are you doing?" I asked.

"I'm keeping Jack company," Chuck said, indicating the locked door with an exaggerated gesture. "We've been talking all day." There were little balls of gray carpet caught in the stubble on his cheek.

"Has he answered you?" Lindsey asked.

"Not as such," Chuck admitted, taking a generous swig of the Bushmills. "He's my imaginary friend. But I was alone here all day while you were out gallivanting around—"

"We were at a funeral, remember?"

"Whatever." I could see he'd drunk about a quarter of the whiskey in the bottle. "The point is, I wanted someone to talk to, and I figured Jack could use the company. I think we've grown much closer."

"Where's Alison?"

"Napping."

I started to say something about it being a little early in the day to be drinking, but Lindsey was dragging me insistently toward my bedroom. "We'll leave you two alone," she said, kicking open the bedroom door.

"Okay," Chuck said, sounding somewhat befuddled. He rustled the newspaper theatrically. "Hey, Jack, where was I? Umm . . . Fuck it, I'll read you the sports pages."

Making love to Lindsey again was the sweetest of paradoxes, heart-breakingly familiar and excitingly new at the same time. The taste of her skin, the slope of her breasts, the smell of her scalp, the soft crush of her lips, all of these sensations were familiar to me, and yet I felt them all as if for the first time. It was like returning to the home you grew up in and finding it completely unchanged, and yet inexplicably new, because your own memory, incapable of preserving each minute detail, had generalized it in your mind. I kept breaking off kisses to look at her, because I could finally look at her without hiding anything. It was a gentle reunion, slow and easy, uncomplicated by sexual acrobatics or overly strenuous coupling.

Afterwards, I sat up with my back against the wall, pulling her into my lap, her back to my chest, so that we could both look out the window as twilight turned into night and the lights came on around the lake. I leaned my cheek against her temple, inhaling her scent as if I could fill myself with it.

"Well," Lindsey said, rubbing the outside of my thigh. "That was fairly inevitable."

"I know," I said. "I guess I always knew we'd be here again."

"Me too," she said. "Can we keep it this time?"

"You're not worried that I'm on the rebound?"

"You got married on the rebound," she said, pressing her bottom into me. "I was your first best shot."

"What happened to enjoying ourselves without complicating things?" I asked.

She made a face. "Aren't you enjoying yourself?" she asked suggestively, pressing down a bit harder on me.

"Umm, yes."

"Sounds pretty simple to me."

"I love you," I said, reaching under her arms to stroke her breasts. She moaned and stretched herself out in a feline manner, luxuriating in the touch.

"I know," she whispered. Then, in one athletic motion, she flipped herself over so that we were facing each other, and kissed me deeply. I rolled her onto her back and as I kissed her neck, I realized that I'd found one good thing about being thirty: It's an age where maybe, just maybe you can start keeping things.

Later, we were lying in bed speaking softly when Chuck cracked open the door and stuck his head in. "Hi guys," he said. "I was wondering when you'd get down to business."

"Hi, Chuck," Lindsey laughed, pulling up the blanket to cover herself.

He took that as an invitation and plopped down on the bed, lying across our feet. "Maybe now you guys can stop eyeballing each other at meals, you know? You were putting out all this sexual tension, it was like Mulder and Scully." He sat up and sniffed the air. "Ah," he said. "The smell of fresh sex. I have just got to get some of that." He still had a nice buzz going. I kicked him from under the covers so that he fell off of the bed. He lay on his back looking up at the ceiling, his knees bent as if he might do some sit-ups. "Jack says he's not feeling too well. He asked me to slip some aspirin under the door."

"Did you?" I asked.

"I don't like the idea of giving him any drugs at all," Chuck said. "But he's probably running a low-grade fever, which is standard for cocaine withdrawal. He's also probably suffering from exhaustion right now, also par for the course, but it probably isn't helping the fever. I should probably go in there and check him out. He said he'd fix the door so that I can come in."

Just then Alison stuck her head in the room. "Hi guys," she said drowsily, and then actually took the scene in. "Oh!"

"Hey," Chuck greeted her from the floor.

"Finally," she said with a smile, jumping onto the bed and giving me a hug. She reached over and grabbed Lindsey's arm "I knew you guys would get it together."

"Was it that obvious?" I asked.

"Um, yeah," Alison said with a grin. She leaned forward to look down at Chuck. "What are you, the referee?"

"We're going in to visit Jack," Chuck said, sitting up. "Wanna come?"

"You bet."

"Okay," I said. "Can you guys just give us a minute to get dressed?"

"Sure," Chuck said, making no move to leave. "Take your time."

"Come on, Chuck," Alison said with a laugh, pulling him out of the room.

"For Christ's sake!" he objected as he went. "I'm a doctor. You think I haven't seen a naked woman before?"

Lindsey rolled over and kissed me. "We'll pick this up later," she said.

"When?"

"I don't know. What are you doing for the next forty or fifty years?"

"Rocky II," I said, identifying the quote as I pulled on my pants. "When he proposes to Adrian in the zoo."

"One of my favorite movie scenes," she said, buttoning her shirt.

"So was that a proposal?"

"Better," she said, quickly arranging her hair with her fingers. "That was a promise."

24

Jack had the shakes. His eyes were sunken and bleary, his lips dry and chapped, his complexion pallid. He flashed us an anemic smile when we entered, and then went back to doing what he'd been doing, which was lying under the blankets in a sheen of sweat, shivering. The room still smelled of smoke, but there were competing odors of perspiration and vomit.

"Oh my god!" Alison exclaimed, nearly tripping over the shattered television set as she ran over to sit on the edge of the sofa bed. The place was still a huge mess, what with Jack's raging fit the night before last and then last night's fire. She placed her hand on his forehead, then her lips, while brushing the sweat-soaked hair out of his face. "He's got a fever."

Chuck came out of the bathroom with a soaked towel, which he placed on Jack's forehead. "I'm dying, man," Jack said, closing his eyes as rivulets of water ran over the bridge of his nose and his eyebrows. "Give me some aspirin."

"You're not dying," Chuck said. "But you're malnourished and you've got a low fever." He turned to Lindsey and me. "Go downstairs and make him some toast and eggs or something light like that." He turned back to Jack. "You haven't been eating much, have you?"

"Just give me some fucking aspirin, man," Jack said. "Please."

"Can't we give him something?" Alison said.

"I'll give you some Excedrin," Chuck said. "After I see you eat everything on your plate."

We all sat around with Jack while he ate dinner. At first he was tentative, even unwilling, but the aroma of Lindsey's hastily prepared cheese omelet overcame him, and soon he was stuffing himself greedily. Alison would occasionally try to slow him down, but her efforts were in vain. Within five minutes Jack had polished off the omelet, two English muffins with margarine, and a tall glass of orange juice. He sat back with a contented belch, and Chuck brought him out a glass of water and three Excedrins which he popped into his mouth and swallowed in one gulp.

"Thanks for dinner," he grumbled.

"It's the least I can do after practically electrocuting you," Lindsey said. Jack flashed her a confused look, and I realized with a start that he had little if any recollection of the previous night's insanity.

"Why don't you take a shower, Jack," Chuck said. "Get yourself cleaned up a little."

"Yeah," I said. "You do smell like shit."

"We'll change your linens and clean up the place a little while you're in there," Alison said.

"Okay," Jack said. It was odd to see him so compliant. The animosity had been drained out of him, replaced with a trancelike indifference to all of us. I realized that I preferred the animosity.

He pulled off the blankets, revealing to us that he was stark naked under them. He sat up, oblivious to Alison's sharp intake of breath as she quickly looked down into her lap. Even in this dilapidated state, Jack's movie star body was the epitome of lean muscularity as he got up and headed toward the attached bathroom. As he walked, I noticed two red marks like a vampire bite, where Lindsey's stun gun had made contact with his lower back. "Where do you think you're going?" he asked Chuck, who was following him into the bathroom.

"I'm just going to sit in there while you shower," Chuck said. "You're still pretty weak. I don't want you to fall and hurt yourself."

"You going to hold my dick for me while I pee?"

"Whatever floats your boat, Hollywood."

"Well," I said as the two of them went into the bathroom. "At least we know now that Jack doesn't color his hair."

Alison, who had already begun stripping the bed, let out a snort. "That's not funny," she said, smiling in spite of herself. "Now go get me some new sheets from the linen closet before I throw something at you."

We cleaned up Jack's room, sweeping away the ashes and the broken glass, and dragging the larger debris downstairs and into the garage. Alison changed the sheets while Lindsey cleared away all of the dirty Tupperware scattered around the room. Many of the containers still had the food we'd put in them over the last three days, and there were cold-cuts packages lying unopened where we'd slid them under the door. We'd assumed Jack would eat once we got the food to him. We'd been wrong.

When he came out of the shower, Jack looked a bit more like his old self. He still had about five day's growth of a beard, since he'd been unshaven when we abducted him, but his hair was ten shades lighter and surrounded his head in a healthy golden mane.

Chuck leant him a clean pair of scrubs that said "Property of Mt. Sinai Hospital," and Jack climbed back into bed.

"Do you still hate us?" I asked him.

"I don't know," he said, rolling onto his side. "Am I still a prisoner?"

We looked at each other and then at Chuck. "Why don't we discuss that tomorrow," Chuck said.

"Whatever," Jack said.

"I'll stay in here with you tonight, Jack," Alison said.

"No thanks," Jack said. "I'd prefer to be alone."

"Are you sure?"

Jack turned away from us all. "Close the lights as you leave, please," he whispered.

25

I was never able to sleep after making love. Sex always left me wired and inexplicably restless in bed beside the sleeping form of my partner. It was amazing how so soon after the most intimate of unions I could feel myself alone again.

After we got Jack into bed, Lindsey and I made love again, this time with a little more abandon than we had that afternoon. Soon afterwards she was fast asleep while I, true to form, was ready to run a marathon. As thrilled as I was to be sharing a bed with her again, I was much too fidgety to stay in it.

I went downstairs and watched the end of the late news. Sports and weather. Happily, I missed the meat of the newscast, so I had no body count for the night. After the news I flipped between a *Cheers* rerun and *Baywatch*. I realized that I still thought of *Cheers* as new, even though it had run for ten years and was now only in syndication. I thought about Lindsey, and prayed that this time was for keeps. At some point I dozed off.

I was awakened by the sound of the refrigerator door closing.

I rolled over on the couch, and saw a lean form come out of the kitchen.

"Who's that?" I whispered.

"It's just me." As the figure approached, I realized that it was Jack.

"What are you doing down here?" I asked him, only half conscious. In the dim light, he appeared to be shirtless.

"It's okay," he whispered. "Go back to sleep. I just needed a drink."

"But how . . . ?" I didn't finish the question, because I closed my eyes and sleep claimed me again. After what felt like a few seconds I opened my eyes again, as if suddenly remembering something, but Jack wasn't there anymore and I wondered if he'd ever been. I fell back asleep and dreamed that Jack was on *Baywatch*, walking up the beach in his red lifeguard trunks carrying the red life preserver over his shoulder. I sat in a lounge chair near the ocean, waiting until he got closer to me so that I could congratulate him for being on the show. In the reverse logic of dreams, being on *Baywatch* was somehow a greater achievement than his movie career. As he walked by me I called out to him, but the pounding of the surf drowned out my call, and he didn't hear me. I screamed his name again, but his eyes remained fixed on some distant point ahead of him and I could only watch helplessly as he strolled down the beach, until he was out of sight. For some reason, it didn't occur to me to get up out of the chair and follow him.

The next morning Chuck woke me up by urgently shoving my shoulder. "He's gone, man."

"What?" I rolled over on the couch, my face peeling off the leather like a sticker off wax paper.

"Jack's gone. He's not anywhere in the house."

Even in my groggy state, I was not completely surprised. "What time is it?"

"Ten-thirty."

"How'd he do it?" I asked, sitting up and stretching my arms behind me. Looking out the window I saw that it was raining hard, and only then did I hear the steady pounding of water on the roof.

"He took the hinges off the door."

"That can't be easy," I said with admiration. "He must be feeling better."

"Well, I'm sure he's feeling great," Chuck said sarcastically. "Because he's probably high as a kite right now."

"Maybe he just went for a walk. To clear his head or something."

Chuck raised his eyebrows. "Yeah."

"Does Alison know?" I asked.

"She's out looking."

"Where?"

"I don't know," Chuck said with a sigh. "Around. She's driving around town."

"Where's Lindsey?"

"Still sleeping, I guess. I thought you were in there, too, so I didn't go in."

"Never stopped you before," I said, standing up to stretch.

"So," Chuck mused. "You're in bed with the woman you've been in love with for years, and you decide tonight might be a good night to sleep on the couch? What's wrong with you?"

"I'm funny that way," I said, heading up the stairs to wake Lindsey. Before I was halfway up, though, the doorbell rang. I turned around and sat down on the stairs while Chuck crossed the foyer to open the door. It was Jeremy, in a bright yellow slicker that covered him from head to ankle. I remembered what it felt like to hear the rain from underneath a plastic hood, and felt a stabbing jolt of yearning for childhood, for walking through the woods in camp, insulated in my rain slicker, looking for the sala-manders and slugs that came out during summer rainstorms.

"Hi, Jeremy," I said. "What's up?"

"I can't find the Darth Vader mask," he said, pulling back his hood to see me better. "I left it on the porch last night and it's gone now. Did you take it back?"

"No, of course not," I said. "Maybe your mom brought it in."

"Nah. She didn't," he said, looking crestfallen. "I was gonna wear it for Halloween."

"Well listen," I said. "I'll come over a little later and help you look for it, okay?"

"Okay," he said.

"How's your mom doing?" I asked.

"She's okay," he said, turning to leave. By the way he said it, I could tell he'd been asked a little too much lately. "She said I have to go back to school soon."

"I'm sorry to hear that," I said.

Alison returned an hour later, worried and distracted. By then I'd awakened Lindsey, who smiled at me and said, "Still walking off good sex, I see. How late did you stay up?"

"Late enough," I said, plopping down beside her on the bed. She wrapped her legs around me and I pressed my face into the pocket of her collarbone. "Jack's gone."

"What?"

"He pulled the hinges out of the door and took off last night."

"Shit," she said.

"Yeah." I found myself selfishly considering the implications that Jack's disappearance would have on Lindsey and me. If Jack was gone, there was no longer any reason to stay at the Schollings's lake house. We'd all go back to Manhattan, to our homes and lives, and the details and trivialities of daily existence would begin their subtle assault. I didn't want us to be exposed to that yet. Lindsey and I had just been formed and we hadn't had time to harden yet. We were still vulnerable. I wanted to keep us in the private protection of the mountains and the lake until we were better defined.

I was scared shitless of reality. That it might be something other than this.

26

With no idea of where to even begin looking for Jack, Chuck and I took the Taurus and drove into town, which felt more like doing something than sitting around waiting for Jack to maybe show up, which we left Lindsey and Alison to do. "I think I saw him," I said to Chuck, who was peering intently over the steering wheel into the rain.

"What? Where?" he braked instantly.

"No, not now. I think I saw him last night."

He flashed me a hard look. "You saw him leave? Why didn't you stop him?"

"I was sleeping on the couch. I thought I was dreaming."

Chuck frowned at me and then fiddled with the windshield wipers. "Brilliant," he said.

"It may have been a dream," I said weakly. "I'm not sure."

"Whatever. I guess it's all academic now," he said, but I could tell that he was pissed.

Main Street was pretty much deserted because of the heavy rain, but we drove up and down the length of it anyway, peering intently at every person we saw darting between buildings or into parked cars. Every time we passed a restaurant or coffee shop, Chuck would stop and I'd run in and look around. Neither of us harbored any real hope that we would suddenly come upon Jack, sitting comfortably in a booth with a sandwich and a coffee, but like I said, we needed to do something. After we finished with Main Street, we started on Maple, checking every storefront and alley, but Jack stubbornly refused to appear.

"This is a waste of time," Chuck complained as I climbed back into the car for the fortieth time. "He left hours ago. He could be anywhere by now."

"You have a better idea?" I asked him, wiping my now-soaked hair out of my face.

"Anything would be better than this," he muttered.

"At least you're dry," I said, wringing out my shirt.

"Yeah, whatever."

We drove in silence for a few moments. "Okay," I said, as Chuck executed a jerking three-point turn and headed down Maple again. "You're Jack. You just escaped from the house. Where do you go?"

"If I knew that, I guess I wouldn't be driving around in circles now, would I?" Chuck snapped at me.

"Excuse me, but what the fuck is your problem?"

Chuck pulled over in front of a corner luncheonette and threw the car into park. "I think I'm done with this," he said.

"What do you mean?"

"Which word didn't you understand? I mean I'm finished. I've had it with him, with all of this. I'm out of here." He looked at me. "It's gotten way out of control."

"I don't understand. You're just giving up?" I asked.

"Don't give me that shit, Ben," he said angrily. "This is way more than any of us signed on for." He looked away for a minute. "I mean, for how long and at what cost do we keep trying to help a junkie who doesn't want to be helped?"

"He's our friend, Chuck. Or maybe that doesn't mean anything to you."

"He's a junkie!" he shouted. "Cut that self-righteous crap! He can have all the movie premiers and Hollywood blow jobs he wants, he's still a goddamn junkie and as much as I want to help him, I'm not going to let him destroy my life along with his!"

"Listen," I said, turning in my seat to face him. "Let's not get carried away here."

"No, you listen, Ben!" Chuck said, hitting the steering wheel in frustration. "I'm not the one getting carried away. We came up here for him, and what's he done for us? He's broken my nose, demolished their house and come closer to burning us to death than you might want to believe. I mean Jesus, what's it going to take? Does one of us have to fucking die for you all to get that this isn't working?" He stared at me, the veins in his neck throbbing, his face flushed with intensity.

"Nothing like that's going to happen," I said.

His eyes bulged and he hit the steering wheel again. "I don't believe you, man." He pushed open his door and stepped out into the rain, walking first one way, and then the other, kicking up a spray from the puddles in front of the car. I'd never seen Chuck lose it before. I stepped out of the car and approached him, sitting down on the hood of the Taurus which made my ass feel oddly warm in the cold rain.

"What's this really about, Chuck?" I asked him, shouting to be heard above the rain, which fell in a frenzied patter on the street around us. "Why is this different for you than for me?"

Chuck turned to me, now completely soaked, his hair matted to his pink scalp, his face dripping. "Because I have something to lose!" he shouted at me. "I took a big risk, doing what I did back in the hospital."

"We're all taking a risk," I said.

"Bullshit, Ben!" He spat out, his voice trembling with rage. "I could lose my residency, or worse! I could lose my license! Then what am I? What the fuck do you have to lose?" He pointed an accusing finger at me. "You hate your job, you hated your marriage. You had nothing, man. You come up here, it's fucking summer camp for you! Your friends, your old girlfriend. You see Jack leaving, what do you care? Let him go. I mean, what the fuck do you have to lose?"

"Shut the fuck up," I said.

He pushed the finger right up to my face. "Answer me, man. What do you have to lose?"

"Shut up!" I yelled, slapping away his hand. He swung it back in a fist and hit me across the side of the face, catching me completely off guard. I flailed out blindly as I fell, catching the collar of his jacket, which I pulled with me as I went down. He landed on top of me and began pummeling my sides furiously. Squirming on my back underneath him I punched up, hitting my elbows on the pavement each time I pulled back. He let out a bloodcurdling scream when my fingers swiped against his swollen nose and we rolled over into the glare of the Taurus's low beams, wrestling and swinging wildly.

The gunshot was absolutely deafening, and the force of it separated us with a jolt. Standing above us under the awning of the luncheonette was a tall, hulking man in denim overalls, with a woolly, slightly graying beard and a pump-action shotgun which was now aimed directly at us. He had tattoos up and down his meaty arms and a bandanna wrapped tightly over his skull. He looked like a Hell's Angels version of Paul Bunyan. "Just what in the hell do you think you're doing, fighting in front of my place?" he asked. Sitting on our butts on the wet pavement, we just sat there staring at the man and his shotgun. My ears were still ringing from the gunshot. "You going to answer me?"

I looked at Chuck, and then raised my hands over my head and began to get up, which isn't as easy as it sounds. I made it onto one knee before falling back, my ass hitting the pavement with a wet plop. "I didn't tell you to get up," the man said. He made no move to lower the shotgun, which I found very disconcerting.

"Sir," I said. "I'm sorry for the disturbance. We just had a minor altercation." He turned to look at me, which also meant pointing the gun directly at me. Although it seemed highly unlikely that he was going to shoot me, I'd never faced the business end of a shotgun before, and I felt a cold stirring deep in my bowels. I looked around helplessly, but the street was completely devoid of pedestrians. Only a complete jackass would be out in this rain.

"You had a minor altercation," he repeated, mimicking me. "I don't know where in the hell you're from, but it ain't here."

"No, we're not."

"Where then?"

"Can you put that gun down?" I asked him.

"I don't have a gun," he said condescendingly. "What I have is a 12-gauge, twenty-four-inch Winchester and one hell of an easy target."

"Well, do you think you could point it somewhere else?"

"You didn't answer me," he said, pumping the shotgun, which made a dangerous clicking sound.

"New York," I said. "Manhattan."

"Big mistake," Chuck muttered under his breath.

"You say something?" the man said, pointing the shotgun at Chuck.

"No sir."

Paul Bunyan looked at us thoughtfully as we began to shiver in the rain. "You city boys thinks its okay to come up here to the sticks and carry on like that in a place of business?"

"No sir," Chuck said. "We're very sorry. Truly. And if you'd just let us get up, we'll get out of here and you'll never see us again." His teeth were starting to chatter from the frigid rain.

The man considered us thoughtfully for a moment. "I'm going to go back into my restaurant," he said. "I think the two of you need to sit here for a while and think about what you've done. I can see you from my window. If either one of you gets up off that street before I tell you, I'll come out here and put some buckshot in your pants. You got it?"

We looked at him incredulously. "You're punishing us?" Chuck said.

"Damn straight," said Paul Bunyan, slinging the Winchester comfortably over his shoulder. "Teach you to respect someone else's place of business." With that he walked back into his restaurant frowning at us from his stool behind the counter.

"I don't believe this," I said. "We're being disciplined by a redneck. This is a joke."

"You want to get up first?" Chuck asked.

"After you."

Neither one of us moved. As humiliating as it was for the two of us to be so intimidated by one guy, its was downright emasculating to be scared into place by him when he wasn't even standing there anymore.

"You look pretty uncomfortable. That's why I asked," Chuck said.

"Yeah well, you hit like a girl."

"And you fight like an old man," he said with a grin. "If I'd known what a shitty fighter you were, I would have kicked your ass years ago."

Although it was still coming down hard, our ears had adjusted to the sound of the rain, relegating it to a background din the way your eyes adjust to the dark, and we could now speak without shouting. "I'm sorry, Chuck," I said softly.

"It's all right," he said, rubbing his nose. "Like I said, you fight like a geezer."

"No, really. I'm sorry about not considering what you have at stake here. You're right, I had nothing to lose."

"Hey," he said. "I didn't mean all that. Really."

"No, you were right," I said, leaning back on my elbows, my feet stretched out in front of me, and tilting my head back to swallow some rain. "I guess I hit rock bottom right before we came up here."

"Ah, you're okay," Chuck said, assuming the same position. "You were just in a funk. Happens to us all."

"Well, anyway, I'm sorry," I said.

"Forget it. The truth is, this whole thing was my idea in the first place. I knew what I was getting into. Mostly."

"That's right," I said. "It was your idea, you bastard. I forgot about that. This whole thing is your fault. I can't believe I apologized to you."

We lay there on the street for a few minutes and I had to laugh, in spite of everything, at the absurdity of the whole situation. Chuck turned to me with a smile. "I'm sorry I hit you," he said. "I guess after getting the shit kicked out of me twice, I needed to just hit someone."

"If you count now, it seems to me that you got the shit kicked out of you three times."

"Now?" he asked. "I beg to differ. I was so winning that fight."

"You were so not, tough guy."

"I was pounding your sorry ass."

"Uh, no. You were getting whupped, and I know that for a fact because I was there."

"Assface."

"Dickhead."

The door to the luncheonette opened and we both ducked instinctively as Paul Bunyan stepped out under the awning again, sans the Winchester. "Soup's on," he called.

"What?"

"Minestrone," he said. "You want some?"

"Are you kidding?" Chuck said.

"I never kid about lunch," said the man, before stepping back inside.

We climbed to our feet, and I could feel a river running between my toes. "What do you think?" I asked Chuck.

"Soup sounds good," he said with a shiver. "You buying?"

I shrugged. "Let's go."

27

We walked into the Schollings's house around noon, dripping rainwater with every step. "What the hell happened to you guys?" Lindsey asked, staring at us.

"We got you some soup," Chuck said, handing her a paper bag.

"Thanks," she said absently, still staring at us, not speaking the questions in her eyes.

"I take it there's no news?" I said, pulling my sweatshirt over my head and dropping it to the kitchen floor like a twenty-pound weight.

"No," Alison said. Her face looked positively drained, her eyes frantic.

"You guys better get into a warm shower fast," Lindsey said, putting her hand on my chest. "You're soaked through."

Chuck showered in the hall bathroom and I went into the master bathroom where I discovered that Alison's parents took their showering very seriously. The shower was its own little room within the bathroom, behind a frosted glass door, with auxiliary heads along opposite walls so that you could be hit from five spots at once. I stood in the center with my chin to my chest luxuriating in the steaming assault of the hot spray. If I'd known about that shower when we first got there, I'd have logged some substantial hours in it.

I was still standing there fifteen minutes later, letting the water pound my chest and scalp, humming an old Thompson Twins song, when I heard the bathroom door open and shut. I looked up, hopeful that Lindsey had come in to join me, but then the shower door swung in and Chuck stuck his head in and said, "Hey dude, what's taking so long?"

"Do you mind?" I said, slamming the door against his arm.

"Don't be so sensitive," he said with a chuckle. "I'm sure it's very impressive when you're aroused."

"Fuck you."

"With that thing? I probably wouldn't even notice." He then sat down on the toilet lid, having filled his dick joke quota for the time being. "Listen," he said. "I know I got a little out of hand out there, but still, I meant what I said."

"Which part?"

"The part about this having gone too far. The part about it being time to cut our losses and go home."

"Oh," I said. "That part."

"Yeah. Well, anyway, I think we should all talk it out, you know? Just kind of air out all of the opinions and see where the chips fall."

"I agree. But maybe this time without the wrestling."

"Deal. I think we should do it right now."

"Well, I'm a little naked right now," I said.

"Little being the operative word," he said with a snort, standing up and lifting the toilet seat. "I meant when you get out. You are planning on getting out of there sometime soon, aren't you?

You've been in there for a half hour." I heard the jiggle of his belt buckle.

"I know you're not going to piss in here while I'm taking a shower," I yelled at him.

"Just be glad I don't have to take a dump, dude."

I stuck my head back under the main shower head and tried not to hear him as he urinated. Keeping my eyes shut as the water flowed down across my face, I leaned against the cool tiled wall, tracing the grout with my fingernail.

"So things seem to be pretty good with you and Lindsey, huh?" Chuck said.

"Uh huh."

"That's good. I'm happy for you, man. She's really much better for you than Sarah was."

"Thanks."

"Way hotter, too." He did a little shake dance and pulled his pants up.

"Thanks again," I said, reluctantly turning off the shower as he flushed.

"I never really developed a rapport with Sarah. I'm not sure why," Chuck said, vigorously scrubbing his hands in the sink. He washed his hands the way he must have been trained to scrub in for surgery, which was something I'd never noticed before.

"Sarah hated you," I said, stepping out of the shower.

"That may have been a contributing factor," Chuck admitted, handing me my towel. "Here you go, junior," he said with an exaggerated look at my crotch, just as Lindsey walked into the bathroom, her eyes widening in puzzlement.

"Am I interrupting something?" she asked with an ironic smile. I could be naked in front of Chuck and I could be naked in front of Lindsey, but somehow being naked in front of both of them was more than I could handle. I quickly wrapped the towel around my waist, wondering at how every so often life could feel exactly like an episode of *Three's Company.*

"Guy talk," Chuck said, heading for the door. He turned and gave me a meaningful look at the door. "I'll see you downstairs in a few minutes?"

"Sure," I said, pushing my wet hair out of my face.

"So," Lindsey said after he'd gone. "What happened out there with you two? You guys looked really beat up when you got back."

"We had a pretty intense argument about what to do now that Jack's gone AWOL."

"You want to give me the highlights?"

"Nah," I said, grabbing another towel for my shoulders. "I have a feeling we're going to have the whole argument again anyway."

When I came downstairs ten minutes later, Alison and Lindsey were eating the soup we'd brought them in the kitchen and Chuck was watching a rerun of *Magnum P.I.* in the living room. "You know what always bugged me?" he said. "Tom Selleck was considered the hottest guy in the early eighties. *Magnum* was a hugely popular show. And yet, they could never get a single decent-looking female to guest star. Every time he gets involved with someone, she's a dog."

"Standards were different then," I said, joining him on the couch.

"Bullshit. *Charlie's Angels* came before *Magnum* and they were all hot. But this show is demoralizing. If a good-looking guy who drives a Ferrari isn't getting any, what hope is there for anyone else?"

Chuck always employed the Socratic method of viewing television shows. He didn't seem able to enjoy himself without his pointless commentary. How come whenever there was a band in a sitcom episode, they could never make it look like they were really playing? Were we really supposed to believe the cops on *21 Jump Street* could pass as high school students? Didn't you ever want to see Alex and Mallory get it on on *Family Ties*? How the hell did Mulder and Scully justify their travel expenses? At first it was annoying, but after a while I learned to tune him out.

The women finished eating and joined us in the living room. "I think we should split up and go look some more," Alison said. Chuck snapped off the television and looked at me expectantly, as if it were somehow my responsibility to start this discussion, but I didn't want any part of it. Alison looked completely strung out, and not in the mood for conversation. Better to spend a few more hours of futile searching before we grappled with the ramifications of Jack's disappearance. It would give us all time to think about the situation, and our own places in it. I tried to signal that to Chuck with a look, but it was a bit too much for my eyes to convey alone, so I made a small gesture with my hand and shook my head slightly and Alison picked up on it immediately. "What?" she asked, looking at me.

"Nothing," I said with a frown. "I just . . . nothing."

"What?" she repeated impatiently.

"Nothing," I said again, getting up from the couch in order to more effectively ignore the exasperated look I got from Chuck. "Let's look now. We'll talk later." I took Alison's keys from her. "You and Lindsey stay here, in case he calls. Chuck and I will split up and look some more."

Chuck followed me out onto the porch shaking his head in disgust. It was still pouring, and the occasional clap of thunder could be heard in the distance. "What the hell was that?" he asked. "You said we'd talk about it."

"You were free to chime in at any time," I said.

"Come on, Ben. You know if it came from me she'd go apeshit."

"Let's just give it a few more hours," I said, looking at my watch. "We'll meet back here at three and by then maybe Alison will have had some time to think about things."

"You're just putting off the inevitable," he said with a frown, fishing his car keys out of his jeans.

"That's what I do," I said, pressing the button on Alison's key chain. The Beamer beeped twice and flashed its headlights. "I may even be the best in my field."

"I'll see you at three," Chuck said darkly as we stepped into the rain.

"Hey, think positive," I said. "We might actually find him. Or he might come back on his own."

"Yeah," Chuck muttered, pulling up the hood of his anorak and stepping off the porch. "That'll happen."

Chuck took the Taurus and drove north up 57. I drove the Beamer south, away from Carmelina. I knew Alison had driven this route earlier, but there was just nowhere else to look. Who knew? Maybe I'd find Jack strolling along the blacktop in the rain, waiting for a ride. The rain pelted a smattering rhythm on the sunroof in a minor key that harmonized perfectly with the Counting Crows disc playing on the car stereo. Opaque blotches of water formed on the windshield, refracting the beams of oncoming cars. Not a great day to be outside. Jack had left without anything. Alison's examination of his room showed that he'd taken only his wallet, not bothering with his shoes, or even his shirt for that matter, and according to Alison, no clothing was missing from the house. As far as we could tell, Jack was out in the rain with nothing but the pants of the hospital scrubs he'd been sleeping in. I was still fairly certain that he couldn't have gotten very far. His only means of transportation would have been hitchhiking, and few drivers would be inclined to pick up a half-naked, fully soaked stranger.

A flash of lightning illuminated the dense gray and black clouds that covered the sky, and off to my left I saw the actual bolt over a tree-topped mountain peak. The storm was shifting into high gear. As I rounded the next bend, I saw a back-up of four cars, unable to continue because of a felled tree that was blocking the road. "Where are you, Jack?" I said out loud, turning the car around and heading back toward the house.

The suddenness with which the deer appeared in front of me was shocking. It didn't wander onto the road from the forest as much as it simply materialized in the center. I fruitlessly stomped on the car's waterlogged brakes and then there was a sickening, crunching impact—felt more than heard—which instantly evoked the soft-hard nature of the animal as it became one with the car. My hands grasped the wheel as I shouted an electrified denial, the brake pedal vibrating furiously under my toes, the high-pitched scream of hydroplaning wheels giving voice to the mute animal as we careened off the blacktop and into the mud-filled gully that separated the road from the forest. The force of our momentum lifted the deer onto the hood of the Beamer, its wet back pressed against the windshield so that all I could see were the perfect zigzag patterns of its sand-colored coat until the airbag exploded into my face as we hit the far side of the gully.

The first thing I became aware of as my senses gradually returned from the gray mist of semiconsciousness was that the Counting Crows were still singing, oblivious to the collision. But the music had separated. Somewhere to my left was the acoustic guitar, strumming methodically, while the piano notes floated above my head. The drums were beating off to the right, and Adam Duritz's disembodied, whining voice was coming from somewhere behind me. The bass seemed to be coming from inside my belly. Heard with such utter clarity, it wasn't music anymore, but disconnected sounds that made no sense. My face was still numb from the impact of the airbag, but I could feel a hot tingle beginning in my cheeks, growing incrementally with every passing second. My hands still clutched the steering wheel in a death grip, the muscles of my arms locked into place. The rest of me hadn't checked in yet. I unclenched my right hand from the wheel with difficulty, that simple motion sending the nerves in my arm and shoulder into an agonized frenzy, and punched off the stereo. Suddenly, silence was everywhere.

Gradually, as if someone was turning a volume knob, the sound of the rain hitting the roof of the car got louder and louder, ushering me back to reality. I fumbled for the door, feeling the spray of rain on my face as it swung open. I experienced one truly terrifying moment when I found myself unable to rise up from the seat, but then realized that I was straining against my seat belt, and I managed to undo the clasp and climb out of the car. I walked around to the front of the car on wobbly legs, taking in the crushed grille, the twisted green metal that had once been the front of the hood. Twenty feet away was the deer, lying in a mangled heap that rendered only its legs recognizable. "Where are you, Jack?" I muttered nonsensically as I approached the deer, my shoes sinking heavily into the mud. Its head was twisted completely around on its neck, the ears still standing up, its freckled snout pointing skyward. There was surprisingly little blood, but the deer's crushed body, like the music in the car, no longer made any sense. As I stood over the dead animal a few drops of blood appeared on its long neck, only to be washed away by the driving rain. A few more drops reappeared and vanished before I realized that the deer wasn't bleeding, I was. I held my hand against my nostrils and it came away bloody. Suddenly, the deer's body began to vibrate as I watched with horror, scared that it wasn't dead yet, but as with the blood, my perspective was off. The deer wasn't vibrating, I was. The last remnants of strength left my legs and I sat down hard into a puddle. I was aware of a great, elemental sadness that seemed to have been growing in me for years like air constantly being breathed in and never breathed out. The rain poured over me, cold needles invading me at every point on my body, and I felt myself dissolving.

I don't remember who arrived first, the ambulance or Lindsey and Chuck, who'd grown alarmed when they couldn't reach me on the Beamer's cell phone, but later Chuck told me that when they found me I was crying like a baby.

28

I awoke in an empty hospital room, blissfully numb from morphine and thinking about Sarah. I looked down at my body, covered from the waist down by a thin white blanket, as if it were an inanimate object, just another part of the bed. It had nothing to do with me. Sarah didn't know that I was hurt. That seemed wrong. I was floating above the bed, couldn't feel the sheets under me, the soft pressure of the mattress against my back. Where are you, Jack? I thought. There was a fresh bouquet of flowers on the end table. Birds of paradise, carnations, tulips, and baby's breath. A splash of color in the otherwise sterile room. I floated above the flowers and could see the petals stretching outward, blooming in fast motion. Sarah didn't know I was hurt. She was my wife. Not anymore. Still, it seemed wrong.

I leaned over and lifted the telephone from the end table. After a few misses, I managed to dial Sarah's number. "Hi," I said when she picked up the phone. "It's Ben."

"Ben?"

"Yeah."

There was a pause. "What's wrong?"

"I was in a car accident," I said.

"Oh my god! What happened? Are you okay?"

"I guess. I just thought you should know."

"Where are you?" Sarah asked urgently. "Do you need me to come?"

"I don't know," I said. "Some hospital."

"Which hospital, Ben? Where are you?"

"I don't know. In the mountains."

"The mountains? What are you talking about?"

"I killed a deer," I said, and felt a great wave of sadness wash over me as the recollection took hold. My eyes were starting to feel very heavy. "I have to go now."

"Wait a minute, Ben. Is there a doctor there? Is anyone else there?"

"No." I was suddenly feeling very tired. It was beginning to dawn on me that I shouldn't have called Sarah. "I have to go."

"Don't hang up!" she shouted. "Tell me where you are."

"I shouldn't have called you," I said. "I have to go." I hung up the phone and closed my eyes. This is your brain on drugs, I thought as I nodded off.

A little while later I opened my eyes to find Lindsey sitting in a chair by the side of the bed. "Hey, Benny," she said softly, running her hand lightly across my forehead. "You're okay. You had an accident, but you're okay." I could tell she'd been crying.

"What time is it?" When I spoke, I could feel a stiffness in my cheeks, as if they were made out of some particularly dense putty.

"It's around five. You've been out for a few hours."

"I killed a deer," I said, and felt my eyes fill with tears.

"I know, sweetie," she said, leaning over in her chair to gently press her forehead against mine as she rubbed my temples. "I know." She rubbed her cheek against mine, as I cried into the softness of her neck. I couldn't remember the last time I had cried and it felt strange, like an old childhood T-shirt that shouldn't have fit anymore but somehow did. Lindsey held me, quietly rocking back and forth until I was done, which wasn't too long since I discovered crying was hell on my bruised ribs. After I had stopped she handed me a tissue to blow my nose, and it was only as I pressed it to my face and yelped in pain that I realized how swollen it was.

"Does my face look bad?" I asked her.

"Define bad," she said with a light grin. She rummaged through her bag and came up with a make-up mirror. I held it in front of me and observed the purple bruises under both of my eyes. My nose was a reddish brown, and blown up to twice its normal size. I looked like a Muppet.

"Jesus," I said.

"That airbag did quite a number on you," Lindsey said sympathetically, standing up to stretch her legs. I wondered how long she'd been sitting there. She walked over to the flowers and began rearranging them as she spoke. "Chuck and Alison went downstairs to get some coffee. They'll be up in a minute. You should have seen Chuck. He was giving the ambulance guys all these instructions. He rode with you in the ambulance, do you remember?" I didn't. "Anyway, he walked into the emergency room like he owned the place, telling everybody what to do."

"Go Chuck," I said softly, feeling myself inexplicably begin to withdraw again.

"He was like one of those guys on *ER*, you know?" Lindsey continued. "Start a Lidocane drip, give me a chest film, a G.I.

series, fifty ccs of this or that." She giggled. "The doctors down there were ready to kill him. They had to kick him out of the emergency room, but he did manage to negotiate this private room for you."

"Was I conscious?"

"You were in and out, and then they gave you something that just put you out for good." She turned around and sat back down. Somewhere outside a car alarm was blaring. "You gave us a real scare, you know?"

"I'm sorry." For some reason, I couldn't bring myself to speak more than a few short words at a time.

"When we drove up and I saw the car, and I saw you on the ground like that—" her voice broke and a tear rolled out of her left eye and down the side of her cheek before she could catch it with her finger. I watched the tear and felt a sense of guilty pleasure that she was crying for me, that I was enough of a presence inside her to send out that liquid signal. That I belonged to her. "We just found ourselves," she whispered, but the thought went unfinished as Chuck and Alison came into the room carrying Styrofoam cups.

"You're up!" Alison exclaimed, coming over to give me a kiss. "How are you feeling?"

"Lousy," I said.

"You look it," Chuck said brightly, expertly thumbing through the charts clipped to the end of my bed. "You were very lucky," he said, looking up at me. I found myself studying the bruise that remained on his face, although it wasn't much more than a faded yellow smear by now. "No broken ribs, no internal injuries or bleeding. Just the bruises on your face."

"My body," I said, trying to wiggle my shoulders. "Its sore."

"You probably strained all your muscles at the moment of impact."

I saw the deer's back as it hit my windshield, its matted fur crushed against the glass. I closed my eyes and leaned back into my pillows, exhausted and depressed.

"We'll leave you alone for a while," Alison said. "Let you get some rest."

I woke up a little later feeling a bit better, but still inexplicably sad and unwilling to speak. I knew I was upset about killing the deer, but the sadness in me transcended that. It was as if the jarring nature of the accident combined with my recent reunion with Lindsey had stripped me of all the emotional buffers I'd come to rely upon over the last few years. The effect was that I was experiencing the past year of loneliness and despair all at once. I was like something knocked loose off its foundations, weak and somehow smaller, reduced by my experiences. This was not something I could even begin to articulate, but Lindsey, who stayed in her seat by the side of my bed humming quietly, her hand resting gently on my hip, seemed to understand that I just needed some time to absorb everything and come out of it on my own.

By evening I had pretty much regained my equilibrium. Alison and Chuck had gone home, to be there in case Jack called or showed up. Lindsey sat Indian style at the foot of the bed, my legs on either side of her, massaging my feet through the blanket as we talked. Outside, the onslaught of the rain continued, the water streaming down the window in jagged rivulets, like brushstrokes on our reflection. I studied our reflection of us in the window, watching how every time the evening sky was brightened by lightning we became translucent, ghosts floating in the rain-filled sky. I imagined credits scrolling up the window, as if we were the last scene in a movie.

A weary-looking nurse carrying a tray entered the room briskly, her rubber souls squeaking on the waxed linoleum. She threw a disapproving glance at Lindsey perched on the bed and then dropped a paper cup with some pills on my end table. "That's to get you through the night," she said in a surprisingly soft voice. "The doctor says you can check out first thing in the morning."

"Thank you," I said.

She flipped off the light switch and turned to face Lindsey. "Your friend needs his rest and visiting hours are over. I'm afraid you're going to have to leave."

"Okay," Lindsey said pleasantly, hopping off the bed. She bent over me and kissed me lightly, once on the forehead and twice on the lips. "Feel good, Benny," and then, brushing back my hair with her fingers, "I love you."

"I love you, too."

I listened as Lindsey's footsteps and the nurse's squeaks faded down the hallway. Once I was alone, I swallowed the pills and turned onto my side to watch the rain for a while. It poured with determination and a purity of purpose, and I sensed a profound peace somewhere within the pulse of the raindrops, an unhindered expression of nature's raw energy. Hypnotized, I drifted off to sleep.

A short while later I was awakened by someone pulling the blanket up off my chest. "It's me," Lindsey whispered, her lips pressed against my ear. "You didn't think I was going to let you spend the night alone in here, did you?" She slid easily into the bed on her side, threw her arm over my chest, and molded herself into my body, pulling the blanket over both of us. "Besides," she said, "I didn't have a ride." I covered her hand with mine, our fingers intertwining, and for the first time since the accident, I felt whole again. I fell asleep to the tempo of Lindsey's steady breathing in my ear, the soft pressure of her chest rising and falling against my side. Some time during the night it finally stopped raining.

29

The next morning was radiant, which always seems to be the case after a good storm, the air rinsed clean of the gray film that tends to accumulate as a biological by-product of supporting life. Alison came to get us in Chuck's rental, and I wondered if this was thoughtfulness on her part, or if I'd actually totaled her BMW. "I'm sorry about your car," I said, climbing into the back seat. Lindsey sat up front in the passenger seat.

"Don't worry about it," she said sincerely. "Insurance will cover it. I'm just glad you weren't hurt."

"Still no word from Jack, huh?" Lindsey asked.

"Nope." I could see Alison's eyes in the rear view mirror, red-rimmed, with dark shadows under them. When she smiled at me, they watered slightly. We passed the local high school on our left, where hordes of teenagers were filing across the lawn toward the large, red-brick building with a white cupola and the words "Thomas Jefferson High School" engraved into the marble marquis. The kids looked unhurried, almost lackadaisical, as they made their way into the building in their jeans and sneakers, the boys in baggy, un-tucked button-downs, the girls either in skin-tight shirts or sweaters. I felt an instant longing to be one of them, deliberately careless, having all the time in the world. I remembered being that way once, feeling myself on the cusp of some great adventure that lay ahead. Never guessing that the cusp could go on forever.

Jeremy was playing one-on-one with Chuck when we got home, with Taz napping on the grass beside the driveway. Hearing the car, Taz shook himself awake and came over to greet us, followed by Chuck and Jeremy. "Wow!" Jeremy said, looking at me. "You look worse than Chuck!"

"Thank you," Chuck said. "I've been telling him that for years."

"The bruises will go away in time," I said, supporting myself with my arms as I climbed out of the car. "Just like the last rem-nants of Chuck's hair."

"Don't make me kick your ass again, Ben Boy," Chuck said, lending me a hand as I straightened up. "I might be feeling sorry for you, but I'll bet I can find a spot on you that isn't bruised."

"I doubt it," I groaned.

"You seem to be walking okay," Lindsey said.

"I just don't know which side to limp on."

"Any word?" I heard Alison ask Chuck coming up the stairs behind me.

"Negatory."

"How's it going, Jeremy?" I said.

"Okay. How do you feel?"

"I've been better."

"Yeah, well, you're lucky you didn't get a coma."

None of us knew quite what to say to that.

"Did you find the Darth Vader mask?" I asked, leaning over to give a scratch to Taz, who was nuzzling my crotch insistently.

"No. I think someone stole it."

We entered the house and I eased myself onto the couch. "Who would steal a mask?" I asked, wincing as Taz involuntarily bumped into my legs while clamoring to get next to me on the couch.

"Hey," Chuck said. "Did they send you home with any pain killers?"

"You bet," I said, pulling the rust-colored prescription bottle out of my jeans pocket. I pulled out two of the small gray tablets and popped them into my mouth.

"Whoa," Chuck said, leaning over and confiscating the bottle. "Those aren't candy. You get hooked on these we'll have to hand-cuff you to the bed next to you know who."

"Who?" Jeremy asked.

"Nobody," Chuck and I answered in unison.

"There's a guy in this chat room that says he saw Jack playing tennis in Miami yesterday," Chuck said. It was evening, and he was surfing the Net, sharing little bytes with me as I lay prone on the couch alternately watching television and slipping into codeine-induced catnaps. Jeremy had gone home a few hours ago to figure out what he would wear for trick-or-treating, which was only three days away. "Someone else just checked in and said Jack's in Israel, vacationing at the Dead Sea. He was taking a mud bath and he swears the guy next to him was Jack Shaw."

"How many Jack Shaw Web sites are there?" I asked.

"Over a thousand, according to Yahoo."

"God. Do people really have nothing else to do?"

"It's just a diversion," Chuck said. "The majority opinion is that Jack's disappearance is a publicity stunt, something to do with the plot of *Blue Angel II*."

"That's what they're saying on television now, too," I said, and I would have known since I hadn't left the couch all day. Jack's disappearance was the lead story on most of the news programs.

"Of course, a publicity stunt would work better if they actually had a film to publicize."

"True," Chuck said, his right hand clicking away on the mouse. "It sounds like there's already a breach of contract lawsuit in the works."

Lindsey came in, carrying a tray with turkey sandwiches and Cokes which she placed on the coffee table before sitting down on the floor in front of the couch. "Who's suing, Luther Cain?"

"I don't think the director sues," Chuck said. "It's probably the producers, or the studio."

"So much for all their concern over Jack's whereabouts," Alison said bitterly. She was sitting on the floor, flipping through the phone book and scribbling the names of local hotels and motels that Jack could have walked to onto a yellow legal pad.

"That's why its called show *business*," Chuck said. "The bottom line is the bottom line."

"Just like medicine," I said.

"Bite me."

The doorbell rang and Alison ran to answer it. "Oh my god!" she whispered, looking through the peephole. "It's the police."

Chuck and Lindsey got up, and I sat up on the couch so that I could see over the back as Alison opened the door and the officer walked in. He was a tall, lanky man, in a khaki uniform and a brown jacket, his hat already in his hands. "Good afternoon," he said, stepping through the door and into the foyer. "I'm Deputy Sheriff Dan Pike. Do you live here?"

"Yes?" Alison said, her voice nervously rising at the end, as if her answer were actually a question, which I guess it was. "I'm Alison Scholling?"

The rest of us all said hello. He looked over at me. "I take it that you were driving the BMW?" He asked, indicating the car by pointing his thumb over his shoulder.

"Yes sir," I said. "But I'm afraid the deer was worse off than me."

"Is that right," he said, smiling. He had a bushy mustache that all but obscured his upper lip, but not enough to hide the insincerity of his smile. The perennial movement of his eyes in their sockets and the grim set of his mouth gave him the appearance of a man who'd spent his whole life trying to catch up. "Every year Route 57 kills almost as many deer as the hunters. I keep telling the county to put up fences . . ." His voice trailed off. He did not come across as the kind of man you wanted to see splitting quantum particles.

"Are you here about the accident?" I asked.

"What? Oh no. Not that." He scratched his chin thoughtfully. "Is one of you a doctor?"

"I am," Chuck said. "Are you feeling okay?"

"I'm fine," Deputy Dan said. "Say, you weren't in the car, too, were you?"

"No."

"Oh. I was just noticing . . ." He ran his finger across his face, under the eyes, indicating Chuck's bruises. "Kind of a funny coincidence, you and your friend both getting banged up in separate incidents."

"Hysterical," Chuck said. "Hurt like hell actually."

"Is that right?" Deputy Dan said. It was clearly a stock phrase of his, something he said while his brain digested information, kind of like the farting sound a computer makes after you hit save. I was starting to find his slow, deliberate way of speaking annoying. He'd clearly watched his share of detective shows, and had become convinced that slow, confident banter was a standard investigative procedure.

"If you're not here about the accident, why are you here?" I asked.

"There's a doctor's jacket in the back window of the Beamer," Deputy Dan continued.

"That's mine," Chuck said.

"It appears to have some blood on it."

"That's because it does."

"I'm wondering whose blood that might be. Of course, I've got two choices right here, since both of you men look like you've done a little bleeding recently." This guy was really right out of a *Columbo* episode.

"Sheriff," I said.

"Deputy."

"Okay, Deputy. Are you telling me that you were driving by this house, saw all the way up the driveway to the back window of the Beamer that there was some blood on Chuck's jacket, so you pulled in to investigate?"

"I'm not investigating anyone," Deputy Dan said. "But I would like an answer to my question."

"I'm a doctor," Chuck said, and I could tell he was as irked as I was. "I deal with blood every day."

"Is that right?"

"Let me think a minute," Chuck said sarcastically. "Yes, that is right. Say a sheriff gets himself shot—"

"—Deputy sheriff," I corrected him.

"I'm sorry, a deputy sheriff gets himself shot," Chuck said, staring intently at Deputy Dan. "I could get an awful lot of blood on my coat pulling out those slugs."

"I see," Deputy Dan said, a hostile glint appearing in his eyes as he frowned at Chuck. "So would you like to tell me whose blood that is on your doctor's jacket?"

"I would," Chuck said.

"Good."

"But I can't."

"Excuse me?"

"That's privileged information between the doctor and his patient. I'm ethically bound to keep it confidential."

"Excuse me," Lindsey interjected. "But what is this all about? I'm sure you didn't just come in here to argue with us. What's going on?"

"I'm not at liberty to say right now," Deputy Dan said. "It's part of an ongoing investigation."

"Is that right?" I said.

"Well then," Alison said, stepping forward. "I'm going to have to insist you stop questioning my guests like this. As far as I can tell, you have no just cause for coming in here, so unless you have something specific to ask, I suggest you end this visit now."

"You a lawyer or something?" he asked.

"I am."

Deputy Dan grinned at her, a condescending grin to show her just what he thought of lawyers. "Well," he said, replacing his hat. "I guess I'll be leaving for now." Alison pulled open the door for him. "Say," he said turning to face us just before he stepped over the threshold. "How long will you people be staying in Carmelina?"

"I'm not at liberty to say right now," I said. I knew I was pushing it, but the codeine was making me bold.

"What's your name?" Deputy Dan asked me.

"Ben."

"Well, Ben, you're a real clever guy, you know that?"

"I've been told."

"Well, for a real clever guy, you're not too smart. I'll be seeing you." With that, Deputy Dan nodded to us and turned on his heel, Alison closing the door behind him.

"What the hell was that?" Lindsey said.

"Do you think they found Jack?" Alison asked

"No. If they'd found him they wouldn't be asking us. They'd be telling us." Chuck said.

"Well," I said, "they obviously know something."

"Is that right?" Chuck said, and we all lost it.

"Cut it out, man. It hurts when I laugh," I complained.

"This isn't funny," Alison said through her giggles. "We could really be in trouble."

"Then why are you laughing?" Chuck challenged her.

"I'm just laughing at my life," she said with an exaggerated sigh that somehow set us off again.

"That guy," I said, "is depriving a village somewhere of an idiot." We cracked up again.

"I can't believe you guys," Lindsey said, coming to sit with me on the couch. "You two really pissed him off."

"You think?" Chuck said.

"It's probably a safe bet that he's got bigger problems," I said.

"That's true," Lindsey said soberly. "But do we?"

"What do you mean?" Alison asked.

"I mean, they know something. I agree with Chuck that they didn't find Jack, but somehow they suspect we're involved with his disappearance. That's why that deputy was so interested in your bruises and the bloody coat. He's looking for signs of violence. And that means that someone tipped him off as to what was going on here."

"So there are a number of possibilities," Chuck said. "One. They know we kidnapped Jack but have no proof. Two. Maybe someone heard Jack tearing the place apart a few nights ago and reported it."

"Then the police would have come a while ago," I pointed out.

"Seward," Alison said.

"What?"

"Seward. It's got to be him."

As soon as she said it, we all knew she was probably right. After all, he'd known, or suspected, we were involved from the beginning, and after the incident with Chuck's pager he wasn't going to just sit back and see what happened. He had too much riding on Jack not to follow up every lead he got, especially after catching Chuck in an outright lie.

"You think he called the Sheriff's Department?" I asked.

"Why not?" Alison said. "He tells them he has reason to believe we're involved, and asks them to just come out and check it out. He knows they'll do it, because what the hell else do they have to do?"

"Good point," I said. "But now what?"

As if in answer to my question the telephone rang and Lindsey snatched up the portable, which had been discarded on the stairs by whoever used it last. "Hello," Lindsey said softly. Of course, the moment demanded that the caller be Seward, or the Sheriff's Department, or even Jack, calling to tell us where he was. But this was real life, and perhaps the biggest difference between movies and real life is that real life rarely concerns itself with plot development.

Lindsey's face suddenly became an unreadable mask, her expression not quite changing but rather freezing into place, a subtle clenching of microscopic facial muscles all but undetectable, except to someone who knew her intimately. While it remained a mystery who was on the phone, it was clear to all of us that the call was in no way related to our current conversation. It was equally clear to me that Lindsey was disturbed by the call. "Hi," she said atonally. "How are you? . . . Uh huh. . . . Oh, he did? . . . uh huh, no it's fine, he's fine . . . yeah."

She looked up at me then, and I felt a sudden chill on my spine, just the tiniest psychic *uh oh!* before she extended the phone to me and said, "It's for you."

"Who is it?" I mumbled, taking the proffered telephone. "Hello?"

"Ben?" It was Sarah. Shit. Lindsey looked at me for a moment and then went into the kitchen.

"Hi," I said.

"Who's that?" Chuck asked intently.

I covered the mouthpiece with my hand and told him who it was. While he and Alison exchanged puzzled glances, Sarah said, "I was worried about you."

"Why?"

"You called me, remember? From the hospital?"

"Oh. Yeah. How did you know where to find me?"

"You said you were in the mountains. This was the only place I could think of that you might be. I still had the number in my address book."

"Oh. I shouldn't have called you," I said. "I was on some heavy medication." Chuck and Alison exchanged glances and went into the kitchen to give me some privacy.

"I was worried," Sarah said quietly.

"Yeah, well I'm fine," I said quickly, needing like hell not to be on the phone with her.

"Fine," she said testily, and I could tell I'd hurt her feelings.

"Look, Sarah," I said, feeling rotten. "I hate like hell to be rude, but I can't tie up the phone right now . . ."

"Yes," she said, her voice now ice. "I certainly didn't mean to interrupt anything."

I decided that a response to the implication she'd floated would only prolong the discussion. "I know you didn't," I said.

"Well, do me a favor. If you ever get it into your head to give me another call like that, don't."

"Deal," I said. I couldn't believe I'd called her in the first place.

I'd never been a slave to good judgment, but this bordered on self-immolation. "I must have been really fried," I muttered.

"Excuse me?"

"Okay," I said and hung up. Only my battered condition prevented me from throwing the phone across the room. There were so many things bothering me about the call I didn't know where to begin cataloging them. I didn't want to be cruel to Sarah, and I didn't want to hurt Lindsey either, and I'd apparently managed to do both by making one stupid, sentimental call from my hospital bed. Without warning my vision suddenly began to blur and I felt myself grow lightheaded. I lay back on the couch, my eyes at half mast, and felt the room begin to spin. My recent codeine dose was kicking in. I was divorced and that was bad, not because I still wanted to be married to Sarah, but because it was the first concrete sign that irrevocable things were starting to happen to me. Change was something I'd never dealt with gracefully, as evidenced by the fact that I'd even called Sarah to begin with. I probably meant to get off the couch right then and straighten things out with Lindsey, but the codeine was taking no prisoners and without any further preamble I fell into a dark, dreamless sleep.

30

As it turned out, I didn't wake up until morning. At some point while I was asleep someone had thrown a blanket over me. I hoped it had been Lindsey, but I wouldn't have bet my life savings on it. Actually, the way things had been going for me lately, I probably would have bet my life savings on it. The aroma of eggs and coffee came floating in from the kitchen, and I realized that I was starving. I took a quick roll call of my body parts and determined that all of them had shown up to work that day, although some more enthusiastically than others. I carefully rolled off the couch and hoisted myself into a standing position, taking a few seconds to dig my toes into the carpet and wiggle them around. For some reason I'd been finding the sensation of carpet between my toes oddly soothing since the accident. I walked toward the kitchen, the static electricity between my feet and the carpet crackling like a Rice Krispies commercial. I found Chuck and Alison glumly eating breakfast together.

"Hey," I said, pulling up a chair.

"Good morning," Alison said.

"How are you feeling?" Chuck asked, spreading some scrambled eggs onto toasted white bread. I waited until he was done and then grabbed the piece off his plate.

"Hungry," I said, biting into the toast. "Needs salt." I reached across Alison and grabbed the salt shaker.

"Everyone's a critic," Chuck said, grabbing another piece of toast off the plate in the center of the table.

"Where's Lindsey?" I asked.

"Down by the lake," Chuck said. "And if you ask me—"

"I'm not."

"She looks none too pleased," he finished.

I took another bite of toast and eggs and then pushed myself away from the table. "Here," Chuck said, reaching into his pocket. "You'll need it." He pulled out my prescription bottle and cracked one of the pills in half. "Daytime rations," he said, tossing me the fragment. I popped it into my mouth and washed it down with his orange juice. "I'll see you guys later," I said.

I was almost at the door when Alison softly said, "Ben."

I turned to look at her. "Yeah."

"Whatever the problem is, get it worked out now, because we have bigger things to worry about."

"What's the matter?" I asked.

"He's been gone two days, Ben," she said, looking at me intently. "That's two days and two nights."

"I know."

"No," Alison said, her voice catching. "You don't know. None of us knows. He could be hurt, he could be dead, we don't know a goddamn thing."

"Jack can take care of himself," I said weakly.

"Yeah right," she retorted. "If Jack could take care of himself we wouldn't be here right now."

"So what are you saying?" Chuck asked her. "What do you want to do?"

"I don't know," Alison said, running her finger introspectively around the rim of her juice glass. "I think it's gone too far. Maybe we should speak to the police."

"They'll arrest us," Chuck said. "Do you know what an arrest could do to my career? Or yours? You could be disbarred, and I'd lose my license."

"We're talking about Jack's life!" Alison shouted at him, slamming her hand down on the table so hard that I saw bits of egg jump into the air. "How selfish can you be, Chuck?!"

"Hey!" Chuck shouted back. "I came here to help Jack, didn't I? I got my goddamn nose busted trying to help my buddy Jack. But Jack didn't want our help, and maybe it's time you thought a little about that. Jack said fuck it and fuck us and took off. Right now he's sitting in a hotel room somewhere stoned out of his gourd, picking his nose and laughing at us, and I'll be goddamned if I'm going to piss my future away while that's happening. You want to flush your career down the toilet over our junkie friend, you be my guest. You've been martyring yourself for Jack for years now, what's one more sacrifice? But I came here to help a friend, not be destroyed by him!"

Alison just stared at Chuck, ignoring the tears as they descended from her unblinking eyes to the corners of her mouth, which hung open in anguished disbelief. I must have been staring at him, too, or maybe it was just too hard to look at the raw pain on Alison's face, because Chuck suddenly turned to me and said, "What?! You know I'm right."

We stared at each other for a moment. "As long as we all agree then," I said quietly and retreated from the kitchen.

I found Lindsey sitting on a large rock that jutted out over the lake, her chin on her knees, digging out small pebbles from the crevices in the rock and tossing them into the water. She was wearing faded black jeans and a violet NYU sweatshirt, her hair pulled back in a ponytail that disappeared into the crumpled hood of the sweatshirt. She didn't turn around, but I knew she'd heard me come by the way she cocked her head.

"What's all the shouting about?" she asked, her voice carefully neutral.

"Slight difference of opinion concerning the Jack situation."

"Oh."

"Yeah," I continued, rambling nervously. "Alison thinks Jack's lying dead in a ditch somewhere. She wants to call the cops." Lindsey didn't respond, but simply tossed another pebble into the lake. It hit the water with a soft, dignified *ploop*. When it became apparent that she intended to say nothing, I quickly continued. "Chuck thinks Alison has unresolved Jack issues that she needs to explore and is convinced Jack is holed up somewhere, stoned out of his gourd."

Ploop . . . Ploop.

"Chuck is very against calling the cops. He's sure we'll all be arrested." *Ploop.* "What do I think? I think they're both right and they're both wrong and would you please just turn around and talk to me for a second?"

There was a final *ploop* and then Lindsey pulled a stray hair out of her mouth and turned to face me. "You know what your problem is, Ben?"

I briefly wondered at the way those seven words seemed to find their way into the mouth of every woman I've ever known. "No," I said. "Well, yes actually. That is, which problem are you talking about?"

"You can't accept the fact that life doesn't come with the closure and symmetry of a movie. You hate the loose ends, the knowledge that there are things in life that get screwed up and will remain irrevocably screwed up."

This sounded so much like what Sarah had said to me when we got divorced that for one paranoid instant I actually considered the possibility that the two had discussed it between themselves. "I don't want Sarah back," I said.

"I know you don't," Lindsey said with a tender smile. "I'm not worried about that. But you don't want her to resent you or hate you either. And you can't accept the fact that you left something behind, something messy. You want to keep going back to see if you can somehow clean it up, make it more tidy in your mind, but it isn't going to happen."

"I know that," I said.

"And while you're busy looking back," she continued, "you're not looking at what you have right here in front of you. I don't know," she exhaled slowly. "Maybe that's why you write, so that you can give closure to everything, you know? Achieve resolution."

"I know what I have here," I said. "You know I've always been in love with you."

"I do, but it's not enough. I love you, but I'm looking forward, not back." She leaned forward, pulling her knees to her chest. "You screwed up in the past. Well, shit happens. You learn what you can, you scrape it off your shoe and you move on. If you can't do that, you'll never get the chance to get it right."

"I *was* heavily medicated," I pointed out.

"Bullshit, Ben," she said. "Divorce means you've been permanently changed, and that terrifies you. But without change there's no future for you. For us. So I need you to start accepting things. To start looking forward."

The good old days weren't always good, I thought to myself. *And tomorrow ain't as bad as it seems.* I thought about that for a moment, then about the wisdom of looking to song lyrics for direction, and then I climbed onto the rock to sit with her, facing the lake. My fingers found a small pebble and I tossed it into the lake. *Ploop.* There was an answering *ploop* as Lindsey tossed a pebble, and in that way we sealed our pact. I leaned against her and she ran her lips over my forehead.

I noticed our breath as it formed and mingled in front of us, a faint white vapor in the cool morning air. It wasn't cold yet, but the weather was turning. The lake was absolutely still under the gray sky, its current undetectable, as if it too was sensing the approach of yet another winter and was preparing to freeze. Suddenly I sat up straight and looked across the lake. "The geese are gone," I said.

Lindsey smiled at me and gave my arm a squeeze. "They'll be back," she whispered. We sat there quietly for a while watching the lake, growing ever so slightly older together.

31

We were still sitting on the rock a while later when Chuck came storming down, with Alison trailing him angrily. They were still going at it fiercely. "I can't believe you're bailing on us," Alison said, hurrying to keep up with him.

"I'm not the one bailing," Chuck yelled over his shoulder. "Jack's the one who cut out." He strode purposefully over to us and said, "We have to talk."

"We can't just leave," Alison protested. "We have to do something."

"There's nothing we can do," Chuck retorted.

Alison's face was flushed with anger as she approached us. "Is that what you all think?" she asked, slightly out of breath from following Chuck down to the lake. "You think we should just go home?"

Chuck gave me an intense look, and I knew I couldn't leave him hanging. "He's gone, Alison," I said slowly. "Wherever he might be, it's out of our hands now. He didn't want our help before. Even if we could find him, what makes you think he wants it now?"

"What are you talking about?" Alison said. "He needs us." She looked at Lindsey and me, her eyes accusing and pleading at the same time.

"I think we need to lay out the options, Alison," Lindsey said softly. "I mean, none of us is thinking very clearly right now."

"My thinking is perfectly clear," Chuck said, raising his voice. "And I don't need to decide this on committee. I'm going home. Jack's gone. He's either found his way to a phone and called Seward to come get him, or he got high, or . . ." his voice trailed off.

"Or what?" Alison said, daring him.

"Or he's dead," Lindsey said, letting Chuck off the hook.

"I called the local hospital this morning," Chuck said. "No one's been admitted since last night, and there have been no DOAs either. Beyond that, I don't see what else any of us can do."

"We can talk to the police," Alison said. "Once we tell them what happened, they'll help us look for him."

"Who? That jerk-off deputy? Yeah, I can see where he might be a big help."

"We can speak to the sheriff or the State Police."

Chuck made a face. "Great! Screw your life up some more over Jack. It's like some sick joke already! But I'm not going to join you. I was set to leave two days ago, but then Ben got hurt so I stuck around. For him, not for Jack. I've taken off a week during a crucial surgery rotation. If I miss anymore, I can't fulfill my requirement and I'll have to wait until spring to start it over again. I'll lose at least six months, and for what? It's one thing to stick your neck out for someone when it might actually do them some good. But now we're just hurting ourselves pointlessly. Ben could have been killed, for Christ's sake." He stopped and looked over at me before turning back to Alison. "Jack also damn near burned the house down with all of us in it, in case you've forgotten. And at no point through any of that did I think about quitting because I still thought we could help him. But now the police are sniffing around, and I think that's our cue to get the hell out of here.... Jack walked out of his own free will, and that's it. It's time to let him take responsibility for his actions. We're done here, Alison. It was a noble effort and it didn't work. It was over the minute he walked out that door, and you're the only one who doesn't know it."

Alison was looking straight at him now, her eyes narrowed into contemptuous slits. "So go home, Chuck. Take care of yourself. That's what you're best at anyway." Her invective was almost verbatim what Luke said to Han Solo just before the Rebellion's attack on the Death Star, but I didn't see any advantage to pointing that out just then.

"You deluded bitch," Chuck said softly.

"Chuck!" Lindsey shouted in surprise.

"No!" he yelled back. "We're all tiptoeing around her, and I'm not going to do it anymore! I care about you, Alison. I know you don't think that's true, but it is. And that's why I'm telling you this. You don't love Jack, you're addicted to him. Or to being a martyr for him, I don't know, but it's not healthy. You can't even see the damage this is doing to you. To all of us."

"Don't you dare try to tell me how I feel!" Alison spat at him. "What the hell do you know about it? You've never loved anyone but yourself."

He started to say something, shook his head and then waved his hand in a dismissive gesture as he turned away and headed back toward the house. "Fuck it," he said. "I'm out of here."

I stood up, panic churning in my stomach. Something was happening between all of us, bending under all the tension and hostility and I had an ominous feeling that when it snapped it would shatter irreparably. The lines were being drawn, and the sides we fell on would divide us permanently. "Chuck!" I called to him. "Wait a minute." He frowned, but he stopped where he was.

"Let him go," Alison said. "He's made his priorities clear."

"Alison," I said turning to her, trying to keep my voice low and steady. "That's not fair. He came for better reasons than the rest of us."

"What the hell are you talking about?" Alison said, still staring at Chuck, who was standing stock still on the lawn.

"It was harder for him to come than any of us. He had the most to lose, and unlike the rest of us, he had nothing else to gain."

Alison turned to face me, her expression a question. "Look," I said. "It's no secret that things haven't been so great for me lately. The divorce, my job, et cetera. This was a welcome break for me. Also, I also knew Lindsey would be here."

"I understand," Alison said bitterly. "So now you're together, you both got what you want, and Jack doesn't matter anymore. Is that it?"

"Jesus Christ!" Lindsey said, smacking the rock in frustration. "No one is saying that. Will you grow up already?"

"Please, Alison," I said. "The point is, unlike Lindsey and me, Chuck has a major career going, and he had put it at risk because he had a friend who needed help. He came out here to help Jack, and to help us. End of sentence. No other reason. So if you want to argue about whether or not we should call it quits you can argue, but be fair about it. Jack goes postal and tries to burn the house down, and you get pissed at Lindsey for using her stun gun. Chuck brings up the possibility of going home and you bite his head off. We're your friends, Alison. Don't push us away."

"I'll tell you something else," Lindsey said, getting up and walking over to face Alison, who was now standing on the far side of the rock. "I came here for you too, more than for Jack. Because you're my closest friend and I love you. You've always been there for me and I can't stand—" She swallowed hard and continued. "I can't stand to watch you get hurt over and over again by him." She punctuated her sentence with a stiff nod and turned away, wiping a tear out of the corner of her eye.

"When we set out to do this we said that there was a risk that we would lose him," I said to Alison as Lindsey sat back down at the edge of the rock. "But now it feels like we're losing you, too."

Alison turned around and looked out over the lake, her arms wrapped across her chest, hands hugging her shoulders. I could see her back contracting and expanding as she breathed deeply. Chuck took a few halting steps forward to the foot of the rock, sensing a change in the atmosphere. "I had another reason, too," Alison finally said. "For coming up here, I mean. I told myself it was all to help Jack, but that's not completely true. I guess I thought that if I was the one who helped him, if I pulled him through, he'd see how much I loved him, and he'd realize how much he loved me. I just—I don't know. . . . I've spent the last ten years holding out for someone who doesn't even want me. Life's moving ahead without me, and half the time I don't even realize it's happening. It's like every so often I look at the calender and I'm shocked to see that years have gone by and I'm still in the same spot. It's lost time, and I have no idea where it went. And I look up one day and I'm thirty years old and no closer to having a husband and a family than I was when I was in college." She sighed, absently digging her toe into a crevice of the rock. She dislodged a small pebble and kicked it into the lake. I listened for the *ploop*.

"I don't know," she continued, staring into the concentric ripples her pebble had created in the water. "I just know I was supposed to be somewhere else by now. And I guess I thought if I could get him up here, away from all the craziness in his life, we'd have a chance. It was stupid and selfish, but I did it anyway." She turned to face us, her eyes downcast. "It's insane, really. I'm like a stalker, like Kathy Bates in *Misery* or something. I kidnapped Jack to make him love me. I brought you all into it under the guise of saving him from himself, when I was thinking about myself as much as him. And now if he's hurt, or sick or worse, it's my fault. Because I was stupid enough to think I could change him, to make him what I wanted him to be so that my life could get to where it was supposed to be by now."

We all stared at her, stunned by what she had said. I'd always known that Alison was hopelessly hung up on Jack, but it had never occurred to me that she could be experiencing the same combination of disconnection and emptiness closing in on her that I'd been feeling. The sense that time was switching from a jog to a sprint and we weren't even in the race. My heart went out to her, even while my petty misery retroactively welcomed her company. Until you found your way out of the woods, it was reassuring to find other people lost in them with you.

"It's not insane," Lindsey said to her gently. "We're all going through the same things. When you're younger you just take it as a given that certain things will fall into place on their own. Relationships, family, careers, the whole deal. They might not come exactly as you picture them, but they'll come in some form." She smiled ruefully. "You just never figure that they might not come at all. And then you hit thirty and . . . shit! You suddenly realize that they're not necessarily coming and you panic. Or at least, I did."

"It's funny," I said. "I know I was depressed, feeling like my life was nowhere and everything, but I was completely convinced that you guys were all happy with your lives, and I was the only loser. It's somewhat comforting to see that you're all screwed up, too."

"I'm so glad the tragicomic opera that is my life could be a source of comfort to you," Alison said with a quick smirk, and you could feel the pressure around us dissolving.

"And don't think I don't appreciate it," I said.

"Excuse me," Chuck said, stepping fully back onto the rock now. "But is there going to be a bathroom break here? I mean, I enjoy all this sharing and introspection as much as the next whimpering, pathetic loser, but really. There are limits."

"Chuck," Alison said shaking her head sadly. "I'm so sorry about what I said before. Please forgive me, I was totally out of line."

Chuck considered her for a moment and then flashed a mischievous grin. "You weren't out of line," he said. "This is out of line." He stepped forward and without any hesitation pushed her into the lake.

"Chuck!" Lindsey and I shouted in unison.

Alison came up sputtering as she treaded water, but I saw with relief that she was also laughing. "You had that coming," Chuck called to her with a smile. "Just a little something to ease the tension."

"The tension was already eased," Lindsey said, still staring incredulously at Alison who was now doing the side stroke in a little circle, still laughing.

"Don't fuck me up with details," Chuck said and then stepped off the rock, landing with a splash in the water near Alison. "Hey," he shouted up to us. "The water's really warm. You guys should come in."

I looked at Lindsey, who looked back at me with a smile and shrugged. "Let's go."

Lindsey took a running jump, looking like one of those girls in the Mountain Dew commercials, and I gingerly eased myself over the edge of the rock, taking great pains not to stretch or bump my bruised ribs. The water was surprisingly warm, almost room temperature, and we swam in it for a while, joking around and splashing each other. The fall air was much colder than the water, so none of us felt very inclined to get out.

"I've got something to say," Chuck said, while we treaded water lazily in the shadow of the rock. We all looked at him expectantly. "This isn't easy."

"It's easier when you're not wearing shoes," I said.

"Not swimming, you putz," he said, splashing me halfheartedly. "You guys were all talking about how you had these secondary reasons for wanting to do this intervention, and I just wanted to tell you all that I had another reason, too." He paused, but no one said a word. Chuck rarely expressed himself, and we didn't want to do anything to shake his confidence. He grabbed onto the edge of the rock to stabilize himself before continuing. "You see, I've always kind of been the comic relief in our little group here, you know? My love life, my attitude, my language."

"Come on, Chuck," Lindsey said. "You know it's just friendly teasing."

"I know," Chuck said. "And on a daily basis I never minded it. Hey, I bring it upon myself. But over the years it's had the cumulative effect of making me feel like none of you takes me too seriously as a person, which pisses me off. It makes me feel that maybe I'm not such a serious person, but I am. I've devoted my life to healing people, and I'm good at it, I really am. It's ironic, because you guys talk about how you haven't made anything of your lives yet, while I've become a surgeon, and yet somehow I'm still the class clown."

"Chuck," Alison said. "It's not like that."

"It is," he said. "But I don't blame you guys for it. I'm not blind to my own behavior. If anything, I'm upset with myself. I was the fat kid in high school, and I worked my ass off so that in college I'd be taken seriously. Now here I am, years later, and I still have this uncanny knack for making myself seem comical."

"Jesus, Chuck," I said. "I had no idea you felt this way."

"Hey," he said with a smile. "I'm not crying over it. I know none of you mean any harm by it and like I said, it's my own doing. I mean hey, look at this right here." He splashed the water and swam a little backstroke. "I'm asking you to take me seriously while I'm swimming in my clothing."

"There is a certain measure of comedy in that," Lindsey admitted.

"Is that what you're doing, Chuck?" Alison asked. "Asking us to take you seriously?"

He looked at her thoughtfully. "I'm not asking for anything to change. But when we discussed taking Jack up here I thought, now here will be the perfect opportunity to show these guys what I can do, to let you see the doctor side of me for once, instead of just the joker. Like all of you, I wanted to help Jack, but I guess I was also looking for a little respect for myself. For who I am and what I've made of myself."

He finished speaking and looked around sheepishly. The three of us treaded water in silence. "Will someone please say something," Chuck said.

"I never thought you were a joke in high school and I don't think you're one now," I finally said. "It's just this tone that was set, I don't even know when. But I know that we never would have tried this without you, because we think of you as our in-house medical expert. We may not discuss it all the time, but we're all very aware of who you are."

"I'm sure I'm not the only one who calls you for free medical advice," Alison said, and we all smiled.

"Besides," Lindsey said, splashing Chuck playfully. "Don't undervalue comic relief. We do count on you to lighten the mood from time to time. No one's better at it than you."

"Yeah, well I just wanted to say what was on my mind."

"I'm glad you did," Alison said.

We looked at each other, floating in the lake on the four points of an invisible diamond, and there was a symmetry about us that had been missing since we'd come up to Carmelina. We were all pieces in this complex puzzle, taken apart years ago, and with Chuck's remarks the old bond was finally excavated and we clicked into our places in the tableau. The knowledge that we'd all felt a need to come together, to regroup and assess the assorted wounds and scars we'd accumulated in the years since college, united us in a shared sense of well-being.

"We're like plague beetles," I said.

"Come again?" Alison said.

"I saw it on the Discovery Channel. They're these beetles who eat leaves, but they have to eat in groups, many beetles to the same leaf. This way, they dilute the poisonous parts of the leaf throughout the group. If one or two of them tried to eat the leaf alone, the poison would kill them. I feel like we each had our own bit of poison we were dealing with, and by coming up here together we were like those beetles, climbing onto the leaf to do it together."

Everyone contemplated my analogy for a second or two, and then Chuck said, "Ben, I think I speak for all of us when I say you've got way too much free time. I mean, when the hell do you think this shit up?"

I splashed him in the face, laughing. "Let's make a pact," I said. "We should come up here once a year for a long weekend, to just kind of touch base with each other."

"Sounds good to me," said Alison, gently breaststroking in place.

"I'm there," Lindsey said.

"Okay," Chuck said. "We have a year to elect the next candidate for an intervention."

We laughed. I knew that it was highly unlikely we'd actually keep to the pact, but it felt good to make it anyway. It meant that for now, at least, we were all feeling the same attachment to each other. I became conscious of a gradual throbbing in my side, and realized that my battered torso had had it. With a groan I swam over to the rock and guided myself along its shelf to where I could pull myself out of the water. My soaked clothing weighed me down and I grunted from the effort. "You okay?" Lindsey asked, swimming up behind me.

"Fine," I lied, shivering in the cold air. "I could use another codeine fix."

"Okay, let's get out." She pulled herself easily out onto the rock and turned back to Chuck and Alison. "You guys coming?"

"In a minute," Chuck said. "I'm still peeing."

"Chuck!" Alison shrieked and quickly swam over to the rock, laughing as she went.

"Oh, come on," he called after her. "Don't even try to tell me that you weren't doing the same thing!"

32

"You know what really bothers me," Alison said to Lindsey and me, taking a sip from her mug. We'd all showered off the grime from the lake and the three of us were sitting in the living room drinking hot cider while Chuck was upstairs packing. The lake water may have been warm, but the air had been downright frosty as we ran back to the house in our drenched clothing, and we were still coaxing the chill from our bones.

"What's that?" Lindsey said, curled up on the couch, inhaling the steam from her cider.

"Looking back, I can't even say what it is that attracted me to Jack so strongly. I know it must have been something to keep me going all these years, but when I try to quantify it . . . nothing."

"Just cause you can't articulate it doesn't mean it isn't there," I said.

"That's what I tell myself," Alison said. "Because the alternative is even more pathetic, that I hung onto him blindly, more from inertia than anything else. I mean, I'm a smart person, with friends

248

and a career. I don't think I suffer from low self-esteem or anything. So why can't I shake this?"

"I've been asking you that for years," Lindsey said.

"And you know what else?" Alison said. "I have this notion
that it was all timing. That if I'd met Jack even one semester later,
he wouldn't have had the same effect on me. I don't know . . . I
was going through this whole alienation thing with my sisters right
then, feeling like I needed to prove to them how provincial they
were. I mean, it was more about me than them, really. I got to
NYU and everyone seemed so directed, so committed to pursuing
some greater plan, and there I was, raised to think about husbands
and families."

"Cut to ten years later," I said. "And look how all of our great
plans have turned out."

"I know," she said. "And now, of course, everything I was resisting is what I want more than anything."

"I still don't get how all of that led to Jack," Lindsey said.

Alison looked at her with a bemused grin. "If you met my sisters' husbands, you'd understand. They're practically interchange-
able. Ivy Leaguers, corporate champions, weekend athletes. They
even share Knicks season tickets. The truth is, they're actually
great guys. Good fathers, loving husbands. But at the time, I felt
that my eyes had been opened to a whole new world, and I was
determined to break the mold, to come back with something different. Jack was the antithesis of the man I was expected to bring
home, you know? A little wild, a little dangerous, more openly
passionate, less refined. When I met him, he was everything I
thought I was looking for, wrapped up in this beautiful, sexy package." She sighed deeply. "I opened myself up to him so completely, just gave myself over to the possibility of him. And
now, all these years later, I'm still clinging to that possibility. Like
if I can just prove that the girl I was in college was right, it will

be this great happy ending and a justification for the last ten years."

"And if not?" Lindsey asked.

"Then I guess I have to face the fact that I'm no longer that misguided kid," Alison answered. "That now I'm just . . . old."

"Do you love him?"

Alison looked down into her cider. "I do," she whispered. "Terribly. That's the problem."

"Wow, Alison," I said, after a moments' silence. "Who knew you were such a mess?"

"I know," she said with a smile. "I hide it well. You know, I saw a shrink for a while."

That raised our eyebrows. "No way," I said.

"A few years ago. My parents insisted," she said. "I mean, I was like twenty-seven years old. By that age, all of my sisters already had their first babies. I was way off schedule and they were worried."

"How'd that go?" I asked.

"He asked me out."

"He did not!" Lindsey squealed.

"He did," Alison said, smiling.

"This guy knows how you're hopelessly in love with Jack and he asks you out? There's a man who likes a challenge."

"I know. That's what I told him when we broke up."

"Broke up? You mean you actually dated him?" I asked incredulously as Lindsey snickered.

"Sure," Alison said. She was laughing now, too. "He was a good-looking guy, a great listener . . ."

Lindsey burst out laughing. "I can't believe you dated your shrink. You, of all people!"

"How long?" I asked.

"About two months," Alison said. "But two intense months."

"I'll bet," Lindsey said. "Why'd it end?"

"We had sex once in his office, right there on the leather couch. It was actually pretty hot. But as I was leaving his receptionist handed me my bill and—"

"Oh god," I said, now laughing, too.

"It was pretty strange," Alison said, grinning. "I was like, I'm paying for this? How desperate am I? That pretty much did it for me. Seeing a shrink shouldn't make you feel more pathetic than you already are."

"Did you pay it?" I asked.

"Well, that's what made it worse. My parents were paying for it."

Lindsey lost it, almost falling off the couch as she laughed uncontrollably. "Your parents paid for you to have sex!" she stammered. "That's perfect! I can't believe you never told me!"

"It's nothing I was terribly proud of," Alison said, demurely sipping at her cider. "It's a shame though. He was a pretty good guy."

"What's so funny?" Chuck said, coming down the stairs. "What'd I miss?"

"I was just telling them how I slept with my therapist," Alison said.

"Who hasn't?" Chuck replied, plopping down into an armchair. "Wait a minute. You have a therapist?"

"Had one," Alison said.

"Literally," I said, prompting another round of chuckles.

"You also slept with your therapist?" Alison asked Chuck.

"Sure," Chuck said. "But does it count if I made the appointment because I'd seen her in the hospital and I wanted to sleep with her?"

"Judges?" Lindsey said with a flourish.

"I think that's a disqualification," I said.

"It's a common syndrome," Chuck said.

"Patients falling for their therapists?" I asked.

"No. Therapists sleeping with their patients. I've slept with a few therapists."

"It's kind of an expensive way to meet women, isn't it?" Lindsey asked.

"No more expensive than dating, if you think about it," Chuck said. "Plus, you don't have to worry that you're talking about yourself too much because that's what you're supposed to do. And as soon as you want to break things off, you've got the perfect excuse. You just say 'this is wrong. You're my therapist for god's sake!' They feel much too guilty to give you a hard time."

"You should really write a book, Chuck," Lindsey said.

"Is he serious?" Alison asked, turning to me. "I can never tell."

"I've known him too long to rule out the possibility."

"Speaking of serious," Chuck said, sitting up in the chair. "I'm going to head home this afternoon. I can't tell any of you what to do, but there's plenty of room in my car if any of you want to come."

His remark was greeted with a thoughtful silence, as we contemplated what we should do. I'd avoided confronting the issue of going home ever since Chuck had raised it the day Jack disappeared. We'd been in Carmelina for just under a week, but already Manhattan seemed worlds away, and the prospect of going back filled me with a quiet dread. Even though I could picture my apartment and my cubicle at *Esquire*, I could find no trace of myself at either place. It was like looking at photos in an old scrap book, familiar but no longer relevant. I wondered how long it would take, once I returned, for the emptiness to reclaim me. I thought about Lindsey and the logistics of returning to our respective apartments, mine on the Upper West Side and hers in

Soho. After everything we'd been through in the last week, the idea of living separately didn't make any sense, but moving in together after a week seemed equally irrational. Everything that worked perfectly up in the mountains seemed as if it might not hold up under scrutiny when we got back to the city. Still, we were going to have to go back sooner or later.

My mood began to darken as I weighed these issues in my mind, but before I could resolve anything, I looked out the window and saw a police car pulling into the driveway.

Deputy Dan had returned, and this time he wasn't alone. He'd brought his boss with him. Sheriff Joseph Sullivan was right out of central casting, a short, barrel-chested man about fifty years old, with a mottled, fleshy complexion and thin, precise lips. Apparently, he was from the school of thought that as long as you could pull a few measly strands of hair over your gleaming dome of a head you could avoid being legally classified as bald. Sullivan had pale blue eyes that radiated a patient intelligence, a pot belly, and a warrant to search Alison's house. He handed the papers over to Alison while standing on the front porch, content to let her thoroughly examine them before he made a move to enter the house.

"I don't understand," Alison said, her brow furrowed in concentration as she reviewed the document. "On what grounds did you apply for this?"

"We have our reasons," Deputy Dan informed her with a sneer from his perch behind Sullivan's left shoulder.

The sheriff frowned at his deputy, a loaded, keep-your-mouth-shut frown and turned back to Alison. "I'm sure that on his visit here yesterday Deputy Pike told you that we're in the midst of a rather sensitive investigation."

"To be honest, Sheriff," I said, joining them on the porch, "we couldn't make much sense of what Deputy Dan—" I quickly corrected myself, "Deputy Pike, was saying at all. I think you do owe us a bit more of an explanation than this."

"Well, let's not get ahead of ourselves," the sheriff said with a crafty smile. "What I'd like to do is first have Ms. Scholling here take me on a quick tour of the house. Nothing disruptive, just a quick peek into each room. After that, we can all sit down and have a nice chat, turn over our cards, so to speak."

"Can they do that?" I asked Alison. "Can they just storm into your house like that, with no just cause?"

"We've got plenty of just cause," Deputy Dan said.

"No one's talking to you, asshole," I said.

"Hey!" Deputy Dan began, taking a step toward me, but Sullivan cut him off.

"Pipe down, son," he said to me. "You're not behaving like an innocent man."

"What, only criminals think he's an asshole?" I asked. The sheriff actually smiled at that one, for just an instant, but Deputy Dan's hand suddenly move to clutch the top of the hardwood baton clipped to his belt. "Little shit!" he muttered.

"Okay!" Sullivan said, this time with authority. "That's enough! Now this is what's going to happen. The three of you," he indicated Chuck, Lindsey, and me, "are going to sit on this porch with Deputy Pike. You're all going to get along famously. In the meantime, Ms. Scholling and I are going to take a short walk through the house. If everything's in order, I promise you that I'll sit right down and explain to you what it is that's going on. If it's not," he fixed me with a dour expression, "then you'll all be the ones doing the explaining."

He beckoned to Alison, who flashed us a helpless look and pulled open the front door. Sullivan followed her inside, closing the door behind him. The three of us sat on the top stair while Deputy Dan stood fuming over us on the porch. Chuck, whose

face had been drained of all color the moment Sullivan had produced the warrant, stared straight ahead with wide eyes. Lindsey,
sitting between us, leaned against me and I sat back against the
stair post keeping my eyes on Deputy Dan. To my surprise, I
wasn't terribly dismayed by this turn of events. There seemed to
be a surreal inevitability to everything, as if I'd subconsciously
known all along that we'd end up in this situation. Besides, I truly
felt that Jack would never press charges against us. We'd come up
here to help him, it was too crazy to think we could end up in jail
for that.

I was so certain of all this, so convinced that everything would
turn out fine, that it took an extra few seconds to register when
Sheriff Sullivan reappeared with an expressionless Alison and
asked us if we all wouldn't terribly mind climbing into the back
of his car for a ride down to the Sheriff's Office.

33

Contrary to what I'd expected, the Sheriff's Office was not in the center of town, but stood by itself just beyond the Sunoco station on Route 57. It was a solitary, square, one-story building situated in the center of a concrete lot, with a slatted, wood facade on the front, but raw bricks and cinder blocks on the other three sides. Sullivan led us in through a small waiting room comprised of a couch, a low end table with an ashtray, a red plastic 'no smoking' sign right next to it, and some *People* magazines. The top magazine had a picture of Jack on it, and across the picture, printed in bold-faced block letters was the word "MISSING." Above the table was a window that looked into the dispatcher's office. One of the dispatchers, a matronly, older woman who wore a beige cardigan that was definitely not standard Sheriff's Department issue, smiled at Sullivan and pressed a button on the underside of her desk to buzz us through the locked wooden door. "Hey, Rhoda," Sullivan greeted her.

The other woman, ten years younger with industrial strength blond hair, was speaking into her headset while typing into a computer screen. "Well, don't you think it's a bit early to be drunk already, Earl?" she was saying. "I know that, but she's locked you out of the house because you're drunk, and you remember what happened the last time you got drunk." She put her hand over the mouthpiece and turned to Sullivan. "Earl Pender's drunk again and Millie locked him out of the house." Sullivan sighed and turned to Deputy Dan. "Why don't you get him, Dan. I'll take this from here."

"But we're in the middle of—"

"I got it covered, Dan," Sullivan said, with just the slightest edge in his voice. "You go get him and drop him off at his brother's place, okay?" Deputy Dan glared at him, but nodded in submission, then glared at us for good measure. I smiled my best fuck-off-little-man smile and he marched off in disgust. Sullivan led us back through a bank of empty desks and past his office into a small conference room that, judging from the condiments stacked on the counter, also doubled as a lunch room. "Debra," he called before he closed the door. "tell Millie we're dropping him off at Ray's." He closed the door, tossed his hat onto the table, sat down at the head and motioned to the rest of us to take seats as well.

We sat around the table, the four of us and Sheriff Sullivan, each of us trying to decide where to look. He looked at us and we looked at him. He looked at his watch and we looked at each other. This went on for a long enough time to make us all uncomfortable. I thought of the interrogation rooms on *NYPD Blue* and looked for a two-way mirror but there were no mirrors at all in the room. Sullivan scratched his chins thoughtfully, the tips of his fingers disappearing into the folds of flesh above his neck. Finally he cleared his throat and said, "Jack Shaw."

Even Jack's name could make a dramatic entrance. Sullivan's utterance created an instantly tangible change in the air, as if the temperature had just fallen ten degrees. He looked at all of us, gauging our reactions, and his eyes finally settled on me, waiting expectantly.

"The movie star?" I asked.

He smiled, or at least his mouth smiled, but his eyes hadn't gotten the memo, and they continued to bore into me with a cold stare. "Son," he said to me. "Don't piss on my leg and tell me it's raining." He turned away from me to look at everyone else. "I think you're all smart enough to realize that I know quite a bit more already than you first supposed. What we have here is a famous movie star who has disappeared under suspicious circumstances, and four people connected with him staying together, for no apparent reason, in a house where one room was clearly used as a cell of some kind. Two of you look like you got the shit beat out of you, one apparently from a car accident and one from who the hell knows what."

"Are you accusing us of kidnapping Jack Shaw?" Alison asked.

"Oh, I know you kidnapped him," the sheriff said with a grin. "I'm just wondering where he is now, and if maybe you killed him, too."

"That's ridiculous," Lindsey declared. "We're all good friends of Jack's. Why would we want to hurt him?"

"That's what I'm working on," Sullivan responded, scratching his neck again.

"Something's missing," I said.

"What's that?"

"There's something you're not telling us. You obviously have a reason to think we're involved with Jack's disappearance, and I'm hoping, for your sake, that it was more than just a paranoid call from Seward." Sullivan's eyes darted away when I mentioned Seward, and I knew we'd been right.

"Now how would you know about that?" Sullivan asked.

"How else would you have come to us?" Chuck asked. "Who are you, Columbo? We know Seward thinks we're involved. He called us, too."

Sullivan frowned and I could tell that Seward had neglected to mention that small detail. "Mr. Seward did call us," Sullivan admitted. "Which is why I sent my deputy to check it out."

"But something happened after that," Alison said, thinking out loud. "Something happened that gave you enough to go for a warrant."

Sullivan didn't answer her. Instead, he leaned his chair onto the two back legs, his belly pressing insistently against his uniform shirt, and opened up the door a crack. "Rhoda, you want to get me the paper bag on my desk," he called. He closed the door and for a second it looked like he was teetering, like he might actually fall over backwards, but then he threw his weight forward and came down with a solid thud. A few seconds later, Rhoda stuck her head in, smiling kindly at us as if we'd come over to have milk and cookies with the sheriff, and handed him a white paper bag, the kind they give you when you buy a greeting card. "Some kids were playing over by Horn's Creek and they found this in the water." He reached into the bag and pulled out a dark, square object. "Their parents made them turn it in." He tossed the object onto the table and it landed with soft, slapping noise. It was a wallet. More specifically, it was Jack Shaw's wallet.

Of course, we didn't instantly recognize it as Jack's. I mean how well do you examine your friend's wallet? But why else would Sullivan be showing it to us? Still, Chuck had to open it and pull out Jack's waterlogged driver's license, still New York, probably the only state that persists in not laminating them, and a couple of credit cards before we could all accept it as such. It seemed strange that Jack should even own a wallet. Didn't his people handle things like cash and spending? Did movie stars really pull out their own wallets to get the check for dinner?

Alison held onto the wallet, rubbing the damp leather between her thumb and forefinger, her lower lip visibly quivering. Lindsey quickly put a hand on her lap and said, "It doesn't mean anything."

"Oh, it means a few things," Sullivan said. "I don't know all of them yet, but I know a bunch."

"What's Horn's Creek?" I asked.

"It's a small tributary off the Delaware that runs through a good part of the north woods here," Sullivan said. "I take it," he added skeptically, "none of you has ever been there?"

"I have," Alison said, her voice admirably steady. "We used to go hunting for salamanders there when I was little. It runs through the woods on the opposite side of the road from my folks' place, about a mile down."

"That's right," the sheriff said. "Now listen. I've been extremely forthright with you all. Now it's time for you to tell me what's going on." We all looked at each other. "Look," he said, his voice softer now. "I can tell you're all good people, and that maybe something was going on here that may have gotten a little out of control. But it's clear that Jack Shaw is, or was in these parts, and you all have something to do with that. Right now I'm thinking worst case scenarios, like kidnapping and murder. Why don't you tell me your side of this, and let's see if we can't get this whole mess straightened out."

Alison suddenly stood up, the metal legs of her chair screeching against the floor. "Are we under arrest, sheriff?" she asked.

He considered her briefly. "Not yet," he admitted.

"So you don't have enough to formally charge us," Alison said. "Which makes everything you just said nothing more than a theory. We have been worried about our friend for some time now. He has been battling a drug addiction and we offered him some help. As far as I know, he may have been on his way to see us when something happened to him." Her voice wavered a little as she said that, no doubt wondering what had happened to Jack. "So instead of sitting here spinning theories, I'd recommend that you do your job. You've got a missing person here," she held up Jack's wallet for a second and then tossed it back onto the desk, in front of Sullivan. "Find him."

There was a palpable silence when Alison finished her speech. None of us had ever seen her assert herself like that. We all looked over to the sheriff, waiting to see his reaction. He continued to look at Alison with a knowing smile, which I now realized was an affectation and not an indication that he actually knew anything worth smiling about. He picked up the wallet and considered it for a second before placing it back into the paper bag. "And how do you explain that room in your house?"

"Frankly, I don't know how to explain it," Alison said. "You'd have to ask my folks. It's their house."

"And where could I find your folks?"

"They're in Europe, but I don't know how easily you'll find them."

The sheriff stood up and walked across the room, so that we all had to turn in our chairs to look at him. "You all probably think I'm a real annoying hick, just some redneck county sheriff who doesn't know his ass from his elbow." He looked at us, as if waiting for someone to confirm that yes, that was about the sum of it, but no one said a word. "Well let me tell you what's going to happen now, what I was hoping wouldn't have to happen now. I'm going to have to call the FBI about this," he waved the white bag with the wallet at us, "and the FBI is going to send someone down here to ask a lot of questions. I'm sure they'll be particularly interested in the four of you." Sullivan turned and fixed his gaze on Alison, who was still standing. "And young lady, all your due process isn't worth shit to the FBI, you mark my words. They will have their way with you if they feel like it." He turned back to the rest of us. "In the meantime, you've got two little boys and their mothers who turned in this wallet. You can bet that by morning every farmer and his cow around here is going to know that Jack Shaw's wallet got fished out of Horn's Creek, and you know what that means?" He scowled, his eyes turning to slits, as if he'd tasted something particularly vile. "That means media, my friends. Trucks with satellite dishes, obnoxious reporters, and photographers running around this town like they own it." He leaned against the wall, placing his hands with Jack's wallet behind his back like a cushion. "Feebies and reporters, and god only knows what other kind of parasites are going to come up here to turn this town upside down, looking for their lost movie star. I need that," he said, picking his hat up off the table, "like I need a third armpit."

Sullivan finished his speech and put his hat back on his head in a practiced motion designed not to upset the carefully arranged remnants of his hair. The rest of us just stared at him, somewhat taken aback by the venom in his voice. He was probably sincere in his reluctance to call in the FBI, but not, I guessed, for the reasons he'd stated. Sullivan had wanted to crack the case himself, wanted to be the hero who discovered Jack Shaw's whereabouts. If he had pulled that off, I don't think he would have minded a media invasion. He'd be waiting for them with a smile and a freshly pressed uniform, standing so that the cameras caught his better side. If he had one.

"Can we go?" Lindsey asked him, sitting up in her seat.

"You're free to go," Sullivan responded bitterly. "But I wouldn't leave town. Like I said, the FBI's going to want to talk to you."

"We're not going anywhere," I said.

"I'm going to see to that. I'm going to have a deputy watching the house. And I'd appreciate it if you'd all give Rhoda your driver's licenses on the way out for a quick photocopy so that I can include it in my report. Unless," he flashed Alison a humorless grin, "your lawyer has a problem with that."

We emerged a few minutes later to wait for the car service Rhoda had ordered for us. The sun was high overhead, but the air hadn't warmed up much since that morning. We stood around in the parking lot, a subdued bunch, our thoughts filled with Jack and what possible string of events could have led to his wallet being found in the creek. I came up with a number of scenarios, some more imaginative than others, none very positive.

"Well, that tears it," Chuck said with a frown. "I guess I'm not going home after all."

Lindsey put her hands in her pockets and bounced lightly up and down, trying to resist the chill. "What are we going to do?" she asked.

"There's nothing we can do," Chuck said. "You know, when you operate on someone, the surgery can go perfectly, or you can have some rough moments. Either way you do the best you can and you sew 'em up, but you never know, not right away, whether you've solved the problem or not. There can always be post-op complications. You learn not to pat yourself on the back until you've seen the patient come out of it okay."

We all stared at Chuck, wondering what the hell he was talking about. "And this is related to our situation how?" I said.

"What we did was like surgery. We operated on Jack," Chuck said. "We did our best. We just don't know yet if he came out of it okay or not."

"Now you're a philosopher?" I said.

"Fuck you. It was a good metaphor."

"Simile."

"Whatever. I might as well take up philosophy. Once the FBI arrests me for kidnapping I'm not going to be a doctor anymore."

We all looked up at an approaching Buick, wondering if it was our cab, but it passed us to pull into the Sunoco station. A teenage boy got out and worked the pump while studying his reflection in the car window.

"Jack's dead," Alison said quietly. We all looked at her.

"You don't know that," Lindsey said. "There's barely a reason to even think it."

"I just wanted to say it," she said. "To see how it sounded."

"It sounded fucking grim, that's how it sounded," Chuck retorted. "Jesus, Alison!"

"Come on," she said. "We're all thinking it."

"I don't think he's dead," I said.

"Why not?" Alison asked me.

"I just can't be bothered," I grumbled, wondering if it was too soon for another codeine pill. Another approaching car slowed down, and this time I could see the plastic sign attached to the roof. "That's our ride," I said.

We all climbed in, Chuck in the front seat and the rest of us in the back. "Where are you all headed?" asked the driver, extinguishing his cigarette.

"Well, that's the question isn't it?" Chuck said.

34

At about three in the afternoon we got our first reporter. Her cameraman waited below while she knocked on the door.

"Who's there?" I asked, although we'd all watched her approach from the living room window, an attractive woman in her late twenties, with silky blond hair and a chocolate suit cut to show off her long, shapely legs. She strode up the lawn with a practiced air of confident indifference, and although she looked familiar, none of us was sure if it was because we'd seen her on television or because she just looked like we should have.

"My name is Sally Hughes, from Fox News," she said, the words carefully modulated so as to avoid being a rhyming couplet.

I opened the door, casually standing at an angle that kept me out of camera range. "Hi," I said. "Can I help you?"

"Is this 32 Crescent Lake Road?"

"What gave it away?" I said, looking pointedly at the gold numbers on the outside of the door.

"This is the Scholling residence, correct?"

"No," I said, doing my best to look perplexed. "The Schollings are in 42, around the other side of the lake."

"Really?" she said, annoyed. She pulled a folded sheet of note paper out of her jacket pocket and glanced at it, her brow furrowed. "They told me 32."

"Well, they were wrong then, weren't they?" I said, offering up an apologetic smile before closing the door. We watched her storm down the front walk, cameraman in tow, and into the blue van parked on the shoulder of the road. They pulled out fast, leaving tire marks on the road. "They're in an awful hurry," Lindsey remarked.

"Just looking to scoop the competition," Chuck said. "She'll be back."

And she was, ten minutes later, with a fresh coat of lipstick over a smile that seemed even more fake than it had the first time. She didn't even wait for her cameraman, but came walking hurriedly up to the front door while he was still climbing out of the van. This time Chuck went to the door. "Hello," Sally Hughes said to him. "I wonder if you'd care to be interviewed."

"For what show?" Chuck asked. At this point the cameraman caught up and she made a quick, practiced gesture for him to start filming.

"Fox News."

"Fox News," Chuck repeated. "Is this live?"

"No, it's for a segment we'll be doing live in a little while."

"What's the subject?"

"The disappearance of Jack Shaw."

"The movie star?"

She cracked a cynical grin. "Are you going to deny that you and the other people in this house are friends of Jack Shaw?"

"I don't know," Chuck said. "Are you going to accuse me of it?"

"I recently spoke with Jack Shaw's agent, Paul Seward, who is convinced that a group of Jack's friends kidnapped him and brought him to this house," Sally Hughes declared smartly. "Would you care to comment?"

"That's a lovely blouse you're wearing," Chuck said. "It shows off your breasts to great advantage."

"Excuse me?"

"Your breasts," Chuck said, speaking louder and exaggerating every syllable as he leaned into her microphone. "Your blouse shows them off well."

She made a frustrated signal at her cameraman, who stopped filming and lowered the camera, while unsuccessfully trying to hide his grin. "What are you doing?" she asked Chuck.

"You asked for a comment."

She was about to say something else when another van appeared on the road, pulling in behind the parked Fox van. "Hey," I said to Chuck. "NBC is here."

"Cool," Chuck said.

"Shit," Sally Hughes muttered, turning on her heel and storming back to the road.

"Oh man," Chuck said, watching her go before closing the front door. "That is one hot reporter. Did you see the legs on her?"

"This is getting interesting." Alison called to us from the living room. We all ran to the couch to watch the commotion outside. Sally Hughes and her legs were arguing with the man who'd climbed out of the NBC van, pointing to the house and then back down the road. Meanwhile, a white van with the ABC logo drove up from the other direction and parked across the street from the other two vans. The ABC van had a woman reporter as well as two men, who jumped out of the van and began hurriedly fiddling with the satellite machine on their roof.

"I'm having an OJ flashback," Chuck said.

"We'd better lock the gate," I said.

"We don't have a gate," Alison said.

"Oh. Don't bother then."

"Man," Chuck said, indicating Sally Hughes again. "Is it just me or is she seriously hot?"

"Are you ever not thinking about sex?" Lindsey said.

"Sex is like air," I said. "It isn't important unless you aren't getting any."

"Point taken," Lindsey said, patting Chuck sympathetically on the shoulder.

"Screw the both of you," Chuck said.

Within an hour there were six vans and a number of cars crammed onto the shoulders of Crescent Lake Road, and twenty or so news people and cameramen scurrying back and forth. All of the major networks seemed to be accounted for, as well as some of the tabloid television shows. Deputy Dan, who'd been parked down the road ever since our visit to the Sheriff's Office, couldn't help but be drawn into all the excitement. He parked his cruiser on our side of the road, blocking off the Schollings's driveway, and radioed for a pickup truck to come and deliver blue police barricades, which he used to cordon off the reporters on the opposite shoulder. Once he had the media penned in, Deputy Dan stood in the road, waving along the rare passing car and chatting with the reporters.

Pretty soon there were live broadcasts going out on all the networks, news correspondents earnestly telling the masses that Jack Shaw's wallet had been found in a creek not far from this house, in which four of his friends were staying under suspicious circumstances. That was pretty much all anyone knew, but they knew how to tell it over and over again, adding irrelevant bits of stray data and cautious speculation, as well as the occasional interview with an overly eager Deputy Dan.

"Does the Sheriff's Department believe that Jack Shaw was abducted?" asked Sally Hughes from Fox News.

"I can't comment on that at this time," Deputy Dan answered enthusiastically, staring directly into the camera as if searching for the millions of viewers he was addressing.

"Isn't it true that Sheriff Sullivan obtained a search warrant for this house?"

"I'm afraid I can't comment on that, either," he answered, although it was clear he was dying to. Sullivan had obviously had a session with him, telling him to keep his mouth shut or else.

"We have information that after finding Jack Shaw's wallet in a nearby river, Sheriff Sullivan searched this house, and subsequently questioned the four people staying here, people known to be friends of Jack Shaw's."

Deputy Dan stared at her uncertainly. "Um, was that a question?"

You could see the exasperation in Sally's eyes. "Can you confirm any of these facts?"

"Oh," said Deputy Dan, relieved to have located the question mark. "No comment."

"Will the FBI be interviewing the occupants of this house?"

"I assume so," Dan said.

"So the Sheriff's Department has notified the FBI?"

Deputy Dan looked positively crestfallen at his screw-up. "Now wait a minute . . .".

"You just said they would be questioning the occupants of this house, which means there has to be at least a suspicion of wrongdoing on a federal level, isn't that right?"

"You said that," Dan said defensively and you could see the fear in his eyes. "I never said that . . ."

"She is good," Chuck said appreciatively from the couch, where we were all spread out to watch the news.

"She's not a bad news correspondent either," Lindsey teased.

"I'd give her an exclusive," Chuck remarked salaciously.

"It's only an exclusive if you're offering something no one else has had," I said.

"True," Chuck admitted.

"I would almost welcome the FBI," Alison said. "At least then we'll know someone is out looking for Jack who's more competent than this loser."

The television was now showing stock footage of Jack from *Blue Angel*, standing in a restaurant with a cocky expression on his face as he addressed a mob boss who was eating there. The mob boss was played by a character actor whose name I couldn't remember, but I knew I'd seen him on Broadway in something or other. On TV Jack seemed fake, a product of Hollywood, like those computer image dinosaurs they used in *Jurassic Park*. The unreality of the whole situation suddenly hit me. Who was Jack Shaw? Was it this man on the screen, neatly sidestepping a lunging attacker and kicking him into the salad bar? Because that person was a stranger to me. And yet I recognized him as my friend Jack. We thought we knew the real Jack, that we could help him because he was our friend, but seeing him on television now, for the first time I found myself considering that this was the real Jack Shaw, and that our friend was just a piece of his past, left behind like the rest of us.

"We made a mistake," I said.

"What?" Alison asked, turning to look at me.

"We were so sure we were right," I said. "We were sure that we knew the real Jack, and that the famous Jack Shaw was just a job, or a persona, but it wasn't." I pointed to the screen, where Jack was now riding a motorcycle into the desert. "That's the real Jack Shaw," I said. "The person we knew isn't the real Jack, it's the old Jack, and he's gone."

"What are you saying?" Alison asked, pulling herself off the couch and turning to face me.

"We meant well," I said. "We meant to help him. But he wasn't ours to help. Not anymore."

Alison lifted the remote off the coffee table and turned off the television. She stood there for a moment, looking at the blank screen and then with a quick movement hurled the remote across the room, where it hit the wall with a hollow thunk just below a framed Monet poster and burst into pieces. In the instant of impact the television went on again, the remote managing to send out one last electronic signal before its annihilation.

"Hey!" Chuck yelled, jumping up from the couch. We watched her apprehensively, but throwing the remote seemed to have assuaged whatever tension that had been building up inside of her. She turned to me with a weary expression, and I found myself wondering again how much of a toll all of this was taking on her. "You're only half right," she said. "The question isn't which Jack is the real one. They're both real and that's the problem. There are two Jacks, and if you find that confusing, imagine how he must feel. He doesn't know who to be anymore."

We considered that for a moment. "Which one's doing the drugs?" Chuck asked stupidly.

"Shut up, Chuck," Lindsey said. "Alison, have you talked to Jack about this?"

"We used to talk about it," Alison said. "Before . . ."

The picture on the television was once again the front of the Scholling house, as Sally Hughes earnestly summed up her report. "*Once again, we are live in Carmelina, New York, in front of the house where it is now believed that Jack Shaw had been taken. Whether or not he was brought here of his own free will, and whether or not he is even still here, are questions to which we still have no answers. Town records show that the house is owned by one Leslie Scholling, although we do not know what connection if any she has to Jack Shaw . . ."*

The notion that this was going on right outside the house was somewhat unreal to me. I stared at the television, wondering if somewhere within the grainy image of the house was a group of electrons that represented me. I waved my arm, but it had no visible effect on the screen. Alison walked across the living room and drew the curtains, and on the screen I saw them move across the window. "Cool," Chuck said quietly, but then gasped as the screen suddenly showed him, standing in the doorway and smiling at Sally Hughes. "Shit!" he shouted, jumping up and pointing at the screen, as if we couldn't see it. They were showing the footage from Chuck's earlier interview, but they'd muted the sound so that Sally could speak over it. *"This man, who declined to give his name, is one of the people staying in the house, suspected by the police of having something to do with Jack Shaw's disappearance."*

"She can't do that!" Chuck said. "I'll lose my job!"

"Oh, relax," Lindsey said. "If you didn't want to be on television you shouldn't have jumped to open the door before."

"He was jumping at the reporter," I said. "Not the camera."

"Damn straight!" Chuck said, staring dumbstruck at his image on the screen. Then he quieted down and, running his fingers through his scalp said, "Man, is that how I look? I'm getting seriously bald." Suddenly, Sally Hughes was back on the screen, looking directly out at us. "We'll stay here as events develop. For Fox News, in Carmelina, New York, I'm Sally Hughes." I noticed that she had once again avoided rhyming Hughes and news. Chuck watched the screen intently until they cut back to the studio in Manhattan, and then sat back thoughtfully on the couch. "She's not going to get away with that," he said.

"Umm, she just did," Alison said. Chuck's beeper went off. He grabbed it off of his belt and frowned at the screen "Shit," he said, thumbing the button. "My mother." It went off again and he threw it across the floor, where it skidded into the debris of the remote control, scattering black plastic across the carpet. Not a good day for electronic appliances in the Scholling home.

"I'm hungry," Lindsey suddenly said, apropos of nothing. "Is anyone else hungry?"

"I could eat," I said.

"Me too," said Alison.

"Let's go out," Lindsey said.

"Out?" Chuck repeated, glancing skeptically through the blinds. "What will they do if we go out?"

"Probably follow us," I said.

"Who cares?" Lindsey said. "We're not prisoners."

"What about the cops?" Chuck asked. "We're not supposed to go anywhere."

"We'll be going right into the center of town," I said. "Surrounded by the paparazzi. What more could they ask for?"

"A white Bronco and a suicide note?" Lindsey offered.

Alison disappeared for a second and returned having thrown a bomber jacket over her sweatshirt. We all looked at her, smiling in the doorway. "Let's go," she said.

Jack once told me the trick to handling the paparazzi when they swarmed was simple. "Never back up." This way, he explained, they can't pin you down. "If you're walking, you keep walking. If you're standing, you keep your spot. It not only keeps you in control of the situation, but you look better in the magazines and on television."

The minute we stepped outside, the reporters and cameramen, as if responding to some invisible cue, charged as one, all discipline and adherence to the police barricades forgotten. We moved quickly toward Chuck's rental, but the mob was upon us. I stood my ground as per Jack's philosophy, only to get my toes stepped on and nearly smashed in the face by a television camera. Lindsey hustled me into the back seat with her, slamming the door on someone's overhead sound boom, which broke with a satisfying snap. Chuck and Alison made it into the front seats, and all the while the questions never stopped, the flashing lights and cameras circling us like gnats. "Have you been formally charged?" "Where's Jack Shaw?" "Which one of you is Alison Scholling?"

The cameras surrounded us, banging on the windows as the reporters clamored around the car. I saw Sally Hughes immediately to the left of a fat cameraman by my window. "Jesus," Lindsey muttered.

"Hey," Chuck yelled. "Watch the car!" He turned the ignition and threw it into gear. The reporters failed to back away in fear. Chuck rolled down his window halfway. "Can you please clear out there?" he asked.

His request was met with a frenzy of queries. "Are you leaving for good?" "Where's Jack Shaw?" "Are you going to see him?" "What are your names?"

Chuck stuck his arm out the window and waved his hand in a gentle up and down gesture, like someone waving an audience to silence before giving a speech. The reporters, sensing their evening sound byte, converged roughly on Chuck's window, pushing and squirming as they jockeyed for position. "What are you doing, Chuck?" Alison asked him through a false smile.

"Don't worry," Chuck said. "I know what I'm doing."

"That doesn't necessarily make it a good thing."

Chuck flashed her a devilish grin and then looked out at the reporters. "I know you have many questions and we want to answer them all," Chuck said. "You want to know where Jack Shaw is. So do we. We have not been charged with anything because we haven't done anything wrong. We're here because we're worried about our friend." There was another furious spate of questions, but Chuck waved them away. "From this point on," he declared, "I will speak only with Sally Hughes."

There was an angry, confused murmur from the crowd. "Why her?" someone asked.

"Because of her personal relationship with Jack Shaw," Chuck said matter-of-factly. "They were an item. I thought that was common knowledge."

There was a collective gasp from the crowd, and suddenly they all turned to face Sally Hughes. "Oh, for Christ's sake," she said. In the sudden lull, Chuck found the break in the crowd he was looking for and with tires screeching he peeled out of the driveway, leaving the reporters in a cloud of dust.

"What the hell was that?" I asked.

"It worked, didn't it?" Chuck said proudly, as he turned onto Route 57. On our left I saw Deputy Dan running toward his car at full speed while attempting to unholster his radio at the same time. The radio suddenly flew out of his hands and went skittering across the dirt shoulder of Route 57. Yet another electronic appliance biting the dust. I briefly searched for some significance in that observation and, finding none, returned to the matter at hand. "I'm not familiar with this particular technique, Chuck," I said from the back seat. "What did we actually accomplish back there?"

"*We* accomplished nothing," Chuck remarked, glancing at me in his rear view mirror. "*I,* on the other hand, accomplished a great deal."

"And that would be?"

"Foreplay," Chuck said.

"Pissing off Sally Hughes was foreplay?" Alison asked.

"You betcha."

"How so?"

"It's a thin line between anger and lust," Chuck said.

"Oh my god," Alison said. "And you believe what you're saying, don't you?"

"Absolutely," Chuck said. "You have to admit, she's thinking about me now."

"She's thinking about how she'd like to strangle you."

"Strangle me, mount me. It's all a question of sublimation."

"And I thought men didn't care about foreplay," Lindsey remarked wryly.

"Hey!" I said.

"Present company excluded, of course."

"Look," Chuck said, slowing down to take a curve. "Right now she's thinking about me and she's feeling something, right? Maybe it's negative, but it's still something. She's no longer indifferent to me. Now I've got something to work with. Between anger and indifference, I'll take anger every time."

"The saddest thing about this whole theory," I said, "is that on some level I actually agree with it."

"This sounds like a *Seinfeld* episode," Alison remarked.

"A bad one," Lindsey said.

"Hey, slow down," I said. We were passing the bend in the road where I'd hit the deer. There were black streaks that indicated the path of the Beamer's tires where they'd skidded off the road, and a jagged set of tire tracks cut deep into the grass all the way down to the shallow gully where I'd finally come to a stop. Here and there was a smattering of shattered orange and clear plastic from the front lights of the car. I'm not sure if I was steeling myself for a cinematic flashback, or hoping for one, but none came and we rounded the curve, leaving the site of my accident behind.

35

"A jelly jar . . . a garden hose," Chuck murmured thoughtfully. "A cheerleader's baton."

"No way," said the girl above the breasts Chuck was addressing. She was dressed in tight black slacks and an even tighter blue polyester shirt, the bottom three buttons opened to reveal her flat, tanned belly. She seemed very skinny for the breasts she was carrying.

"I'm telling you," Chuck said. "It's more common than you'd think."

"What else?"

"Cucumbers, an electric toothbrush."

"*Shut up!*" the girl squealed in delight.

The topic was *Things I've Pulled Out of People's Asses in the Emergency Room*, one in a handful of popular conversational gambits Chuck employed when flirting in bars. I was often skeptical that scatological talk could work as an aphrodisiac, but Chuck had proven the method successful on more than one occasion.

"I'm serious," he said, catching the bartender's eye and indicating the two shot glasses sitting in front of him. As the bartender filled them with Glenfiddich, Chuck straightened his back and rocked on his stool as he stretched, a move that expertly moved him a few inches closer to the girl he was talking to.

"He's good," Lindsey said appreciatively. We were watching from our vantage point a few stools down, eating a meal of grilled steak sandwiches and mashed potatoes.

"She can't be older than eighteen!" Alison said.

"She got in," I said, pointing to the bouncer, who sat on a stool by the door checking ID's. "She's at least twenty-one."

"A Cookie Monster finger puppet," Chuck said, tossing back the whiskey.

"No!"

"Oh, for heaven's sake," Alison groaned.

We were in a pub called McAvoy's, eating the house specials while we watched Chuck work on the girl. It was a dimly lit, wood-paneled room, with tables off to one side, and a recessed floor that had the bar, a small dance floor, and a pool table. The walls were adorned with framed, autographed pictures of aging celebrities and politicians, with nothing in common except that they all fit into the category of *People Who Would Never Be Caught Dead In Carmelina*. Frank Sinatra, Ed Koch, Marlon Brando, George Bush, Muhammad Ali, Buddy Hackett, and a host of others. Two lazy ceiling fans, installed ostensibly to disperse the thick smoke coming from the grills in the kitchen, seemed instead to be weaving the smoke into something thicker that hung suspended above us, creating a murky sense of intimacy. We'd been momentarily concerned that our notoriety would cause us some problems, but, if anything, the clientele seemed excited to have some quasi-celebrities to gawk at. It certainly wasn't hurting Chuck any. Walking in he'd slipped the guy at the door a fifty and said, "Please keep out the cameras, okay?" A quick nod, the money disappeared, and we went inside to eat. The dinner crowd was just beginning to taper off but the place was still full, and we'd only been able to get seated at the bar.

A few minutes after we'd arrived, Deputy Dan burst through the front door, stopping short when he saw us at the bar. He seemed very flustered, and unsure of what his next move should be. Lindsey smiled and waved to him and he reflexively waved back, which seemed to add to his confusion. Finally, he did an about-face and walked out of the pub. I walked over to the window and saw him double-parked across the street, smoking a cigarette and glowering at the reporters who clamored around the pub's window trying to get a glimpse of us inside.

Chuck and his new friend hopped off their stools and went over to look at the jukebox. A skinny guy with cratered skin and a mustache stopped behind us at the bar and tapped me on the shoulder. "You're the ones on television, huh?"

"That's us," I said.

"So, where is he?"

"Where is who?"

This seemed to confuse him. "You know who," he said. "Jack Shaw is who."

"You got me," I said.

He frowned, clearly disappointed with the way the conversation was going. "I saw Alec Baldwin once," he said. "Guy was real standoffish, you know?"

"I hear you," I sympathized.

"You really his friend?" he asked.

"I've never met Alec Baldwin."

"Nah. I mean Jack Shaw. He's your buddy?"

"Uh huh."

"How about that." He considered this intelligence for a few moments before nodding politely and moving on.

"Boy," Lindsey said as I turned back to the bar. "If being famous meant having scintillating conversations like that every time you went out, I'd be doing coke, too."

"Come On Eileen" began playing on the jukebox. I looked up to see if it had been Chuck's choice and saw him smiling at us as he led the girl back to the bar.

"This song always brings me back to high school," Lindsey said, singing along quietly with the too ra loo ra yays.

"What else?" I asked.

"I don't know. Men at Work, Pat Benatar, Simple Minds, you know, the theme from *The Breakfast Club*."

"Human League," I said. "You know, 'Don't You Want Me.' And everything by Duran Duran."

" 'Tainted Love,' " Chuck offered, leaning between us to grab some beer nuts off the bar. " 'Hurts So Good,' 'Safety Dance.' "

"Who sang that again?" Lindsey asked.

"Men Without Hats," I said. "But as far as I know, they only sang it once."

"Never heard of them," said the girl with Chuck, and I wondered how old she'd been when the eighties one-hit-wonder bands had played. "Do you like any old bands?" I asked her.

She thought about it for a minute, licking her lips. I noticed that she had a barbell through her tongue. "Pearl Jam," she said, after a little bit.

I gave Chuck a look. "What?" he asked with a grin, leading her away from the bar. "They're pretty old."

"You're older," I said to the back of his head, then looked over to Alison, who was sipping her beer thoughtfully. "What's on your mind?" I asked.

"Three guesses."

"Where do you think he is?" I asked.

"I have no idea," she said. "It really makes no sense."

"We'll find him."

"We aren't even looking."

"I mean, he'll turn up."

"I hope so," she said with a sigh. "I keep thinking that if we hadn't tried this, he'd be back in California, and I'd be able to speak to him, the same as always, you know. Aside from all the worry about what might have happened to him, I just miss him, you know?"

I saw Lindsey looking over my shoulder, slightly alarmed, and I spun around on my stool to find myself face to chest with Paul Bunyan from the luncheonette. My heart skipped a beat, but I quashed the reflex to bolt from my chair. After all, I saw no sign of the Winchester, and the guy had served us some good soup. "How you doing?" he said.

"Good," I said hesitantly.

"You and your friend get everything worked out?"

"What? Oh yeah, sure. Thanks."

"I just wanted to tell you thanks," he said, rubbing the bandanna on his skull.

"For what?"

"For them," he said, pointing out the window at the reporters. "I did more business today then the last two weeks put together."

"Really?"

"You bet. I've even got a Jack Shaw Special now. Any sandwich and a beverage for three bucks."

"Good idea," I said.

"They're eating it up." He put a huge paw on my shoulder. "No hard feelings about the other day?"

"Of course not."

"I hope your friend turns up okay. I like his movies."

"Thanks."

"Okay then," he said with a gap-toothed smile and lumbered out of the bar.

"What the hell was that about?" Lindsey asked.

Before I could answer we were approached by a man in a navy suit and a crew cut who pulled over a stool and said with a grin, "Hi. Do you mind if we talk for a minute?"

"So much for keeping out the reporters," Lindsey said. "We have no comment."

"I'm Agent Don Allender, with the FBI," he said, his grin never faltering. It was certainly an effective conversation stopper.

"This day keeps getting better and better," I muttered, but quietly since I was a little scared of him.

He studied me for a moment. "What'd the other guy look like?" he asked.

"Huh?"

"Your face," he explained, pointing to my eyes. I had forgotten for the moment that they were still fairly bruised. I told him about the deer and he nodded sympathetically.

"You're here to find Jack?" Alison asked, turning fully around to face Allender.

"Not exactly," he answered, unbuttoning his suit jacket to sit more comfortably. He looked like he was posing, and I wondered if the FBI actually had classes on how to sit and stand while on duty.

"What then?"

"Well, I'm here to ascertain whether or not there's a reason for us to be involved."

"And what would constitute a reason?" I asked.

"If you kidnapped him, that would pretty much do it for me," he said pleasantly.

"Well, I'm sorry to disappoint you," Lindsey said.

"Wait a minute," Alison said. "If he hasn't been kidnapped, then you don't bother looking for him? Either way he's missing, isn't he?"

"Oh, we're looking already," Allender said.

"Really?" Alison asked skeptically.

"You bet," he said, with just enough Midwestern twang to go with his ruddy complexion.

Chuck joined us, leaving his new acquaintance to consult excitedly with two other girls standing near the pool table. "Who's this?" he asked.

"Don Allender," said Don Allender.

"FBI," I said.

"New York office," Don added helpfully.

"No way," Chuck said.

"Way," Don smiled.

"I never met an FBI agent," Chuck said. "What's it like?"

"It's all right," Don smiled. "Beats working for a living."

"I bet."

"How old are you?" I asked Allender.

"What does that have to do with anything?" he asked, mildly taken aback.

"Just curious."

"Thirty."

"Us too," I said, indicating our group. There seemed to be something less intimidating about the FBI when you realized the agents were your age.

"It's a weird age, isn't it?" Don said, surprising us all with his conversational tone. "Leads to a lot of annoying introspection."

"Tell me about it."

"So," Don said, almost apologetically. "Did you kidnap him?"

"Are we on the record?" Alison asked him.

"Would you like to first talk off the record?"

We looked around at each other. "Could we have a minute?" Alison asked.

"Sure," Don said, getting up and grabbing a stool at the end of the bar. He asked the bartender for a Molson and turned around with his back to the bar, looking around the room with a wistful expression on his face.

"I think I want to level with him," Alison said.

"We'd be incriminating ourselves," Chuck objected.

"We haven't done anything wrong, really," Alison said. "He seems like a friendly guy, like a guy who would understand."

"They all seem like that!" Chuck retorted. "It's to catch you off guard."

"And you've talked to how many FBI agents?" I asked. I agreed with Alison. Don seemed okay.

"I agree with Alison," Lindsey said. "He's not like Sullivan or Deputy Dan, who are looking to be heroes. He seems like a decent guy with no real agenda. I think we can trust him."

"I never trust anyone over thirty," Chuck grumbled.

"Which explains your taste in women," Alison said.

"Oh, bite me."

"I'm too old for you, Chuck," she said with a giggle and then, inexplicably threw her arms around him. He still looked pissed, but he returned the hug. "Okay," he said. "But if we wind up in jail over this, I'll hold you personally responsible."

"Ben?" Alison turned to me. "Are we unanimous?"

I looked over at Don Allender, sipping at his beer thoughtfully. That didn't seem like proper behavior for a federal agent. I reminded myself that he had entered high school the same time I did, listened to the same bands and watched the same television shows. It was probably a lonely job, running around wherever the FBI sent you. He certainly seemed eager enough for conversation.

The fact that he was drinking a beer while on duty made him seem even less threatening. "Okay," I said. "If we're going to make a new friend, he may as well work for the FBI."

The rest of the night passed in an increasingly drunken haze. We told Don everything, and it turned out that he'd already pieced most of it together. When we asked him how all he would say is, "Hey, did I mention I work for the FBI?" After he'd agreed with Alison that it didn't seem likely that we would face prosecution, we were so relieved that we started a tab and began celebrating with tequila shots. Don removed his jacket and joined in the celebration. "I've been on the road for the government for over three years," he complained while licking the salt off his hand. "I turned thirty and suddenly I was alone in the world. No family, no friends. No real relationships of any kind." He downed the tequila and squeezed a lemon rind into his mouth. "I mean, what are we living for?"

Later:

"Do you watch *ER*?" Don asked Chuck.

"Sometimes," Chuck said.

"Do you, like, sit there and point out everything that isn't realistic?"

"Nah. They're pretty well researched, they've got doctors on staff. The only part that's really bogus is the way they spew out all that technical jargon while they're running around. If we really shouted out all those instructions so fast there would be a shitload of mistakes."

"Really?"

"Also, that guy Carter. He's an intern but he's always on E.R. rotation. That's not how it works. Hey," Chuck said. "Do you watch *The X-Files*?"

"Sure."

"Do you sit there and point out all the FBI bullshit there?"

Don looked up from his beer chaser and, wiping his mouth with his shirtsleeve, said, "To whom?"

Later:

I made my way somewhat unsteadily toward the jukebox, a fistful of quarters in one hand, a Sam Adams in the other, with the aim of playing every song from high school that I could find. "Centerfold," by the J. Giles Band, "Ninety-nine Red Balloons," by Nina, Billy Idol's "Dancing with Myself," Howard Jones's "No One Is to Blame," and "Space Oddity," not David Bowie's but that other one, with the bouncy synthesizer, by Peter something or other. The jukebox was like an eighties time capsule. I noticed the "Theme from *St. Elmo's Fire*," but by then I was out of change. I'd surpassed my personal limit on tequila, but rather than feeling sick, I was suffused with a warm, expanding laziness. My mouth was still tart from the lemons and salt. Lindsey moved toward me with liquid grace, as if in slow motion, and asked me to dance. "I taste like lemons," I said, sucking on the insides of my cheeks. "Umm," she murmured, "let me taste," and pressed herself hard up against me, her tongue slipping between my lips before her kiss even got there.

Later:

The girls went off to the bathroom. The television over the bar was showing a commercial with Michael Jordan and Bugs Bunny, which prompted Don, Chuck, and me to have the obligatory sports conversation. Was Jordan really the best ever? Don't look at his points, look at his shooting percentage. And what about our own pathetic Knicks? It's too bad Ewing's ego can't play center instead of him. At least the Yankees look good for next year again. Don told us about how he played football in college. "I mean, I'm not saying I was the greatest, but I was good enough in high school to get a partial scholarship to Indiana. So I'm playing there freshman year, doing all right, you know? Nothing to write home about, but I'm starting to develop some real ability. Anyway, we're at practice one afternoon having a scrimmage, you know, white shirts and colors, and I'm running long for a pass, and my foot comes down on something funny, twists my ankle all out of whack, rips a bunch of ligaments." He made a circular motion with one hand, a kind of italicized et cetera symbol while chugging on his beer with the other. "Turns out some guys had been drinking on the field the night before and someone left a beer can. That's what I landed on." He frowned and shook his head sadly, as if reliving the injury. "You just don't expect, in a program like Indiana University, to have fucking beer cans on the field during practice. It's not professional." Chuck and I nodded in drunken agreement. "I mean Jesus, a beer can . . ."

Later:

McAvoy's was packed. The song playing on the jukebox was Madonna's "Crazy for You," and everyone was on the floor for a slow dance. I wrapped myself around Lindsey, her right leg planted firmly against the inside of my thigh, her head bumping softly against my chin as we danced, like a boat tied up at the dock. A few couples away, Chuck was dancing with the girl who thought Pearl Jam was an old band. She nuzzled his neck while he whispered to her, running his hands provocatively up and down her sides. On the opposite side of the small dance floor, Alison was dancing companionably with Don, her back to us, her head resting on his shoulder in quiet meditation. Her hair hung down behind her, covering his hand which rested on her back. I saw him move his hand out, looking at the hair spilling over his fingers as if he couldn't believe it was really there. He let it drop against her back and unconsciously brushed out the loose tangles with his fingers, a gentle gesture that seemed, for no apparent reason, to express a profound sadness within him. For a moment, it felt like college again, and I closed my eyes, trying to submerge myself in deja vu. I inhaled softly, smelling the uniquely familiar combination of beer, smoke, sawdust, and shampoo and for a moment the illusion was complete. But then the song ended and Third Eye Blind came on, singing "Semi-Charmed Life," as nineties as you could get, and Chuck's date began churning and gyrating with delight, waving her hands and letting out a whoop as her decade reasserted itself, and the moment was gone.

Later:

McAvoy's was closing and we were all too wasted to drive. I suggested asking the reporters for a ride home since they would no doubt follow us there anyway, but when we got outside we found that they'd called it a night. Deputy Dan was sleeping in his car across the street, and we decided to let him be. Eventually Paul, the guy who worked the door, offered us a lift home. We all piled into his old blue van, which smelled of yeast and coffee. Don declined the lift, explaining that he was staying at an inn down the block. There were handshakes and hugs all around, and Don promised he'd be out to see us tomorrow. We watched him from the rear window of the van, waving wistfully at us until we turned the corner. The benches in the van weren't bolted too tightly, and they rocked every time Paul accelerated. Only after he'd dropped us off did it dawn on me that we were only three. Chuck and his new friend had disappeared.

36

The next morning I staggered into the kitchen, queasy and dehydrated, to find the girl Chuck had been hitting on last night sitting in one of the kitchen chairs, eating a hard-boiled egg and thumbing through a Sharper Image catalogue. "Hi," she said, her voice reverberating off my eardrums like they were rubber. I muttered a hello, and shoved a mug under the coffee maker. Bart Simpson stared up at me from the side of the mug, recommending that I not have a cow. My brain seemed to be struggling with the urge to burst out of my head and find a dark, quiet cave to crawl into.

"Hangover?" she asked brightly. I couldn't tell if it was her mouth or my head that needed a volume control. Probably both.

"Thanks, I've already got one," I said, sitting down in the chair across from her, holding my mug in both hands as if I could somehow absorb the coffee quicker that way.

"Ha ha," she said, taking a dainty little bite out of her egg.

"Where's Chuck?" I asked after a long sip.

"Who? Oh, he's sleeping like a dead man."

I raised an eyebrow. "You didn't kill him, did you?"

"Hardly," she said with a lascivious grin.

"I don't think I caught your name."

"Jenna."

"I'm Ben."

"Hi," she said, rather pointlessly. "What happened to your face?"

"I was born like this."

"Oh shit, I'm sorry," she exclaimed and then, getting it, giggled. "Oh. Very funny."

We sat in silence for a moment, I sipping my coffee intensely, she taking ridiculous little bites from her egg, holding it between her thumb and forefinger as if she were afraid she might crush it. "Who the hell buys these things?" she said, and for a second I wondered if she meant the egg, but then I saw that she was indicating one of the gadgets in the catalogue, a key chain/pepper spray/laser pointer. I decided the question had been rhetorical. The next one wasn't. "Say, Ben, do you think you could give me a lift?" I saw some egg yolk caught under the metal barbell running through her tongue, and the reason for her peculiar little bites became clear.

It was still pretty early, and the media camped out across the street were still shivering over their first coffees of the day, so we were able to get into Chuck's car, which he'd somehow managed to drive home last night, and out of the driveway before they could scramble to their cameras. The steering wheel felt like an icicle in my hands, and my chest muscles contracted in the cold air. "Jesus, it's cold," I hissed, turning the heat up full blast, which served only to blow a jet of frigid air into my face. Jenna giggled and waved at the reporters, twisting around in her seat until they were out of view. "Cool," she said, plopping back down in the passenger seat.

"I can't believe Chuck drove home," I said. "He was pretty wasted."

"I drove," she said proudly. I didn't bother pointing out that she'd been drinking, too. Jenna pulled some makeup out of a small leather knapsack and began applying it, pulling down the sun visor to use the mirror on it. When she was done, she cracked the window and lit up a cigarette. She leaned over and proffered the pack to me, shrugging when I declined and tossing it back into the knapsack. "It's here, on the right," she suddenly said.

"What, the high school?" I said.

"Yep."

"You've got to be kidding me."

"Everyone thinks I look older," she said boastfully.

"Older than what?"

"What?"

"Please tell me that you're eighteen."

"Okay. I'm eighteen," she said with a smirk.

"Really?"

"Maybe."

"You don't think your parents missed you last night?"

She dismissed my concern with a carefree wave. "I was sleeping at a friend's."

"Well, I guess that's sort of true."

"You don't tell and I won't."

I pulled over to the curb, staying well behind the buses that were parked in front of the school letting out a seemingly endless flow of students, who broke ranks as soon as they exited the buses, mixing effortlessly into the youthful chaos of the school's front yard. Despite the cold, no one seemed to be in a rush to get inside. Why try to be older, I thought to myself, when you could still be here.

"Thanks for the ride, Ben," said Jenna, leaning over and planting a warm kiss on my cheek. "You're the best." In one fluid motion she was out of the car and strolling toward the school gates. Feeling oddly paternal, I watched as she bounded gracefully up the three stairs and in to the front yard, where she turned to give me one final wave before the crowd consumed her.

When I pulled into the driveway, the reporters were back at their posts across the road, cameras and microphones in hand. There seemed to be more of them than yesterday, all packed into the barricaded area. I noticed a number of men holding still cameras with large telephoto lenses and judged them to be freelance photographers. The paparazzi had arrived. I drove by them with my windows closed and pulled into the driveway. I hoped for Chuck's sake that none of them had gotten a good view of Jenna. I heard the sound of a bouncing ball and looked up to see Jeremy standing in the driveway. Taz sat on his haunches on the grass behind the basketball hoop, his attention alternating between furiously cleaning his front paws and alertly watching the reporters below. Jeremy was wearing a hooded sweatshirt under his windbreaker, which must have made it a bit difficult to shoot. As I stepped onto the court I could hear the faint clicks of the cameras from down on the road, and I wondered what they were going to do with pictures of me.

"Hi," Jeremy said.

"Hi yourself." He passed me the ball and I tossed in a lay-up. I felt my bruised muscles groan in protest, but it felt good to move. "Still playing hooky?"

"I guess." He took my pass and put in his own lay-up, which rolled lazily around the rim before falling through the net. "Did you really do it?" he asked me.

"Do what?"

"Kidnap Jack Shaw. They're saying on TV that you all kidnapped him."

"Do I look like a kidnapper?" I asked him, stopping my dribble.

"No."

"Jack's my friend."

"So why are they all here?" he indicated the press down on the street who, for lack of anything else to do, were idly snapping a few pictures of us.

"Listen," I said, turning him away from the telephoto lenses. "If you had a friend who was in trouble, wouldn't you do anything you could to help him?"

"You mean if he was on drugs?"

"Okay, yeah. If he was on drugs."

Jeremy thought about it for a minute. "Yeah, I guess so. But I wouldn't kidnap him."

"Well," I said, sitting down on the ground. "What if you knew you could help him, but he was so messed up he wouldn't let anyone help him. So messed up that you were worried he might die before anyone helped him?"

"He was really that messed up?"

"He was. And we were desperate, because we thought our friend might die." It occurred to me that Jack was Jeremy's idol, and I hoped I wasn't ruining that for him. The kid had been through enough disappointments already.

"So you brought him here to help him?" Jeremy asked. "To get him off the drugs."

"That's right," I said. "But don't tell them that." I pointed to the reporters.

"So where is he now?"

"That," I said, pulling myself up to my feet, "is the question."

"You don't know?" he asked, shocked.

"He escaped," I confessed.

"And that's when they found his wallet?"

"Yep."

Jeremy took the ball and tossed it in the air thoughtfully. "Do you think he's dead?"

"I hope not, but we're all really worried about him."

There was a pause. "Tonight is Halloween," he finally said.

"Is it really?" I said, surprised that I wasn't aware of it.

"I don't think I'm going to be able to trick-or-treat," He said.

"The mask," I remembered. "You never found it?"

"Nope. Besides, my mom won't let me go out alone, and my sister doesn't want to go."

"You can come over and hang out with us if you want."

He looked up at me. "Are you going to dress up?"

"I don't know. I haven't really thought about it."

"It's Halloween," Jeremy admonished me. "You're supposed to dress up."

"That's the law, huh?"

"Yes."

"Well, why don't you come over for dinner and I'll see what I can do."

"I'll have to ask my mom."

"Okay."

We heard a rumbling sound and looked down the road to see a white school bus pull up to the front of the house. The doors opened and a slew of teenagers began filing out and onto the roadside where the press was camped. Most of the kids were girls, in jeans and jackets, but I noticed a handful of boys scattered throughout the mix. Deputy Dan came running over, waving his hands in frustration, but the kids seemed to be ignoring him for the most part. The last kids to get off the bus were carrying sheets of white oak tag, which they handed out to a few of their peers.

The members of the media scrambled to their cameras and began filming and interviewing a number of the teenagers, who seemed only too happy to comply. From where Jeremy and I were standing, we could make out the writing on the oak tag. *Bring Back Jack; We're praying for you, Jack;* and simply *Where's Jack?* In all, I counted about thirty kids.

"What are they doing?" Jeremy asked.

"It looks like they're going to hold a vigil," I said. Deputy Dan had now run back to his car and was jabbering excitedly into his radio. The media, grateful for something to do, were swarming around the kids now, searching for faces and sound bites to put on their next transmission.

"What's that?"

"They're going to stay there until Jack turns up."

"Why?"

"I don't know," I said. "I guess it beats school."

"They're going to get pretty cold."

We stood there for a little bit watching the scene on the road as if something might happen at any second, but for the most part the kids just seemed to be standing around. The problem with vigils is that, aside from actually being there, there isn't really a whole lot to do. Some stood, some sat on the ground, some smoked, some huddled for warmth. After a few minutes the reporters lost interest and went back to the warmth of their vans to await further developments. After a minute more, Jeremy and I went to our respective houses to do the same.

37

There are doubtless many ways to react upon learning that you may have inadvertently committed statutory rape. I wasn't sure what Chuck's way would be, but I had a feeling it would be something extreme. Either furious denial or complete indifference. And then there was the not unreasonable possibility that it wouldn't be news to him, that he'd known all along that she was in high school. I wasn't sure how I felt about that, but I knew I wasn't in the mood to hear the justifications that would come, regardless, so I elected not to mention the high school to him. Besides, my impression of Jenna was that she had certainly done this sort of thing before and seemed perfectly happy about it, so I didn't think she'd make any trouble for Chuck.

I found him sitting at the kitchen table eating a bagel and drinking coffee while flipping through Carmelina's local paper. He didn't seem remotely hung over or concerned that Jenna was nowhere to be found. His ease with the one-night stand bespoke a long-standing familiarity that made me suddenly feel sorry for him. I wondered if he ever got lonely.

"Are we in there?" I asked.

"Front page." He said it with a mouth full of bagel, so it came out "mom mage." He finished chewing and said, "It's pretty even-handed though. They're making a much bigger deal about Jack's wallet than about us. All it says is that the sheriff questioned some friends of Jack's vacationing in the area. It doesn't draw any conclusions. Maybe things are dying down a little."

"Look out the window."

"What?"

"Just look."

He got up and walked over to the living room window. He stood there looking out for about thirty seconds. "Holy shit," he finally said.

"Exactly."

"Where'd they come from?" he asked, as I joined him at the window.

"I don't know, maybe the local high school."

We watched as one of the guys turned on a boombox and began shuffling in place. Two girls in skintight leggings and sweatshirts jumped up and began dancing with wild abandon, as if it were the most natural thing in the world to be dancing on the shoulder of a road in the middle of the day. They were probably dancing to keep warm, and it must have been working because one of the girls removed her sweatshirt and tied it around her waist, never once stopping her hip-grinding motion. Chuck whistled appreciatively and said, "Dude, you gotta love high school girls."

Don Allender showed up around lunchtime. By then the crowd had swelled to over fifty kids who had nothing better to do, and

Deputy Dan had been forced to set up additional barricades at the foot of the Schollings's lawn to keep them from crossing the street and running up to the house. Alison and Lindsey had awakened with hangovers even more severe than mine and were sitting in the kitchen with the lights out, hydrating themselves by alternately sipping coffee and cold water. Chuck and I were watching the crowd from the living room when Don arrived, ignoring Deputy Dan's urgent protests as he pulled his rented car into the driveway behind Chuck's. It was starting to look like a Ford dealership out there. We watched him emerge from the car in his freshly pressed navy suit and flip his badge for Deputy Dan. A small conversation between the two men ensued, with a good deal of frowning on the part of Deputy Dan.

"That guy" Don told us when we greeted him on the porch, "got into the gene pool when the lifeguard wasn't watching."

"He definitely has severe delusions of adequacy." I agreed as we stepped inside.

"It's such a cliché," Chuck said. "The small-town deputy with a room temperature IQ Like that deputy on *BJ and the Bear.*"

"Perkins," Don said, impressing me. "He worked for Sheriff Lobo."

"Have you met the sheriff?" I asked.

"He's a fictional character."

I grinned. "I mean Sullivan."

"Sure. We actually spent the morning together, canvassing all the motels and inns in the area."

"No luck, I take it."

"None. The truth is, he could be anywhere."

"Do you think he's dead?" Chuck asked.

Don took a deep breath. "I have no way of knowing," he said. "But for a guy as famous as Jack Shaw to not be spotted for three days . . . It doesn't look good."

Chuck motioned to Don to be quiet as Alison and Lindsey joined us in the living room, but Alison said, "It's okay. He isn't saying anything we aren't all thinking."

"I'm sorry," Don said. "I wish there was more I could do."

"That's how we all feel."

"Well, if it's any consolation, if he were my friend, I would have done the same thing you all did."

"We all allegedly did," Chuck reminded him.

"Right." Don smiled. At some point the night before he had become our ally, and while I didn't quite see how or why it happened, I was suddenly grateful for his reassuring presence.

"So," Lindsey said. "What do we do now?"

"We wait," Chuck said.

"Are you going to be sticking around?" Alison asked Don.

"I'm not sure," Don said to her, and I thought he might have been blushing ever so slightly. "I'd like to stay a little while, see if anything happens." It occurred to me that Don had a crush on Alison.

"Well," I said, "tonight's Halloween and we need to throw a little party." They all looked at me with puzzled expressions. "I kind of told Jeremy that he could hang with us tonight, you know? His mom's not letting him trick-or-treat."

"I guess we might as well do something," Alison said.

"We don't have to do much," I said. "We can just have some dinner and watch whatever Halloween movies are on TV."

We were interrupted by a knock on the door. I opened it to find Deputy Dan standing there. I thought about Chuck's *BJ and the Bear* reference and smiled. "Yes?" I said.

"There's a guy down there who said you want to see him. Wants me to let him come up to the house."

I looked over his shoulder and saw Paul Seward pacing by the police barricades that protected the Schollings's property. The crowd behind him had swelled, and all of the cameras were on Seward as the reporters surrounded him, assaulting him with questions. "Um, guys," I said.

They all came over to see. "I was wondering when he'd turn up," Chuck said bitterly.

"Do we want to see him?" I asked. I could tell by Deputy Dan's expression that he did not relish the idea of returning to Seward with a negative response. "He really wants to talk to you," the deputy encouraged. "Said he wasn't leaving until he did."

"We'll think about it," Alison said, abruptly shutting the door on the hapless deputy. "That prick left me waiting in the lobby for over an hour when he sneaked Jack out back in New York. Let him hang out for a while."

"Why do we need to see him at all?" Lindsey asked.

"Maybe he's heard from Jack," Chuck surmised.

"If he knew anything, why would he come to you?" Don said. "He knows less than you do."

"How scary is that?" Alison said.

"What?"

"That someone knows less than we do."

38

One of the earliest memories I have of my father is of him urinating. Not so much the sight of it, because his back was to me,
but the surprising force of the sound of his urine hitting the water
in the toilet, a powerful bass so much stronger and deeper than
the sound of my own urinating, which was more of a high-pitched
tinkle. I was probably around four years old or so, and I can no
longer recall the circumstances that led to my being present while
my father evacuated his bladder. Maybe he'd been giving me a
bath, and didn't want to leave me alone in the tub while he went
to a different toilet. Maybe we were together somewhere in a public restroom, I don't know. All of the details, save for the sound
of his stream and the image of his posture, slightly stooped with
one arm disappearing around his hips to his groin area and the
other holding onto the slack of his belt, have been wiped clean
from my memory. But it was the sound alone that truly struck me.
What must it be like, I wondered, to unleash so much power
through so flimsy an attachment? As I grew, I always associated

the sound of a powerful urine stream with manhood, taking pride in mine when it resonated deeply, and suffering momentary insecurities when it seemed feeble or unsteady.

I didn't know why I found myself thinking about that as I taped a cardboard, glow-in-the dark skeleton to the Schollings's front door. I decided it was probably because I was thinking about Jeremy, and the loss he had just sustained. To lose your father at that age, when he's still such a powerful presence in your life, constantly shaping your perceptions both intentionally and accidentally with every seemingly insignificant word or gesture, was a loss I would never comprehend. If my father died tomorrow, I would lose the man who had been responsible in many ways for the man I was, but Jeremy had lost his father while he was still a work in progress. Who knew what impressions had already been formed, and how much more would now have to come from a host of external sources. Thinking in those terms, I could only imagine the confusion and uncertainty that would follow him for years.

In a way, I thought as I secured the left leg of the skeleton and started on the right, it explained why he'd reached out to me so quickly, the first adult male he'd encountered after his father's death. And my strong, almost paternal response to him may have been due to the unconscious faith implicit in his attachment to me, that I was a fully formed adult who could be looked to for guidance, to fill the void. Maybe it was through his eyes that I was finally beginning to see myself as an adult, someone who was no longer being shaped by another, but was now a whole person capable of forging someone else's perceptions of the world.

There was something both comforting and frightening in that thought. As a child, I heard my father urinate and the boy I was had his first dim notion of manhood, of a strength and sturdiness borne of experience, instantly forgotten but stored securely in my psyche. I wanted to tell Jeremy that he had forgotten memories of his father like that in him, memories that would continually emerge as he grew up, reaffirming the living bond he had with his father. If I could make him understand that, I thought it would offer him some comfort, and he would be justified in having looked to me for guidance.

I stood back to review my handiwork and then leaned in to bend the grinning skeleton's posable knees into a more realistic stance against the door. I checked the crowd, looking for Seward, but he'd apparently grown tired of waiting and, I hope, freezing his nuts off. Satisfied, I gathered up my tape and went inside to see if Lindsey wanted to go with me to get a pumpkin. I was feeling a sense of well-being and contentment that I'd been missing for so long that it felt almost alien to me. My new, young friend and my rekindled relationship with Lindsey now seemed to me as parts of a greater whole. After turning thirty I'd been ruminating on all of the things I could no longer be for myself, but now I'd discovered that there were new things that I could be for other people, and it felt good. For the first time in my life I thought of myself not as an impostor but as a complete person, a true adult, and to my great surprise, I didn't mind. I kind of liked it, actually.

"Wow," Lindsey said when I shared those thoughts with her. We were driving the Taurus down 57 to where I remembered seeing the pumpkin stand. "It sounds like you had a real epiphany."

"Maybe," I said, checking my rear view mirror. As far as I could tell, the press had not opted to follow us this time. "It's weird. I haven't felt this good since I don't know when. I actually feel a bit guilty about it. Jack's missing, and here I am . . . happy."

"Here *we* are," Lindsey said. "Don't forget about me. It's like, Jack got lost but we found ourselves, and each other."

"Can I ask you something?" I said.

"You just did."

"Why did you agree to this intervention?"

"I'm sorry?"

"Aside from the obvious. Everyone's given an ulterior motive except you." I said.

She chewed her lip thoughtfully for a minute. "I don't know," she said. "I know you and Chuck and Alison really wanted to help Jack. I didn't know if it would do any good or not, I've never really been as close with him as you. Like I said, I wanted to help Alison even more than Jack, she was so torn up about the whole thing. But more than that, and this is going to sound selfish, I guess I wanted to help myself, too. Nothing was really happening for me, and I couldn't seem to get my life out of neutral. Being with you guys . . . I thought it would remind me of who I was, you know? Because I always felt so secure in who I was when we all hung out. And I guess knowing that you would be there . . ." Her voice drifted off thoughtfully and she looked at me, wincing gently at her own honesty.

"It was the same for me," I said, feeling both guilty and re-lieved. "I think maybe we all needed to shake things up a little. Jack had the major addiction, the one we could all hang our hats on, but we all had our own minor addictions bringing us down."

"Like what?"

"Where should I start? Alison has her Jack addiction, I'm stuck on the past, you've been unable to settle down . . ."

"Right," Lindsey said. "What about Chuck?"

"I don't know," I said. "I can't pinpoint it exactly, but he's got his own issues."

"He's addicted to minors," Lindsey said, groaning at her own pun.

"Whatever. The point is, I think we all came up here looking to kick some habits."

"Does that make us selfish?" Lindsey asked.

"Maybe, a little. But I don't think a little selfishness is necessarily unhealthy. It's just possible that—"

"Stop!"

"What? I'm just saying—"

"No. Really, stop." She pointed out her window and I saw that we were about to pass the pumpkin stand. I braked and pulled into the parking lot, the gravel crunching and popping like gunfire under the Taurus's tires. "So," she said, after I'd turned off the engine. "It was an intervention for all of us."

"Hey," I said. "The Scarecrow, Lion, and Tin Man weren't just helping Dorothy for the hell of it. They all had their own reasons for wanting to see the Wizard."

"I still feel a little guilty," Lindsey said, blowing her hair out of her face as we stepped out of the car.

"So do I," I admitted.

"But I also feel good about us, and about myself."

"So do I."

"We finally feel good and we have to feel guilty about it."

"That's life," I said. "If irony's your bag, there's never a dull moment."

She smiled, took my hand, and we walked over to look at the pumpkins.

Dusk was falling when we returned to the Scholling house. Even before we rounded the last curve we began to see scattered cars parked haphazardly along the shoulder of the road. "Uh oh," Lindsey muttered. The crowd in front of the house had grown significantly, probably since school was out for the day. There must have been over a hundred kids jammed into the small grass clearing on the shoulder of the road, many now in Halloween costumes. The theme, I noticed, was *Blue Angel*, with boys in leather jackets and the wraparound shades Jack wore in the movie, the girls in sad clown faces, in tribute to the villain of the film. Somewhere, a boombox was blaring Stone Temple Pilots. A number of kids in rubber horror masks were leaning against the police barricades and posing for the cameras with a long sign that said "Come Party With Us Jack."

"It appears our secret hideout has become Carmelina's newest hot spot," I said.

"You think?" Lindsey said.

As we pulled past the crowd, a number of kids crept under the barricades and ran into the street directly in front of us, leaving me no choice but to hit the brakes. "Oh, Christ!" Lindsey said.

"Where's Jack?" shrieked one of the girls wearing a sad clown face. "What have you done with him?" Her friend, another girl dressed identically but with a happy clown face stood directly in front of the car holding up Jack's picture. Before I could respond, there was an amplified squawk and Sheriff Sullivan pulled up from the opposite direction. The girls screamed gleefully and fled back under the barricades. Sullivan pulled up so that his open window was opposite my closed one. As he waited for me to lower mine, I saw that our little meeting had captured the attention of the crowd. "Good evening," Sullivan said with a smile.

"Hello," I responded. Someone from the crowd lobbed a raw egg, which landed a few feet in front of our car with a thin splat.

"Heard from your friend?"

"Nope."

There was a musical chant coming from the crowd, the kind you hear at hockey games, which sounded something like *"Bust his ass, Sheriff, bust his ass."* Sullivan smiled. "Your fan club," he said, indicating the crowd.

"I don't suppose you're going to disperse the crowd," I said.

"Nah. They'll get bored with it in a few hours," he replied. "Besides, Halloween night these kids are usually up to all sorts of mischief. It makes my job easier, having them all right here where I can see them." Just then there was another wet, crunching sound and Lindsey and I both ducked involuntarily as another egg hit our front windshield.

"Well," I said, inching forward. "I'll let you get back to your crime fighting." Without waiting for a reply I made a sharp right and pulled up into the Schollings's driveway. I could see in the mirror that the back of the sheriff's car had been egged a few times as well.

Alison and Don were sitting on the porch sipping Diet Cokes, lazy spectators to the frenetic festivities going on across the street. "Getting crazy out there," Don observed as I carried the pumpkin from the car.

"That's one ugly pumpkin," Alison said. Our last minute shopping hadn't left us with too many choices, but what our pumpkin lacked in symmetry it made up for in sheer audacity, with misshapen lumps and wells marring its rough orange surface.

"It's supposed to be," I said. "You know, Halloween and all."

"Right."

I found Chuck and Jeremy inside, watching a Halloween *X-Files* rerun. Mulder and Scully were having one of their routine arguments in the front seat of a car as they drove through a cornfield. "Those two should just get a room already," Chuck said.

"Ignore him," I told Jeremy, plopping down between them, after carefully placing the pumpkin on the coffee table. "He's a highly disturbed individual."

"Where'd you get that pumpkin, Chernobyl?" Chuck asked.

"You think it's scary now, wait till we get done carving it."

"What's Chernobyl?" Jeremy asked.

While we watched the end of *The X-Files*, Alison and Lindsey prepared potato salad, corn muffins, and cranberry sauce while periodically checking on the turkey they'd stuffed and placed in the oven. Then Chuck got up to make a salad, which was always his job since he could cut like a Japanese chef, a fringe benefit of his surgical expertise. I would pass a vegetable and call out a number somewhere between ten and thirty. Chuck would repeat the number as he studied the vegetable for a second and then launch into a series of speed-cuts, the knife pounding the cutting board in a fast, steady rhythm while I counted out loud. He always fit in exactly the amount of cuts I had specified, and the vegetable was always cut with perfect symmetry. "Seven years of medical school," Alison observed wryly. "That is one expensive salad."

"It's a gift," Chuck said.

I hoisted a tomato and looked over to Jeremy, who was watching with awe. "Twenty?" I asked.

"Twenty-five," he said with a smile.

"Amateurs," Chuck grumbled. He made a show of studying the tomato and then attacked the chopping board.

"Cool," Jeremy said.

"You should see me operate," Chuck said through gritted teeth as he finished his dicing. "Next."

Later, while Chuck and Don watched *Cops*, Jeremy and I used scalpels from Chuck's medical bag to carve a face into the pumpkin. First we cut off the top and scooped out the "brains" and then set to work carving a jagged grin. We had just finished one eye when Alison took out the turkey, so we decided that a cyclops pumpkin was a fine way to go. I wedged a candle into the goop left in the bottom of the pumpkin and we carried it onto the porch, where Jeremy lit it. The effect was satisfying and we both stood there admiring it for a moment. "Pretty good, hey?" I said.

"Yep," he said, smiling at me. I smiled back and it was a nice moment. You can't smile at adults the way you can smile at a kid, with no sarcastic remark or shifted gaze to keep things from getting too personal. Out on the porch we were simply two people, connected by circumstance, sharing a smile as dusk fell. Three, if you counted the one-eyed pumpkin.

39

The first explosion caused us all to jump in our seats, and Lindsey, who was passing a bowl of potato salad to Don, dropped it onto the table with a jarring crash. "What the hell?" Chuck said. Don, who was on his feet before the potato salad hit the table, ran across the room and positioned himself to the side of the living room window, his back to the wall, his right hand resting on his shoulder holster. His pose looked extremely professional. "Everyone stay where you are," he ordered. No one argued. A second blast rattled the window and then Don took a quick peek out of the corner. I saw his right hand first relax and then leave his shoulder holster altogether, which I took to be a good sign.

"What's going on?" I asked.

"They're shooting off fireworks," he said, puzzled.

"Who is?"

"You got me. Someone in the crowd."

We all got up from the table and joined him at the window, just in time to see a bottle rocket go up and burst into green and red sparks. "Whoa," Jeremy said, impressed. There was a series of rapid, machine-gun type bursts as someone set off a handful of firecrackers, and then a small explosion of red and yellow sparks that spun around on the ground like a twister. The crowd had moved to one side of the clearing, in order to watch the fireworks while maintaining some distance. Sullivan got out of his car, megaphone in hand, and began shouting a warning to the kids in the crowd, but his voice was drowned out by more explosions as two more bottle rockets were launched. The crowd applauded appreciatively as Sullivan put down his megaphone and began a purposeful walk from his car over to the crowd. We couldn't see who was setting off the pyrotechnics because of the crowd surrounding them, but that meant they couldn't see the sheriff approaching either. Suddenly there was a loud, hissing noise, followed by a short, muffled blast and a flash of green light and then the dull thud of an unseen impact. "That was too low," Don said, concerned.

"What?" I asked.

"That explosion. It was in the crowd." Before he even finished speaking, we heard some anguished shouts. "Oh, shit," Chuck said, heading for the front door. "Call 911."

They'd been using three lead pipes, each no more than two feet long, which they'd planted into the ground at various angles to launch the fireworks. Each pipe had an opening cut into it right before the shaft disappeared into the earth, so that they could slide the fireworks into the pipe and still have access to the fuse. It was a crude launch pad, but it did the trick. The kids lighting the fuses were too caught up in their task to realize that each blast was rocking the pipes in the ground, loosening them, until finally one of the pipes had taken off with the bottle rocket it was launching. The charge had apparently exploded within the rusty pipe, sending lead fragments shooting like shrapnel into the huddle of journalists who were covering the vigil, the largest piece ricocheting off one of the news vans and into the shoulder of the Fox News cameraman, where it embedded itself painfully. The bottle rocket itself, freed of the pipe, had pierced the throat of a young girl, whose heart Chuck was desperately trying to restart.

The crowd was deathly silent as Chuck worked on the girl, pumping and counting as he tried to breathe life back into her. As he breathed into her, he gently moved the stem of the rocket, still stuck in her throat, out of his way, taking great pains not to dislodge it. He worked with rhythm and determination, oblivious to the crowd around him. Sheriff Sullivan leaned over the wounded cameraman, calming him down and wrapping him in a blanket, while Sally Hughes sat on her knees, her hand on his chest. She was bleeding from a nasty gash on her left temple, although she didn't seem to have noticed it yet.

A number of other kids had been hit by flaming debris from the rogue missile, and Don, Alison, Lindsey, and I moved between them, assessing their injuries as best we could. They all had suffered some mild burns, but nothing that looked very alarming, so we just calmed them down and Don procured some ice from one of the media vans to apply to the burns until they could be treated.

Carmelina had only one ambulance and when it arrived the two paramedics took in the scene and for a moment they seemed overwhelmed by the crowd. "Over here," Chuck called to them. "I've got no respirations." As Chuck spoke, the medics pulled open the girl's shirt and began placing electrode stickers on her chest. "She's got a puncture and burn at the base of her neck," Chuck said through grunts as he continued to press down on her chest. "Just above the sternal notch." The monitor the medics set up came alive with two loud beeps and Chuck automatically turned to look at it. "She's in V tach, let's hit her with three-sixty."

I turned away as the paramedics placed the paddles on her and yelled "Clear!" There was a small, popping sound and the faintest smell of smoke, and then Chuck said, "We've got a pulse!" There were scattered cheers from the surrounding crowd as Chuck and the paramedics worked to stabilize the girl and move her onto the stretcher. I found myself filled with admiration for Chuck, for his expertise and confidence. I wondered what it felt like to be so adept at something, to be able to walk fearlessly into such a horrifying situation and know how to make it better.

A few minutes later they loaded the girl into the ambulance, followed by the wounded cameraman, and the ambulance took off. Chuck looked over the three kids who'd been burned and, determining that they were in no serious danger, sent them off to the hospital with Deputy Dan. Sullivan patted Chuck on the back and gave him an appreciative nod before wading into the crowd to determine who was responsible for the fireworks. It was then that Chuck saw Sally Hughes leaning against her news van, pressing some blood-soaked paper towels to her wounded temple. "Who says there's no god?" he whispered to me with a smile, before heading over to examine her. "You're going to need a few stitches," he told her with a frown. "Why don't you come into the house and I'll take care of you."

"Will you tell me about Jack Shaw?" she asked weakly.

He smiled incredulously. "You're losing blood and all you can think about is how you can use it to get a story?"

"You're going to use it to get a date, aren't you?"

"Touché," Chuck said, and, offering her his arm, led her across the street.

"Well, I'll be damned," Alison said.

"Come on, cut him a break," Lindsey said. "He was great out there."

"He was," Don agreed.

"And she is of legal age," I pointed out.

"Okay, okay," Alison smiled. "Let's just get inside. It's freezing out here."

Chuck worked on Sally Hughes from Fox News in the kitchen, while the rest of us sipped hot apple cider in the living room. Don got a fire going in the fireplace and we all sat back to warm up. In all the confusion of the last half hour, none of us had realized how cold it was outside, and only once we entered the relative warmth of the house did it occur to us that we were freezing. Jeremy, who had been ordered to stay in the house when we all ran out, had been watching anxiously from the window, and he insisted on full details, which we gave in bits and pieces as we all relived what we'd seen. A little while later Chuck joined us with Sally, who now sported a gauze bandage on her temple, and introductions were made all around.

Alison remembered that we hadn't eaten dessert and she brought out a batch of marshmallows and brownies, as well as some long hot-dog tongs we could use as spits to roast the marshmallows. In all the activity, no one but me heard the three short knocks on the back door. Given the insane nature of the evening so far, I was only mildly surprised when I opened the door to find Darth Vader standing on the Schollings's deck. "Can I help you?" I asked the Dark Lord of the Sith.

"Let me in, Ben," Jack said, his voice muffled by the mask. "I'm freezing my ass off out here."

I stood aside mutely as he walked into the house and followed him into the living room, where he effectively silenced the conversation as everyone stared at him with varying degrees of concern. Alison stood up slowly, gaping at Jack, who finally reached up and pulled off the Darth Vader helmet. There was a crackling of static electricity as the mask came off and it caused Jack's hair to float comically around his head. He used his fingers to brush some greasy strands out of his face, smiled uncertainly and said, "Miss me?" Alison walked slowly across the room, her face twitching with emotion and Jack fell into her arms.

"That," Jeremy announced, "is my mask." We all laughed and the laughter seemed to break the spell on Chuck, Lindsey, and me. The three of us jumped up and ran to hug Jack and Alison and each other, patting and holding each other with tears in our eyes, acknowledging the enormous stress of the last few days now that we could finally relieve ourselves of it.

"Where were you man?" Chuck kept asking him. "Where the hell were you?" But Jack just held onto Alison with his eyes closed, not responding to any of our exhortations, until, as he began to slip down and out of her grip, it finally dawned on us that he had passed out.

Don and I carried Jack over to the couch and laid him down as Chuck ran into the kitchen to get his medical bag. We all watched as Chuck examined Jack, who by now had regained consciousness and was muttering to himself. "He's dehydrated and he's got a high fever," Chuck said, frowning as he pulled out a stethoscope and slid it under Jack's black T-shirt. I wondered where he'd gotten the shirt. "He may also have low-level hypothermia. Someone get some blankets."

As Chuck continued to examine him, I noticed that Jack had a fair amount of cuts and scrapes on his neck and arms, as well as his chest. "Jesus," I said. "Where the hell was he?"

"I don't know," Chuck said. "He's suffering from exposure. It looks like he was outdoors for some time."

"Is he in any danger?" Alison asked as Lindsey came downstairs with a load of blankets.

"Nah," Chuck said. "I don't think so. He just got himself sick."

"High?" I asked, quietly.

"Can't tell," Chuck said. "Although the fever could be part of withdrawal, which would be a good sign."

"Not high," Jack mumbled, opening his eyes. "Just fucking cold."

"You sure?" Chuck asked.

Jack grabbed Chuck's wrist. "No drugs!" he whispered, his voice scratchy and hoarse. "I'm clean, man. Sick and sober."

"Okay then," Chuck said. "I believe you."

"Better believe it, man," Jack said, closing his eyes. "Better fucking believe it."

Chuck wrote out some prescriptions, and Don drove into town to fill them. Lindsey made some vegetable soup, which Jack began to devour as if he hadn't eaten in days. "Easy," Chuck said, pulling the bowl away. "You want to keep it down, you have to go slow." Jack nodded in understanding, but as soon as Chuck moved the bowl back, Jack began wolfing it down again. He just couldn't help himself. Within a minute he began retching and Chuck took the bowl away. "Forget it," Chuck said. "You'll eat through your arm for the time being." He produced an IV drip and inserted the needle into Jack's arm. He had no stand for the bag, though, so he called a wide-eyed Jeremy over and had him perch on the sofa back holding the bag. "Just hold that until it's empty," Chuck told him. "It should take about forty-five minutes."

"Okay," Jeremy said gravely.

Chuck left to put away his bag and get a drink. Jack opened his eyes weakly to find Jeremy staring down at him in wide-eyed fascination. "Who're you?" Jack asked him.

"Jeremy Miller."

"Oh," Jack said and closed his eyes again.

"He's still pretty out of it," I told Jeremy.

"I can't believe that this is really him, you know?" Jeremy said. "Blue Angel. Right here on the couch."

"When I see him in the movies, I think the opposite," I said. "I think, I can't believe that's my friend Jack up there on the screen."

"Do you think he'll be okay?"

"Yeah," I said, although I was wondering about the long-term prognosis.

40

"I was in the forest," Jack told us the next morning, as if that made sense. We were all eating breakfast in the living room. His fever was down and some of his color had returned, although his face still appeared somewhat haggard. There were still dark pouches under his eyes, but he seemed bright and focused and significantly improved from last night. "I got this crazy notion that I had to get back to nature, you know? Like get born again or something, so I just took off into the woods."

"Why the woods?" Alison asked. She was sitting by his feet at the edge of the couch, where she'd no doubt spent the night. Lindsey and I were on the love seat, and Chuck was on the armrest of the easy chair across from us. I'd walked a reluctant Jeremy home the night before, when the IV bag had been depleted. He was in school now, probably finding it almost impossible to keep the secret I'd asked him to for at least another day. As Don had been leaving last night he'd promised to stop by on his way out of town, but he had yet to show up, so for now it was just the five of us, which was really the way it needed to be anyway.

"I don't know," Jack answered Alison. "I wasn't thinking too rationally. When I left the house, I was planning on getting to town, calling Paul, and getting the hell out of Dodge, you know? I was going to have him wire me a ticket, and get my ass back to LA. I was already a little feverish, I think." He stopped for a moment, a perplexed look crossing his face. "I didn't even think to put on a shirt," he said in disbelief. "Jesus, can you imagine that?"

"Get to the part where you become Tarzan," Chuck advised him.

"Can I have a cigarette?" Jack asked.

"No, but you can have some oatmeal," Chuck said.

"Christ," Jack complained, but he didn't turn down the oatmeal when Chuck put it in front of him.

"Slowly," Chuck cautioned him.

We all watched Jack eat three or four spoonfuls as if it was the most fascinating spectacle we'd ever seen. It occurred to me that this must be what it's like to be Jack Shaw the movie star. Everywhere he went, people surrounded him, trying to get a glimpse of even the most mundane aspects of his life.

"Anyway," Jack continued, wiping his chin with his forearm. "I'm walking down the road, trying to hitchhike, but there's like no one out there, and the few cars that go by don't stop. It didn't occur to me what I must have looked like. I thought for sure someone would recognize me and stop. Every time I go out I hope no one will spot me, and the one time I want to be spotted, no one does. Go figure. Anyway, I thought, no sweat, I'll just walk. So I'm walking down the road and I'm looking at the mountains on both sides of the road, with all those trees and everything, and they just looked so quiet, you know? And I thought about what would happen when I made it into town, and when I made it back to LA, between work and the media and all, and I just figured I'd be high again before too long. I'd either score something here, or Paul would have something for me when I got back—"

"Paul gives you drugs?" I asked incredulously.

"Yeah," Jack said simply.

"That bastard," Lindsey said

"He doesn't shove them up my nose," Jack said pointedly. "I'm the one who takes them."

"It doesn't matter," Chuck said. "Your agent is a fucking drug dealer. You have to get rid of him."

"It's not that simple," Jack said.

"It ought to be," Chuck retorted angrily.

"Let it go," Alison said softly. "We'll deal with it later."

Jack looked at her appreciatively. "Listen," he said to Chuck. "I'm not denying that he's part of the problem, okay. But I just don't want to fall into the trap of pushing the blame onto anyone else. The problem is me and me alone, okay?"

"Okay," Chuck said, although he clearly remained unconvinced.

"Anyway," Jack said, after a few more spoonfuls of oatmeal. "I'm walking down the road, looking at these mountains, and it starts to rain, just this light drizzle, you know? And I feel the rain on my skin, and it feels good and clean, like the first clean thing I've felt in months. And I don't know what happened then. I was just standing in the middle of nowhere, and it was dark as hell and there were these quiet mountains all around and I felt alone, but not in a bad way. I just felt like I was alone with myself for the first time in so long, you know?"

I'd lost count, but it seemed like the fifth or sixth "you know?"

in Jack's narrative. He desperately wanted us to understand, to affirm his experience. Alison was nodding and I saw that her eyes were moist. "And I just thought," Jack continued, "if I could just be alone like that for a while, I could somehow get a handle on myself, kind of get back in control. And the mountains and the forest just looked so peaceful, and one thing I was sure of was that I'd have one hell of a time trying to find any cocaine up there."

"So you just walked into the forest and set up residence, like Thoreau?" I asked.

"Yeah, I guess," Jack said. "I wanted to sort of beat myself down. No food, no distractions, kind of like the Indians used to do, you know, to become a man."

"You had a Native American bar mitzvah," Chuck remarked, eyebrows raised.

Jack smiled. "Something like that."

"And we were worried that an intervention would be too dramatic," I said wryly.

Lindsey laughed. "We should have known we'd be outdone by a true professional."

"What the hell did you do in the woods for three days?" Chuck asked him.

"I meditated mostly," Jack said. "I thought about all of you and me and my life and the drugs and my career and everything, you know? I played these games where I would organize and reorganize my priorities. And I walked a lot, all over the woods, up one mountain and down the other. It's really an amazing thing. Your natural instinct when you're in the woods at night is to be afraid and get the hell out you know? And your natural instinct when it's raining is to find shelter. And when I forced myself to ignore those instincts and just relax and embrace the rain, the cold, and my fears it was very liberating. And once I found myself liberated from those needs, stopping the cocaine didn't seem like such a big deal anymore."

"So why come back now?" I asked. "Aside from the fact that your friends were sitting here with their lives on hold worrying themselves sick about you."

Jack smiled sheepishly. "It was just so fucking cold, man." Everybody laughed. "Next time I go out to commune with nature, I'll be better dressed for it."

"Where'd you get the shirt?" Lindsey asked him.

"I don't remember," Jack said, frowning. "Where is it?"

"I threw it out," Alison said. "It stank."

"I don't know. I must have found it in the woods."

"You know you lost your wallet?" I asked him.

"I didn't lose it," he said. "I threw it into a stream. I didn't want to be tempted to go into town and buy drugs. Wait, how do you know about that?"

I told him about how his wallet had been found, and how we'd all become suspects in his kidnapping and possible murder. "Jesus!" he said, breathing out slowly. "I don't know what to say. It didn't occur to me that it would be found."

"I'm just curious," I said, annoyed in spite of myself. "What did you think we'd all be doing here while you were gone?"

"What do you mean?" he asked.

"I mean, did you think we'd all just go home and give up on you? Did you think we would all quit our jobs and just stay here until you resurfaced?"

"Ben," Alison said, trying to cut me off.

"No," I said, surprising myself with the force of my resentment. "I want to know. Did it occur to you we might be worried? Did you even think about us?"

Jack looked up at me, his gaze unswerving. "No, I guess I didn't, Ben, and I'm truly sorry about that, because you're all pretty much my only real friends. I was just zoned out, you know? I was in another world, and I guess I just figured you'd be here when I got back."

"And here we are," I grumbled, my anger dissipating in the face of his honesty.

"I knew I could count on you," he said with a grin.

"Fuck you."

"I love you, man." He stood up and came over to hug me.

"No, fuck you," I said, putting up my hands.

"I love you, Ben."

"Fuck you," I said again but by then I was laughing and he was hugging me and I realized that I was really, truly, glad he was back and that he was okay.

"So," Alison said, interrupting our horseplay. "Do you think it worked?"

"What?"

"Your trip. Your time up there. Do you think you've kicked the habit?"

"I don't know," Jack said. "I certainly don't feel any craving for coke, not like I used to."

"Well," Chuck said, "medically speaking, it's out of your bloodstream by now."

"I know," Jack said. "I feel like I somehow purified myself. Like it's no longer a part of my life."

"Could it really be that simple?" Lindsey asked.

"There was nothing simple about it," Jack said good-naturedly. "You go try and live in the woods for three days."

"So," Alison said, stretching her arms over her shoulders. "What happens now?"

"Now," Jack said, "I think I ought to see about getting my job back."

I remembered the time I'd asked Jack about the future and

he'd said, "This is the future." It was ironic, I thought, that his philosophy of living in the moment and not getting bogged down with worries of the future was actually the cornerstone of most addiction recovery programs. One day at a time, wasn't that what they said? I felt an irrational surge of optimism at the notion that Jack's own nature might actually serve him well in his struggle to stay sober. Then again, it could be a load of crap and Jack could be high again in a week.

41

We spent the rest of the morning watching with fascination as Jack pulled together the scattered strands of his career. His first call was to Luther Cain, whom he awakened at home. Despite being accustomed to Jack's fame, watching him dial an Oscar-winning director's home phone number from memory was still impressive. Their conversation was surprisingly brief, but Jack explained that Cain was not a "phone guy" and would be immediately flying by private jet into Monticello, along with Craig Schiller, one of the producers of *Blue Angel II,* and they would drive down to meet with him in person. "He needs to see for himself what the story is," Jack explained matter-of-factly, as if it were no big deal that one of Hollywood's biggest names would be dropping by the Schollings's place. I guess it wasn't so outrageous when you considered that one of Hollywood's other biggest names was making phone calls from the living room couch in shorts and a Tommy Hilfiger T-shirt. But still, it was pretty cool.

The plan, devised with Alison's help, was that Jack would forgo his twelve-million-dollar salary and work for scale, allowing Cain to reimburse the insurance company for the lost days so that no one was out any money except for Jack. It was Alison's hope that by establishing a position of goodwill with the insurance company, they wouldn't refuse him coverage on future projects. Jack was confident that if he could get Cain in his corner it would give him the credibility and the muscle to salvage his career.

"You know Cain's already brought a lawsuit against you," I reminded Jack.

"That's just business," he said. "It's no big deal."

I had to admit that there was something intoxicating about living in a world where million-dollar lawsuits were tossed casually aside, and severe grievances were resolved with a quick phone call. I could see how, after living in that world for a while, you tended to take a light view of consequences. No damage was too great to be undone by the big business of entertainment. I knew that was a simplification, but not by much.

Jack was already signed to two other projects after the *Blue Angel* sequel, and even though he was itching to speak to the producers of those films, he decided that the prudent thing to do was to first arrive at an agreement with Luther Cain. "Then I'll be dealing from a position of strength," he said.

"You see," Chuck said to him. "You can handle your career. You don't need that fucking guy."

"It's not that simple," Jack said with a frown. "There are contracts. Agreements. There's history there."

"A history of drug abuse and exploitation," Alison said sharply.

"The guy owns a piece of me for the next few years," Jack said, shrugging his shoulders.

The next item of business was an exclusive interview with Sally Hughes. Chuck had extracted a promise of secrecy from her the night before, after considerable negotiation and flirtation, by guaranteeing that she would be the one to break the story in a one-on-one interview. Sally originally wanted to do the interview live via satellite feed, but after consulting with her bosses decided to videotape it so that it could be edited into a cleaner segment. Chuck went outside and ushered Sally and her crew through the media throng, past Deputy Dan and the police barricades and into the house. The competing journalists reacted in a panic of shouted questions and demands, furious at being scooped. Sally now had replacement cameramen, two of them, who'd driven through the night to be here for what she'd called in as an exclusive with the alleged kidnappers of Jack Shaw. If they were surprised to see Jack himself actually sitting there waiting for them, they were professional enough to contain themselves. A sound guy and a makeup person were there as well, and they got to work setting up klieg lights and umbrellas to mute them, moving the furniture, and basically turning the living room into a mini-studio. Chuck introduced Sally to Jack, and Sally did her best not to seem too impressed or excited, and failed sensationally. This was clearly the biggest interview of her career. Jack went upstairs for a quick shower, and the camera guys put Chuck on the seat next to Sally to do some lighting tests. Chuck flirted with Sally the whole time, posing and leaning in to whisper to her while they shot her from different angles. She made faces at us, but she didn't seem to really mind. If anything, his clowning around seemed to calm her down.

Jack returned about twenty minutes later, looking clean and composed in black jeans and a denim shirt he'd taken from my suitcase. While the makeup guy worked on him, Jack chatted amicably with Sally, listening attentively as she mapped out her plans for the interview and offering a few suggestions of his own, which she hastily scribbled down.

The rest of us retreated to the back of the living room, well behind the cameras, and the interview began. "You've been missing now for almost seven days," Sally said, after a short preamble. "Where have you been?"

Jack smiled and said, "First of all, I've only been missing for three days. Up until three days ago, I was staying with my friends."

"Staying here in this house?"

"That's right."

"But you told no one."

"I chose not to alert the media, if that's what you mean."

Watching Jack under the lights and in front of the camera was really something. There was nothing about him you could point to that was different, but his smile seemed that much more radiant, his demeanor that much more commanding. It wasn't that something changed in him when he was in front of the cameras, but rather he became something that was always in him, lying just beneath the surface. It was this intangible, indescribable quality that Jack brought to the screen, but seeing it in person from ten feet behind the camera was a remarkable experience.

We had discussed whether or not Jack should publicly admit that he'd been taking cocaine, or just claim the ever-popular addiction to painkillers like so many other celebrities did. We'd come to the conclusion that there had been too many public displays for plausible deniability. "Better to just come clean and move past it," Jack said. "The industry isn't known for its long memory, you know? Besides, there's already a protocol to the whole rehab thing that the studios and press have to come to expect. Misbehavior, confession, and most of all, contrition. As long as you play the part, they'll give you your shot at redemption. If you improvise, you can bring down a whole world of shit on yourself."

I don't know how calculated Jack's performance was, but he pulled it off beautifully. He was quietly confident without seeming brash, and while he was apologetic he didn't ask for sympathy. He was a slightly subdued, wiser Jack Shaw who was now ready to make amends and pick up his career where he'd left off, with a new commitment and a clear perspective. I hoped that was really the truth, and not just Jack getting into character, and I wondered if, for someone like Jack, there was actually a difference.

"Many speculated that your disappearance was drug-related. Is there any truth to that?"

"Drugs were part of it. But it was more than that. I was having some troubles that needed to be worked out. Unfortunately, my schedule didn't allow me the time I needed, so I was forced to take some unscheduled time."

"Were you addicted to drugs?" Sally persisted.

"I was using cocaine," Jack said simply.

"And now you're not?"

"I will never take cocaine again."

"Can you tell us by what means you conquered such a powerful addiction in only a few days?" Sally asked.

"I wouldn't say I conquered it," Jack said, looking introspectively at his hands. "I would say I got the drug out of my system, got rid of the immediate craving for it, and, with the help of my friends, established a strong foundation for keeping myself sober."

"You mentioned your friends," Sally said, leaning forward like Barbara Walters. "Is there any truth to the rumors that your friends actually had to kidnap you?"

Jack laughed. "I hadn't heard that one," he said. "Is that really what they're saying?" He delivered this line with the same easy tone he'd used when he declared that he wouldn't do coke again. He lied so effortlessly that for an instant even I believed him. With a jolt of dismay, I realized that I was no longer capable of distinguishing the truth from the lies when Jack spoke.

They went on for another ten minutes, Jack dishing the bullshit and Sally eating it up, until Jack started to look tired and distracted. Sally sensed she was losing his attention and brought the interview to a close. The cameramen went outside to shoot some filler of the mountains and the house, and Jack lay back on the couch with a tired smile. "When will it hit?" he asked Sally.

"We'll edit it in the van," Sally said, flushed with excitement. "It will probably take about a half hour, then I'll go live with a quick update and introduce the segment."

"The other guys out there are going to go nuts," Lindsey said from the window.

"I know," Sally said, unable to conceal her pleasure. "They'll be storming the house." She turned to Jack. "Remember, you agreed not to talk to any other networks until after the late news tonight."

Jack lifted his head and looked at her. "Once was enough," he said. "No offense."

"None taken."

Sally got up, shook Jack's hand and took herself and her now irrepressible smile to her van to work on her story. I sat down beside Jack, who was sipping at a Coke thoughtfully. He looked exhausted. "So," I said. "Was that acting, or was that really you?"

"That was really me acting," Jack said.

"What do you mean?"

"The really great actors not only convince the audience," Jack quoted, standing up and stretching. "They also have to convince themselves." He smiled at me.

"Profound," I said.

"And maybe just a bit pathetic," he said, putting down the soda can and heading for the stairs. "But believe it or not, it actually works."

"It must be tough," I said sincerely. "Having no clear line between your reality and your bullshit."

"There's a line," Jack said. "It just moves around a lot."

"How do you deal with it?"

Jack said "Drugs." We both laughed.

"Jesus, I'm wiped," Jack said, turning at the banister. "I'm going to catch a few z's."

"Don't you want to see yourself on TV?"

"Nah," Jack said, yawning as he started up the stairs. "I hate that guy."

Don said he couldn't stick around to meet Jack, who was still napping when he came to say good-bye. He didn't even take off his suit jacket. "I'm heading back to Manhattan," he told me, handing his business cards to Chuck and me. "Give me a call when you get back, we'll get a few drinks, play some ball, whatever." It struck me that he really liked us, and that maybe he didn't have too many friends in his line of work. I tried to remember the last friend I'd made as an adult, not counting some of the people at *Esquire*, and couldn't. At thirty, friends are pretty much like bone mass. Whatever you've managed to store up until now starts to diminish and is rarely replaced. I told Don I'd be in touch, and I meant it. He shook my hand and Chuck's and gave Lindsey and Alison quick hugs, saying how glad he was that everything worked out. I thought that assessment might be premature, but it was nice of him to say. Alison walked him to the door and he stopped for a moment and looked at her, clearly wanting to say something more to her, something specific. His behavior confirmed my earlier suspicion that he had more than a passing interest in her. He hesitated, opened his mouth, and then closed it again. "I'll see you," he said.

"Thanks for everything," Alison said.

He waved it off. "I'll call you in a little while, okay?" he said, not making eye contact. "See how everything turned out."

"Okay."

"All right then," he said, and stepped out of the house.

"I think he likes you," Lindsey said to Alison.

"He's just a nice guy, that's all," Alison replied, closing the front door.

"What, a nice guy can't like you?" Lindsey persisted.

"Leave me alone."

"He really is a nice guy," I said, not to bug Alison but just because I was thinking it.

Chuck said, "I wonder if he's ever, you know, killed anyone."

42

Sally Hughes's interview with Jack hit the airwaves at about one o'clock and we amused ourselves by monitoring the various networks as the news spread. Within ten minutes of the story breaking, all the other networks were interrupting their programming with live reports from the correspondents outside the house, as if they'd uncovered the news by being there, as opposed to seeing it on television like everyone else. After all the live reports went out, we noticed a change in the behavior of the news people outside. They began moving all over the place with their cameras, climbing up on top of their vans finding any possible vantage point from which to aim their cameras at the house, all in the hopes of getting a shot of Jack. They were undoubtedly catching hell from their bosses for his having made it safely past them into the house, and now the pressure was on them to deliver something. Some of the photographers were even climbing the trees.

By the time Jack awoke two hours later, Fox had aired snippets of the interview twice more, and a crowd of fans easily twice the size of last night's vigil had begun descending on the scene. Sullivan wasn't equipped to control the crowd and called in the state police, who arrived in a commotion of sirens and lights and began erecting more prominent barricades. When the crowd continued to swell, they were forced to close off the road, and within a few minutes the road had become a large pedestrian mall. Jack peeked out under the shades for a second, careful to hide his face from view, and whistled softly. "Word sure gets around in these small towns."

"It helps to have the networks camped out on your doorstep," I said.

"Man," Chuck said, watching a group of young girls holding posters of Jack. "You must get laid everywhere you go."

"Yeah, whatever," Jack said distractedly.

"Hey," Lindsey called. She and Alison were still in front of the television. "Seward's on TV"

We all turned to see Seward, in a black suit and blue and red tie, walking past a group of reporters as he made his way through the crowd outside. There were beads of sweat under his perfectly gelled-back hair, probably due to the fact that he'd had to abandon his car and walk the last mile, and an annoyed arch to his eyebrows, which was probably congenital. He carried himself with a nervous arrogance and had the weathered good looks of an ex-athlete except for his eyes, which seemed too dark and small for his face. "We're all relieved that Jack's okay," he said, in answer to an unheard question. "Beyond that I have no comment."

"Have you seen Jack Shaw since he returned?" someone shouted. "Have you spoken to him?"

"Yes," Seward lied. "We spoke briefly yesterday." He stopped in his tracks. "People," he said, condescending to address the media. "I'm going in there to speak with Jack right now. I hope I'll have more to say to you after that. For now, I'm asking you to please get out of my way." With that he strode up to the barricade, where he was stopped by a state trooper. The trooper spoke to Seward, who looked irate and began gesticulating wildly with his hands until finally a second trooper joined the conversation, followed by Sheriff Sullivan. Seward pointed an angry finger at Sullivan's chest, but Sullivan didn't seen impressed.

"We might as well let him in," Jack said uncertainly. "I mean, I'm going to have to deal with him sometime."

"No you won't," Alison said. "You never have to see him again. He needs you, you don't need him."

"That's not how it works," Jack said. "We have contracts. He's a player. I can't stonewall him."

"Let's let him in," I said. "What's the worst he can do?" I stood up and opened the front door, and there was an audible "Ooooh" as the crowd hushed. I was suddenly very conscious of the fact that I was on live television. The reporters began shouting questions to me, but they were too far away to be understood. Still, I knew the cameras were all zooming in on me, and many of them were in the middle of live feeds, so I smiled and made a few peace signs, which made me feel like an idiot. When you're not in front of cameras every day, you have no damn clue how to act and you just become this wooden dolt. I called to Sheriff Sullivan, who turned to face me, and I pointed to Seward.

"Is he okay?" Sullivan asked.

"Nah, he's a prick, but he can come up," I called back, hoping that the cameras had picked that up.

Seward stormed past the troopers and headed up the lawn with a purposeful stride. Someone in the crowd started a chant of "We want Jack," and within seconds the whole crowd, easily a few hundred people, was screaming and whistling for Jack. I nodded at Sullivan who flashed me a sarcastic half-grin, as if to say all his worst expectations had been realized. I guess he had a point, see-

ing as how we'd turned his town into a circus. He blamed us for
the crowds, the closed road, the humiliation of having to call in
the state troopers, and probably last night's injuries too, but there
wasn't a damn thing he could do about it. And now that Jack was
back safely, he couldn't even save face by arresting us. I didn't
know how the hierarchy worked out here, but someone had to be
coming down hard on Sullivan for all of this. Basically, it sucked
to be him today.

Seward blew by me and said, "fucking lightweight," out of the
side of his mouth, which was a kind of nebulous rank out, and I
responded with, "dickhead," which was, I thought, much more to
the point and followed him into the house. Seward walked right
across the living room, ignoring everyone in it, and leaned over to
hug Jack on the couch. "Thank god you're okay, man," he said.
"Thank god. You had me worried sick. Where the fuck were
you?" Jack just shrugged and sat back in the couch. "It's okay,"
Seward continued, hurrying to fill the silence. "We'll work everything out. I'll get on the phone with Luther and the studios and
we'll smooth it all over. We might need to make a few minor
concessions, but they'll be so glad you're back they'll be kissing
our asses to make it all work. Don't worry about anything, I've
already got a few scenarios in mind. We can go over them on the
plane."

Jack, who had maintained a stone face through his agent's entire
rap, straightened himself out on the couch and softly asked, "What
plane?"

"Back to LA, Jack," Seward said, speaking as you might to a
mildly retarded young boy. "We have to get back there as soon
as possible. We've got to meet with Cain and Schiller and put a
new deal together. We've got to resolve the breach of contract
thing—not that it will be a problem, I've already got it worked

out, pretty much, and then we've got the insurance issues. We'll also have to do a little spin control, I mean your little interview was okay, but we've got to tighten it up for the trades . . ."

Watching him talk at Jack, I began to understand Paul Seward's operating style. His technique was to make everything seem overly complicated and involved so that his clients, actors like Jack, would want to sit back and let him sweat all the details, which left Seward in the driver's seat. I would have fallen for it myself, had I not watched Jack work most of it out with one phone call that morning. Seward might have been a good agent, but he was also a bullshit artist, which I guessed was what qualified him for the job in the first place. What I was having a little more trouble understanding was Jack's seeming inability to stand up to Seward. Jack was never one to lack confidence, yet as soon as Seward entered the room Jack became quiet, almost meek, as if Seward instantly sucked all of the resistance out of him.

Jack sat back on the couch staring at the ceiling, and the longer he stayed quiet the more Seward bombarded him with plans and strategies. While Seward paused briefly to catch his breath, Jack flashed me a quick, meaningful look, which I took to mean he wanted a little help with Seward.

"Do you mean Luther Cain, the director?" I asked Seward, who was about to speak again. He flashed me an annoyed look, and said, "Yes, of course that's who I mean," in a patronizing voice before turning back to Jack. "Now I'd like to arrange for a car to come get us to the airport—"

"The reason I ask," I interrupted him, "is that I spoke to Luther Cain this morning, and he didn't say anything about you being at the meeting."

That got his attention. "You spoke to Luther Cain," he said skeptically.

"The director," I added helpfully. He looked at Jack, raising his eyebrows in disbelief, as if we might be playing a joke on him, but Jack nodded quietly.

Seward now turned his full attention on me. "You spoke to Luther Cain," he repeated between clenched teeth. "Do you realize the damage you may have caused? Who the fuck do you think you are? Jack," he turned to look at Jack again. "Did you know about this?"

"Yeah," Jack said.

"Of course he knew," I said. "Listen, arrangements had to be made."

"Arrangements?" Seward shouted incredulously. "Arrangements! Who the fuck are you? I am Jack's agent, and I make the fucking arrangements."

"You weren't here," I pointed out.

Seward opened his mouth to speak, but all that came out was an incredulous gasp, and he actually clenched his hands in frustration. I noticed a vein throbbing alarmingly in his temple and briefly wondered if he ate a lot of red meat. "If you called and harassed Luther Cain," he finally spat out, "you may have put Jack in a very bad position."

"I thought I did okay," I said.

Seward took a deep breath, and exhaled into his hands. When he looked up he had a new, fake smile plastered to his face, which looked doubly ridiculous in light of his recent outburst, the kind of smile that often precedes psychotic violence. "Look," he said, running his trembling fingers through his sticky hair and wiping the residue on his pants. "I'm sure you thought you were just helping out Jack, but you have to understand, there are complicated contracts that need to be worked through here, obligations that must be met in one way or another, and you couldn't possibly begin to work your way through them. Still," he turned to Jack.

"I'm sure when we meet with Cain we can straighten this all out. He's a stand-up guy, and he and I go way back. We'll get on a plane this afternoon and I'll have a meeting set up by tomorrow—"

"Jack, you can't go back to LA today," I said. "You have a meeting at seven this evening."

"Oh, for Christ's sake, will you cut that shit out!" Seward screamed at me, his voice tinged with hysteria. "You're not helping here. Do you understand?"

"No," Jack said. "I do have a meeting this evening."

"Jack, who could you possibly be meeting with here? Now I don't know what these people have told you, but—"

"We're meeting with Cain and Schiller," I said. I was really enjoying myself now.

Seward looked as if he'd just been punched in the stomach. "Luther Cain is coming here?" he said softly. I nodded but he'd already turned away from me and plopped down on the sofa next to Jack, staring straight ahead at nothing in particular. "Jack?" he said softly, not looking at him.

"Yeah?" Jack said, also staring straight ahead.

"Luther Cain and Craig Schiller are coming here?"

"Yeah."

Seward nodded, as if he'd just asked Jack the time. "What's going on Jack?"

Jack turned to look at Seward, who continued to stare straight ahead. "I don't think we can continue with business as usual, Paul." The use of his agent's first name as well as Jack's soft tone made me acutely aware of how hard this actually was for Jack. He'd been with Seward for almost ten years and they'd enjoyed stratospheric success together. Then somehow along the way, Jack became addicted, and when he wanted his drugs Seward had delivered, the same way he delivered anything else Jack asked for. It was Seward's job to keep Jack happy, and he'd done that job well, but in the end he did it too well, and for that he was being fired. Jack felt like a shameless hypocrite, a typical Hollywood bad boy, blaming everyone else for his troubles, making a public scapegoat out of his agent. Seeing it that way, I suddenly felt bad for Seward.

"Are you firing me, Jack?" Seward asked without a trace of emotion in his voice.

"Yeah," Jack said. "I just think I need to start again, you know?"

Seward nodded. "Start again," he nodded. "Sure. Whatever. If you think you can do better, then by all means . . ."

"It's not about doing better, Paul," Jack said quickly.

"I'm just curious, Jack," Seward said, and I now realized that his carefully modulated voice was not without emotion, but brimming with rage. "Do you think it's my fault that you're a fucking cokehead?"

Alison gasped and I started to interrupt, but Jack waved us away. "It's okay," he said quickly. "No, Paul, I don't think it's your fault. You worked to get me to the top and I didn't handle it well. But now I've got to try to move on, and I have to stay clean."

"What am I, a goddamn vending machine? If you don't want to do drugs, don't do drugs. You're a pain in the ass on drugs. Puking and crying and making a mess everywhere you go. If you kick the habit, no one is happier than me."

"I needed help, Paul," Jack said. "I needed someone to tell me that I was out of control. I needed someone stop me. But you just kept getting me more."

"I got you to work every day," Paul said, finally turning to face Jack. "If it weren't for me, you'd have slept for days, missed appointments, missed shooting. They'd have buried you!"

"I didn't need work. I needed to get out of work and deal with this."

"We had obligations! You signed contracts! This isn't a fucking game! You don't just call time-out and leave the studios to sit there and jerk off while you fly off to some spa to clean up."

"I was in trouble," Jack said.

"You were making millions of dollars, Jack!" Seward shouted.

"So were you, Paul," Jack said. "And you didn't want to risk stopping, even if it meant watching me slowly kill myself."

"I don't believe this," Paul said, getting to his feet to face Jack. "This is a business, Jack. You're expected to suit up and show up, like any professional. You work out your problems on your own time. I will not apologize for being a professional, for being good at what I do!"

"I'm not asking for an apology," Jack said. "I'm asking you to resign."

"You ungrateful prick!" Seward hissed. "I brought you to the top! Every goddamn movie you made, every dollar you made was because I negotiated it for you. I did everything and—"

"Which is why I'm giving you the chance to spin it any way you want," Jack said. "After this whole disappearance thing, nobody would blame you for not wanting to represent me anymore. You have your reputation to think about. You honored your obligations and I was screwing up."

"You owe me, Jack," Seward said, but his energy was waning now.

"I know it," Jack said. "You'll get your percentage of *Blue Angel II* and *Crossed Wires*. You did both of those deals." I didn't think it prudent to point out at that instant that Jack had negotiated away his salary for *Blue Angel II*, and that Seward's percentage would be chump change.

"It's not that easy, Jack," Seward said. "Our contract is for the next five years. I know you don't think much of contracts, but I'll fight you over this one."

"No you won't," Jack said. "You know you'll take a settlement. You fight me and you may as well find a new line of work, because no serious actor will touch you with a ten-foot pole."

"That's bullshit and you know it."

"We'll see."

"Go and try dealing with Cain and Schiller without me," Seward said, pacing. "It'll be a fucking joke. You'll be a joke. You're damaged goods, Jack. Everyone knows you've got rusty pipes."

Jack sat back in the couch, closing his eyes. "I think you'd better go now."

Seward looked around at us. "I hope you're all pleased," he said with a maniacal smirk. "You just watched your friend destroy his career."

"I feel okay," I said.

"I'm thrilled," Alison said.

"Happy as a pig in shit," Chuck said. "Nothing personal."

"You're all fucking lightweights," Seward said. "You have no idea what you're dealing with."

"They made you agents look so much more likable in *Jerry Maguire*," Lindsey said.

"Jack," Seward said, making one last desperate plea as Alison opened the front door. "It doesn't have to be this way."

"It does," Jack said, without opening his eyes.

Seward stared at him for a few more moments and then buttoned his suit jacket. "Okay then," he said, composing himself. "It's your funeral." As he walked through the door past Alison, she handed him a card. "What the hell is this?" he asked.

"That's my friend Don, who works for the FBI," Alison said. "You missed him by about two hours. You may want to give him a call. He'll be more than happy to open a full investigation into who might have been supplying all those drugs to Jack, you know what I mean? Then again, he might be too busy."

"What are you, threatening me?" Seward asked incredulously.

"Jack's going to let you spin this however you want," Alison said, ignoring the question. "You quit, you were fired, whatever you want to say. And he's going to offer you a fair deal for terminating your contract, which is in everybody's interest here, including your own." She paused to fix Seward with a hateful stare. "My advice? Shut your mouth and take the deal. It's more than you'll ever be worth."

Seward dropped the card where he stood and started to respond, but Alison quietly closed the door on his face. "You go, girl!" Lindsey said appreciatively.

"Whew," Chuck said, sitting down next to Jack on the couch. "We should really have him over more often."

43

"What's going to happen now?" *Ploop. Ploop.*

"I don't know." *Ploop.*

"Are you going back home to the city?" *Ploop.*

"I guess." I was sitting on the rock by the lake with Jeremy, skipping stones. He'd come running over breathlessly after dinner to see Jack, but Jack was in his meeting with Cain and Schiller, so Jeremy joined me outside, where I'd been sitting by myself for some time already, pondering the exact question Jeremy had just asked. What happens now?

After Seward left we'd all eaten a late lunch together, but there was a disjointed feeling to the conversation. It was as if now that Jack was safely back and ostensibly on the road to recovery, the very thing that had brought us out here was gone. Our private world was dissolving, like when the lights come on at the end of a movie and real life starts again. I felt an acute sense of sadness at the notion of all of us going back to our separate lives again. I knew we'd all stay in touch, at least marginally, just like before but there was something special about us as a group, something we'd rediscovered in the last week that wouldn't be sustained once we separated. The closeness we had from our college days was still there, but time would continue to work on us, to change us or make us grow into whatever was inside of us waiting to emerge.

But there was something more. We'd put our lives on hold to help Jack, but now that it was time to resume my life, I couldn't seem to manufacture even the smallest thread of enthusiasm. And as I sat by the lake with Jeremy, I realized that I didn't want to go back to the life I was living. It was empty, and it wasn't fair to expect Lindsey alone to fill it. Lindsey was a great start, a miracle actually, but like Jack I needed to make some changes. The problem was, I didn't know where to begin. I wanted to be a real writer, not a glorified list maker, but you didn't just wake up one day and say, today I'll be a successful novelist. Jack planned on going into counseling when he got back to LA to maintain his resolve. The question was, what would I do to maintain mine? I looked out onto the still, empty lake and thought about the geese. I wondered if they'd made it safely to their destination yet, and when they'd be coming back.

"Do you like living in Manhattan?" Jeremy asked me.

"Sometimes," I said.

"Not always?"

"No. Not always."

Ploop.

Luther Cain and Craig Schiller emerged from the living room with Jack in a flurry of smiles and handshakes. The rest of us, including Jeremy, were sitting around in the kitchen waiting to see how everything turned out. I had to admit, it was pretty cool to meet Luther Cain in person. He told us that he'd had his own drug problems when he was starting out and he was going to work closely with Jack to get him back on track. He was convinced of Jack's determination and announced that he would be his sponsor in a twelve-step program. Schiller, a heavyset guy with a beard and a ponytail, just nodded and smiled, deferring to Cain. Whatever they'd worked out in their meeting seemed to make all of them happy. Jack walked them both to the door, careful to stay out of camera range, and promised to meet them the following morning at their hotel, from which they'd all fly back to LA together. Before he left, Cain turned to us and said, "Jack's lucky to have friends like you." It was corny, but we all smiled like little kids because, for Christ's sake it was Luther Cain!

Jeremy was unimpressed with Cain, but the minute the director had left, he began bombarding Jack with questions about his movies. Jack had been brought up to speed about the boy by that point, and spent a good hour talking to him. At my request, Alison produced a camera and I shot some photos of Jeremy with Jack for him to hang on his wall next to his *Blue Angel* posters. I knew he'd treasure the pictures and I also wanted him to have proof in case any of his friends ever doubted his story.

Our last dinner together at Crescent Lake was a long, almost festive affair. Chuck made his usual garden salad while I made a huge bowl of spaghetti in marinara sauce. Alison and Lindsey took care of the baked salmon and garlic bread while Jeremy and Jack set the table. We sat for a few hours, talking about Jack's upcoming movies, reminiscing about college, teasing each other, and having a general good time, but I could sense the melancholy creeping in. Jack's head was already back in LA, Chuck was itching to get back to Mt. Sinai, and I had no idea what Alison was thinking, but I could sense her withdrawing as the meal progressed. When we were finally done, Alison began washing the dishes while Jack dried. Lindsey hinted that it might be a good time to leave them alone, so the rest of us walked Jeremy back to his house. "When are you leaving?" he asked me at the foot of the stairs leading to his back door.

"I don't know," I said. "Sometime tomorrow, I guess."

"Before I get home from school?"

"No. I'll make sure I'm still here to say good-bye."

"Okay," he said. "Do you think I should live in the city?"

I smiled at him and patted his shoulder, a gesture that made me feel oddly adult. "No," I said. "You belong right here. This place beats the city, hands down."

"So why don't you move here?" he asked.

"It's not that simple."

He shrugged. "That's what you always say."

Back in the house, Jack and Alison had disappeared, leaving a mess of unwashed dishes cluttered around the sink. "Well, I'll be damned," Chuck said. I smiled. "Do you guys have any idea whether or not they ever, you know?" He made a pushing motion with a fist and raised his eyebrows suggestively.

"Nope," I said.

"No clue," Lindsey said. "But I don't think so."

"Man," Chuck said. "Ten years they know each other, and you think he never banged her even once? Is that possible?"

"You knew her for ten years, too," I said. "How many times did you bang her?"

"It's not the same," Chuck said. "He could have had her any time he wanted. I mean, Alison's hot. I would have if I could have. If you knew you could have a girl like that any time you wanted to, would you wait ten years?"

"I think you may be simplifying the situation just a tad," Lindsey said.

"I just don't think it's possible," Chuck said, shaking his head.

"Can I ask a question?" I said.

"Yeah."

"Why are we whispering?"

We looked at each other, and then up at the ceiling, smiling. "Ten years," Chuck said, opening the fridge and pulling out some beers. "They deserve some quiet."

"Maybe they're just talking," I said with a grin.

"Then they'd still be washing dishes," Chuck said. "Jesus, I'm going to be the only one in this house who doesn't get any to-night."

"Why don't you go find your reporter friend," I said, heading for the stairs.

"Where the hell are you two going?" Chuck asked.

Lindsey gave him a kiss on the cheek. "To get some," she said.

"I'm just wondering," I said to Lindsey a little later as we lay together, our hips gently touching. "You want to be a teacher, I want to be a writer. Why do we have to live in the city to do that?"

"We don't," she said, running her fingernail down my side. "Why? What are you thinking?"

"I don't know," I said. "I just want to stop running in place already. We're thirty years old, we should be building a life already, you know?"

"I know," she said. We looked at each other for a long minute and then she gave me a soft kiss on the forehead. I could feel her smiling. "You know what I think?" she said.

"What?"

"I think I'd like to be here when those geese come back."

44

When Lindsey was asleep, I went down to the kitchen for a drink, restless as usual from my nooky high, and giddy at the prospect of the major change we had discussed. I was actually humming a happy little tune when I came upon Alison in the dark, sitting on a stool by the counter, thoughtfully sipping hot tea. She was wearing a sweatshirt and shorts, her straight hair uncharacteristically messy. "Hey," I said, thinking about Chuck's ten-year remark.

"Hey," she said.

I poured myself a cup of orange juice and pulled up a stool. "Where's Jack?"

"He's sleeping," she said, and smiled shyly at me, confirming our earlier speculation.

"Was that the first time?" I asked. "For the two of you, I mean."

She took another sip. "That was the first and second time," she said with a wicked grin, but there was a sadness behind it.

"So what's wrong?" I asked. "Is ten years of foreplay too much to live up to?"

She smiled again. "No, nothing like that."

"So what then?"

"He asked me to come out and live with him."

"What, in Hollywood?"

"Yep."

"That's great," I said, but Alison just sipped at her tea. "That's not great?"

"I told him no," she said.

"Oh."

She sighed deeply. "I think, after all these years of waiting for him to get his act together with me, I'm finally ready to move on. We came up here to get him off drugs, but I think I also came to get me off him."

"You know he loves you," I said.

"I know," she said softly. "And I love him. But he'll never be who I want him to be, which is the Jack I knew before he became 'Jack Shaw.' " She put up her fingers to indicate quotation marks. "And he'll never love me the way I want to be loved. Now he's been shocked into this awareness that he's somehow been changed, and that terrifies him, so he wants me to be with him, to somehow prove he's the same guy he always was. But he's not, and as much as I love him, I can't go with him just because he's scared. I deserve better than that." She looked at me.

"You've thought about this," I said.

"Yeah," she said. "And I'll probably be second-guessing myself as soon as he's gone, kicking myself for not going with him, but right now I'm sure I'm doing the right thing. He and I are actually in the same position now. We'll both be looking to find another way to make the world go around. Him without his coke, and me without him."

"Man," I said, reeling from what she'd just told me. "This must be so hard for you."

"I know," she said. "All those years, wishing he'd just tell me he wants me. Now he does, and I don't want to go. I must be crazy."

"You sound pretty rational," I said. "How'd he take it?"

"Okay. We had sex."

"After you said no?"

She laughed. "You didn't think after ten years I wasn't going to at least get a taste."

"Slut," I said with a grin. "You know, you'd be surprised at how similar you and Chuck are sometimes."

"Please," she said. "I'm depressed enough already."

I finished my drink and got up. "I'm going to sleep," I said, giving her a small kiss.

"Ben?" she said.

"Yeah."

"We did the right thing. For Jack, I mean."

"It looks that way," I said.

"You think he'll go back to doing drugs?"

"I don't know," I said. "I don't think so, but I didn't think he'd take drugs to begin with."

"Yeah," she said. "Well, if he does, he's on his own. I have a strict once-in-a-lifetime intervention policy."

"I agree," I said, setting down my glass in the sink.

"Have a good night," Alison said.

"You okay?"

"Sure."

"Well," I said, pausing in the doorway, "it sounds like you know what you're doing."

"Yeah," she said sarcastically. "I'm a big talker. Watch. Next week I'll be jumping on a plane to go see him."

"I don't think so," I said. "I think we all found some new direction this week."

"Oh, is there something you guys haven't told us?"

"Tomorrow," I said. Alison smiled at me and I turned and headed back up the stairs.

The reporters went berserk when Jack stepped out of the house the next morning. They were literally climbing all over each other to jockey for position and it was all the troopers could do to keep them behind the barricades. Jack walked calmly down to the front of the lawn and stood there for a few minutes, smiling and engaging in good-natured banter with the reporters. Most of the non-professional portion of the crowd had disappeared overnight, but there was still a pretty impressive throng of media, all clamoring for a bit of Jack's attention. NBC, CBS, ABC, CNN, *Hard Copy, Access Hollywood, Entertainment Tonight, Extra, The National Enquirer, The Globe*, and a whole slew of local affiliates I didn't recognize. After he'd given them about fifteen minutes he came back into the house and we all made our good-byes.

"What do you think, Ben?" he said to me after giving me a hug. "This whole thing would make a pretty cool novel, huh?"

"Could be," I said.

"Well, if you do it, I get first dibs on the film option."

"Deal."

He looked at me. "Thanks again, man, for everything."

"Just stay sober, so we can feel like we actually accomplished something."

"Oh, I think you accomplished something," he said, indicating Lindsey. "Don't thank me, I'm just glad I was able to bring you two together."

"Right."

"Hey, it was all part of the plan."

He gave Lindsey a hug, and then Chuck, who gave him a few hard pats on the back just to keep everything hetero. "Take care, Hollywood," Chuck said. "Stay in touch."

"I will," Jack said. "I want to have you all out for the premier when we get this movie done. They're looking at Labor Day."

We all said okay, but I wondered if we'd really go. Then he and Alison stepped outside and got into Chuck's rental. She would drive him to Cain's hotel, and Jack would go back with Cain on the studio jet. We watched them as they pulled out of the driveway, Sheriff Sullivan riding in his police car behind them to make sure none of the press tried to pull a Princess Di pursuit. I think he also wanted to make sure Jack got the hell out of his town.

"Well," Chuck said. "I guess that's that, then."

"You headed home now?" I asked him.

"As soon as she gets back," Chuck said. "I'll probably be on call for the next year straight after the shit I just pulled."

"You love it," Lindsey said.

"It's a living. You guys packed?"

We looked at each other. "What for?" Lindsey said.

45

That was four months ago, and Lindsey and I are still in Carmelina, which is already starting to feel like home. The lake is frozen now, a phenomenon that continually fascinates me. Most nights we go walking on its icy surface after dinner, holding hands as we slide around. Sometimes we bring out a blanket and sit in the middle of the lake, just listening to the silence and looking up at the stars.

We stayed in the Schollings's house for about two months, until mid-December when we closed on a small house on the other side of the lake. It was a stiff asking price, but Jack helped us out by paying for it in full. Now we make interest-free payments to Jack, who insists he'd like us to forget about the whole thing. "Consider it a Christmas present," he says. Maybe in a few months we'll agree, but for now pride keeps us writing the checks even though he has yet to deposit any of them. The house has three bedrooms, a cozy living room with a fireplace, a study, a dining room, and plenty of windows. The master bedroom has a small terrace with a full view of the lake, and when you stand on it you can see the Scholling and Miller houses across the water. Every few days Jeremy and I meet out on the lake and go ice skating while Taz slips and slides clumsily along with us.

Lindsey got a job teaching at the Carmelina Elementary School. She actually filled the slot left vacant by Peter Miller, but we don't get morbid about it and Jeremy doesn't seem to care. A few weeks after Jack returned amid great media fanfare to Los Angeles, Dave Boim, my boss from *Esquire*, got ahold of me and told me he thought it would be a good idea if I tried to write the story of Jack's intervention for an upcoming issue. I called Jack to see what he thought and he said, "No problem, it's a good idea. It'll warm you up for the novel and screenplay." I laughed, but not as much as I would have a few months ago. The article came out in January, and Jack agreed to do the cover to help push the issue, which yielded some very big numbers for *Esquire*. I'm actually putting together some notes for the novel. I've gotten a number of calls from some other magazines, and while I'm not an overnight smash, I'm a real freelancer now, not a list maker. There are a few writing assignments I might take, but right now I'm working primarily on writing fiction. Dave told me that now that I'm a contributing writer, he'll make sure that Bob Stanwyck gives any short stories I submit serious consideration. I'm also teaching English and creative writing at Thomas Jefferson High School in Carmelina. I originally took the job just to pay the bills, but I'm enjoying it a lot more than I thought I would, although walking through the halls sometimes makes me feel old.

The night before we moved into our new home, I stepped out of the shower to hear the Schollings's piano being played downstairs. It was a powerful piece, with strong minor chords and a soft, haunting melody. I ran downstairs to find Lindsey sitting at the piano, her body swaying as she played. I waited dumbfounded until she was done, and then, as she quietly closed the lid I said, "That was incredible!"

"Thank you," she said simply.

"When the hell did you learn to play?"

"I've always been able to," she said. "I just never played in front of anyone before."

I was floored. "I can't believe you can play the piano and I never knew."

"There's a lot you don't know about me," she said with a teasing smile.

"Like what?"

"Like, I'm pregnant."

"No way."

"Way."

Alison and Don have been dating for about six weeks and things sound pretty solid. She turned him down twice, but the guy just kept coming at her. I know she still speaks to Jack every week, but I guess that's a lot healthier than every day. Despite what she said that night in the kitchen, she didn't break down and go out to LA. I don't envy Don the baggage that probably comes with Alison from her Jack years. Still, they seem happy, and I hope it works out because I like Don and it's always a good time when the four of us get together.

Chuck's been seeing Sally Hughes on and off ever since he went home, and every once in a while he talks about getting serious with her, but so far it's still pretty casual. Neither of them seems at all interested in settling down. The last time I spoke to him, he mentioned that he was looking into a hair transplant, which I didn't take to be a good sign.

Jack finished shooting *Blue Angel II*, which will come out on Labor Day, and went right to work on *Crossed Wires* with Julia

Roberts. It's his first romantic comedy and he's really jazzed about it. He's also signed on to do two indie films over the summer, to build his credibility as a serious actor. "When you get your start in action," he explained to me, "it's an uphill battle to get any other kind of roles. The sooner you cross over, the better off you are. Otherwise, you'll be playing the same character for the rest of your life."

After he got back to LA he did the whole talk show thing, apologizing to Oprah and everyone else and talking about his rehab. He's got a new group of agents at CAA. and he swears by his drug counselor, with whom he meets weekly. He's also taken up yoga and has been flirting with Scientology. Despite all of that, or maybe because of it, I still worry about him. There's a certain desperation in the way he needs to fill every hour with something. It's like he's still searching for the discipline that will become his anchor, that will keep his addiction at bay.

We try to stay in touch, but we're both pretty busy. I've discovered, to my dismay, that I'm already thinking of him more and more as Jack Shaw the movie star and less as the Jack I used to know. It was probably inevitable, but it still depresses me. Time's surface is slick as oil, and there's just no way to hold on. Whatever it was that held the five of us together has grown up and moved on. There was a shot of Jack in *Entertainment Weekly* last week, stepping out of a restaurant with a striking brunette. I asked him who it was, but he dismissed her as just a friend of his. It may be true, but I know there will always be a part of his life that he doesn't share with us. If anything major happens, I guess I'll have to rely on *Entertainment Tonight* or *Access Hollywood* like everyone else.

I haven't told my parents yet that they're going to have another grandchild. I don't know what I'm waiting for. My mother will be horrified that we're not married, and I don't think I'll be able to make her understand that it just feels tacky to get married in the same year I got divorced. My dad, as usual, won't say much, but I think he'll be happy. I have to admit that I get a little kick out of being an unmarried, expecting father. It has the same effect as a temporary tattoo, making me feel like I'm on the edge, but only for a little while. I'm sure we'll get married one of these days.

Life's not perfect. Sometimes we hit cash crunches and I'm periodically flustered by the antiquated plumbing in our new house. But we're both happy. Our life together is a full one, and sometimes I get this overwhelming feeling of sweet anticipation that brings a lump to my throat. I'm looking forward to being a father, and I'm amazed at how ready I feel. Thirty is a fine age to become a father. Jeremy Miller is a fixture in our house, and we're looking forward to seeing the next *Star Wars* films together. And this spring I'll sit by the lake with Lindsey and our unborn child, watching for the return of our Canadian geese. More than anything, I'm looking forward to spending the rest of my life with her.

Basically, I'm looking forward.